THE SISTER BETWEEN US

HAILEY DICKERT

This novel is a work of fiction. Names, characters, places, and incidents are either products of the author's imagination or are used fictitiously. Any resemblance to actual events or locales or persons, living or dead, is entirely coincidental.

First released April 2023.

ISBN: 978-1-960497-00-0

Developmental Editing: Alli Morgan and Anonymous
Proofreading: Alli Morgan
Cover: Books and Moods
Cover Image: Adobe Stock with commercial licensing permission

Published by Hailey Dickert
www.haileydickert.com

Author's Note

To anyone who's been swallowed by the darkness of grief, unsure if you'll ever return to the light, the day will come when you'll remember them and smile without the tears. This one's for you.

This book contains topics that could be difficult for some readers. For a complete list, please visit: *haileydickert.com/tsbu-authors-note*

Should you be having a mental health crisis, please reach out to 9-8-8, the National Suicide and Crisis Lifeline. Your mental health is important. Your life is important.

For my grandpa, who encouraged me endlessly to pursue a career in writing before I even knew I wanted one.

Look at me now, Pop-Pop.

I'm doing the damn thing.

Your copy is waiting in Heaven's library – please skip over the spicy stuff.

“Darkness cannot drive out darkness;
only light can do that.”
—*Martin Luther King, Jr.*

Playlist

Not Like I'm In Love With You – Lauren Weintraub

Butterflies (Acoustic) – Abe Parker

Little Things (Acoustic) – Jade Facer, John Buckley

this is what falling in love feels like – JVKE

Best I Ever Had – Drake

What Keeps You Up At Night – Dan + Shay

die first – Nessa Barrett

Bigger Than The Whole Sky – Taylor Swift

Safe & Sound – Taylor Swift

when the party's over – Billie Eilish

I Lost a Friend – FINNEAS

you'd never know – BLÜ EYES

break my heart – Matt Hansen

Turbulence – Jonah Kagen

i wish u knew – vaultboy

broken – Jonah Kagen

I'd Run to You – CJ Starnes

Something in the Orange – Zach Bryan
blue jean overalls – Wilfred
Ghost – Micky
WYD Now? [Feat. Zai1k & Zakhar] – Sadie Jean
Breakups – Seaforth
Locksmith – Sadie Jean
Forget About You – Devin Kennedy
Doppelgänger – Joshua Bassett
the way i used to – Kelsea Ballerini
25 in Barcelona – JP Saxe
Halfway – Ber
ceilings (sped up + reverb) - pearl, fast forward >> & Tazzy
Amsterdam – Wild Rivers
Till Forever Falls Apart – Ashe, FINNEAS
this is how you fall in love – Jeremy Zucker, Chelsea Cutler
Until I Found You – Stephen Sanchez, Em Beihold

Prologue

What would you do if the most important person in your life vanished?

One second, they're there.

The next?

Gone.

Unfortunately, you can't always protect the people you love.

No matter how much you wish you could.

No matter what you'd give up to do so.

Split-second moments change the trajectory of our entire lives. We often don't realize how impactful the moment is until much later.

The first stroke of a paint brush that ignites a new passion.

A single second of eye contact with a stranger who becomes your lover.

An accident that has irreversible consequences.

You weren't aware it was coming, and you could have done nothing to prevent it, yet the entire direction of your life is flipped upside down, for better or worse. The previous version of yourself is yet to exist ever again.

The last moment I remember is her telling me she loves me.

Then it all goes dark.

1
Jake

I'm yanked back to reality by scalding grease splattering my skin.

"Shit!" I jump away from the sizzling skillet, patting my exposed stomach in an attempt to brush away the pain.

A mild burning smell reminds me to flip the pancake in the other pan.

"If you'd put a shirt on, you wouldn't have that problem," my younger sister, Sophia, snarks from her position next to me on the white marble countertop. She supervises as I struggle to make the most basic damn meal of the day—breakfast. I know I don't have to do this, but I want things to feel normal for the girls. I don't want them to notice the gaping hole in our life the way I do.

So I make the bacon.

And I scramble the eggs.

And I burn the pancakes.

Every Saturday, we used to wake up to the house filled with the smell of freshly cooked maple bacon. That was our cue to get out of bed and come to the kitchen. It was highly effective. Mom even bought a bacon-scented candle once to test if it would get us downstairs as quickly. It worked. And I was pissed. The mouthwatering smell and no bacon? Come on.

"But then I'd have bacon grease on my shirt," I say pointedly. "And Mom's the only one who can get that shit out."

"Well, maybe you should learn," she sasses with raised eyebrows.

"Maybe *you* should learn." I smirk while pointing the spatula at her. "You're almost ten. Plenty old enough to help with the laundry."

I pick up the finished plate of bacon and turn around, setting it on the kitchen island. The middle of it, where a vase of fresh tulips used to frequent, is bare. Dad and I are doing our best to fill the voids, but these things are still noticeable… at least to me.

I finish preparing the eggs and cut up a watermelon while Sophia makes toast.

"Can you get the girls?" I ask her as I carry the trays of food to the table.

"You got it." She snaps and points finger guns at me. I chuckle and shake my head as she hops off the counter and leaves the room.

A few minutes later, my twin sister, Chloe, her best friend, Leah, and Sophia all walk in giggling. I'm glad some of us are finally feeling some happiness and normalcy.

"Nice of you to join us, ladies," I tease.

"Good morning to you too, Jake," Chloe says as she walks to the sink to wash the wet clay off her hands. She's been obsessed with pottery ever since she took it as an elective freshman year of high school. It's an interesting, messy, and expensive hobby.

"Jacob," Leah says, grinning, clad in leggings and an oversized

T-shirt splattered with bright colored paint. She always calls me by my full name when she wants to annoy me. I relish in the split second her gaze flicks down to my exposed abs, then back to mine.

"Le," I return with a smile. My nickname for her, although it can hardly get shorter than Leah.

"Cute braids," Leah says, pulling on the end of one of Sophia's janky braids that has blonde hair sticking out every which way.

"I did my best!" Sophia whines, throwing her head back.

"You look great, Soph," I tell her before turning my attention to Leah, giving her a *what the fuck* look.

"Come to my room after breakfast," Chloe says, chuckling. "We'll teach you how to do a perfect french braid."

"Yeah, you'll be the talk of the fourth grade." Leah winks.

"I better be." Sophia giggles, flipping her golden hair behind her tiny shoulder.

I pour myself a steaming cup of black coffee, the strong, nutty smell energizing me before I even take a sip, and make my way to the large round wooden dining table with five navy blue chairs around it. Leah is here so often she even has her own seat. There used to be six chairs, but we moved one to the garage to avoid spending every meal staring at Mom's empty seat.

The center of the table is packed full with overflowing plates of bacon, scrambled eggs, pancakes, sliced watermelon, and toast.

I hope it's enough.

Dad walks through the front door from his overnight shift just as we're sitting down at the table. He shrugs off his EMT jacket and places it on the coat hook in the hallway.

"Morning, kiddos," he says, with a broad smile, joining us at the table.

"Morning," we all chime simultaneously.

"This looks great, thanks." He gives me a knowing smile. "So what are you kids up to today?" Dad asks while piling a hearty helping of scrambled eggs onto his plate.

"We're going to the springs with our friends," I respond between bites of watermelon, the juices dripping down my chin.

"That sounds fun." Dad smiles. "What about you, Sophie Bear?"

"Sage and her mom are picking me up and we're going to the Tampa Zoo to see the koalas," Sophia says right before stuffing an entire burnt pancake in her mouth without a single complaint.

"Well, now I wish I wasn't going to be sleeping half the day so I could tag along," Dad says sadly.

"Sleep is for the weak," Sophia says, pointing her fork at him.

"Yeah." Dad sighs. "Maybe next time, Bear."

We scarf down breakfast and after cleaning the kitchen, we all split to get ready for the springs.

I pop my head in the open door of Chloe's bedroom. The girls are holding up bathing suits in the mirror against their clothed bodies. "Be in the Jeep in thirty minutes or you're walking."

Without looking away from the mirror, they simultaneously flick me off. I swear they practice that move. I raise my eyebrows and fold my arms across my chest, searching for Chloe's gaze in the mirror.

"Yeah, yeah, don't get your panties in a wad, Jake. We'll be there."

Thirty minutes later on the dot, I'm sitting in the old black four-door Jeep Wrangler Chloe and I got for our sixteenth birthday. It sucks we have to share it, but I'm just happy to have some wheels. I spend a few minutes looking through music options for the drive and finally settle on a Drake playlist before giving the horn a few quick honks. I'm one minute from leaving their asses behind. They know I'm serious. I've done it before.

Finally, Chloe and Leah walk out our red front door, laughing like they have all the time in the world. When they're almost to the car, Leah throws her head back, groaning—the telltale sign she's forgotten something—and mutters something to Chloe before jetting over to her house next door.

"What else could she possibly need?" I ask Chloe as she hops in the passenger seat. "Your bags are already overflowing."

"Cool your panties, Jakey," Chloe quips. "She needs her sunscreen."

A few minutes later, Leah walks out of her house, bottle of sunscreen in hand, and *finally* gets into the Jeep.

"You *sure* you didn't forget anything else?" I ask her with a cocked brow as my eyes flick down to her exposed legs. "Maybe some pants?"

She narrows her eyes at me and smirks. "We're going to the *springs*, not church, Jacob."

"Mm-hmm," I hum.

"Why are you in such a rush, anyways?" Chloe asks me. "Worried all the hotties will be taken by the time we get there?"

"Yeah, Chloe, I'm *terrified.* It would certainly ruin my evening plans." I wink.

"You are such a douche canoe," Chloe says, rolling her eyes as I put the Jeep in reverse. My gaze flicks to Leah as I back out of the driveway. She's grinning out the window, trying to hide her expression, but her cute dimples give her away completely.

I pull into the springs gravel parking lot and find a spot. We all hop out and I open the back of the Jeep. The girls each grab a large beach bag. I haul out the cooler filled with Publix subs—God's gift straight from heaven—and our liquid courage.

As we unpack, the familiar rumble of an old two-door Ford truck pulls up next to us carrying a sausage fest in the truck bed.

"Funny seeing you here," Matt, my best friend, says, hopping out of the driver's seat as the rest of the guys jump out the back hauling coolers.

"Well, if it isn't the two most beautiful ladies in all of Longwood." Matt smirks, directing his attention to Leah and Chloe.

"Hey, Matty," the girls coo with wide grins plastered across their faces.

"I can carry that for you." He gestures towards the bag weighing down Leah's shoulder.

"What a gentleman." She beams, handing it to him.

I was gonna offer to do that.

A silver Honda Civic parks next to Matt's truck, carrying a few senior girls my friends forced us to wait on. Their arrival finally allows us to start our way toward the springs.

Laura, a friend from school, is walking next to me, making small talk about our college plans, which bores the shit out of me. She's cute, but I don't have any interest in leaving the friendzone.

I can't help but overhear Leah's conversation as she walks ahead of me with Matt. I ignore the sinking feeling in my stomach as I realize Leah and I only have one class together this year, while she and Matt have almost identical fucking schedules. My jaw clenches, and I try to ignore that too.

"So, you looking forward to our final school year?" Laura asks, pulling my attention back to her.

"Oh, uh, sure. One year closer to flying this hick town, right?" I sigh. Most kids grow up in Longwood and never leave—but that won't be me. I'm getting far away as fast as possible. I love my family, but if I stay here, I'll end up at some boring, dead-end job with a perfectly nice wife and two or three cookie-cutter kids. Born here. Raised here. Die here. The thought of that terrifies me.

There's got to be more to this world than the forty square miles making up our little podunk town. I love this place. It made me. It raised me. But I have *got* to get the fuck out of here. Maybe that's how Mom felt when she left. She was born here, raised here, and I guess she didn't want to die here too.

"Yeah, I can't wait to get out of here." She laughs weakly. "How are your offers so far?"

"I've gotten some interest, but it'll depend on this season before I really commit anywhere." A heavy weight rests on my chest thinking about how important this season is.

In ninety-nine percent of America, football is the popular high school sport, but in our small Florida town, for some reason, it's soccer—and I happen to be pretty damn good at it. While I'll admit I have a lot of natural talent, I work my ass off on that field, and it's paid off. I've been team captain since the beginning of last season. Even took us all the way to the state championship before a team from Jacksonville beat us out.

Getting a full ride on a soccer scholarship is the best chance I have to pay my way. Although he won't admit it, Dad is struggling with the bills. Mom left Dad with all that when she blew town. Her half of the mortgage, and I guess her half of the kids too.

"Well, I'm sure you'll get tons of offers." She smiles, nudging my shoulder with hers.

We're finally at the end of the trail exiting the tree line towards the springs below. Teenagers are scattered everywhere—lying back on beach towels, sitting on lawn chairs, playing flip cup, running in and out of the springs, splashing around—all soaking up the final Saturday of summer.

As we're setting out our things, Laura places her towel next to mine, and I notice Leah eyeing her with an unreadable expression. I'd like to imagine she's jealous, but it's probably just curiosity. Leah has never shown much attention to my dating life unless it's to make it the end of a punchline.

Our spot is finally set up. Matt brought a Bluetooth speaker, which is now emitting Childish Gambino loud enough to DJ for the whole spring, but no one minds. This is where teenagers come to party.

I pull my Longwood High soccer T-shirt off over my head and kick off my sandals, now wearing nothing but my favorite black swim trunks and matching Ray-Bans. I finally sprawl on the laid-out towel, and the blazing sun embraces my skin like a warm blanket. I can't help the aching feeling in my chest at the reminder that this is the end of summer and these days with my friends at the springs are almost over. Next year, we'll all be off to college or on other adventures, so this is it.

Leah stands near me clad in an oversized white button-down dress, her black bikini faintly visible through the thin fabric. Her fingers fumble with the top button before it pops free and in what feels like Baywatch-style slow motion, she undoes button after button, revealing more of the bikini and exposed skin underneath.

Thank God for my Ray-Bans. My hungry eyes drink in every movement. The way the dress drops, exposing her shoulder as she tugs the sleeves off her arms and tosses it to the ground in a heap. How she runs her pointer fingers between the back hem of her bikini bottoms and her adorable little ass, readjusting it evenly into place. Enough hidden to make any sane man want to know what's underneath. Every drop of blood in my body rushes south.

Fucking hormones.

I force my eyes away before she, or anyone else, for that matter, notices I'm staring. I flip over on the towel, move my Ray-Bans to the top of my head, and lie on my stomach, trying to hide my *frustration.*

I've sworn up and down to myself I'll never do anything about these lustful feelings. I blame them on male hormones and genetics.

Leah's always been a part of my life. Me, Leah, and Chloe were like the three musketeers until puberty happened and we drifted apart. My little crush on her never felt like something I could act on, not without risking our friendship.

Not without risking *everything.*

"Hey," Leah bellows to Chloe a few yards away. "Can you put some sunscreen on my back? I'm still fried from last week."

"Have Jake do it. I need to pee, and I'm seriously about to burst." She squirms.

"Your bladder is the size of a walnut," Leah says, laughing.

"Right?" Chloe groans. "Nature calls, I'm answering. I'll be right back."

Leah shakes her head, grinning, then reaches around her shoulders in a failed attempt to apply sunscreen to the middle of her sun-scorched back. She looks towards me with an unreadable expression raising her eyebrows, the bottle of sun lotion dangling from her fingertips.

"Would you mind? If I get any more sun, I'll turn into a *Jobster.*" She snickers at the last word, unable to maintain her composure. When we were eight, Leah spent an entire summer with our family at a beach house in the Florida Keys. I got so sunburnt, the girls called me Jobster for a month. Like Jake, mixed with lobster. *Hilarious.*

I scrunch my face at the horrible nickname that's been completely overused in the past ten years. While the joke has lost its luster, the corners of my mouth upturn at her inability to maintain a straight face. Somehow, it still makes the girls giggle. Every. Damn. Time.

"Fine," I groan in an attempt to sound annoyed.

I feel a lot of things about putting sunscreen on Leah, but annoyed isn't one of them.

I reach down and readjust myself before standing up, hoping my previous frustration isn't noticeable.

I walk over and immediately notice a little blue speck on her collarbone.

"You have a little paint there," I say, pointing to it.

"What?" She tries to look down and puffs out her perfect chest in the process.

My breath hitches, and I avert my eyes in an attempt to maintain my composure.

"It's fine, I can…" I reach out, gently rubbing the paint off with my thumb, and the small fleck flutters to the ground. "Okay, it's gone." I smile and allow my hand to linger against her skin a moment longer than necessary before holding out my hand face-up. She squirts a generous amount of cream-colored lotion into my palm and turns around. Leah wasn't kidding. She's two shades away from crimson. She winces beneath my touch. "Sorry," I mumble.

"It's okay, just sensitive."

I lessen the pressure, sliding my palms gently along her spine, between the string of her bikini, down to the dimples of her back, and against the sides of her soft hips.

She adds another dollop to my hand, and I apply it to the center of her back, using my fingers to connect her splattered freckles like the constellations of the night sky. Goosebumps ripple across her body, and I force myself to look away. *This girl is trying to kill me.*

I don't know if you can die from blue balls, but if you can, I'm a high-risk patient.

2
Leah

Jake rubs in the last bit of sunscreen between my shoulder blades, and my heart pounds so hard in my chest I struggle to breathe. I'm self-conscious of the stupid freckles all over my skin, and I wish they would disappear as he touches every single one of them.

"Thanks," I manage to choke out.

"Anytime," he replies, seemingly unaffected.

I turn away just as one of the hottest guys I've ever seen walks up to us with a wide smile plastered across his face.

"Jake?" he says, laughing and running a hand through his dark brown hair.

"Hey!" Jake says enthusiastically with a smile. "We're gonna kick your ass this season, Danvers."

"You mean how you guys beat us last year?" he refutes with a breathtaking smile.

"Whatever, man." Jake laughs.

The mystery guy must've noticed I was giving him the once-over because his next words are, "Well, hello there, gorgeous."

My cheeks flush at the compliment. "Hi." I bite my bottom lip to stifle a smile. "I'm Leah."

"Hi Leah, I'm Cole," he offers with a seductive grin.

Chloe and her boyfriend, Trey, walk up, and she mouths *oh my God* at me with a huge smile.

She's so damn nosy.

"Is this that hot twin sister of yours everyone's been talking about?" Cole asks Jake, pointing a finger directly at me.

"Actually, *I'm* the hot twin sister," Chloe interjects. "But this is my equally hot, *extremely single* best friend." She gestures to me with a smile before taking a swig from her water bottle. *She's the absolute best wing woman.* Trey grins and throws his arm around her, planting a kiss on her head.

"Ohhh." Cole's eyes bounce between Jake and Chloe. "I guess I see the resemblance."

I'm not sure what resemblance he's referring to considering Chloe is bleach blonde and thin, a mirror image of Lysa, whereas Jake is tall and broad with dirty blonde hair. Their only similarity is a matching set of emerald-green eyes.

"And good to know." Cole chuckles, returning his attention to me. "I also happen to be *extremely single* myself."

"Interesting revelation." I grin while toying with a strand of my auburn hair.

"I suppose it is." He bites his lower lip as the corner of his mouth turns upward.

"Cole, come on, let's go," a guy yells impatiently from a few yards away.

"Give me a minute," Cole responds, then turns back to me. "Sorry… I have to give him a ride home."

"Oh… okay." I smile faintly. "Well, it was nice meeting you."

"You too, beautiful. Maybe next time we can talk with less…" He glances around at the others. "Distractions."

"Yeah… maybe." I smile, watching Cole as he walks away and disappears into the tree-covered path. When I turn to throw the sunscreen bottle on my towel, I find Jake and Chloe's eyes glued on me.

Chloe's grinning ear to ear, and Jake looks like he's constipated.

I don't bother asking either of them what their problem is.

Between the booze and the blazing sun, the whole day has faded away. I'm sitting by a bonfire near the water's edge, and the smokey smell is seeping into my hair worse than a trip to Benihana's. Trey and Chloe are across from me, snuggled up on a log, talking and laughing.

"Here." Jake sits down next to me, holding out a wine cooler.

"Thanks." I take it from his hand, our fingers brushing in the process.

He smells like coconut sunscreen mixed with sweat—but not the gross kind of sweat, the intoxicating I-want-to-smell-more-of-this kind. With each inhale, goosebumps scatter up and down my arms. Without standing up, Jake pulls off his Longwood Soccer sweatshirt, which has Summers written on the back and the number eight.

"Here." He places the sweatshirt in my arms without asking or waiting for an answer.

"Oh, thanks," I say, awkwardly pulling the sweatshirt over my head and tugging it into place.

We sit in silence for what feels like forever, although it's probably only one or two minutes. He's scratching off the label on his brown glass beer bottle. *I wonder what's bothering him tonight. The last time he looked this way was after Lysa left.*

"Are you okay?"

"Honestly?" He sighs. "I don't know."

"Have you heard anything from your mom?" I ask hesitantly. Finding out your mom is gone and you have no idea where she is or if she's coming back is a tough pill to swallow. Chloe, Jake, and Sophia hardly left the house for weeks.

"Not a damn thing," he mumbles. "No calls. No texts. Just radio silence."

"And you still have no clue why she left or where she is?"

"No, I hear Dad on the phone with her sometimes, but he won't tell us shit." He shakes his head. "I mean, who fucking does that? Just up and leaves their children in the blink of an eye." His knee bounces uncontrollably as he brings the amber bottle to his mouth and takes another long pull of the beer. "Apparently she doesn't give a fuck about us."

"I really think you need to talk to Will and tell him how much it's eating at you," I say, looking over at him and placing a firm hand on his leg to stop his bouncing knee. His leg stills as he glances down at my hand, then back at me.

"Yeah, you're probably right..." He looks directly into my eyes. "And I know you miss her too." He places his hand on mine, squeezing before quickly pulling away, and heat radiates up my arm from the brief contact.

"Yeah..." I sigh, rubbing my thumb up and down the condensation of my seltzer can. *I definitely do.* "How's Soph handling it all?"

"She's... adapting. She's happier when you're around." He smiles, nudging me against my shoulder, and I blush.

"Thanks, I love that little bug."

"So, are you looking forward to senior year?" he asks in an obvious attempt to change the depressing subject.

"I guess so." I smile faintly. "You?"

"Yeah, it's just all becoming real…" He picks at the label on his bottle. "And there's a lot of pressure riding on me this season."

College scouts have been watching Jake for years, which I'd think would be exciting for him.. I know he can't wait to blow this town. But I also know he puts a ton of pressure on himself to be the best.

"Yeah, I bet. Have you gotten any offers yet?" I inquire to avoid what I really want to ask. *Will you miss me when you're gone?*

"Yeah, the Crystal Bay University scout was at a game last season, and they've already offered me a full ride. Told me I should keep the talent in the state that grew it. I think it was some bullshit orange growing analogy?" He laughs, and I do too. The Stingrays will say anything to make sure they have the best athletic teams in the state, and they usually do.

"But you don't want to go there?"

"Honestly, I want to get as far away from this place as possible. At least for a little while."

I nod, attempting to mask the storm of sadness brewing inside of me at where this is leading.

"So ideally you'd like California or…?" I ask hesitantly.

"I mean, yeah, UCLA has always been my dream school. But Europe's a possibility too. That's what my coach told me at least."

Europe? I assumed he could go as far as California, but I never imagined him going overseas. My chest tightens, and I toy with the gold ring around my middle finger.

"They don't give scholarships or anything. But I could forego college, play for a league team, and actually get paid. It wouldn't be much till I earned my spot, but it's at least something. And if I want,

I can still take classes over there. College is basically free in most of Europe."

"No shit?" I exclaim, attempting to sound enthusiastic. "That would be cool."

"Yeah, I guess," he replies with a shrug and smile that doesn't quite reach his eyes. "Dad is totally against it. He says I need to make sure I have a degree to fall back on if the whole soccer thing doesn't work out. Says I should play in college and then can play professionally after I've earned a degree."

"What would you want to fall back on if you had to?"

"For my degree? I have no fucking clue. My actual fallback plan is probably opening a bar," he says with an eyebrow waggle and a smirk.

"Oh my God," I gag out, rolling my eyes. "You are *such* a guy."

He chuckles, throwing his head back while holding his stomach. "Kidding, sort of."

"Uh-huh. Sure you are." I narrow my eyes at him with a grin. "Come on, be serious."

"I guess a business degree could be a good option. It would help with opening the bar." He grins, nudging me with his shoulder.

"Mm-hmm," I hum and roll my eyes at him.

"Have you convinced your parents to let you do an art degree yet?"

The question is a knife to my already bleeding heart. "No." I shake my head. "They 'don't believe art is a profitable career' and would rather I do basically anything else," I say, rolling my eyes.

"I know you want to make them proud," he says hesitantly. "But you shouldn't have to give up something you love in the process."

"Yeah…" I stare down at my feet.

I wish it was that simple.

"Have you heard from anywhere yet?"

"Not yet. I think they'll send out responses by December for early admission applications."

Chloe and I have already applied for early admissions at the

University of Florida and Crystal Bay University but haven't heard back from anywhere. We've talked endlessly about going to the same university. UF has an incredible art program, and even a ceramics track Chloe is obsessed with, so that's our number one pick. I have no idea what I'll do if we don't get into the same schools. She's been there for me through everything—and I mean *everything*.

I got my period during math class in sixth grade and bled through my pants. Chloe found me crying in the bathroom, stripped down her jeans, and gave them to me, no questions asked. She put on her gym shorts even though they were against the dress code. The principal gave her detention, and she never even mentioned my name.

My entire life, it's been Leah and Chloe. Chloe and Leah. Who would I even be without her?

"Well, your GPA is near flawless, so I'm sure you'll get in everywhere." Jake smirks.

"Jake, come here," Matt yells from the other side of the springs, and Jake glances over his shoulder towards the noise.

"Uh, I guess I better get over there," he says, pointing his thumb behind him.

"Yeah, of course," I respond with a tight-lipped smile as he stands. "See you."

"Later, Le." He waves, then turns his back to me and walks away.

I sigh and stare at the crackling fire, thinking of all of the things I wish I'd had the courage to say instead.

Will we still talk?

Will you miss me?

Will you forget about me?

3

Leah

Senior year starts tomorrow, and since I spent all of yesterday at the springs, I have to get my stuff ready today. Most people dread it, but the prep work is my favorite part of going back to school.

The sound of turning a fresh, crisp sheet of notebook paper, the smell of ink gliding across the page, new binders with color-coded tabs for each class, sharpened pencils with fresh erasers ready for removing all of my inevitable mistakes, pens with ink that glides right out—man, I'm such a fucking nerd.

I'm putting my school supplies in the new backpack Mom bought me on Friday during our annual school shopping trip when there's a knock on the door.

"Come in," I bellow as both my parents stroll into my room with giddy smiles.

"Hey, honey," Mom says. "We were thinking… since your senior year starts tomorrow, we could take you to a nice lunch at your favorite Thai restaurant downtown."

Uh-oh. Bribery with food... They make it hard to resist. I would rarely turn down Lotus Thai, but Mom and Dad have been badgering me about my college plans, and it's driving me crazy.

What school do you want to go to?

What do you want to major in?

Art's not a real major.

What about business?

Do you think you should take the SATs again? I'm not sure your score was high enough.

They mean well, I know, but it still drives me absolutely batshit.

"Oh, I actually already promised Chloe we could pick out our first day outfits. I also have to go to BCD and grab a few last-minute things for school," I lie.

BCD—aka Books, Crafts, and Drafts—is a small local store that sells, you guessed it, books, craft supplies, and beer. It's full of gorgeous abstract art, tipsy college students studying, and smutty romance novels. They do have a few things I could use for school, but I'm actually hoping to buy some supplies for painting at Chloe's later. Lysa brought me there for the first time when I was eight to buy me my first paint set, and I've been obsessed ever since.

"Okay, sweetheart," Mom says sadly. "Well, let us know if you change your mind."

Dad pulls out his wallet and hands me a twenty. "Here. For the *school stuff*." He winks.

He knows me pretty well for never being here.

"Thank you." I kiss them both on the cheek, and they leave my room.

I've found three new acrylic paints and am browsing through the romance section. I finally settle on *The Fault in Our Stars* by John Green since I'm in the mood to be emotionally destroyed.

I turn to walk towards the register, looking down to check the price on the book, when I run directly into someone. Before I can see their face, I smell Chanel No. 5.

"Are you fucking kidding me?" Katelyn McClaire, Longwood High School's resident mean girl and Jake's ex, spouts, looking down at her white sundress now drenched in beer. *Oops.* Her sister is the bartender and is apparently stupid enough to serve a minor.

"Sorry, Katelyn, it was an accident," I say genuinely. *Yeah, a happy accident.*

"Mm-hmm, sure." She crosses her arms and bodychecks me with her shoulder as she continues past.

That girl is Satan incarnate.

I don't know what Jake saw in her. I mean, sure, she's beautiful—a tall, lean figure with golden skin, chestnut brown hair, and ocean blue eyes—but her heart is as black as they come, and her mouth only spits straight garbage.

"Okay, well, see ya around." I wave awkwardly, resisting the urge to put down every finger except one.

"Yeah, I might be in your neighborhood later to come by and see Jake." I spin around to her smirking face. "We have some... *unfinished* business."

A burning sensation creeps into my stomach. "Considering you and Jake broke up four months ago, I'm not really sure what there is left to talk about," I scoff.

"Who said anything about *talking*?" she clarifies with a devilish grin, trying to get a rise out of me.

When Katelyn and Jake were dating, she fought with him constantly about the fact that I was always around. She was jealous of me, which I thought was absurd, since nothing has happened in the fifteen years Jake and I have known one another.

Jake has always been a no-fly zone. Especially since our eighth-grade field trip to Sea World when Chloe cried to me after a few girls pretended to be her friend just to get close to her brother. As soon as Jake formed his own friendship with them, they dropped Chloe completely. I've been her ride or die for fifteen years, but I still never want her to worry or wonder about my motivation for wanting to spend time with her.

"Guess I *will* see you later then." I smile at Katelyn sweetly. "I'll be over at Jake's tonight too."

"Lovely," she sneers, scrunching her nose with upturned, pursed lips. She turns around and stomps toward the bathroom to undoubtedly try to get the beer stains out of her soaked dress.

I'm sitting on the baby pink upholstered armchair in Chloe's room, watching as she throws almost every item in her closet onto the floor.

"This is ridiculous. I cannot find *one* single thing in my closet that is worthy of the first day of senior year."

I shake my head and laugh. "Chloe, has anyone ever told you you're a bit dramatic?"

"Excuse me?" She throws a hand over her chest. "I am the *queen* of dramatic." I giggle and chuck a throw pillow in her direction, which she karate chops away. "Besides, this is our *senior* year. And I have a *hot* boyfriend now. I've gotta show those bitches that they don't have a chance."

"Chlo..." I stand up, taking her hands in mine. "You're a freaking bombshell, and Trey's lucky to have you. Anything you wear tomorrow is going to look incredible. So for the love of God, would you pick something so we can go to the studio?" I tap my forehead against hers, and she smiles while narrowing her eyes.

"Fine, but if I don't look hot as shit tomorrow, I'm blaming you," she says, shooting finger guns at me, Sophia-style.

"Blame away, darling," I reply, taking a bow.

"How was your day?" she asks while draping yet another sundress in front of her in the full-length mirror on the wall.

"It was okay. Just got ready for school and went by BCD."

Footsteps echo from down the hall, and Jake appears in the doorway with a devilish smirk on his face. His attention is focused solely on me. My heart is racing, and my cheeks turn bright red.

"Um, can we help you?" Chloe says without turning away from the mirror.

He narrows his eyes at me, amused. "Did you spill a beer on Katelyn at BCD today?"

My eyes go wide, and I gasp. "I can promise you, it's not what it sounds like." I laugh, remembering the look on Katelyn's face.

"Excuse me, you did *what* now?" Chloe shrieks, spinning around, throwing the sundress on the chair next to her.

"Okay, okay," I say through fits of laughter. "Listen, I was walking to the counter to pay and accidentally... *accidentally*," I emphasize, looking at Jake, "bumped into her, causing her to spill a beer she somehow had all over herself." He stands there smiling, with folded arms, not saying a word.

"Karma is a *biiiitchhh*," Chloe singsongs, laughing.

"Anything else?" Jake asks, obviously amused.

"She did mention that she was coming by tonight due to some 'unfinished business' the two of you had," I say with a cocked brow.

"She did *what?*" Chloe echoes behind me, and I giggle at her dramatics.

"I guess that's what inspired her little *revelation* earlier." Jake's eyes are glued on mine, and he's unable to stifle the breathtaking grin that overtakes his face.

"Revelation?" I echo with a cocked brow.

"Yeah, Katelyn texted me earlier asking to come over. Said she's made the biggest mistake of her life to let a fine ass snack like me walk away."

Chloe and I both roll our eyes and stare at him.

"Okay, fine." He waves a hand in the air. "I may be slightly paraphrasing. But yeah, she asked to get back together and wanted to come over tonight to *seal the deal*." He waggles his eyebrows. "And that part was *not* paraphrasing."

"Ugh, disgusting." Chloe scrunches her face. "What time is she going to be here? So we can make sure *we're* not." The thought of him and Katelyn getting back together makes me nauseous.

"Chloe." Jake sighs, finally turning his attention to her. All the amusement is gone from his face. "Do you really think I would get back together with Kate after the way she acted and the way she treated the both of you?"

His eyes land on me when he says "you." I didn't think he noticed all the ways Katelyn bullied me, or us, but I guess he's more observant than I thought.

One time when Katelyn was over, she stopped me on my way to the bathroom.

"If I ever find out something happened between you and Jake, I'm not just going to ruin your reputation. I'm going to ruin your entire goddamn life," she promised before spinning around and walking away.

I believed her. She's vicious. I was so shocked I couldn't even reply, standing there like a scared idiot with my mouth hanging on the floor.

"I am totally over her," Jake says. "I was over her before we even broke up. And besides, there's a new girl I have my sights on anyways." His gaze connects with mine again for a brief moment, and a breath catches in my throat.

"Who—" Chloe starts, but Jake is quick to cut her off.

"Don't bother asking, because I'm not telling." He glances around Chloe's room. There are clothes thrown haphazardly, covering every available surface. "What the fuck is going on in here? You guys rob a Target or something?"

"Ha ha. Just trying to look our best for the first day," Chloe retorts. "Some of us actually *care* about our appearance," she says while eyeing Jake's outfit choice, which consists of a faded and worn-out pair of gym shorts from our sophomore year and a Longwood High School Soccer T-shirt with the sleeves ripped off.

"Some of us have to actually get shit done and can't just sit around all day playing fashion show like a little kid." Jake glares at her.

"Oh, fuck off."

"Okay, okay, people, no need to get hostile," I say in an attempt to ease the tension.

"Whatever, I'm out," Jake says as he strolls out of the room.

"I don't know what the fuck that was about. He's never usually that touchy," Chloe says.

"Fuck if I know." I shake my head.

I'm sitting on the comfy chair, looking around her disaster of a room. The one organized portion is the wall of pottery next to the closet that hosts everything she's made since starting ceramics class three years ago. It's so cool to see how her earlier pieces compare to the newer ones. The first ones are little blobs of clay, and the new pieces are, well, gorgeous. She's incredibly talented.

My eyes snag on a framed picture sitting on one of the shelves of Jake, Chloe, and I in an enormous bathtub with bubbles filled up to our chins.

When we were seven, Will and Lysa took us kids down to Key West for a little vacation. The pool was closed after dark, so they used the huge, jetted tub in their room to make us a "bubble pool." We were having so much fun, we didn't notice it was spilling over the sides until Will came running in, slid through water and bubbles, and jumped in the tub to turn it off. Lysa must have heard the ruckus and came barreling in too. She stopped short when she saw Will standing soaking wet in the tub, fully dressed, and burst into a fit of laughter. Soon we were all laughing, and after Will got out, Lysa snapped that picture of us.

I used to be so annoyed that she was taking pictures all the time. We would have to pause the fun we were having until she could get the perfect shot. Now that we're older, I'm happy to have those frozen moments in time. Perfect memories that the universe can never take away from us, regardless of the future.

I know how much Chloe and Jake miss Lysa, how hard they took her leaving. I've tried to be there for them while they mourn someone who didn't die, just abandoned them. But I'm experiencing the same pain. With my parents being gone all the time, the Summers took me in, and Lysa always treated me like a daughter. It feels like she left me too. I just wish I knew where she is. As much as I don't want to, as much as she hurts the people closest to me, I miss her.

I miss those simpler times when we were just little kids with happy parents. When the pool being closed at sunset was our biggest problem.

Chloe and I are in our favorite room in the house, the garage, aka our art studio. Lysa had Will and Jake clean out a section of it last summer so that Chloe would have room for her potter's wheel and kiln. When they unveiled it, there was already an easel, canvas, and some paints set up for me too. Will and Lysa have always been so supportive of our art, which makes it hurt that much more that my parents don't believe in me.

We're both hot messes covered in either clay or paint, working furiously to finish our current projects before the chaos of the new school year starts tomorrow.

"What was Jake's problem earlier?" I ask Chloe, unable to stifle my curiosity at his weird outburst.

"I don't know." She shakes her head and throws another clump of wet clay onto the potter's wheel. "Honestly, he's been short-tempered since right before summer."

What she means to say is "since Mom left," but Chloe refuses to mention her. My heart tightens in my chest at the thought of Lysa. *Is it possible to miss someone and hate them at the same time?*

I don't know if I could ever hate Lysa, but I do hate what her leaving has done to the family.

"Yeah," I say, remembering how anxious Jake was last night.

"We just all need to move forward." Chloe slaps hard at the clay. "New year and better vibes."

"New year and better vibes," I repeat in agreement.

Beep. Beep. Beep.

An alarm goes off, letting us know that the bowl we made before going to the springs yesterday is ready to be removed from the kiln.

Chloe and I walk over to it, buzzing with excitement at seeing how it turned out. Chloe makes the ceramics, and I etch the designs and paint them. We're a perfect team.

Chloe pulls the small bowl out of the kiln and… *Wow, it looks incredible.*

It's one of the best we've ever made.

It's perfectly round, with leaves I etched into it and a turquoise glaze. "Oh my God," I say. "It looks so good!"

"I know, I'm obsessed." Chloe smiles and wiggles with excitement. "We should put our bugs on the bottom."

I take the bowl from her. "Sure thing, Lovebug." That's been my nickname for Chloe since we were in fourth grade. There was a swarm of lovebugs on the playground, and Chloe ran straight through them like a psychopath while the rest of us ran the other way screaming. Ever since then, she's my Lovebug, and since I was such a scared little shit, I'm her Scaredybug.

I bring the bowl over and flip it upside down on our work desk.

"What's up, buttercups?" Sophia says, striding in.

"Hey, Soph," I say, squirting some white paint on a tray.

"Finally ready for your first day tomorrow, little lady?" Chloe says to her, laughing. Sophia has been "prepping" all day. She's going to be the most prepared kid in the fourth grade.

"Getting there." She shrugs, then walks over just as I'm finishing writing our nicknames in script on the bottom of the bowl.

"Hey… what about me?" Sophia pouts.

"Well, I guess you need a bug first, huh?" I tilt my head at Chloe and smile.

"Hmm…" Chloe taps a finger on her mouth. "I guess we can call you our little *Ladybug*," she says, squeezing Sophia's shoulders.

"Yes! Ladddyyyybuggggg," Sophia replies, dancing and singing the word.

We all three laugh, and it's the sweetest sound I've ever heard.

I add "Ladybug" in red paint to the bottom of the bowl, initiating Sophia into our swarm.

4

Jake

It's almost eleven o'clock, the night before our first day of senior year. I open Instagram and after aimlessly scrolling for a while, I land on Leah's profile. Somehow, I always end up on her profile like a stalker. The most recent picture is of her and Chloe lying on top of an enormous pile of clothes, laughing up at the camera with the caption: *First day ready! #senioryear*

The second most recent picture is from her at the springs yesterday in her little black bikini. It should be illegal to post a photo like that on the internet. She's angled away from the camera with her strawberry hair thrown over her shoulder, allowing a full view of her backside from her neck to her toes. Her face is looking to the side, and she's smiling like she saw something funny.

I wish I was on the other side of that smile.

I like both photos and contemplate sending her a DM before deciding against it. I always chicken out when it comes to Leah. There are too many what-ifs.

What if it's all in my head and she doesn't feel the same?

What if we give it a shot and it doesn't work out, and it ruins our friendship, or her and Chloe's friendship, forever?

Or worse, what if she hates me?

I throw my phone on the bed and decide to take a shower, where I will definitely try *not* to think about that photo I just saw on Leah's profile.

As I'm undressing to get in, my phone vibrates. *I might as well check it before getting in the shower.*

My heart rate quickens as I see a notification from Leah. We rarely text outside of the occasional random funny meme or to coordinate a ride somewhere.

LEAH

Leah

Saw you liked my picture. Can't sleep either?

Me

Nope :(

Smooth, idiot. What would she even respond to that?

Me

How did the fashion show go?

Leah

Fine. Chloe found her perfect "I'm Trey Blake's girlfriend" outfit lol

Me

Lol okay

I'm so bad at this, it's pathetic.

Me

What about you?

Leah

What about me?

Me

Did you find your perfect girlfriend outfit?

Leah

I mean I'm not anyone's girlfriend, but I guess I found my perfect make me your girlfriend outfit.

Who does she want to make her boyfriend?

My jaw clenches. I forego my plans of showering and plop back down on my bed.

Me

Send me a picture

Leah

Of?

Me

Your make you my girlfriend outfit 😜

It's been five minutes, and she still hasn't responded. The low light is still on in her bedroom, which is visible from my window. *Why hasn't she answered yet?* I throw a pillow over my face, ready to end my misery, when the phone buzzes again.

Leah

I never said it was to make me YOUR girlfriend

Me

Just show me the outfit and then we can talk about it

Good job, Jake. Keep saying that flirty stuff and don't sound like a fucking idiot.

Leah

Fine

A photo pops in of Leah smiling in the mirror. I can tell she just took it because her hair is in the awkward updo she always wears to bed and there's no sign of makeup on her face. My favorite look of hers. She's wearing a light blue-and-white floral sundress that looks flawless on her. I scan down her long legs and she has on a pair of white Converse.

Me

Woah

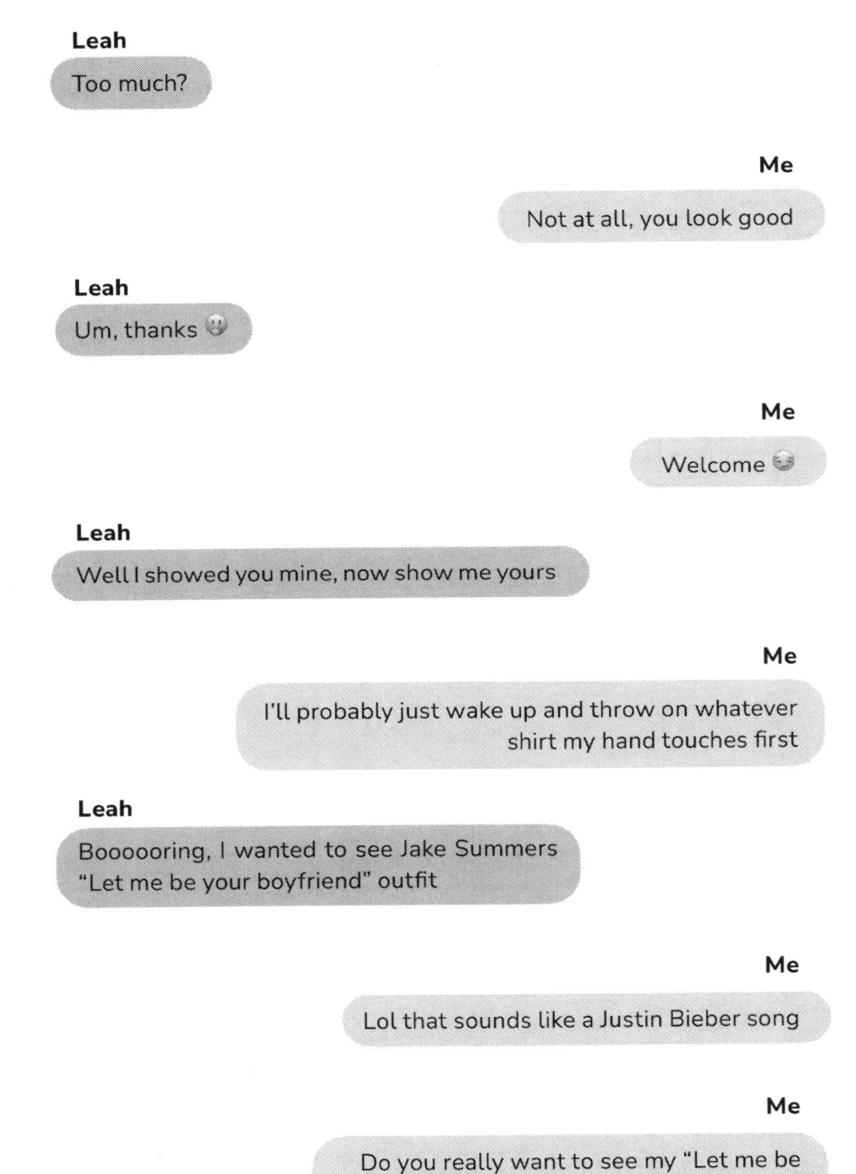
Leah
Too much?
Me
Not at all, you look good
Leah
Um, thanks
Me
Welcome
Leah
Well I showed you mine, now show me yours
Me
I'll probably just wake up and throw on whatever shirt my hand touches first
Leah
Boooooring, I wanted to see Jake Summers "Let me be your boyfriend" outfit
Me
Lol that sounds like a Justin Bieber song
Me
Do you really want to see my "Let me be your boyfriend" outfit?

Leah

Yes 😇

Hmm, how should I play this…

I'm so sick of playing it safe, but if I'm wrong about this and Chloe finds out, she'll never stop giving me shit.

Fuck it.

I look down and realize I'm practically naked from my earlier attempt to take a shower. I'm wearing black American Eagle boxers and nothing else. I lean back and opt for a top-half selfie, showing off my hard-earned abs. I take about ten photos, choose the least douchey looking one, and hit send before I can change my mind.

It feels like hours have gone by waiting for her response.

Maybe I was too forward.

Finally, after what was actually only about two minutes, I get a response.

Leah

Usually an outfit consists of clothing

Me

A suit is clothing, and it's my birthday suit 🎂

Leah

My favorite kind of suit 😏

Me

😉

I wake up in the morning with no new messages. I guess we both fell asleep after I sent her my last text. Even though texting her exhilarated me, I was exhausted from helping Dad around the house all day and passed right out.

I forgot to set an alarm and only have twenty minutes until we have to leave for school. I hurry to shower, do my hair, brush my teeth, and like I told Leah, throw on the first thing my hand touches. Which did just so happen to be a fitted navy blue-and-white Hollister button-up, dark wash jeans, and white Nikes. Shockingly, Chloe is already waiting for me when I get in the driver's side of the Jeep.

"Jesus, I thought we were going to be late," Chloe chides.

"Calm down, Chlo, we live ten minutes from school. And what's gotten into you? Aren't I usually the uptight, punctual one?"

"It's hard to be calm, Jake. This is the last first day of high school." She taps her foot, shifting restlessly in her seat.

"Besides, we're still waiting on Leah," I point out.

"She's coming out now."

I look towards Leah's house just as she walks out of the front door. She's wearing the same dress and shoes she sent me a photo of last night, along with her backpack, which looks way too full for it being only the first day of school. Her strawberry hair is styled in large curls, and she has makeup on, including some glittery stuff on her cheeks. I don't know what it is, but she looks cute. Although I still prefer the makeup-free version I saw last night.

"Hey, guys," Leah says as she hops in the back seat.

"Hey," Chloe and I chime in unison. I want to comment on her dress, but I'm afraid it would be too obvious to Chloe, and I'm not ready to go there. Especially because I don't even know where "there" is yet.

Chloe glances between Leah and me, narrowing her eyes. "Aww, you guys match perfectly. How cute." She smirks.

I turn around to back out of the driveway, my eyes snagging on Leah's, and I try my damndest to stifle the smile threatening to bust across my face.

We get to school within ten minutes as promised. Chloe jumps out of my car before it's even in park.

"Where are you..." My words trail off when I spot Trey's white Toyota Camry parked a few spaces away from ours.

Leah and I grab our backpacks, get out of the Jeep, and begin walking towards the school together. Chloe is in the passenger seat of Trey's car, and they're kissing like starved animals. I mean, good for her, but I'd rather not see it.

"Nice dress," I say to Leah with a smirk.

"Thanks. You don't look so bad yourself. Decided to forgo the birthday suit?" She eyes my outfit up and down, and I can't help but wonder if she's thinking about what's under my button-up.

"Yeah, I didn't want detention the first day for breaking dress code."

"True, I'm not so sure Principal Langly would have approved."

"And you?" I grin down at her.

"What about me?"

"Would you have approved?"

"If you wore your birthday suit to school?" she asks incredulously as her cheeks turn pink. I can't help but smile. I love teasing her.

"Yes," I say with a straight face.

"I'm not sure, Mr. Summers. It is, after all, against the school dress code," she says in her most convincing Principal Langly impression. "I may just have to give you detention."

"Is that a promise?"

She stifles a laugh. "Afraid so, Mr. Summers."

"And what would that en—"

"Hey!" Chloe pops up in between us as we're just about to enter the front doors of the school.

"Jesus Christ," I yelp, throwing my hand over my chest. "Where the fuck did you come from?

"You scared the shit out of me," Leah squeals.

Well, I'm glad I'm not the only one.

"Sorry… Ready for class?" Chloe asks Leah. "I'm so excited we have the same homeroom this year."

They both start jumping up and down like they did when Mom and Dad said they were taking us all, Leah included, to Disney World for vacation a few summers back.

They're gone before I can even blink, and now I'm nostalgic thinking about that trip.

"I can't believe you talked me into this," Leah says, looking around at the "scary" decor lining the dilapidated walls surrounding us as we're in line for the Tower of Terror.

"Leah, we're at Disney, how freaking scary can this thing be?" I say pointedly.

"Scary enough that I was the only one stupid enough to go on it with you, apparently," Leah replies.

We shuffle forward in the line, and a woman dressed in ghost makeup directs a large group of us into a round room that looks like an old library. We're shoved in here like sardines and considering its July in Florida, it smells like it too.

The doors shut, the sound of lightning cracks, and then the room goes pitch-black. Leah throws her arms around my waist, and I hold her as she clings to me. The lights are flickering and people are looking around at the dramatics, but I can't pull my eyes away from Leah's head nuzzled into my chest.

I inhale the sweet smell of coconut and peppermint and rub my arm along her shoulder.

The lights flicker back on, a telltale sign that the show is over, and I'm immediately disappointed.

She looks up at me with her beautiful chestnut eyes and laughs. "I'm sorry."

"That's okay," I say as we remain clinging to one another. Her smiling lips are only inches away from mine. All it would take to taste them is a slight dip of my head.

"Alright, folks, this way," another "ghost" shouts, and the crowd starts pushing us towards the actual ride.

We untangle from one another, and my body immediately aches from the loss.

That was the first time I ever thought about kissing Leah Stone.

5

Jake

It's Friday afternoon, ending the longest first week of school I've ever had. Soccer practice has been grueling, and our teachers are power-tripping by starting the semester assigning us a billion bullshit projects. I drop my backpack on the kitchen island, then grab a protein bar from the pantry. The house phone rings, startling me.

Who even has a house phone anymore?

"Jake, can you get that?" Dad hollers from upstairs.

"Hewlo," I mumble into the phone, a protein bar hanging out of my mouth.

"Hello, this is a prepaid call from…" an automated voice says. I begin to pull the phone away to hang up. "Elysabeth Marie Summers." My hand freezes at the sound of Mom saying her name, and I return the phone to my ear. "An inmate at Athens County Jail." *What the fuck?* "To accept the charges, press one. To refuse the charges, press two."

I fumble the phone in my hands, pressing one firmly before returning it to my ear.

"Will?" Mom's trembling voice says on the other end of the line. "Will, can you hear me? I've fucked up. Big time. I need your help."

"Mom?" I croak out.

"Jake," she gasps.

"Why are you calling from Athens County Jail?"

"I, uh, oh this is, uh—"

"Mom, you can tell me. I'm not a little kid," I say, cutting off her rambling.

She breathes in and exhales loudly, and the faint sound of women chattering in the background comes through the line.

"I was arrested."

"Seriously?" I ask, calmly trying to process the information. "Are you okay?

"I'm fine, honey." She sighs.

"Why were you arrested?"

"I–it doesn't, it's just, it's nothing for you to worry about," she stutters nonchalantly.

"Nothing for me to worry about? Are you fucking kidding me, Mom?" I snap, unable to contain my anger. "You left without even so much as a fucking note!" I yell into the phone, seconds from crushing the cheap plastic in my hand. "Don't you think we've been wondering where the hell you've been? And the first phone call we get after months is from a fucking jail? And you can't even be honest about *why* you're in there?"

"It's just a misunderstanding. I should be out of here in a few days and then I'll come home. I promise." Her tone is anything but believable. "Could you please get your dad? I need to talk to him so he can help sort out this mess."

My temper has completely snapped just as Dad runs into the room.

"What's going on?" he probes with wide eyes. "Who are you talking to?"

"Your selfish fucking wife has been arrested. Did you know about this? Is that where she's been all this time and you just didn't bother to tell us?" I scream at him.

"What? No. Is that her on the phone? Let me talk to her," he commands, extending an open hand.

"She's all yours." I toss the cordless phone at Dad before hightailing it to my room. I throw on my running gear. I may have just practiced my ass off, but if I don't run this rage off, I'm gonna end up throwing my fist through a fucking wall.

I run seven miles before I trudge back through our red front door, dripping in sweat. Rage is still bubbling under the surface, but it's at least marginally contained.

"Jake, come here," Dad bellows from the living room before I can even shut the door.

"What, Dad?" I snap.

"We need to talk."

"Yeah. You're damn right we do. Where are the girls?"

"Chloe is out with Trey tonight, and Sophia is sleeping at Sage's house."

"Okay… Shouldn't they be part of this? At least Chloe?"

"Jake." Dad sighs. "I know this is asking a lot, but I need you to keep this between us for now."

"Why? So there can be more lies in this house?"

"The girls are finally coming back into a sense of normalcy since your mom left. Chloe is bouncing around the house like a lovesick puppy. I've never seen her this happy. And Sophia is thriving at school, making new friends. I don't want that to change. That *can't* change. You guys are just kids. You need to be having fun and worrying about the future. Not worrying about your mom." He snarls the last part with a wrinkled nose.

"How can I *not* worry? It's Mom. Why is she in there?"

"Jake," Dad says with pursed lips.

"If you want me to keep it from the girls," I say, crossing my arms over my chest, "you have to at least tell me why the hell she's even in there."

"Fine, but then you promise we can keep this between us a little while longer?"

I have to know what the hell she did, and if this is the only way to get that information, I'll happily agree. "Yes."

He exhales heavily. "She was arrested for drug possession."

"What?" I scoff. "No fucking way. How? Why?"

"Do you remember last year when your mom had that knee surgery?"

"Yeah, but she was walking normally within a few weeks. What does that have to do with this?"

"Well… the doctors prescribed her an opioid to help with the pain." He looks at me expectantly as if hoping I'll put the confusing as fuck puzzle pieces together. "She never stopped taking them."

"But I don't understand. There's no way a doctor would keep prescribing those a year after the accident," I say, shaking my head.

"A doctor didn't prescribe them, Jake," he admits. "She found other ways to buy them."

I sit down on the nearby kitchen chair, overwhelmed by Dad's confession.

"But why did she leave?" I ask, looking in his eyes, begging for the truth. "Doesn't she realize what it's done to our family?"

"Addiction makes you too selfish to care what you're doing to the people you love. Her leaving had nothing to do with you or your sisters. It's about her, her and her addiction. Until she decides herself that she doesn't need it anymore, it will always have a hold over her. Her desire to get high is stronger than her ability to be your mom. And I couldn't allow that. Not in my house. Not with my kids."

"What do you mean?"

His shoulders rise and fall with the release of a large exhale. "Your mom didn't just leave you guys out of nowhere. I made her leave," he admits.

"What?" I balk as my eyes almost pop out of my skull. "What do you mean, you *made* her leave?"

"A few days before your mom left, I came home from work early. Sophia was in her room, and I found your mom lying on our bathroom floor next to an open bottle of pills. I thought she'd overdosed. I ran to grab my phone to call for an ambulance but by the time I came back, she'd burst into manic laughter. Her eyes glazed over. I see that look twenty times a week. She was fucking high." He shakes his head. "It turns out she wasn't hurt, just too drugged to stand up, which she thought was just hilarious. She was supposed to be watching our child, but she was too fucking high to even get off the damn floor," he spits out, tears full of anger brimming on his eyelids. "What if Sophia had found her like that? We fought for hours until she finally told me where she got the pills."

"Jesus, Dad," I mutter.

"I gave her two options: she could stay at home with us, we'd get her help and move past this as a family, or she had to be gone by the end of the week. I guess you know what option she chose."

"So you didn't make her leave. She chose to. She chose drugs over us," I say, dragging my hands through my hair.

"Jake, she loves you all so much," he says, putting a hand on my shoulder.

"Yeah, she just loves the pills more," I say, shaking my head and standing up.

He pulls me to him, wrapping his arms around me. "Jake, I'm sorry. I wish I didn't have to burden you with all this. You need to remember that her leaving had nothing to do with you guys and everything to do with her."

"So what's going to happen to her now?" I pull away and look at him. "She said she needed your help. Are you going to bail her out?"

"No way." He shakes his head. "This is the best place your mom could be. I begged her to go to rehab, but I guess she wasn't ready, and now the decision has been made for her. Hopefully, she'll use the time to move past her addiction and prepare herself to be a part of your lives again."

"I guess you're right." I sigh heavily.

"I've got to work the night shift tonight," Dad says, reaching for his keys, ending the conversation. "Are you going to be okay here alone?"

"Yeah, I'll be fine."

"And I know it's asking a lot of you, Jake, but *please* keep this between us. I just want you kids to be happy," he begs with pleading eyes.

"Okay."

"Love you, kid." He kisses the side of my head before leaving the room.

"You too," I mumble under my breath after he's already gone.

As much as everything he said makes sense, I can't shake the sinking feeling knowing he's kept this from me all summer. The one person I trust without question hid something so massive from me. If he could do that, could he also have lied about what happened with Mom? I need to know. I have to hear her side of the story too.

I need to see my mom.

6
Leah

I wander through the Summers house in search of Chloe. When I finally get to her room, I see that it's empty, just as the garage was, so I pull out my phone.

CHLOE

Me

Where are you? 😶

A text bounces back immediately.

Chloe

I'm out with Trey tonight. Sorry I didn't tell you! He surprised me with a last minute date and I couldn't say no. 😶

Me

That's okay, have fun 

We didn't exactly have set plans, but we always hang out on Fridays. *Is it so hard for her to at least keep me in the loop?* I'm happy for her. I really am. It's just, Chloe and I have been a package deal for our entire lives. I don't even know what to do with myself without having her around all the time. Even at school, we now sit with Trey and his friends at lunch. That does include Jake, which is a bonus, but it doesn't take away the sting of feeling like I've lost my best friend. I know she'll always be there for me for the important stuff, but being alone in our art studio this week just felt wrong. I missed the sound of her throwing clay or cursing the pottery wheel when it wasn't cooperating.

A rustling sound comes from Jake's room.

"Hey, Jacob," I say, waltzing in without bothering to knock.

"Hey," he clips with his back facing me while stuffing various items into a backpack. My mouth goes dry at the sight of him. He is clad in black gym shorts, no shirt, and his hair is wet like he just took a shower.

"What are you up to?" I question, moderately distracted by the rippling muscles of his back.

"Nothing." He unplugs his phone charger from the wall and shoves it into his bag.

"Are you okay?" I press, walking closer to him.

"I'm fine." He exhales heavily while grabbing a tube of toothpaste off the bed. He's throwing things in his backpack like he's about to flee the country.

"Are you going somewhere?"

"Leah," he snaps, spinning around. "What's with the third degree?"

"I'm sorry," I apologize with wide eyes. "I just—you don't seem okay."

He sits on the bed, and his toned shoulders slump as he rubs his hands over his face.

"Jake…" I kneel down, placing a hand on his knee, willing him to look at me. When he finally does, he looks absolutely broken. Red-rimmed eyes and a solemn expression. The last time I saw him so distraught was after he broke his leg freshman year and was told he might not be able to play soccer ever again. "What's going on?"

He's shaking his head like he doesn't want to tell me, but the look in his eyes says otherwise.

"You can talk to me." I rub my thumb against his knee, and he looks down at it.

"I can't." He sighs as a lone tear falls down his cheek, and I wipe it away with my thumb.

"Why not?"

He opens his mouth to speak but closes it again. "You'll tell Chloe."

"Jake, if the only reason you're hesitating to tell me whatever is going on with you is because you don't want Chloe to know, I promise I can keep this between us. Okay?" I take his hand in mine and squeeze it gently.

I hate keeping things from Chloe, but Jake looks completely and utterly broken. If I can help ease just a fraction of that pain, I'll willingly bear the burden.

He scans my expression, looking for any sign that he shouldn't trust me but finding none.

"Fine." He frowns with pursed lips. "But you're going to need to sit down for this." He tugs my hand and pulls me to sit next to him on the bed, then fills me in on his entire fucked-up afternoon.

"Holy shit," I bark out, now pacing in Jake's room. "So what, now you're just going to drive to Georgia by yourself to see Lysa?"

"That's the plan." He shrugs, still sitting on the bed.

"I can't let you do that." I shake my head and sit down next to him.

"Well, you sure as hell aren't going to stop me," he snaps.

"That's not what I meant." I put up my hands in defense. "I mean I can't let you go alone."

"You want to come with me?" he asks with furrowed brows.

"Yeah?" I mirror his expression. "I'll just tell my parents I'm spending the night with the Summers. It's not a lie." I grin, and he throws his arm around my shoulders, tugging me in for a tight side hug. His scent envelops me completely to the notes of pine, temptation, and everything I want but can never have.

"You would really do that for me?" He holds me against him, and the faint smell of peppermint on his breath is a fucking narcotic in itself. He kisses the top of my head, and while the gesture seems platonic, it doesn't stop my heart from nearly bursting out of my chest.

"Of course." *I would do anything for you.*

We're only halfway through our eight-hour drive, and it's already past midnight. Jake is quiet and completely focused on the road. The mellow playlist coming through the speakers is the perfect backdrop for our comfortable silence. I'm gazing ahead when the Jeep swerves slightly off to the shoulder to the right. I gasp, gripping the handle tightly as my heart rate accelerates before Jake jerks back onto the road, shaking his head and readjusting his grip on the steering wheel.

"We should pull over for the night," I suggest once my breathing steadies.

"I'm fine," he argues, white-knuckling the steering wheel.

"No. You're not fine. You're exhausted. You had practice *and* you said you ran another five miles earlier."

"Seven." He grins.

"Sorry, *seven*." I roll my eyes, smirking. "Like I said, you're exhausted. The visiting hours don't open until nine anyways, and we're only like four hours away. We still have plenty of time."

He lets out a heavy exhale before conceding. "Okay."

Ten minutes later, we're pulling into a rest stop on the side of the highway. Jake opens the sunroof and we lay our seats back, staring up at the stars.

"What are you going to say when you see her?" I ask hesitantly.

"I haven't gotten that far." He sighs.

"What would you say if she was here right now?"

"Honestly?" He turns his gaze on me. "I'd ask her how she let it get this far. When she left, she might have been too addicted to quit on a dime. But there was a day before that when she looked at the tiny pill in her hand, knowing what the repercussions could be if she didn't stop taking it, knowing she had a family depending on her, and decided to swallow it again anyways."

"Jake…" I turn my body towards him, reaching across the center console to place my hand on his bicep. He covers it with his warm hand, giving it a small squeeze. "I can't even begin to imagine how hard this must be for you."

"Le." He turns his concerned gaze on me. "You *have* to stop doing that."

"Doing what?" I ask with furrowed brows.

"Acting like you don't feel as broken as we do about her leaving," he says softly.

"I just... She's *your* mom. It feels wrong to act like... I don't know," I say, exasperated, as a lone tear escapes and slides down my cheek. He turns towards me and places his palm on my face, brushing it away with his thumb.

"You've been at our house every day for the last fifteen years, been on every family vacation, been there at every holiday. I know how much you love her. How much she loves you. Hell," he says, chuckling while pushing a strand of hair behind my ear, "sometimes I think you're her favorite, always bonding over all the artsy stuff."

My cheek is on fire from his touch. I can't remember the last time I've had this amount of direct eye contact with Jake. His intense stare steals the breath from my lungs.

"That's not true." I smile and try to think of something to say that could lighten the mood of this moment. "She likes you a decent amount."

I feel his rumbling laugh all the way to my toes, and I'm thankful for his response to my attempt at humor.

He sighs. "God, I'm so mad at her." He runs his warm palm down my arm and takes my hand in his, holding it against his chest. "What she's done to us, to our family... to *you*."

I squirm in my seat. It's all too much. His stare, his touch, his concern. I should be the one consoling him, not the other way around. My heart is pounding so hard in my ears that I may go deaf.

"I feel like such an idiot." He shakes his head. "Just thinking about all the shit she missed out on before she left, it all makes sense now..."

"What do you mean?" I shift my focus, giving him my full attention.

"She was the perfect mom," he says wistfully. "Always. To us. To you. She was at every game, tournament, parent/teacher conference, art shows for you and Chlo. Made cupcakes from scratch for our bake sales. She *never* missed anything." He exhales loudly. "Then she started missing *everything*. No mom screaming her head off in the crowd during my games. Letters sent home from teachers because she missed the parent/teacher conferences. Sophia even called me because Mom forgot to pick her up from school a few times… Oh, and no *fucking* cupcakes!"

I can't stop the laugh that bubbles out of my mouth at the last point on his list, and his lips tug upwards too. "Sorry." He chuckles. "Food on the brain."

"That's okay, I know the way to your heart is through your stomach… and bacon works the best." I grin, and he smirks at me as his thumb rubs over the inside of my wrist, causing my body to shiver. *Hopefully he didn't notice.* "Well… at least tomorrow you'll get some answers."

"Will you see her with me?" he asks as his breathtaking green eyes bore into mine. Eyes that I couldn't say no to if I tried.

"I assumed you'd want to talk to her alone," I say weakly.

"Honestly?" He shifts position so we're holding hands on the center console. My gaze is frozen on the spot where we connect as he rubs circles on my palm with his thumb. "You being there with me would make it a hell of a lot easier to handle."

My heart constricts at the idea that my presence would have enough of an effect on Jake to help ease his worry. "Okay, I'll come."

"Thank you." He smiles softly.

"For what?"

"For this." He squeezes my hand. "For coming with me so I didn't have to face it alone. I'm so grateful for you."

"Jake, I'm always here for you," I say quietly.

"I know that. It's just, I know it's half my fault, but as we've gotten older, I feel like we've drifted apart. And I hate it. We used to be best friends. Don't get me wrong, I'm glad you and Chloe are still so close. I guess I just—I miss this. Us hanging out. Talking. Being real with each other."

"I know. Me too."

"Thanks for being my friend again," he says with a sleepy smile as he rubs his thumb softly against my hand.

"Yeah, of course," I manage to croak out.

If he wants to pretend that this touch is friendly, I'll play along, but we're fooling ourselves to act like this is anything other than what it is. A match dropped on a gunpowder trail, slow burning towards dynamite.

Jake closes his eyes and after a few minutes, his breathing steadies into a rhythm. His hand is still, no longer tracing circles on my palm. Eventually, my heart rate returns to normal, and I allow myself to relax too, savoring the protective grip of his warm, rough hand in mine.

7
Jake

Leah and I are sitting side by side in a dimly lit room full of strangers, all mirroring a similar position.

My hands are folded on the cold metal table in front of me as my right leg bounces uncontrollably. Leah reaches out and places her hand on my knee to steady it, and I'm instantly more relaxed.

I hear a buzzing sound and glance at the door to see female inmates trickling into the room wearing blue shirts and matching pants with plain white tennis shoes. A tall, thin blonde walks into the room, looking around anxiously. *There she is.* Her search stops when her gaze gets to our table, and she walks over with a blank expression. Leah removes her hand from my leg and folds her hands in her lap.

"Hey, Mom," I say, staying seated as she reaches the table.

"Hi, Lysa," Leah says uncomfortably.

"Hey, kiddos," she replies, sitting opposite of me.

She places her hands on the table, and they're trembling. I wonder if she's nervous or in withdrawal. She reaches out to grab my hand and the second her skin touches mine, I yank mine back, uncomfortable with the contact.

"Jacob," she pleads, with tears brimming her sunken eyes. Her once perfectly polished face now looks worn and tired. "I'm so sorry… to both of you… to all of you."

"We don't need your apologies, Mom." I sigh.

"Then why are you here?" she asks, holding herself.

"I don't know." I shake my head as my leg starts to bounce again. "I guess for answers."

"What do you mean?" she asks with furrowed brows.

"How did you end up *here*?" I throw my hands up and drag them through my hair. Her nose is running, and she uses her shirt to wipe it. Leah places her hand on my leg again, pushing it down forcefully to stop the anxious bouncing.

"You already know the answer to that." She cocks her head to the side.

"How would I know?" I ask with furrowed brows.

"Your dad called this morning and said you might be showing up," she says with a half smile. *Damn, that smile reminds me so much of Chloe.*

"I never told him I was coming." I narrow my eyes at her.

"He's a smart man. Give him a little credit." *I probably should have at least left a note…* "I am a bit surprised to see you here though, Leah," she says with raised brows. "Do Paul and Nora know you're here?"

"Do Paul and Nora know *you're* here?" Leah responds, and I have to bite my lip from laughing at her response. Mom purses her lips with a frown and sighs.

"Why were you arrested, Mom? Your version," I demand.

"I, Jake, I—there's just…" she sputters, folding her arms across her chest, rubbing her palms along her biceps.

"Mom, just spit it out." I wave a hand in the air towards her. Leah squeezes my leg, which I'm sure is her way of saying, *relax.*

"It was honestly stupid." She looks away from us and shakes her head. "I was driving home from dinner, and I took out my phone to text a friend… and I just took my eyes off the road for a second and somehow hit a parked car."

"And?" I press, knowing there's obviously more to the story.

"Well, the cops showed up and decided to search my car. I protested, but they did it anyway." She rolls her eyes. "Anyways, they searched my car and found my friend's pill bottle in the glove compartment. It wasn't my prescription, so they arrested me for drug possession."

"Seriously, Mom?" I deadpan.

"She had forgotten them in there. I was going to give them back to her next week." *Liar is written all over her face.*

"What was your friend's name?" Leah asks, seeing through her bullshit as easily as I can.

"Oh, uh, she—" Mom stutters, looking between Leah and I with wide eyes.

"Damn it, Mom," I whisper shout, slamming the metal table between us. A guard looks over and starts walking towards us. I put my hands up to show him everything is fine, and he settles back against the wall. "I'm sick of the fucking lies." I shake my head again. "There was no friend. The friend was you. *You're* the fucking addict."

"No, I'm no—"

"The first step to recovery is admitting you have a problem," I snap.

"Jake, like I said, it was a misund—"

"This is un-fucking-believable." I shake my head and stand up. "Let's go, Le. We're leaving."

Leah stands quickly, and I take her hand in mine.

"Wait!" The sound of a metal chair screeching against the linoleum floor, paired with Mom's desperate tone, has me turning back to face her. "Please."

"No," I say firmly. "You have a family who fucking loves you. We're all here for you. But if you can't at least admit you have a problem, I don't want you in my life, and I'm damn sure never letting you around the girls." The guard is eyeing me suspiciously, but I don't care. She needs to hear this. "How long are you in for?"

"Three to five, depending… Maybe earlier if I can get out on good behavior," she replies quietly, looking down at the table.

"Months?" I hold my breath for her answer.

"Years…" Her sad eyes connect with mine.

"Fuck, Mom." I sigh loudly. "You're going to get clean in here. If not for me, then for the girls." I risk a quick glance Leah's way, and she's trying her damndest not to cry. I squeeze her hand three times. *I'm right here, Le.*

"Jacob," Mom says, pulling my attention back to her. "I already told you they weren't mi—"

"The first step is admitting you have a *fucking* problem."

It's already dark when we arrive back in Longwood. Neither of us were really in the talking mood, so we listened to the radio and drove in comfortable silence. Most people would find it uncomfortable spending eight hours in the car with someone and barely speaking, but I guess when you've been friends for so long, it kind of takes away the awkwardness.

Leah was nervous that Chloe was going to text or call her asking where she was, and she would have to lie about it. She's a horrible liar and keeping stuff from Chloe eats at her, but her worries were unfounded because she didn't hear a peep from Chloe all day. She kept checking her phone and nibbling at her nails, which she typically only does when she's nervous. I think hearing nothing from Chloe bothered her even more.

"Thank you again for coming with me," I say as I pull into the driveway and kill the engine.

"Like I said before, you need me, and I'm there. Okay?" She smiles softly.

"Okay." I grin, jumping out of the Jeep.

"See ya." She waves before spinning around and walking towards her house.

"See you." I'm unable to take my eyes off her until she disappears inside.

I walk through the front door, and Dad's leaning against the kitchen counter, staring at me with his arms folded. *Shit.*

We stare at one another for what feels like hours before Dad finally breaks the silence. "Did you get the answers you were hoping for?"

"Not really," I admit, walking closer to him in an attempt to decipher his mood.

"Do you want to talk about it?"

"You know what?" I throw my backpack on the floor with a loud thud. "Yeah, I do want to talk about it."

"Okay," he says, waiting for me to elaborate.

"I can't believe she did this," I shout in frustration. "When did she become so damn selfish?"

"I'm sorry, Jake." He sighs. "I just, I wish I had the right words to make you feel better but I just… don't. I guess that's why I've avoided this conversation."

"The girls are going to be devastated," I croak out.

"I know." He kisses my head.

"We can't tell them," I say firmly.

"What?" he asks, surprised.

"Just like you said yesterday, they're finally happy. Mom's already ruined us once, and they're finally getting back to a new normal. I don't want to wreck that." I can tell I'm not going to have to fight Dad hard on this one. "She won't even admit she has a fucking problem. I can't just tell the girls we found her but still don't know when or if she's coming back. Not yet."

"We'll tell them by Christmas?" Dad asks hesitantly, and I can tell he's as frustrated with all of this as I am.

"Okay," I agree.

He pulls away and demands my eye contact. "I know you weren't alone." He smirks.

"Are you going to tell Paul and Nora?" I ask, holding my breath for his response.

Please don't tell Leah's parents. They're so hard on her. She'll be grounded until graduation.

"No. I'm not going to let that girl be punished for something she can't control."

I look at him with furrowed brows. "What do you mean?"

"Come on, Jake. You just spent twenty-four hours alone with the girl, and you really have no clue what I'm talking about?"

I shake my head, praying he'll elaborate.

"You two have been running circles around each other, literally and figuratively, since you were three years old. She would do anything for you—including leaving the state to visit a jail hours away at a moment's notice. That girl is special, and I hope to God you figure that out for yourself before it's too late and some other idiot comes and snatches her away for good."

My jaw is hanging to the floor. He rarely comments on my dating life and has never—ever—said anything to me that would allude to him thinking there could be something between Leah and me.

"All I'm trying to say is life is short. Don't waste it playing games."

"When did you get so wise, huh?" I tease in an attempt to lighten the mood.

"I just know what it's like watching someone you love fade away." He sighs, looking down to the floor with empty eyes. "Regardless of the reason."

For the first time in months, I really look at him. I notice how completely and utterly broken he is. I've been so focused on the fact that Mom left me and the girls, but she left him too. She woke up one day and said, *I love my husband, but I love the pills more.* My chest aches as I stare at the broken man in front of me. The man who always stands up straight, towering tall and strong in every room. The man who always smiles and jokes, making sure those around him are okay.

"I don't want you to spend a single minute being unsatisfied with your life, Jacob. If there's something you want, go for it and don't look back."

"Dad…" I smile tenderly, pulling him to me for a tight hug.

"But if you ever leave the state again without even so much as a note, you will be grounded for the rest of your life. You understand?"

"Yes… I'm sorry."

"Alright, go get some rest. You must be exhausted," he commands, ending the conversation abruptly in his usual fashion. He's definitely right about the exhaustion. I barely make it to my room before collapsing on my bed, not even bothering to take a shower and rinse off the prison stench. I avoid thinking about the conversation with Mom and focus instead on how my body ignited in flames every time Leah's fingertips grazed my skin.

My muscles relax as the smoldering memory allows me to drift peacefully to sleep.

8
Leah

I walk through the Summers' red front door, hoping to find Chloe or even Sophia for some company.

"Hey, Leah," Will calls from the kitchen. "Are you hungry?"

"I could eat." I shrug, walking into the room as he constructs a sandwich on the marble island. He grabs another plate and two slices of bread. "It's so quiet in here."

"Yeah, all the kids are out," he says sadly. My heart breaks seeing him like this. Will has always been the fun dad. The never-let-you-notice-anything-is-wrong dad. I fucking hate what Lysa leaving has done to this family.

"Not all of them," I say, smiling and putting my hands under my face.

He chuckles and slides the sandwich over to me. "You're right, thanks for keeping an old guy company."

I take a bite of my sandwich and look around at the empty house, ignoring the sinking feeling in my stomach. I used to come here every day after school, and Chloe would be waiting for me so we could hang out, go to the studio, listen to music. Now I only really get to see her at school. She's either busy with Trey or studying for her AP classes. I know that we're growing up and getting lives of our own, but it just feels like I'm getting left behind. I'm trying to figure out who the hell I even am without Chloe.

"You doing okay, kiddo?" Will asks, snapping me out of my thoughts.

"Yeah," I say, attempting to put on a brave face and failing miserably.

"Listen, Leah." He exhales heavily. "I'm really sorry you had to get involved with this whole mess with Lysa." I look down at my plate, unable to think of any words to respond. I'm not shocked. Jake told me Will knows I went with him and isn't going to tell my parents. "But the other part of me is thankful that you're able to be there for Jake. He's hurting more than he lets on, and I think you might be the only one he actually opens up to… So thank you."

His words surprise me. Since going to see Lysa, we haven't really talked much, and when we do, it just feels like there's this tension I can't explain.

"Of course," I say, trying to muster a smile back at him.

"I need a new painting for the downstairs bathroom. Think you could make us something?" he asks, smiling with a tilted head.

"Yeah," I say, grinning. "I think I can come up with something."

"Okay, great. I've gotta go pick Sophia up." He places his plate in the sink, then grabs his keys off the counter. "Just lock up if you head out before we're back, okay?"

"Sure." I wipe my hands on a napkin and throw it on my plate.

"Hey, Will?" I say as he's walking towards the front door, and he spins back around. "Thanks." I smile genuinely.

"Anytime, kiddo." He shuts the door, and I'm left in the empty house. It's nice knowing Will cares, but it also reminds me just how *uninvolved* my own parents are. I've been walking around lost in thought for at least a week, and neither of them have even asked once if I'm doing okay.

I wash our plates and put them on the drying rack, then go to the art studio to do the one thing that brings me distraction from the guilt of not telling Chloe about Lysa.

The one thing that makes me forget how damn lonely I am.

9
Jake

"Pass, pass!" Coach Hamilton bellows from the sidelines. It's Thursday night, game night, and we're already three matches into the final season of my high school career. So far, our record is three to zero. If I have any hope of getting out of this town, state, or maybe even country, I need to get us to the state championships undefeated. My teammates are good, but they don't all take this shit as seriously as I do. I'm the striker, so there's a lot of pressure on me to catch the passes and make it into the net. Not to mention the fact that unless I get a full ride, I'll probably end up at Longwood Community College and my soccer dreams will die along with my soul.

Trey, who's a midfielder, intercepts the ball from going out of bounds and dribbles it downfield. He looks up, eyes connecting with mine, then launches the ball directly towards my zone. I sprint to ensure I'm in the right position before stopping it with my chest. The ball falls to the ground. I dribble closer and closer to the goal. Breathe in. Breathe out. I cock my foot back, and in one fluid motion, I launch the ball towards the goal. My breath hitches as it flies through the air, just barely grazing the fingertips of the opposing team's goalie before landing safely in the back of the white net.

Hell. Yes.

Moments later, three long blows sound from the referee, signaling the end of the game. We beat Jenkins High by one point, continuing the season's undefeated streak. The bleachers erupt in loud cheers as my teammates rush to me on the field. We form into a circle, arms slung around one another's shoulders.

"Stallions! Stallions!" I chant our school's mascot, with my teammates falling in sync.

"Stallions on three," I shout.

"One. Two. Stallions!" The team howls unanimously, shooting goosebumps down my spine. There is something incomparable about being part of a team like mine.

After we shake hands with the opposing team, we make our way back to the side of the field to start gathering our belongings.

Chloe sprints to me with a huge smile and tackles me with a hug. "Congratulations, big bro!"

Her hair is in high pigtails with ribbons. She's sporting a Longwood Soccer shirt with Trey's and my numbers hand-painted on the front in alternating school colors, blue and yellow, and the same color paint under her eyes. She has a perfect stallion painted on her cheek—Leah's doing, I'm sure. I've never seen Chloe look happier, and it just confirms the decision not to tell her about Mom.

"Thanks, Chlo," I reply, my smile growing wider as I spot Leah standing behind Chloe wearing a similar outfit, except she's sporting the hoodie I gave her at the bonfire before school started. It's humid as hell, so I have no clue how she can stand being in it, but I'm not complaining. It looks fucking hot on her, and not just because my last name is blazoned across her back.

"Congratulations, Jakey." Leah grins awkwardly while giving me a side hug. I put my arm around her, holding her a second longer than necessary before she pulls away. I hate this weird tension between us. I've hardly seen her since we saw Mom two weeks ago, and we haven't had any more late-night conversations. I barely have a free minute from the time I wake up until my head hits the pillow at night, and I'm so tired I fall asleep the moment I get in bed. *Excuses. Excuses. Excuses.*

"Hey, Jake," Laura says, walking up to us, her high ponytail bouncing with each step. She's wearing her Longwood High cheer uniform, and I can admit she looks good. "Great game," Laura says, smiling and opening her arms for a hug.

"Thanks, great cheering," I say, embracing her. I pull away and look down at her face. My jersey number is painted on her cheek in blue. *Hmm, okay.* "Nice number," I say, narrowing my eyes at her with a smile.

"Oh," she says, laughing nervously. "Everyone on the team picked a player."

And she picked me... Interesting.

"Love your face paint, guys," Laura says, turning her attention to Chloe and Leah.

"Thanks," they respond in unison.

"Alright, well, I gotta go. See you at the party later?" she asks, turning her attention back to me.

"Yeah, sure," I say with a weak smile. It's Labor Day weekend, and we don't have school Friday or Monday, so we're kicking off the long weekend by having a big bonfire at the springs. "See you there."

Chloe has wandered off too, no doubt to find Trey. At first, I was annoyed that she was dating a teammate of mine, worried it may throw off his game, but so far, it's been fine.

"Nice sweatshirt," I tease Leah with a sideways grin while taking the fabric on her shoulder between my fingers.

"Oh, uh…" she stammers, glancing where my fingers rest on her shoulder. "Do you want it back?"

She begins taking off my hoodie. The skin of her stomach is increasingly more visible with each inch it glides up her torso. I realize, one: she is probably wearing a crop top, and as much as I want to see what's underneath, I don't want anyone else here to see, and two: I really do want her to keep it. I know she's not technically mine, but her wearing my number means something, at least to me. And as long as she's wearing my number, she's not wearing one of my teammates'.

I reach forward and grab the hem of my hoodie, keeping it in place on her body. My fingers graze down her bare stomach as I pull the hoodie back into place.

"No." I smirk. "You should keep it. It's nice to have a *fan club* in the crowd."

"Ha. Ha. Jake Summers Fan Club, party of two," she says while holding up two fingers like a peace sign.

"Wouldn't it be three?" I tease, pointing towards Laura, who is now standing with the rest of the cheer team. She's watching us and glances away quickly.

"Yeah… I guess you're right. Three." She crosses her arms over her chest, and I swear her chestnut eyes flickered green for a moment.

"Like I said, Le, keep it. Looks better on you than me."

"Thanks," she replies, grinning as her cheeks turn pink. "We came with your dad… so I was hoping you could give me a ride to the party tonight?"

"You're not riding with Chloe and Trey?" I ask before I can think about the words coming out of my mouth.

"I mean, I guess I could."

"I'm kidding, Le, of course I can," I say before she can change her mind.

"Thanks," she says, smiling. "Honestly, being in the car alone with the two of them is like—"

"Trust me, I know," I cut her off, not needing her to elaborate on the ridiculous amount of PDA that Chloe and Trey display on the regular. Part of the reason I've barely seen Leah is because Chloe is spending so much time with him.

"Alright, I still have to go shower, so I'll meet you at my car in like fifteen minutes?"

"You only need fifteen minutes to fix all of… that?" she asks, scrunching her nose while waving her finger towards me. I look down at my sticky, sweaty jersey and the grass stains on my knees. *Maybe she's right…*

"I'm a guy, Le. I don't need an hour in the mirror and five outfit changes to go to a bonfire."

"Just go get cleaned up. You stink."

I meet Leah at the Jeep, and the cute pigtails she sported earlier are gone, along with the face paint and any signs that she was just playing cheerleader at a high school soccer game. High-waisted light wash jeans hug her curves perfectly and—*yep, I knew it*—a black crop top T-shirt shows off just an inch or so of her tan and velvety smooth stomach.

Fuck.

She's holding my soccer hoodie loosely, allowing visibility of the delicate patches of freckles along her arms. Her most beautiful feature.

"Ready to go?" I ask her out of habit as I unlock the Jeep.

"Yep," she says, smiling and hopping in the passenger seat.

Like our trip to Georgia, we ride in comfortable silence except for the background noise supplied by the radio, which is playing our local country station. After ten minutes, "Check Yes or No" by George Strait starts playing through the car speakers. I know the lyrics by heart. It was always one of my parents' favorite songs. When I was younger, they would belt it out as loud as possible every time it came on the radio.

Listening to those lyrics while sitting next to the girl next door, who I've known my whole life—I can't help but feel like it's some kind of sick joke from the universe. I wonder if she would check yes as fast as I would if given the choice.

God, I'm such a sappy fuck sometimes.

Maybe I should stop being such a pessimist and take it as an encouragement to stop being such a damn idiot. There is no awkwardness in the air between us, but I do feel anxious. It's not from the lack of conversation, more so because I can't stop staring at the holes in her jeans giving a slight peek at her long, tan legs or the fact that her right knee is jumping up and down about as fast as my heart rate.

We have spent so much time together over the years but since high school, we've never been alone for more than a few minutes here and there. *Excluding our trip to see Mom.* I think that's also one of the reasons I've never mentioned anything regarding the way I feel about her. I hadn't even admitted those feelings to myself until a few weeks ago after seeing how supportive Leah was during all the shit going on with my mom. The way she made me feel calm even when I was seething with rage underneath the surface. That's the kind of girl—hell, the girl—I want by my side when life gets rough.

The more I stare at her and think about the conversations we've had these past few weeks, I can't help but wonder what it would be like to actually be together.

To fall in love with the girl I've known my whole life.

10
Leah

The Jeep is on *E*, so we stop for gas on the way to the springs. Jake suggests that he could go after the party, but I make the excellent point that getting gas in the middle of the night on an abandoned highway seems like the beginning of an episode of *Dateline NBC*.

I wait in the car while Jake pumps the gas and goes in to pay. Jake exits the store, and a small white plastic bag is dangling from his fingers. He pauses at the driver's side window, rustles around in it, then holds up a pack of sour Skittles and a strawberry Gatorade, smiling at me with a huge cheesy grin and a raised eyebrow. He opens the door and hands them to me, then slides in.

"Got you a little something," he says, his proud smile still plastered wide. He pulls out a blue Gatorade and a pack of regular Skittles for himself.

"Oh, wow." I'm unable to hide the giddy smile on my face.

"Thanks, Jake. These are my favorite."

"I know." He blushes, looking over at me while unscrewing the top of his drink. "You learn a lot about a person when you've known them for fifteen years."

"I suppose that's true." I watch as he takes a swig of the Gatorade—his Adam's apple bobs with each swallow. We've known one another forever, but it's still a surprise when someone else notices these small things about you. Especially when it's someone you thought barely noticed you at all.

Jake puts the car in reverse, places his right hand on the back of my seat, and turns to look out the rear window. His hand brushes my shoulder while he backs up, and my heart races. His thumb lightly grazes my shoulder as he pulls it away, returning his hand to the steering wheel and pulling onto the main road.

"Besides, don't you remember that Halloween when we were nine?" he asks, glancing quickly in my direction before turning his attention back to the road. "Ms. Jansen down the street gave out full-sized sour Skittles and when we got back to the house, you convinced everyone to trade their sour Skittles with you for all of the other candy you had. I begged you to let me keep one bag, and you wouldn't take no for an answer and wrestled me for it." He laughs, shaking his head. "I guess I realized that day you would all but kill a man for a pack of sour Skittles."

My heart rate quickens. *I can't believe he actually remembers that.*

"Oh yeah." I grin, popping one of the Skittles in my mouth. The sour candy fizzles against my tongue with a burst of green apple.

Mmm, so good.

"What else do you know about me?" I challenge, watching his every movement. Curiosity overpowers my desire to play it cool.

"I know that you love strawberries but hate strawberry ice cream.

That you love the beach but hate the sand. You're stubborn as hell when you think you're right but always willing to apologize if you realize you're wrong, which isn't too often. You like salt on your popcorn but not your eggs, and a vanilla iced latte is your caffeine of choice," he says matter-of-factly.

I place my hand over my chest in an attempt to calm my pounding heart. I can barely breathe from the confession. "Oh, wow, J—"

"Your favorite color is light pink because it reminds you of bubble gum. You love country music but also know the words to every Drake song ever written. You'll always choose Lucky Charms, but you only eat the little marshmallows." He chuckles. "If someone is behind you walking out of a building, you always hold the door open for them even if you're in a rush. You still watch Disney Channel after you've watched too much TV that makes you sad or scared, and you love to read trashy romance novels. Which are basically just handwritten porn if you ask me. Oh, and every time you have an exam, you wear the pearl clip in your hair that your grandma gave you for good luck."

My mouth is hanging open, my stomach in knots. I try to speak, but the words don't come out. I know tons of little details about Jake too, but even though we've known one another for so long, I never thought he really noticed me. I mean, obviously we talked and he knew I was around, but I mean *noticed me,* noticed me. Enough to know my likes, dislikes, and little quirks—some that I didn't even realize about myself.

Seconds later, we arrive at the springs, and Jake finds a parking spot near Matt's truck. Unsurprisingly, the lot is already filled with cars from almost our entire school. Most of the attendees tonight didn't need an extra hour to get ready and arrive here.

Jake cuts the engine, and we both hop out of the Jeep.

"Don't forget the hoodie. It's kind of cold," Jake says before I shut my door.

"It's eighty degrees, Jacob." I narrow my eyes at him with a smirk.

"Le..." He sighs. "Could you just..." He gestures to it with his hand. "Please?"

I roll my eyes dramatically. "Fine, *Dad*." I grab the hoodie, slam the door shut, then meet him at the back to start walking toward the springs.

"If you're gonna call me that, I'm going to need you to say Daddy instead," he says in a serious tone as the corner of his mouth twitches upwards. I throw my head back, laughing, and shake my head.

"You're ridiculous," I say, unable to wipe the smile off my face.

"You're ridiculous, *Daddy*," he corrects me, and I giggle while rolling my eyes.

The sun has already set and there aren't many lights on the path to the springs, so it's a bit freaky to walk at night. I'm thankful Jake is here, but I can't stop myself from overanalyzing his confession in the car. He seems unaffected, having the same relaxed, carefree look about him as he always does.

Halfway through our walk to the springs, there's a bustling movement in the bushes. I gasp and grab Jake's arm tightly, pulling him to me. A second later, I make out the outline of a squirrel running up a tree. *Oops.*

"A little jumpy tonight, Le?"

"Hey, it's dark out here." I elbow him softly in the ribs. "You can't pretend you're not even the least bit freaked out."

"A man shows no fear." He puffs out his chest.

"I see no men here."

We walk for another minute before I realize I'm still holding on to his arm.

"Oh, sorry," I mumble, looking at the place where our bodies connect and withdrawing my grasp. Thankfully, it's too dark for him to see the hot flush on my cheeks.

"That's okay," he responds in a tone I can't quite decipher.

We reach closer to the end of the path opening up at the springs. Jake places his hand on my back, guiding me out of the woods. His strong, calloused hand grazes against my skin, leaving goosebumps in its wake. My skin is burning hot, yet somehow the gesture still feels familiar—comforting.

Once we emerge from the trees, he drops his hand, and I immediately ache at the loss of contact.

Half the partygoers are ambling around on the shore, drinking or playing party games, and the others are in the springs, swimming under the moonlight. We really got lucky with the weather. It's in the mid-seventies tonight, which isn't typical for North Florida in early September.

A few girls around the springs are giving me dirty looks as we amble towards the spot where the drinks are set up. Jake may be one of my oldest friends, but I am definitely not blind to the fact that he is one of the—hell, *the* hottest guy in our school. I have been getting jealous looks from girls for years simply from always being around him. I always told everyone he's like a brother to me, although that's hardly the case anymore. At least if I'm reading correctly into our interactions lately. Something has been… different.

"Pick your poison." Jake gestures, waving to the wide array of liquor spread out on the table. There are a few coolers next to the table which presumably contain mixers, soda, water, and beer.

"Uh, I'll have a beer," I request in an attempt to sound cool and casual.

"Okay." He grins, leaning down and rustling ice around in one of the coolers before pulling out a Bud Light. He twists the top off and hands it to me.

He never takes his eyes off me as I bring the cold bottle to my lips. I take a long pull and try as hard as possible to hide the look of disgust on my face as the malty liquid glides along my tongue towards my throat. *This shit is disgusting. Why do people drink this stuff?*

"And?" he probes, arching an eyebrow.

"And what?"

"How's the beer?"

"It's good," I gag out in the most convincing tone I can muster.

He raises his eyebrows at me. "Bullshit. You hate beer. What do you actually want?" Man, he does know me too well.

"You couldn't have said something before I took a sip of this disgusting piss water?" I mutter incredulously.

"I wanted to see how far you were willing to take it." He cackles, throwing his head back while throwing an arm over his stomach to brace his laughter.

"Fine." I grin, unable to hide my smile while narrowing my eyes. "I'll have a Malibu and pineapple juice."

Jake laughs. "One tropical girly drink coming right up. Would you like a little umbrella with that?"

"Why, actually yes, I would," I say with a sarcastic smile, not actually expecting one at this backwoods party.

A few seconds later, he takes my beer for himself, replacing it with a cup that has a pink umbrella sticking out the top, and I can't help but laugh.

"Thanks, bartender, I'll be sure to leave you a good tip," I say, raising my eyebrows.

Did I just flirt with Jake? This was not on tonight's agenda.

"Oh, is that so?" he counters, stepping closer and towering directly in front of me. "And what kind of tip would that be?"

"My tip is to not insult the 'customer' by making fun of their 'girly drink,'" I say using air quotes.

He grins and nods. "Oh, okay, is that all the tip you have to give?"

"Hey, Leah, hey, Jake," says Matt, walking up and interrupting our conversation. "Congrats on the game, man."

"Thanks." Jake responds with a grin, and then they do one of those weird bro hug/back clap things.

"Sorry I couldn't make it. Mom told me if I didn't participate in tonight's family dinner, there was a zero percent chance that I could come to this shindig tonight so—"

"I get it, Matty, no big deal. I would pick a party over your football games any day," Jake says, nudging Matt with a smile. Two of the school's team captains being best friends seems like some kind of cliché, or maybe in a rom-com they would be enemies. I savor the jealous glares I'm receiving from girls around the springs as two of our school's hottest commodities catch up right next to me.

"Hey, Jake." Laura beams, barging into our circle. I've barely interacted with her since we all went to the springs before school started, but I know that she and Jake have a few classes together, and she always talks to him after games. She's perfectly nice, smart, and ridiculously beautiful. Jake's favorite type of girl. *At least his number has been scrubbed off her face from the game earlier.*

"Hey, Laura." He grins. She stares at him without speaking for a little longer than I'm comfortable with.

"Hey, guys," she greets, finally acknowledging Matt's and my existence. Then her attention snaps back to Jake. "Do you, uh, want to go for a walk?"

"Uh..." He glances between Matt and me with a hesitant expression.

Matt chimes in. "I need a partner for beer pong anyways. Leah?"

I am pretty decent at beer pong, and it would be awkward at this point if I denied him.

"Sure." I accept his invitation with a tight-lipped smile.

"See you guys," Matt says, throwing an arm over my shoulder and steering me away from the drink table. I fight all my limbs not to turn around at what I'm sure is Jake flirting effortlessly with Laura. The sound of her laughter tells me all I need to know.

11

Jake

Laura and I walk along the edge of the springs and settle for a long, rough log by the bonfire. The fire is crackling and emitting a light gray, pine-scented smoke. I can see Leah across the water standing around the beer pong table and talking animatedly with Matt. He leans in close, lips brushing against her ear, and she throws her head back, releasing a howling laugh. The muscles in my jaw are tight, and my hands clench so hard against the beer bottle in my hand, I might crush it. *Fuck.*

I take a long pull from the Bud Light, and my mouth tingles from the awareness that Leah's lips were just touching the same spot a few minutes ago.

"You played really well tonight," Laura bubbles, pulling me out of my jealous spiral.

"Oh, thanks," I say with a tight-lipped smile.

"Congrats on your team being undefeated. I bet those college scouts are starting to swarm."

She has no idea… "Yeah, I've gotten some offers."

"Oh! How exciting." She beams, and her expression is a little too over-the-top. "Where to?"

"Um, University of Florida and University of Central Florida. A few others out of state too."

Her face brightens. "I'm actually going to the University of Central Florida. Maybe we'll end up classmates again."

Unlikely. I'd prefer to go anywhere in the world than stay in Florida. "Yeah, maybe."

"Or… more than classmates?" she suggests hesitantly. Her eyes are wide and expectant as she draws light circles on my knee. *Damn, she's forward.* Usually, that kind of confidence is a turn-on for me, but for some chocolate-eyed, strawberry blonde reason, I'm just not interested.

I place my hand over hers. "Look, Laura, you're really nice, and I'm sorry if I gave you any false hope, but—"

She removes her hand from my leg. "It's because of Leah, isn't it?" she says, sighing and looking across the springs.

"What? No, it's just…" I stammer, trying to form a sentence.

"Jake, I see the way you look at her—act around her. I'm not blind, and I'm definitely not the only one who has noticed. I just thought if it's nothing you were ever going to pursue, you'd like to know your other options." She shrugs.

"Oh no, it's not like that with us. She's just like a sis—"

"Don't even finish that sentence. You and I both know that there is no scenario in which Leah is *just like a sister* to you. I guess I can understand when you were kids. But now, and the way *you* look…" Her graze trails the entire length of my body before she bites her lip in approval. "There's no way she sees you like a brother either."

I don't even know what to say. She's right, and the "she's like a sister" excuse is getting really fucking old. Matt has been getting on me for months about growing a pair and admitting how I feel about her. We've been friends for ten years, and he knows me well enough to notice that I'm crazy about her. Though I've never actually admitted it, to him or anyone else for that matter. I'm definitely not about to admit it to the girl who was just throwing herself at me. I don't know her well enough to know if I can trust her.

"Look, like I said, Laura, I'm sorry if I gave you the wrong impression. You're a beautiful girl, but it's just never gonna happen between us. You can think whatever reasoning you want. I'm just being honest." It's not a full-out denial, but it's also not an admission.

"It's fine, I get it." She smiles softly, and I think she means it. "It's starting to get cold," she says, wrapping her arms around herself. I don't feel the urge to rip off my hoodie like when Leah feels that way. "My jacket is back in my car."

"I have to go to the bathroom anyway. I'll walk you to get it." I'm not interested in prolonging this conversation, but everyone knows better than to walk alone in the woods at night, and I'm not a monster. Also, I do really have to go to the bathroom—that Bud Light flew straight through me.

We get up from our position, starting towards the pathway for the parking lot and restrooms. I look over to where Leah and Matt have just started their game of beer pong.

"I'll meet you by the path in a minute," I tell her, walking away without waiting for her response.

I stride over to the beer pong game and let one of my friends know I'll be right back. Definitely not anything necessary to do, but I wanted to get a closer look at Leah in her element. They seem to be beating the opposing team, and I can't help but wish I was her teammate rather than my best friend. Matt looks between Leah and me, raising his eyebrows with a smug smile on his face, and it almost looks like he's challenging me.

He's pressed me so much about being into her that I can't imagine he would go for her. We've never gone after the same girls, and he wouldn't be so fucking stupid. Leah makes a cup and jumps with excitement before turning to double high-five Matt. He laces his fingers between hers and yanks her closer, then taps their foreheads together with a devilish grin. My vision turns red, hands curling into fists at my side as a burning sensation overtakes my stomach.

Fuck this shit.

12

Leah

Matt and I are one cup away from beating William and Brad, two other seniors from our school, and we've only had to down a half cup worth of beer each. I'm hardly drunk but between the beer pong and the tropical girly drink Jake made me, I am starting to get a pretty good buzz.

I've been trying to avoid looking around for Jake, mostly because I'm worried I won't see him and then will wonder what he and *Lauraaa* have been up to for the past hour.

The next time I look around after my turn, Jake is talking with one of his soccer buddies and Laura is nowhere in sight. Although it doesn't answer the missing time, her lack of presence tells me, hopefully, that there's nothing to tell.

Matt has the final throw. He picks up the small white ball, bends his arm back, then throws it skillfully towards the last cup awaiting at the other end of the table. William tries to flick it out but no luck.

"Fuckkkkk," William and Brad gripe in unison before Brad downs the final beer.

"Hell yeah!" Matt and I turn towards one another, and he lifts me by the waist, then spins me around. He holds on a little longer than required for a post beer pong friendly celebration, then leans down and presses his warm, wet lips to mine. *What the fuck?* I jerk away like I've been stung.

"Uh, oh, Matt, I—" I stutter.

He laughs with a devilish grin. "Relax, Leah, it was just a friendly 'we won beer pong, let's celebrate' kiss. It didn't mean anything."

"Okay..." I say, mildly relieved. *Did he really mean that?* He turns his back to me and high-fives our losing opponents. Matt is handsome and perfectly nice, but he's just not... Jake. My heart races from the unexpected physical contact. I glance to the spot I last saw Jake, and he's no longer there. I scan the springs as much as possible in the dim lighting and don't see his lean frame anywhere.

Fuck. I wonder if he saw that kiss.

I wonder if he'd even care.

I wonder if he's off with Laura...

"Good game, Matt. *Boys*," I boast with raised eyebrows, nodding to the other end of the table as I walk away.

"Whoa, whoa. Where are you going?" Matt grabs my arm, spinning me back towards him. "We won. We're supposed to keep playing."

"Oh, uh..." The desire to get eyes on Jake is immensely stronger than my desire to please the Beer Pong Gods. "Sorry, you'll have to find a new partner. I have to go find Chloe." Matt shrugs and walks away, already looking around for a new beer pong partner of the female variety.

"What the *fuck* was that about?" Chloe squeals, running up to me wide-eyed and grinning.

"It was nothing," I retort, rolling my eyes. "Matty said it was, and I quote, a 'celebratory, meant nothing' kiss."

"Well, maybe it could be *moreee* than that?" Chloe probes, waggling her eyebrows.

"Oh my God, Chloe. You know I love Matt, but just *not* like that."

"Oh, come on, he's one of the hottest guys in our class," she says pointedly.

"So I should date him because he's hot?" I laugh.

"You don't have to date him. You could just use him and have sex with him because he's hot." She grins devilishly.

"Chloe," I gasp, both of us keeling over in laughter. "Just because you decided to give your virginity away to Trey tonight does *not* mean I have to follow suit. We don't have to do *everything* together."

Her smile falls to a frown.

"What's wrong?" I ask with furrowed brows.

"Trey doesn't want to have sex tonight."

"Why not?" *What teenage boy doesn't want to have sex?*

"Yeah, I, well—Trey said he didn't think I was actually ready, that it's too soon."

"*He* turned *you* down? What the fuck?"

"Yeah, I don't know. I just assumed he'd been with so many girls that it wouldn't be that big a deal to him, but maybe he's right. It has only been two months since we started dating. I mean, I feel like I'm ready, but I also don't want to beg, you know?"

Trey has a bit of a player reputation, as does the rest of the soccer team, so I am a bit surprised he's not jumping at the opportunity. Maybe he is a genuinely decent guy after all.

"So I guess just keep taking things slow and see what happens?"

"Yeah," she groans. "But damn, I have needs too, you know? And he's *sooo* fucking hot." She studies Trey, who is standing around the bonfire a few yards away talking to some guys from the soccer team along with a few cheerleaders.

"You got a little drool there," I say, pretending to wipe the corner of her mouth.

"Oh, shut up." She giggles, swatting me away. Trey catches Chloe's gaze and waves her over to him.

"It's fine," I assure her. "Go see your man, I can keep myself plenty busy."

"Okay, thanks. I'm sorry, I know I've been a shit friend lately. I promise we'll hang out soon."

I smile with pursed lips, unable to disagree. She hugs me and then quickly skips to Trey. He puts his arm around her and kisses her on the side of the head. I ache to be held like that. So comfortably. Publicly being claimed by another.

I walk towards the cooler for another drink and see Jake emerge from the walkway to the woods… with Laura. *Seriously?* My hands curl into fists as a blazing fire burns in the pit of my stomach.

He's scanning the springs, gaze freezing when his furrowed eyes meet mine. I can't help but be curious if that has something to do with his best friend's public display of affection earlier. Laura leans towards Jake, touching his arm while whispering something in his ear, then walks away before we reach one another.

"Looks like you're enjoying yourself tonight, *Summers*." I smile, unable to keep the bite out of my voice.

"Yeah, you too. Looks like you're having a great fucking time," he spouts through pursed lips.

"What the fuck is that supposed to mean?" I ask with furrowed brows, folding my arms over my chest.

"Nothing, it was just an observation," he says, expressionless, gaze flicking down at my pushed-up chest then quickly back to my eyes.

"An observation of what?" I ask, exasperated, waving a hand in the air.

"Nothing," he says, and his jaw ticks. "I just saw you and Matty *celebrating* your win," he mocks. "So it must be a good night, right?"

"Is that why you're in such a pissy mood? Because Matt and I were *celebrating*?" I scoff.

"Whatever, Le," he spouts, rolling his eyes and shaking his head, looking away from me.

"Jake, what is your fucking problem? *Couples* usually come out happy from the woods," I taunt a little too loudly, waving a hand between him and Laura, who is only standing a few yards away with a group of friends.

Jake laughs in my face. "You have no *fucking* clue what you're talking about."

"I have a pretty good idea," I spit back.

A group of girls stare at us, grinning as they drool over the hottest piece of gossip. Chloe, who's on the other end of the springs hanging on to Trey, has even noticed Jake's and my heated argument. It wouldn't be so interesting for the bystanders except that Jake and I have barely fought in the fifteen years we've known each other. Sure, we banter, but we never full-on argue. Especially not around a hundred other people, and especially not regarding our dating choices.

The only real fight Jake and I have ever had was when we were eleven. Chloe, Sophia, and I were inside playing when I spotted him kicking around the new soccer ball Will and Lysa had bought him for his upcoming tryouts. I excused myself to go outside for some fresh air and, let's be honest, to spend time with Jake. Even back then, my pull to him was like gravity. I always wanted to be around him.

I open the sliding door to the back patio and walk outside. Jake is kicking around the new soccer ball Will and Lysa bought him since he needed an official size for the twelve-year-old league next year. "Can I help you practice?"

"Sure, just don't do anything crazy. I literally got this yesterday," he warns as if I don't already know everything that goes on in the Summers house.

Jake dribbles the ball between his feet effortlessly. After twenty minutes of me attempting to take it with no luck, I stick my foot between his legs and knock it away from him. Yes!

I'm dripping in sweat as I chase after the ball with him quick on my heels. I reach the ball and spin around, kicking it as hard as possible past him.

It hits the side of their garden shed with a bang, and a soft squeaking noise flows through the air as it plops to the ground, unmoving. Jake and I run over to inspect the ball, and there's a gaping hole on the side of it. We look up at the shed, and a large nail is sticking out of the wood.

Crap.

"Are you kidding me, Leah?" he snaps, staring at the deflated ball in his hands.

"Jake, I'm so sorry. I didn't mean to do it," I say with wide eyes.

"Well, maybe you should've just left me alone to practice and I'd still have the ball," he says, throwing it across the yard. "How am I supposed to practice for tryouts now? They're next month! And the size five ball is totally different to handle than the one in the old league."

"Tryouts? Come on, Jake, it's a twelve-year-old league. I'm pretty sure they have to let everyone play," I point out.

"They might have to let everyone on the team, but they don't have to let everyone play. There's no way I'm riding the bench the whole season because you popped my ball."

My stomach is in knots. My heart is racing. He's never been so angry with me before.

"Just relax—"

"Relax?" he scoffs, cutting me off. "You might have messed up my chance for the whole season. Dad told me to be careful, that he was only buying me one."

"I'm sorry, I–I didn't mean to," I sputter out as tears blur my vision.

"Le," he says, sighing.

"I'm sorry!" I scream, then run towards the gate between our houses. I feel awful.

"Le, wait," he calls after me.

The gate slams behind me, and I run into the house and up to my bedroom. I throw myself on my bed, letting out the tears. Jake and I have never fought. Not like this, at least. He's never been so mad at me. I can't get the vision of his furious eyes out of my head. I stare at my dresser, and my eyes wander to the purple piggy bank on top.

I catapult myself out of bed, run over, pick it up, then shake out the contents onto the top of the dresser.

I hope it's enough.

I turn to leave my room just as there's a knock on the door.

I don't want Mom to see me like this... I stay quiet, hoping she'll go away.

"Le," Jake says in a gentle tone. "It's me."

"Come in," I choke out after a moment's pause.

He comes in cautiously with a half smile that doesn't reach his eyes.

"I was just about to come over," I say.

"What's that for?" he asks, pointing at the change and crumpled up dollar bills cradled in my hands.

"Oh... It's to buy you a new ball," I admit, hoping he'll be pleased. "It's only twenty-three dollars and eighteen cents, but maybe we can go to

Wal—"

"Leah," he says, smiling and cutting me off. This time the corners of his eyes crinkle, showing it's genuine. "No. You're not using that on me. You've been saving to buy a new easel for months."

"Well, I feel awful," I say, looking down at my dirty tennis shoes.

"So do I," he admits, and I look at him with furrowed brows. "I shouldn't have yelled at you. It was an accident."

I can't stop the grin from spreading across my face. "Yeah, I really didn't mean to."

"I know," he says, grinning. "I forgive you."

"Good."

"Do you forgive me too?" he asks hopefully.

"Always," I reply.

"Come on. Let's go for a walk," Jake commands, placing his warm hand on my lower back. He steers me toward the same walkway he and Laura just came from, and I try to ignore what this must look like to everyone else.

The moon is high and bright, illuminating the previously shadowy forest. I'm too distracted by Jake's proximity to think about the possible axe murderer that could be hiding behind the trees. *Okay, almost too distracted.* I guess we avoided one possible *Dateline* story for another titled "Young kids murdered in the woods while discussing their not love lives." *Okay, the title is a work in progress, but you get the point.*

We amble the familiar path in silence before Jake leads me down a smaller walkway, ending up again on the springs' edge. We settle onto a large, cool rock overlooking the water, sitting close enough that our shoulders are slightly grazing one another. The aroma of pine and earth fills my nose like a freshly lit candle. The water trickles along, small gusts of wind whistle through the trees, and there's music and chattering in the distance. This spot is definitely more private than the show we were just putting on.

I have no clue what I'm going to say. Why am I even mad? Why is he mad? Do either of us even have a *right* to be mad?

What the fuck is going on?

It feels like an eternity before I finally break the silence.

"I don't understand why *you're* mad at *me,* Jake. You were plenty distracted by *Laura,* so I'm not sure what the fuck *I* could have possibly done in the last hour to justify this level of Jake scrutiny. I wasn't even around you."

He sighs loudly and mumbles something.

"What? Do you think your best friend is too good for me or something?" I challenge, hoping to finally force some truth between us.

"Yeah, that's it," Jake scoffs, shaking his head.

"Well, I guess that would be Matt's decision, now wouldn't it?" I say, even though I have zero interest in actually pursuing anything with him.

His jaw tightens, along with his shoulders. "God, Leah, you are so *infuriating* sometimes. Do you think I really give a shit who Matt kisses? He has a different girl every week."

"Then what the fuck is your problem?" I shout, my entire body trembling with rage.

"*You're* too good for *him.*"

"And why the hell would you care who kisses me? Especially since you were hooking up with Laura not thirty minutes ago, probably in this same fucking spot," I accuse, waving my arms around as my blood bubbles underneath the surface.

"For the record, I didn't 'hook up' with Laura," he retorts, using air quotes. "I was walking back from the restroom, and she was walking back from getting a jacket out of the car, and we happened to arrive back to the party at the same time."

"Uh-huh, sure, well it looked—"

"I don't give a fuck what it looked like. Nothing *happened,* Le," he yells, throwing his hands in the air.

I slide my bottom lip between my teeth, contemplating if I believe him—and also trying to determine if I even have the right to act like I care. Jake has never lied to me, and I have no reason to believe he'd start now, especially over something like this.

"Okay," I muster out. "But you didn't answer my question."

"Which was?"

"Why would you care who kisses me?" Surely, he'll say because he cares about me and doesn't want someone like his little sister dating a player—which we all know Matthew Evans is. But my chest flutters as I hold out hope for a different answer. "And for the record, Jake, nothing happened with Matty either."

"I saw you guys kiss."

"Like you said, it's not what it looked like. I told him immediately I'm not interested like that, and he laughed in my face, saying it was a meant-nothing, celebratory kiss. He clearly didn't give a fuck about my rejection, so I believe him."

Jake stares at me, covering his mouth with his hand. "That fucker." He chuckles, shaking his head.

"What?"

"Matt's my best friend, and I—he knew what he was doing."

"What?" I repeat. "I'm so confused, Jake." I exhale heavily, trying to gather my thoughts. "Can I just be totally honest with you?"

"Please." He sighs.

Thank God for the liquid courage.

"At the beginning of the school year when you texted me about our first-day outfits, it almost seemed—scratch that—you were *definitely* flirting with me. I mean, when have you ever sent me a picture like *that*?" I purse my lips together, unable to stop myself from smirking. "Then we had the road trip, and I know we didn't talk much but I felt like we were, I don't know, bonding? Since then, it's been radio silence from you… And I know the phone works both ways and all that, but I guess I was kind of waiting on your lead because I thought I was imagining it all in my head. Then you said all that stuff you know about me in the car earlier, and now you're acting, well, you're acting like a jealous boyfriend!"

I shout the last sentence, and it sounds absurd coming from my mouth.

"I can assure you. If I *was* your boyfriend, this would be a totally different conversation, ending with Matt having the living shit beat out of him."

The possessive tone, paired with his fiery eyes, sends goosebumps scattering across my body.

"Is that what you want?" My hands tremble, awaiting his response.

"What?" he asks, furrowing his brows.

"To be my… boyfriend?"

Did I really just ask that out loud?

Jake's gaze locks with mine, and the entire world around us has frozen in place. There's no trickling water from the springs or leaves whistling in the wind. My heart has even stopped beating.

Before he can respond, something jostles loudly in the trees above us, startling me yet again. I jump towards Jake, landing partially on top of his muscular lap. His arm catches my waist, preventing me from falling as a flock of birds departs from the tree line into the night sky.

Shit, I'm such a Scaredybug.

He cradles my waist, fingers grazing the exposed skin. A wildfire ignites in the place his warm hand caresses, radiating uncontrollably throughout my body before settling directly between my legs. The only sounds are our heavy breaths and pounding hearts as the aroma of pine and beer wafts off of him, enveloping me completely.

Green, inquisitive eyes glimmer in the bright moonlight as he analyzes every inch of my face—gaze landing upon my wet, parted mouth. His tongue glides along his bottom lip before he bites down on the tender flesh.

Fuck. I'm done for.

My lips tingle at the tantalizing proximity of his mouth. The impending possibility of those beautiful, swollen lips devouring mine.

"You still didn't answer my—"

I'm interrupted by his hungry mouth claiming mine. My muscles freeze for a brief second until my body takes over. Reacting purely on instinct, leaning deeper into the kiss. He pulls back for a moment.

"I was jealous," I blurt out. I'm not sure when I decided to start being so blunt. Apparently, my tropical girly drink and the small amount I drank during beer pong have made me brave—or stupid.

I don't know if I'm more surprised by my admittance or when he responds, "So was I."

His lips crash again with mine. This time stronger, hungrier.

"Why?" I mumble into his mouth, unable to stop myself from ruining this fantasy-like moment we're having. At the game earlier when he complimented me on his hoodie, I convinced myself he was just being a flirt. I guess his kiss should be admittance enough, but I can't help but wonder. "Why now, Jake?"

"Oh, come on, Leah." He pulls farther away from my face, and I'm regretting speaking at all. "Matt's my best friend. He's been pressing me about something I've been trying to deny for… a while now, and I guess he decided I needed a little *push* to face my… feelings."

"And what *are* your feelings?" I probe.

"Well, for one, I can't stand the thought of someone else having their hands all over you. Especially wearing… this." He groans in approval, pulling me on top of him in one smooth, swift motion, forcing my legs to fall to each side of him in a straddle. His warm hands trail along the center of my back, slowly sliding under my shirt to trace the oversensitive skin. Whatever minuscule part of my body was free of goosebumps is riddled with them now.

"I feel the same way," I admit, and his eyebrows fly to his hairline. "I don't know why the hell you're so surprised, Jake. I thought it was obvious?"

"Not even the tiniest amount." He shakes his head.

I guess I should be thankful it wasn't, because if he didn't feel the same way, that would be extremely embarrassing.

"Well… I do," I confirm, pressing my forehead gently against his and nuzzling his nose.

His mouth curves into a devastatingly sexy smile, radiating heat throughout my entire body.

Jake's trembling hands roam to the front of my chest, and he glides his thumbs along the bottom wiring of my bra. My heart pounds in anticipation to the rhythm of the pulsating between my thighs. Any attractive guy touching me this way would get me a little hot and bothered, sure, but having Jake's strong, warm hands this close makes my entire body tremble with anticipation.

My breathing is rapid as Jake closes the distance between us, gently anchoring his mouth to mine. It's less hungry than the unexpected kiss before. His lips are warm like hot coffee on a cold winter night, and he tastes like peppermint and beer. Usually, that would be a repulsive combination, but in this instance, it's a welcome aphrodisiac enveloping me completely.

His delicate fingertips graze my skin like feathers. He explores below my ear, tracing the curve of my neck. I slide my fingers lightly up the back of his neck, then rake them through his silky, tousled hair as my free hand memorizes the rippling muscles of his back under his thin T-shirt. The tip of his wet tongue splits my lips, and I give no protest as our tongues fuse together along with our bodies.

His strong hands ease around my throat, tracing the length of my neck gently with his thumbs. His lips separate from mine again, only this time, instead of speaking, he brushes them against my cheek, suckles my ear. And then his mouth is on my neck, devouring me. A small moan releases from my lips in approval.

Jake hums at the encouragement, grazing his thumb down my neck, along my clavicle, pushing the collar of my shirt towards my shoulder. His mouth angles downward, nibbling the collarbone he just let free. Fingertips trail down my back until they find my ass. He squeezes it as I grind myself against his pulsating cock. The thought of him inside of me has me teetering on the edge of nirvana.

I've never been filled with so much lustful desire before. I'm aching for him to be closer to me. On top of me. Inside of me. I've always considered how I might lose my virginity, but never did I think it would be on a rock at the springs, and especially never did I think it would be with my best friend's brother. Actually, that last part is a lie. I've fantasized endlessly that it would be with Jake, I just never actually thought that it could be a possibility.

Oh fuck. Chloe.

What am I thinking? What am I *doing?*

"Stop," I blurt abruptly, surprising even myself. Jake's muscular shoulders tighten as he stares at me with furrowed brows and wide eyes.

"What about Chloe?" I whisper.

"What *about* Chloe?" he says incredulously, wrinkling his nose.

"What are we going to tell her?"

"*That's* what you're thinking about right now?" he deadpans, not moving his hands—which I'm thankful for, but it also makes it terribly hard to think.

"I'm sorry. It's just, this is obviously..." I search for the right word. "New... And it would be nice to figure out whatever this is before we bring Chloe's strong opinion into the mix." I don't mention the fact that when we were ten, Chloe had me pinky promise I would "never, ever, even if pigs fly" date Jake.

"I don't know. Just tell her we're friends with benefits," he says with a wink.

"Excuse me?" I scoff.

"What?" He chuckles. "We're friends, and this is *definitely* a benefit." He brushes a stray hair out of my face with his fingers, then drags them through my hair.

"Jake." I giggle. "Be serious."

"Leah, you're already struggling with keeping the secret about my mom. You really want to add something else to feel guilty about? And besides, we're not doing anything wrong."

Chloe has told me repeatedly how happy she is to have someone who will always prioritize her over Jake. She's already so hurt about Lysa leaving, I don't want her to have any other reason to feel like she's not a priority.

"Yes, I'm sure," I say with as much assurance as I can muster.

13

Jake

"What were you and Leah arguing about last night?" Chloe bombards me the second I walk into the kitchen the next morning.

"It was nothing," I respond, rolling my eyes, trying to sound casual.

"It didn't look like *nothing*. You had the attention of half the class," she says with raised brows.

"Chloe, it was nothing. I told her Matt was a man whore and to be careful, and she told me to mind my own damn business in typical Leah fashion." The partially true story Leah and I settled on last night since we knew nosey onlookers would be asking.

"*Okayyyy…*" she says, eying me curiously. "Not that I disagree with your judgment, but aren't you supposed to *help* your best friend get girls, not fend them off? Isn't that, like, bro code or something?"

"Yeah, but I also don't want to hear you bitch to me about how I let your best friend date a player and how he's screwing with her head and blah blah blah."

"Yeah… I would like to avoid that. Good point."

"Did *you* have fun last night?" I ask, trying to change the focus off me. If I keep thinking about Leah, then it'll end up with me in a daydream about how good her legs felt wrapped around me as her long fingers raked through my hair.

"Yeah, it was nice. You?" She sounds a bit sad but doesn't elaborate, and I don't push it.

"It was fine."

Sophia comes hurtling down the stairs and into the kitchen. "Jake!" she shouts.

"*Sophia*!" I shout back, dramatically.

"Can we go for a run?" she asks, bouncing on her toes, overflowing with energy.

"Sure, go get changed."

"Yay!" she squeals, barreling back up the stairs.

"What nine-year-old volunteers to exercise?" Chloe says, scrunching her nose in disgust and shaking her head.

"The cool kind," I shoot back, grinning with a cocked brow.

"No way," Chloe says, laughing. "She's just fucking weird."

"Yeah…" I say smiling. "But she's our weirdo."

It's a quarter past nine on Saturday night, and I'm lying in bed, staring at the ceiling. Leah and I have barely talked since I dropped her off at home after the party Thursday night. I should've texted her tonight already, but I don't know what to say. I've typed and erased so many messages it should be illegal. I'm really not great at this whole dating thing. In the past, I've had girls who were so eager to be with me they always made the first move.

Leah and I are keeping things between us for now. She said she wants to "figure out whatever this is" before we bring other strong opinions into the mix. But I have nothing to figure out.

There are three things I want in life: Leah Stone, my mom's sobriety, and a full-ride scholarship to UCLA.

After our make-out session at the springs, we rejoined the party so it wasn't too suspicious. Everyone saw us leave together and if we would've been gone too long, people would have talked. Hell, they probably did anyways. To be honest, I couldn't give two fucks about everyone knowing, but I'll follow Leah's lead. She's already keeping the secret about Mom for me. I can do this for her.

The light flicks on in her bedroom, and I can't stand it anymore.

Alright, play it cool.

LEAH

Me

Hey 😊

Leah

Hey 🥰

Me

What's up?

Leah

Just got home from an exhausting study session at the Brew House 🥵

Me

Aww I'm sorry. Too exhausted to go for a drive?

Leah

Never. Meet you at the Jeep in 10

Me

"Hey there, handsome." She beams, bouncing into the passenger seat before planting a kiss on my cheek. It feels so familiar and normal that it *almost* doesn't surprise me.

"Hey, beautiful." My right hand grips her chin, drawing her warm and willing mouth to mine for a deep, tongueless kiss. Her twinkling cognac eyes capture my full attention as my lips upturn, unable to resist the reflex. I'm grinning like an idiot.

"What?" she asks, biting her lip to stifle a smile.

"I'm just happy," I admit.

"Me too," she says, smiling wide and allowing her dimples to show. "Let's get out of here before someone sees us."

"Oh, you mean like Chloe?" I point towards the back with my thumb. Leah gasps, spinning around towards the empty back seat.

"Jake," she squeals, playfully hitting her fist against my shoulder. "Don't scare me like that."

"Sorry." I chuckle. My hand closes around her small arm, and I pull her towards my lips for another quick kiss. I back out of the driveway, attempting to ignore the annoyance I feel from her not wanting anyone to see us together. I want to show Leah off to the whole fucking world and say, *See that beautiful girl right there? She's mine, and I'm damn proud of it.*

"Where are we headed?" she asks while gazing out of the window as we turn off our residential street onto the main road, snapping me out of my own head.

"You'll see. And just so you know, we have to pick Chloe up at twelve tonight from Trey's house."

"What? Why? How are we going to explain why we are together?" she sputters.

I rest my hand on her thigh. "Leah. Calm down, okay?"

She glances at me, squinting her eyes, and I'm not sure if it's from the physical contact, but I enjoy the surprised look on her face.

"Okay." She eyes me curiously. "But it's just—"

"I want to take you somewhere so we can talk, but I just wanted you to know we are picking up Chloe later."

"Okay… You want to go somewhere and just… *talk*?" She raises an eyebrow, and a devilish smirk forms upon her lips.

"We'll see," I respond, squeezing her thigh with my hand that's still placed possessively on her leg.

I hop out of the Jeep to unlock and push open a heavy metal gate that leads to the field of a local farm. It's ten acres of empty, open land surrounded by cow pastures and farmland on all sides, besides the one hosting the dirt road we drove in on.

"Where are we?" Leah asks, squinting her eyes around the darkness as I drive through the pasture towards the middle, the Jeep bumping along the uneven ground.

"I've been coming here since I got my license. It's the best place in town to see the stars, especially on a clear night like tonight." It's also my refuge whenever I need to get away and think without any distractions.

I stop in the middle of the field, then cut the engine. We get out, rounding the front of the Jeep. I hop up onto the hood and extend my hand to hoist her up. We climb up the front windshield and settle on top of the flat hardtop roof. I lie back onto the cool metal, allowing the intoxicating aroma of country air, freshly cut grass—my doing—and dirt to envelop me. Cows are mooing in the distance, and the warm, humid night air is blowing gently. Our senses are encompassed entirely by the nature around us.

"How'd you find this place?"

"Remember when I did that summer job a few years back for Brahms Ranch?" She nods her head in confirmation. "Well, I was helping one of the ranch hands, Rickie, with some work on the fences over there," I explain, pointing to a fence line you can barely make out in the darkness. "He told me if I came here on a cloudless night, I could see every star in the sky." Leah pulls her gaze away from me and angles her face up towards the heavens. I observe her beautiful features as a confused and curious expression transforms into astonishment.

"Oh my God," she exclaims with eyes wide. "I've never seen stars so bright before. Or so many."

"I know. It's crazy, isn't it? I came here the night Rickie told me about it. For the past few months, I've come back as often as I can. You can't get views like this near the neighborhoods. Too much light pollution."

"And they don't care if you're here?"

"Uh, actually," I say laughing. "I did get caught out here once by Mr. Brahms."

"Really?" she asks with wide eyes. "What happened?"

"He rode up on horseback, pointing a shotgun at me," I say.

"What?" she shrieks.

"After he realized who I was and that I was just needing a little escape from the… noise in my life, he decided not to put a twelve-gauge through me and said if I mow the grass once a month, I can have a key."

"You could've been shot, you idiot," she says, laughing and hitting me against the arm.

"Worth it," I reply, smiling down at her.

"I get it. It's beautiful," Leah exclaims, gesturing her arms towards the star-scattered sky above us.

"Yeah, extremely beautiful," I agree, unable to take my eyes off her. I've wasted way too much time over the last fifteen years thinking about Leah to let her get away from me. "Leah," I say, sitting up.

"Yeah?" she says, ripping her gaze away from the stars and mirroring my position.

"I know you said you want to take things slow, but I just don't know if I can do that."

She looks down at her hands and fidgets with the gold ring I gave her for her eighteenth birthday. I still get a rush every time I see her wearing it. "I… I just…" My choice of words may have had an ulterior meaning, which wasn't my intent.

"I'm not talking about physically. I'm fine if you want to take things slow regarding that."

Her body relaxes. "Then what are you talking about?"

"I'm talking about secrets and sneaking around and not telling people we're together."

"Are we together?" she asks, tilting her head to the side.

"I know I sure as hell don't want anyone else… or for you to be with anyone else." My stomach clenches at the thought.

"I feel the same way," she admits with a soft smile.

"So how about we make this simple and you be my girlfriend?" I grin, raising my eyebrows. Feels so dorky to ask her that. I wonder how our parents felt when they asked someone if they wanted to go steady.

I hope to God she says yes.

"But what about Chloe? What will she—"

"Damn it, Leah," I say with clenched teeth, dragging my fingers through my hair. "I'm not worried about Chloe. She is going to have to be okay with this, Le. She loves you, and she loves me, so how can she not be okay with the fact that we love each other?"

"We... What did you say?"

Oh fuck.

That was not how I intended for that to come out. Hell, it's probably the truth, but I don't think we're ready to jump from friends to lovers in the blink of an eye. I don't want to scare her away.

"I-I, uh, I didn't..." I stutter.

She sighs, sitting up and pulling her legs close to her chest. "Jake, it's fine. I'm sure you meant it as a figure of speech."

Not even a little bit.

I slide down the windshield to the hood of the Jeep and hop off. "Leah, come here," I gesture, patting the hood.

She climbs down and settles on the front of the hood, dangling her legs. Her knees are parted, and I settle between them. The scent of her strawberry lip gloss floods my senses, and her nervous hands tremble as she rests them on my shoulders. I press my forehead to hers, and we gaze at one another in silence.

"Not a single day has gone by in the last fifteen years where I haven't thought about you," I confess. "And now that we've finally started this, whatever *this* is, I can't just sit back and keep it a secret. I'm fucking *crazy* about you, and I want the entire damn world to know. Because if I have to sit there," I say, starting to pace in front of her, "while one more asshole, or even worse, one of my dumbass friends, hits on you or gives you a *celebratory* kiss, *especially* when you're *my* girl, I will lose my fucking shit."

"Jake..." she says with a soft smile, jumping off the hood and grabbing my arm, pulling me back to her. My large frame cages her against the hood of the Jeep. "I have had a crush on you for my entire life. I just—I never would have imagined you felt the same. I even overheard you tell Katelyn once that I was like a little sister and she had absolutely nothing to worry about. I don't think she believed you... but I did."

"Do you want to know why Katelyn and I fought so much?"

Leah looks at me intently with tense, unmoving shoulders.

"Because she saw something that I wasn't ready to admit yet. The way I looked at her was nothing compared to the way I stopped and stared every time you walked into a room."

Whenever Leah walks into a room, all of the oxygen disappears. My eyes pull in her direction like gravity. I forget how to breathe. Hell, sometimes I've even forgotten to listen if someone was talking to me, like Katelyn, which is why she always noticed. I was a shitty boyfriend and in complete denial of my feelings. Was Katelyn horrible? Sure. But I can't imagine having to be with Leah and watch her be in love with someone else. My stomach sours at the thought.

"Yes." Leah smirks before planting a soft kiss on my parted lips.

"Yes, what?"

"Yes, I'll be your girlfriend."

"Oh, fuck yes," I say, bending down and hoisting her over my shoulder. "Leah Stone is my girlfriend. Back off fuckers!" I scream into the nothingness like an idiot while spinning her in circles.

"Jake!" Leah howls with laughter, beating her tiny fists against my back. "You're crazy."

I slide her off my shoulder, down my body, and set her on the hood, where I slide my body back between her legs. "And you're mine."

I drag my lips below her ear, along the edge of her jaw, and exhale my hot breath against her neck. I cradle her face between my hands before pulling those soft, warm lips to mine.

Our mouths are tangled for minutes, maybe hours, lost in one another, and it's still not enough. My hand is cradling her face while the other is placed firmly on her thigh. I'm aching to glide it towards the heat radiating from her center, but I'm hesitant since I just told her it's fine if we take it slow in that department. My phone rings in the car, breaking our trance. I'm prepared to fully ignore it until Leah pulls away. "You should probably at least check who it is."

Oh shit, what time is it?

I grab my phone. Chloe is on the caller ID, so I bring it to my ear. "Hello?"

"Where the fuck are you? It's twelve fifteen. Didn't you say you wanted to get me at twelve cause you have practice tomorrow?"

"Yeah, sorry, we lost track of time." Leah looks at me with wide eyes, mouthing *what the fuck?*

"We?" Chloe probes. "Who are you with?" *Oh, I guess that's why Leah made that face.*

"I'll be there in twenty minutes." It only takes ten, but I'm not quite ready to be done here yet.

"No hurry, you're the one who said twelve," she says before hanging up. Leah is standing next to me and staring at me with a panicked look on her face.

"What?"

"What are we going to tell her?"

"How about the truth?" I offer.

"Sure." She laughs. "So we just pick her up from Trey's and say, 'hey, Chlo, what's up? Yeah, so I know this is sudden, but your brother and I are dating now.'"

"Uh, yes?" *Do girls always make everything this complicated?*

"I think I'm going to pass out."

"Leah, Chloe loves us. How can she not be okay with something that makes us so fucking happy? You're always so worried about everyone else. You're allowed to do something for yourself for once."

"I guess you're right." She sighs, her body tense in my arms.

"Alright, we have to go." She turns to walk towards the passenger side. I grab her arm, pulling her back to me. "But first…" I claim her lips with mine, running my fingers through her hair. "Okay, now we can go." I grin, pulling away, booping my nose on hers.

Leah's buckled in the passenger seat, and I'm driving down the road towards Trey's house. Her knee is bouncing wildly, and I place my hand on her thigh. I can understand why she's so nervous, but I know my sister, and she would just want us to be happy. It's almost twelve forty-five when we finally pull into Trey's driveway, and I text Chloe to come out. The front door opens, and she walks out with Trey trailing behind.

"We can tell her, but just… not now," Leah pleads. "Tonight was incredible, and I don't want to ruin this memory with whatever her reaction will be."

"Okay, whatever you say," I concede, giving her leg a quick squeeze before placing my hand back on the steering wheel. I'm just happy I've finally got the girl. If she wants to wait, we'll wait. Chloe skips to the Jeep and slides in the back.

"Hey, Jake," Chloe chirps while putting on her seatbelt as I back out of the driveway. "Hey," she adds, checking the passenger seat, "Leah?"

Leah glances back at her, smiling awkwardly.

"What the fuck are you doing here?" she accuses, looking between Leah and me. "Missed me that bad, huh?" Chloe chuckles, squeezing Leah's shoulder.

"Uh, yeah." Leah grins, shooting me a *help* look.

"Late night milkshake run," I chime in.

"Then where are the milkshakes?" she asks skeptically, raising her eyebrows at us. *Fuck.*

"Well, I thought you might want one too, so we're going now," Leah replies without missing a beat.

"Oh, I am *sooo* down," Chloe says excitedly, wiggling in her seat.

14
Leah

I stare at the sunlight streaming in through my blinds as the last few days play on a loop in my head.

Did Jake really kiss me for the first time and ask me to be his girlfriend, all within a span of forty-eight hours?

It all happened so quickly I can almost convince myself I imagined it until I spot the McDonald's milkshake cup sitting next to my bed. *Can't believe their ice cream machine was working for once.* Chloe never probed why I was with Jake. I think she really believed I came because I missed her. I almost feel guilty for allowing her to believe I'm playing the part of a doting best friend.

My phone vibrates against the nightstand.

JAKE

Jake

Good Morning Beautiful 

Me

Good Morning

Another reminder that I didn't imagine the last few days.

Being Jake Summers' secret girlfriend is honestly the most fun I've ever had in my life. At school, we've gotten pretty creative in finding places to sneak away for a little privacy—supply closets, the back corner of the library, the locker room during lunch. At home, it's a bit more difficult but definitely not impossible. I go to Jake's when no one's home, and my parents always assume I'm there for Chloe.

"All this alone time with you is making me greedy," I say, straddling Jake on the couch in the Summers living room. No one else should be home for at least another hour. "It never feels like enough."

"Trust me, I know," he replies with a crooked grin, sliding his palms up the outsides of my thighs. "Not being able to touch you at school is fucking killing me. I have to admit, it is pretty hot though, sneaking around with you."

"Is that why you insisted on making out in the living room?" I laugh. "You have a perfectly good bed right upstairs."

He raises his eyebrows and grins. "At least buy me dinner first, baby."

He laughs, and I can't stop the smile from spreading across my face as I shake my head. "The more time I spend with you, the more I hate being alone," I admit, leaning down and kissing his plump lips.

"Well, now you never have to be alone again." Jake drags his thumb along the edge of my jaw, planting kisses in its wake towards my neck.

"You can't be with me *all* the time." I giggle and pull away when he gets to a ticklish spot.

"Why not? I'll just sneak in your window after your parents go to bed." He waggles his eyebrows.

"Jake." I gasp. "Don't you dare. I don't need you breaking your neck trying to climb up the gutter."

"It would be worth it." He leans in, kissing my lips softly. "Even if it was just for five minutes with my girl."

His girl.

"I never would have pegged you as such a romantic." I grin.

"Why not?" he asks, mock hurt. "I'm the *king* of romance."

I giggle, and he narrows his eyes at me. "Prove it."

He glides his long fingers through my hair, then rubs my cheeks with his thumbs as he stares into my eyes. "Baby, you couldn't handle it."

"Try me."

He leans towards my aching lips, then veers off, kissing my cheek and moving towards my ear. He sucks my earlobe in his mouth, nibbling on it, then breathes a hot breath against it that sends goosebumps scattering across my body.

A rustling noise comes from the front door, and we both freeze. The faint sound of keys jingling causes Jake to stand up and toss me to the other end of the couch like a sack of soccer balls. I yelp as I fly through the air and my body falls against the soft cushions, attempting to contain my laughter as I curl up in the corner. I close my eyes, faking a nap, but keep the slits open just enough that I can see Jake.

He sits back down, readjusts himself, then pulls out his phone, pretending to scroll. Will and Sophia's voices come echoing down the halls as Jake's shoulders ripple with laughter on the other end of the couch. I kick him for almost giving us away.

"Hey, kiddos," Will chimes.

"Ello, mates," Sophia says in a horrible British accent.

I open my eyes and fake a stretch and yawn. "Oh, hey, guys," I say, smiling.

They totally bought it. *I think.*

The golden paint gleams as I brush it on with steady strokes. My soul is smiling from finally getting to express itself all over the canvas. My phone buzzes on the bed, and I quickly jump up and stumble over a discarded pile of clothes when running to check if it's Jake.

CHLOE

Chloe

Hey Scaredybug! I miss you. 💕

Me

Miss you too, Lovebug

Chloe

Trey's parents are out of town tomorrow night so he's having a party at his house for his birthday. Be my date? 🥺

Me

Don't you think Trey expects you to be HIS date? Especially since it's his birthday

Chloe

Well his actual birthday is Tuesday, but since his parents are out of town Saturday night... 🥂

Chloe

Besides he'll be so busy with his friends, and we haven't hung out in forever. Pleeeease 🙏

Me

Fine, but on one condition

Chloe

Name your price.

Me

Let's have a girls' night and get ready for the party together. Can Jake drive us?

Chloe

Duh, I already asked him

Me

Okay sounds like a plan 😊 I'll be over at 6 tomorrow?

Chloe

Can't wait 🥳

I'm excited to spend time with Chloe, but I also feel like I have to tell her what's going on between Jake and me before she finds out some other way. I literally blush from the thought of his name. There's also an elephant-sized weight on my chest from not telling her about Lysa. Each little secret is added to a tub of lies, and any second they'll spill out and over the edge, making a mess of my life. Will and Jake want to wait until after Christmas to give the girls a little more time to be happy, and if that's what they want, I'll honor that. No matter how much it's killing me on the inside.

"Knock, knock," Mom sing-songs, popping her head in the cracked door. "We're leaving for the airport." I stare at her with a blank expression and furrowed brows, racking my brain for the information regarding them leaving today and coming up blank.

"Your dad has a business trip to New York and I'm going with him, remember?" she says, irritated.

Barely, but it's possible she told me. I've clearly been distracted. Maybe Jake is taking up more of my thoughts than I'd like to admit. Mom always travels with Dad on his business trips. I used to stay at the Summers' when they'd go, but since last year, they've trusted me to stay home alone.

"Right," I reply with a tight smile. This is a regular occurrence, but it still annoys me that they're barely home. They want to dictate my major and career path but leave me home alone for days at a time without so much as a phone call.

Mom saunters farther into my room, pulling me into her arms and kissing me firmly on the cheek. "We love you, honey." She glances at my painting, then back to me. "And make sure you actually get some studying done and don't waste all of your free time," she says in a disappointed tone.

"Sure, Mom." I sigh. "Love you too."

"Don't forget to set the alarm when you're home at night." She walks back to the door.

"I won't," I grumble. They say it's for my protection, but I'm pretty sure Mom gets an alert every time I set it so she knows when I'm home or not.

It occurs to me that I'm going to have the house *completely* to myself for a week… I'm definitely not the throw-a-rager type, but

I wouldn't mind a little alone time with Jake. Party Saturday, alone time with Jake—it's shaping up to be a pretty good week.

"Hey, Lovebug," I chime as I walk into Chloe's room and tackle-hug her onto the bed.

"Hey, Scaredybug." She chuckles. "What have you been up to today?"

"Not much. Cleaning. Studying. Oh, and my parents are headed to New York for the week."

"Oh, hell yes. Home alone. House party?" she says, waggling her brows. She's *definitely* a psychopath if she thinks I'm going to throw a house party, especially considering her dad is right next door to rat me out.

"Have you lost your mind? Of course I'm not throwing a house party. Do I *look* like someone who wants to be grounded until they're thirty?"

"Okay, okay, you're right. I forgot, you're the *boring* one," she teases.

"Yeah, yeah, more like the wants-to-maintain-her-freedom one," I counter, hitting her with a pillow. "So what'd *you* do today?"

"I went with Trey to a few stores, helping him get ready for the party tonight."

"How many people are coming?"

"I don't know. Some dick from Shorewood's soccer team found out about it and apparently put it on a school-wide blast, so there could be easily a couple hundred people."

"Holy shit!" I squeal, causing Chloe to flinch, throwing her hand over her chest. "A couple hundred?"

Chloe's eyes widen as she nods her head yes.

I don't usually care for house parties with hundreds of people, but it would make it rather easy to sneak away with Jake...

"What the hell has you all smiley over there?" Chloe probes, and I realize I must've not been very good at keeping my emotions under wraps.

"Nothing." I grin, unable to wipe the stupid smile off my face. "I'm just looking forward to finally getting out of the house tonight."

"You know Matt's going to be there," she says with raised eyebrows.

"Okay... and?"

"Maybe you guys could share another *celebratory* kiss. Or more..." She twerks and fake moans, "Oh, Matty, yeah, just like that." Then she keels over in laughter.

"Oh my god, *Chloe*." I laugh, hitting her again with the pillow. "I already told you I'm not interested in Matt like that." *I'm also dating your brother.*

"Uh-huh, I mean, you know it *can* just be for fun? I know Jake was against it but honestly fuck what he says... right?" she says, smirking and cocking a brow. If he could hear her right now, he'd be pissed.

"Like I said, I'm good. Thanks."

"Come on, it's our senior year. Live a little. I wanna go on double dates and swap nasty sex stories," she whines. *Pretty sure she wouldn't want to swap stories if she knew who my love interest was...*

"Swap?" I inquire, eyeing her curiously. "You and Trey finally did the deed?"

"I don't kiss and tell." She beams with an ear-to-ear smile.

"Oh my God, Chloe. Spill," I squeal.

"I mean, there isn't much to spill. It was awkward and awesome all at the same time."

"Did it hurt at all?" Since she's the first of us to lose our V-cards, I'm genuinely curious. I've thought about it hundreds, maybe thousands of times, but I'm terrified it's going to hurt.

"Honestly, a little, yeah. But once we found a rhythm and remembered to use the lube I made him buy, it was almost... magical." She smirks, looking away and sighing with a dreamy look in her eyes.

"Okay, gross," I gag out. "I don't need any more details about Trey's magic dick." She throws her head back, laughing wildly before slamming me with the pillow.

"Fine, I'll spare you the *sex-ay* stuff, but yes, it was awesome, ten out of ten, would recommend. Oh, and the blue raspberry flavored lube..." She holds up both hands. "*Also* ten out of ten."

"Okay." I laugh. "I'll take your word for it."

I'm distracted by fantasies of when it'll finally be my turn. For the first time, imagining it's with Jake doesn't seem so unrealistic.

"Okay, it's already seven-thirty. We should probably get ready so we're not late." Chloe jumps out of bed and puts on our favorite get ready with me playlist, which consists of a variety of cheesy upbeat pop music. We spin each other around singing "Boyfriend" by Justin Bieber at the top of our lungs in between curling our hair and trying on every item of clothing in Chloe's closet. It feels like old times and reminds me how much I've missed spending time with her. Lately, when I'm around Chloe, I'm racked with guilt over all the secrets I'm keeping from her, but tonight has been a welcome distraction.

Seven outfit changes, two bottles of dry shampoo, and one hour later we are both *finally* ready. We've curled our hair into loose waves and applied just enough makeup that we look like prettier versions of ourselves. The outfit I settled on is high-waisted skinny jeans, a tight black bodysuit with a slightly plunging neckline, strappy black sandals, and for accessories, a gold chain link necklace and gold earrings.

"Damn, girl, you look hot," she praises as we check ourselves out in the mirror waiting for Jake to pick us up. He went to dinner with a few teammates after their Saturday practice.

"Thanks, so do you, Lovebug… I missed this."

"Me too." She sighs. "I feel like we never hang out anymore. I know that's partly my fault." *Partly?*

"It's okay. I'm happy that you're happy," I reply.

"I am *sooo* happy. And I know you said you aren't interested in Matt. But I just, I want you to feel like I do with Trey. Are you *sure* there's no one at all you're interested in? Maybe I'd have some sway with them and could talk you up?" she asks, raising her eyebrows.

My heart beats frantically. "Actually, now that you mention it, I have—" A honking sound comes from outside Chloe's window, and she looks through the blinds to see who it is.

"It's Jake. Let's go," she commands, flipping off her bedroom light and walking out of the room. I sigh heavily, annoyed but also thankful for being interrupted, then follow her out.

We walk out the front door, and Chloe spins around to lock it since Will took Sophia and her best friend Sage to the movies. I can feel Jake's eyes on me before I even glance his way. It's dark, but the headlights must give him a good view of me. I slide into the backseat and shut the door while Chloe finishes with the lock. Jake is wearing fitted jeans and a black V-neck shirt that shows off his defined shoulder muscles. My mouth goes dry at the sight.

He's scanning the length of my body with a devilish grin. "Damn it, Leah, how am I supposed to pretend I'm not attracted to you when you get in my backseat looking like *that.* I'll tell Chloe the truth right now just so I can take you right back upstairs." My cheeks flush at the compliment, especially after Chloe's and my sex talk earlier.

I lean forward and squeeze his shoulder. "Sorry, *Daddy.*"

He throws his head back, laughing as I settle back into my seat with a wide grin. The front passenger door opens, and Chloe jumps inside. "You guys ready to go? We're already super late."

"Yep, let's go," Jake agrees as he puts the car in reverse and looks over his shoulder to back out of the driveway. His hungry gaze flicks to mine for a brief moment, paired with a smile so sexy that heat pools between my thighs, and then his attention returns to backing out of the driveway.

If he keeps eye fucking me like that, it's going to be a long freaking night.

15
Leah

We pull up to Trey's, and there are already thirty or so cars in his driveway and lining the street. "Damn, you weren't kidding. There are a fuck ton of people here," I say to Chloe.

"Yeah." She buzzes with energy. "This is gonna be so fun."

I glance up at the three-story mansion with a four-car garage. I was so distracted by Jake when we picked up Chloe the other night, I didn't even bother to look at Trey's house. I knew his family had money, but I didn't realize they had *money*, money.

It's gorgeous. Large stones form the exterior of the house. A dolphin sculptured water fountain sits in the center of the circular driveway. Solar powered torches illuminate the walkway, setting a breathtaking ambiance.

We enter the house through the large wooden double doors, and it's packed. Half our school appears to be here, along with some unfamiliar faces who must be from Shorewood. Jake and Chloe are walking in front of me as I trail a step behind.

"Hey there," the cute guy from the springs, Cole, says, sliding up next to me and placing a hand on the small of my back as he smiles down at me. "I've been wondering when I'd get to see you again."

"Uh, hi," I say, smiling awkwardly.

Chloe and Jake turn around, assumedly after noticing I was no longer following them. I risk a glance at Jake, who's staring at Cole's hand on my lower back with a clenched jaw.

"You look beautiful tonight," Cole says, looking down at me with a seductive grin. I can feel Jake's eyes burning into me, and the unfamiliar jealous glare sends a rush throughout my body.

"Thank you," I say, turning to face him, which forces him to drop his hand.

"It's just the truth." He shrugs, smiling. "Want to get that drink with me?"

"Actually I—"

"In your *dreams*, Danvers," Jake spits, cutting me off. He throws his arm around my shoulder and steers me away from Cole. My body shivers with excitement at the possessive display, a small smile tugging at my lips. Although I hope his jealousy isn't as obvious to Chloe as it is to me.

"Guess you're going to have to work for it," Chloe teases Cole before turning to follow Jake and me.

"That's okay, I like a challenge," he calls after us as we turn to leave. I give him a small wave, and he mouths *later* with a wink. I snap my gaze away to avoid giving him any encouragement.

"What the fuck, Jake?" Chloe screeches as she catches up to us. "You're being such a cock block. Why would you think you get to control who Leah gets to hook up with tonight, anyways?"

"Jesus, Chloe," Jake snaps, removing his arm from my shoulders. "Are you just going to pimp her out to every limp dick at this party?"

"There's nothing wrong with having a little *fun*," Chloe counters. "And besides, maybe you should let *Leah* be the one to decide who she is or isn't going to hook up with tonight."

"You're right." Jake grins. "Leah can *totally* decide that. I promise from here on out, whoever you want to hook up with tonight, I won't deny you. Boy Scout's honor," he says, looking at me while lifting three side-by-side fingers. It takes all my willpower to stop my lips from curling up into a flirtatious, knowing grin.

"Good," Chloe snaps, narrowing her eyes and looking between us. "Stop being so overbearing and give Leah some space, for fuck's sake."

"Chloe, baby." Trey appears, thankfully interrupting this very uncomfortable conversation. "You finally made it," he coos before planting a sloppy, drunk kiss on her smiling lips.

"You know I like to be fashionably late, babe." Chloe kisses him again right before he places a clear plastic cup full of rose-colored liquid in her hand.

"Your favorite." He grins, gesturing to the cup. She swirls the liquid around in her mouth while bringing a finger to her lips and looking up to the ceiling.

"Orange juice… grenadine… and… tequila?"

"Yep, a tequila sunrise for my sunshine."

"Oh my god, you guys are so lame," I spit out, unable to help myself, as Chloe sends me a slap-happy grin. "I'm going to go get a drink. See you guys later," I say.

"They're in the kitchen. Help yourselves," Trey offers.

"Yeah, I could use something too and would honestly rather be anywhere but… here," Jake gags out, gesturing towards the love birds.

"Whatever, losers, you're just single and jealous," Chloe says teasingly before turning to Trey. Jake gives me a knowing smile, and I can't stop the corners of my mouth from curling upward in response.

Jake grabs my hand and interlaces our fingers, pulling me behind him as he wades us through the large crowd. My gaze falls on Katelyn, who's perched on some guy's lap, giving me the once-over. Her eyes pause momentarily on our joined hands, and then she looks away as if we're the least interesting thing in the room.

Maybe she's finally moved on.

After what feels like hours of stopping and talking to friends we know from school or Jake's teammates, we're almost to the kitchen.

I tug his hand to stop him. "I'm gonna go to the bathroom while you get us drinks." I have the sudden urge to get a moment to myself before continuing the incessant small talk.

"Okay, well, pick your poison, Le," Jake requests.

"You apparently know me so well. Just make me my usual," I challenge him with a flirtatious smile. "I'll be right back."

"Okay, one girly drink coming up." He squeezes my hand three times before disappearing into the crowded kitchen. A small smile forms upon my lips at the little gesture that's somehow become ours.

I snake my way back through the crowd in search of a bathroom. There's a door down the hallway next to the living room where a few girls are standing.

"Is this the bathroom?" I ask the one in the back of the line.

"Yep," she says, obviously annoyed at the wait.

After ten minutes, all the girls have gone, and it's finally my turn. Of course no one is waiting after me—I always have shit luck and end up at the back of any line.

Starbucks. Gas station. You name it.

It's a spacious bathroom with a double sink, toilet, and bathtub.

After I pee, I wash my hands and wipe them on my jeans, then grab the handle and open it to walk out. A smiling, handsome familiar face is towering over me just outside the door.

"I hear you've been waiting for me." Cole's deep, husky voice sends a shiver down my spine.

"I what?" My brows furrow. He steps towards me, and I back into the bathroom out of reflex. I don't realize I've stumbled all the way back inside until he shuts the door behind him.

16

Jake

I'm searching for the pineapple juice to make Le's girly drink, but I can't find it anywhere. Matt walks up to me just as I finally find it and twist off the cap.

"What's up, Matty?" I ask, pouring the liquid into the plastic cup.

He doesn't reply so I glance over, and he has an unreadable expression on his face.

"Spit it out, Matty." I laugh, waiting for him to start giving me shit about Leah.

"What's going on with you and Leah?" he asks, smirking with narrowed eyes.

He's so damn predictable. Matt's been trying to pry info out of me since the bonfire, but my lips are sealed. There's no way I can risk telling him before we tell Chloe. Leah would fucking kill me.

"What do you mean?" I ask, trying to sound casual.

"I mean, you almost ripped my balls off for kissing her last week, and you're still gonna keep pretending like nothing's going on between you two?"

"We're just friends." The words taste bitter on my tongue.

"Then it shouldn't be a problem if I ask her to be my beer pong partner again tonight." He smirks, and I want to punch that stupid grin off his face.

"Only if you want to be a dead man." I cock a brow with a straight face, and he laughs. He fucking laughs.

"Fine." He puts his hands up in defense. "But I guess if you're just friends, you won't care if one of Shorewood's guys is making a move on her?"

My heart falls to my stomach, and I clench my jaw. *He fucking knows something.*

"What aren't you telling me?" I ask, unable to keep my emotions level.

"I just saw Cole Danvers follow Leah into the bathroom."

A chill runs down my spine as my body erupts in flames.

I'm going to fucking kill him.

I turn around and push my way through the crowded kitchen.

"Just friends, huh?" Matty says, laughing as he trails behind me.

Once in the living room, I realize I have no damn clue where the bathroom is. I spin back around toward Matt.

"Where the fuck is she?" I spout, breathing heavily. Matt looks to the left of us and tips his chin toward the hallway. I start towards it, leaving him chuckling in the living room.

I get into the empty hallway, and I think Matt was fucking with me until I hear the sound of Leah's panicked voice from outside the door. Their voices are muffled, but she sounds agitated.

"Please!" she shouts, and something inside of me snaps.

My hand flies to the handle, and I throw the door open so hard it slams against the wall with a loud bang. Cole is leaning over Leah against the bathroom wall, and her eyes are wide with panic.

"What the fu—" I snatch Cole by the back of the neck and throw him out of the bathroom before he can finish whatever stupid thing was about to come out of his mouth.

"Don't you *ever* fucking touch her again," I command to Cole, stepping closer to him.

"Stop being a fucking cock block, man. She's just another number to you. Let her be with someone who actually deserves her," Cole spits back, shoving me against the shoulders as the potent smell of vodka hits me like a wall of bricks. *Jesus, dude, did you drink the whole fucking bottle?* I stumble a few steps back, knocking into Leah, who yelps.

All rational thought has gone out the window. The only thing going through my mind right now is pure and absolute fucking anger. I take a step forward, cock my fist back, then swing it toward Cole's face. He puts his hands up in defense, but he's too slow, and my knuckle connects squarely with his jaw. He stumbles backward, hitting the wall, and brings his hand up to his bruised chin. His eyes burn with rage.

"You better shut your fucking mouth," I yell at him with clenched fists.

"Don't like hearing the truth? One day she'll wake up and realize you're toying with her and leave you just like your mom did." *How the hell does he know about Mom?*

I grab the collar of his shirt, then swing forward, hitting him directly on the nose.

And again, hitting him in the eye.

And again, hitting his mouth.

My blood is pumping so hard through my body, I'm starting to see black.

"Jake, stop," Leah yells from behind me, and her panicked voice causes me to pause.

A stone-hard fist slams against my jaw, sending a stinging pain shooting through my face. I step backward, release Cole's shirt, square my shoulders, then cock a fist back to hit him again. His face is covered in blood, and his eye is already swelling shut.

Fuck. How did we get here?

"Jake." Leah steps in front of me, placing her hands on my tense shoulders. I should look at her, but I can't fucking take my eyes off Cole. In my peripheral, our classmates are looking down the hallway to investigate the commotion. "He's not worth it, Jake," she says to me intently.

"Sure, Leah, *I'm* the one not worth it," Cole spouts as blood floods out of his nose.

And just like that, the rage is back. My shoulders tremble. My jaw's clenched so tight I might break a tooth. *Fuck if I care.*

"Jake," she booms, grabbing my chin and forcing my gaze to meet hers. "I'm fine, okay? I'm fine."

Our eyes connect, and we're the only two people in the room. My breathing steadies, and I search her worried eyes. "I'm okay. I'm right here," she repeats, taking my hand and putting it to her face, leaning into it. I rub my thumb against her soft skin, the anger slowly fading away.

"Whenever he dumps you, come find me if you want to know what it's like to be with someone who's *actually* into you and not just looking for a weekend fuck," Cole says, then turns to walk away.

And it's back.

I move Leah gently to the side and step forward, gripping Cole firmly around his neck, then slam him against the wall, causing a picture frame to crash to the floor. "Stay the *fuck* away from Leah." I tighten my grip. "Don't even so much as *glance* in her direction. Do you understand?"

Every muscle in my body is wound up tight. He has to see it in my flaming eyes, how goddamn serious I am.

"Dude, what the fuck?" he says breathlessly, his teeth stained red with blood.

"Say you understand," I yell again in his face before jerking him forward by the neck and smashing him back against the wall.

The guy who never loses his cool is losing it completely.

"I understand," Cole snarls with a grimace. His arctic blue eyes darken as blood drips down his chin and lands on my bent wrist.

I throw him down the hallway, and he stumbles into Trey, who just rounded the corner with Chloe trailing hurriedly behind. *Great.*

"Get out of here, Cole," Trey says, gesturing towards the front door.

Cole looks between Leah and me as the blood runs down his face, his face full of confusion. He opens his mouth to speak, then closes it, shakes his head, and turns around.

Thank God.

I put my arm around Leah's shoulders, pulling her to me tightly. She presses her head against my chest as we watch Cole walk out of the house.

How the fuck did we get here?

Chloe rushes over, attempting to drag Leah away from me to inspect her. I keep my hands placed protectively on her shoulders.

"Oh my God, are you okay? What the fuck just happened?" Chloe asks with wide eyes.

"I... I..." Leah stutters, unable to form a sentence.

"That fucker just tried to force himself on Leah," I snap, trying to calm myself before I go outside and beat him into unconsciousness.

"Oh my God," Chloe gasps. "I'm so sorry. I didn't realize what a sleazebag he was or I would've never even suggested it."

"This isn't your fault, Chlo," Leah mumbles out.

"Well, it kind of is." She looks down at her feet.

"What do you mean?" I bark at her as anger sizzles under the surface. "What did you do?"

"Well, you're supposedly single so I was just relaying the message," she says to Leah with raised brows.

"Yeah, and you also told him earlier that he should work for it," Leah snaps. "And now look what happened!"

"I didn't think he—"

"And apparently that I've been thinking about him for months," Leah says to her with raised brows.

Excuse me?

"What? I nev—"

"God dammit, Chloe," Leah shouts at her, trembling with rage. "Jesus Christ, that guy just cornered me in your boyfriend's bathroom because you can't stop meddling in my love life." I squeeze her shoulders, hard, hoping she'll realize she's gone too far. Chloe's eyes go wide as tears brim in her eyes. "Which you can stop doing, by the way, because I am already *fucking* seeing someone!"

She storms off without even glancing back. Chloe and I watch her as she flies out the front door, slamming it behind her. The music is so loud, no one even hears it, but I can see the door rattle.

Chloe folds her arms and cocks a brow. "Aren't you going to go chasing after her?"

You're damn right I am.

17
Leah

I get to the Jeep, cursing at myself for not swiping the fucking keys from Jake's pocket before I stormed out the door. Did I overreact? Probably… But my body was just filled with so much adrenaline from Jake's fight I couldn't control myself.

"Damn it," I shout, slamming my fist against the hood.

"Le," Jake's rough voice says firmly.

I spin to face him. "God, I'm sorry, I'm just—I'm so fucking mad!" I shout, pacing back and forth.

"Leah," he says again, grabbing my wrist and spinning me towards him. His concerned eyes analyze every crevice of my face in the moonlight.

His muscular arms reach out to pull me to him, and I release a heavy sigh. My hand finds the side of his neck, grasping it firmly, and I melt into him.

"Are you okay?" he asks calmly, rubbing a hand along my back.

"Am I okay?" I ask incredulously. "Are *you* okay?"

"Yes, I'm fine," he replies, sighing. "What happened before I showed up?"

He drags his fingers through his hair so hard I think he's going to end up bald.

"Cole backed me into the bathroom and started hitting on me." I tremble anxiously. "I was pushing him off me, I swear. I told him no. I promise you, I told him I wasn't interested." I look up at Jake, pleading for him to believe me. "I would never cheat on you, Jake. Never." Tears blur my vision as I struggle to steady my breathing. My heart stings, waiting for Jake's response.

Damn it, Cole. You might have ruined everything.

"Le, you don't need to convince me of that, okay?" he says, leaning down and planting a soft kiss on my lips. "I know you're mine." My body starts to relax. "Leah, did he try to force himself on you?"

"No," I say quickly. "Absolutely not. He was just trying really hard to convince me."

"Oh, thank god." He breathes out a sigh of relief. "But this is what I was talking about. If no one knows, then they think they can hit on you, and I have no right to do anything about it."

"He knew we were dating. He didn't care." Jake looks surprised, so I guess he wasn't the one who told Cole. "Pretty sure it wouldn't have mattered if I was your wife... He was pretty insistent," I mumble.

"My wife?" he repeats, raising his eyebrows as the corners of his mouth curl slightly upwards. "Someday." The smile fades, and his eyes turn dark again. "And if anyone touches you without your permission, then you *are* going to have to bail me out, okay? I don't think I'd be able to hold myself back like that again."

"Okay, I promise *if* I'm your wife and *if* you end up in jail because of a fight about me, I'll bail you out. But can we keep the bar fights to a minimum? That was terrifying and exhausting." I grin, trying to lighten the mood.

"Sure, whatever you say, Le," he agrees, running his fingers through my hair, staring at me with furrowed brows and a weak smile. "Damn, I feel like I maybe shouldn't have hit him so hard. I just… I thought he was forcing himself on you, and I just… I fucking snapped, Le." He takes my hand and places it over his pounding chest. "This is what you do to me. You make me fucking crazy. I would do anything to protect you."

"He deserved everything you gave him, Jake." I kiss his face softly. "And you know… you're pretty hot when you're angry."

He steps forward, his tall frame caging me against the hood of the Jeep. A thrill runs through me, knowing how easily we could get caught here, but for some reason, I just don't care.

"Oh really." He smirks. "Well, you know what makes me really angry? The thought of someone else touching you in places I've never even seen."

He rubs his warm palms down my shoulders, waist, hips, then onto my ass. He grips both cheeks and lifts me in the air and places me on the hood, sliding between my legs. My stomach drops, and our mouths fuse again, hungrier. My center is rubbing against his hard stomach, pulsating with impatience as all thoughts of Cole drift into the abyss.

"I want to touch every inch of you before someone else ever has the opportunity," Jake growls into my mouth. "My sexy girl."

My stomach does somersaults at his possessive tone. I'm aching to be somewhere—anywhere—else.

"Take me home," I say to Jake between kisses.

"Gladly," he replies, nuzzling my head to the side and kissing my neck.

"Will you stay with me tonight?" I ask casually as my legs are wrapped around him.

He pulls away and looks at me with furrowed brows as the corner of his mouth curls upwards. "Would your parents be okay with that? What if they catch us?"

"My parents are out of town until next Monday." I waggle my eyebrows dramatically, and Jake's smile spreads ear to ear. I was saving that little nugget of good news for the perfect moment, and this seemed like the right one.

"I get an entire week of you to myself?" He beams, squeezing me tightly and touching his forehead to mine.

"Yep," I say, popping the *p* and pecking him on the lips.

"Then what the fuck are we still doing here? Let's go."

18
Jake

We pull into Leah's driveway, and I park behind her mom's car. Since Dad thinks Chloe is sleeping here anyways, we figured it was the simplest way not to get caught.

"Do you need to grab anything from your room before you come over?" Leah asks.

"Yeah, just go inside. I'll be over in ten minutes."

"Okay."

"Leah," I say as she starts walking towards her dark house. "Lock the door. I know where the key is."

"Okay," she repeats with a grin, giving me a quick kiss on the lips before disappearing into the darkness towards her house. I walk through my house as quietly as possible so I don't wake Dad or Sophia. Since he was expecting me to stay at Trey's tonight, he shouldn't be waiting up for me. This is confirmed by the sound of snoring as I walk down the hall past his bedroom. I tiptoe past Sophia's room, and she's passed out surrounded by her collection of koala stuffed animals. I don't know what her fascination is with them, but she has at least ten.

Finally, I make it into my room unnoticed and flick on the light. At the same time, the light comes on in Leah's room next door. Her curtains are open, allowing me a full view as she walks around her room, anxiously tidying up and hiding piles of clothes. I grin at how adorably frantic she looks. Before she catches me staring, I go to my bathroom to freshen up.

I change out of my jeans, sliding on black sweatpants and my favorite worn-in Longwood Soccer T-shirt. I pull out my backpack and throw in my toothbrush, a clean change of clothes, some deodorant, my phone charger, and an oversized T-shirt for her to wear to bed. I rarely wear it, and I know she'll love it.

I'm at the door about to walk out of my room when I pause. I stride to my bedside table to pull out the pack of condoms and bottle of lube I bought at the store the day after I kissed Leah. Not that I'm expecting anything, but I don't want to be unprepared should the opportunity present itself. I've thought about losing my virginity to Leah since I hit puberty. It never felt right with anyone else. *Man, I sound like a sappy romantic fuck.* After I double-check that I have everything I need, I turn off the light and leave my room to sneak back out of the house.

I'm walking through the kitchen, and the oven light flicks on.

"Shit." I jump, holding my hand over my chest. My heart pounds wildly as I attempt to catch my breath.

"Hi, Jakey," Sophia says, smirking with her arms folded over her chest.

"What the hell are you doing, you little creeper?" I whisper shout at her. "You scared the shit out of me."

"What the *hell* are *you* doing?" she whispers. The curse word sounds hilarious in her high-pitched little girl voice.

"First of all, language—"

"Hypocrite," she mutters with narrowed eyes.

"Second of all, none of your business."

"Oh, it's my business if you don't want Dad to find out." She cocks a brow.

"What do you want, Bug?" I narrow my eyes at her, hoping the use of the nickname will soften her a bit.

"It's *Lady*bug." She narrows her eyes right back.

"Well, I like Bug. It's shorter and cute. Just like my favorite sister."

"Stop trying to sweet talk me," she says, all business.

"Fine, *Sophia*. What do you want?"

"If you don't want me to tell Dad, you have to start running with me five days a week," she says with the best poker face a nine year old can muster.

That's all she wants? To go on runs with me? Easy.

"Three days," I counter, so she doesn't think it's that easy to manipulate me.

"Four days, final offer," she says smugly with an adorable sassy smile on her face.

"Fine, four days." I stick out my hand to shake on it.

"Rain or shine," she commands, holding out her tiny pinky finger, and I laugh.

"Sure, rain or shine." I hook my finger with hers and do a thumb stamp to seal the silly pinky promise.

I finally get to Leah's front door ten minutes later after convincing Sophia to start our runs on Monday and not tomorrow. I dig out the key hidden in the soil of the small potted plant by the front door. The same place it's been for the last fifteen years. Once inside, I lock the door and make my way through the house up to Leah's room. I've been here so many times I can literally do it in the dark with my eyes closed. When I get to her room, she's sitting on the bed, playing on her phone. She's wearing silk pajamas, and it looks like she's washed her face and taken her makeup off. *My gorgeous girl.*

"Hey." She grins, hopping out of bed and greeting me with a breathtaking smile and an even better kiss. "I'll be right back. I have to go set the alarm."

"Okay."

I've been in Leah's room hundreds, probably thousands of times over the years, but I've never actually taken it all in. You can tell a lot about a person from their bedroom. It's like looking into the deepest part of someone's soul. On full display are their likes, dislikes, biggest wishes, and almost maybes.

For example, the guitar sitting in the corner of Leah's room. I haven't heard her play it in years, but I know she keeps it there as a reminder of when things were easier before we got to high school and all the drama and bullshit started. When it was cool out, she used to play with the windows open, and I would hole up in my room and listen to her for hours.

There's a small table set up in the corner with a half-painted canvas and small bottles covered in paint.

She's so damn talented.

I can't help but laugh when my eyes come across the little trophy on the top of her dresser. *Leah Stone - Hustle Award - 6YO PeeWee League.* Chloe was quite literally the worst six-year-old soccer player there ever was and Leah came in a close second, but she sure ran her ass off. She's gotten better over the years from sparring with me.

My favorite part of her bedroom is all the touches of me. I may have just become her boyfriend officially a week ago, but our lives have been woven together for over fifteen years. There's not a spot around the room I can look at without finding a photograph with me in it or some trinket from a memory I'm a part of.

"See anything you like?" Leah says as she walks back into the room holding two glasses of water and a couple protein bars.

"Just getting some insight into you. That's all." I walk over to her window and close the curtains. "And you've got to start closing your curtains. As much as I love getting a free show every once in a while, I'm the only one you should be doing that for in the future."

"You can see me change in my window?" She balks with wide eyes.

"I'm not saying I've watched." I haven't, but I have caught quick glances before forcing myself to look away. "But if I wanted to, I would have definitely had the perfect vantage point."

"So you didn't want to?" she pouts.

"No, I definitely did. I just didn't want to be a Peeping Tom."

"Well, I guess that makes sense you can see in here, given how many times I've drooled watching you walk around shirtless over there."

"Oh, is that so? So you're the Peeping Tom in our relationship?" I tease, narrowing my eyes while walking over to the bed and simultaneously stripping off my T-shirt.

"I guess so." Her mouth curls into a smile as she draws her lower lip between her teeth, and she eyes me up and down like she's ready to devour me at any second. *I hope she does.*

"I said we can take things slow," I remind her. "So if I'm being too forward, just let me know." It's taking every ounce of my willpower not to pull Leah close and show her how much she means to me.

"Jake, listen to me when I say this." She grabs my hand and tugs me down onto the bed with her. "I am so sick of taking things slow.

You have my consent, or permission, or whatever it is you need to do whatever you want, whenever you want to do it. I think it's pretty obvious how we feel about each other and..." She pauses, staring up at the ceiling.

"And what?" I say, dragging a hand through her brushed out curls.

"And..."

"Come on, you can tell me anything. You know that." I graze my fingers down the length of her arm and take her hand in mine.

"No, it's not that. I just..." She sighs. "When Cole had me in the bathroom and was coming on to me, all I could think about was that it would make you hate me—and that would absolutely destroy me. You're the only one I want. The only one I've wanted for years..." She cups my face with her hands and looks me in the eyes. "When you put sunscreen on me at the springs, all I could think about was how good your hands felt against my skin and how I wished we were somewhere private so you could continue exploring every part of me. Jake... I only want your hands, your lips, your breath on me. No one else's. Ever." She kisses the aching bruise on my jaw.

For the first time in my life, I'm completely fucking speechless. Those were my exact thoughts at the springs too, and for the weeks following until I finally got to touch her warm skin again.

"I'm just saying, I know you've already done it before but... I just always kind of thought you'd be my first, and I want to make sure of it." *Wait, I've done what now?*

"What makes you think I've already done it before?"

"Oh, uh... I just assumed," she stammers out. "You and Katelyn were together for like six months. And you look like that. And you're a guy, so..."

"Oh, come on, give me more credit than that." I grin with narrowed eyes.

"Sorry." Her pursed lips curl up at the corners.

"Actually, a big reason we broke up is because she wanted to have sex and I didn't—er—couldn't, rather."

Great, you idiot. Now she's going to think there's something physically wrong with you.

"Why?"

"It just didn't feel right to do something so personal with her when I wasn't in love with her." Which is the truth. Katelyn was a virgin too, and did we do other stuff? Sure. But I could never bring myself to sleep with her. It didn't feel right, and I guess even though Leah and I weren't together, there was some part of my subconscious that hoped this day would come, and I didn't want to fuck it up by busting my nut. Literally.

"So you're a virgin," she repeats to herself out loud.

"Yes," I confirm, and her mouth breaks into a breathtaking smile. Those adorable dimples on full display. "But Leah, are you sure you're ready for that?"

"Jake," she interrupts in her usual way. "I am *so* ready. It's you. It's us. I want this. I want you so bad it hurts. I want you to be the first one to touch me like that."

"I'm the *only* one who's ever going to touch you again." I grin, pulling her on top of me. She squeals with laughter and rests a leg on each side of me.

"Is that a promise?" she asks hesitantly.

"Of course it is," I reply firmly, rubbing my hands up and down her soft, freckled shoulders. She smiles and bends down, planting a soft kiss on my lips. I grab her face in my hands, angling her gaze to meet mine. "Le… I *love* you." Her mouth curves into a wide grin as she bends down and pecks my lips again. "But I don't just love you. I'm *in* love with you. I'm fucking crazy about you. Sometimes, when you walk in a room…" I chuckle. "You just don't know what you do to me, baby. I fucking love you, and I can't go another single day without you knowing how I feel or how amazing you are."

"Jake." She tilts her head and smiles down at me as her auburn hair scatters around us like a curtain.

"It's okay if you aren't ready to say it back. But I just had to tell you." I rub the pad of my thumb against her cheek. "You're it for me."

"Jake… are you kidding? I am so in love with you. I think I've been in love with you since we were twelve." She giggles, and I exhale in relief. "And trust me, my body reacts the same way when you're around. Sometimes I can't even think straight."

I take her face in my hands, looking deep into her beautiful eyes. "I love you, Le."

She smiles softly up at me. "I love you too, Jacob."

It wasn't love at first play date. There wasn't a moment when I was struck by lightning, igniting our dormant connection. There were years and years of exposure to a toxin, forming an addiction I'll never break. It merged with my DNA until it was all-consuming and completely in charge of my entire being.

My life is no longer mine.

Everything I am and everything I'll ever be belongs to Leah Stone.

She plants another soft kiss on my lips, then gets off the bed and turns off all the lights. The glow from a few candles on her dresser dimly illuminates the room. She puts on an R&B playlist, and I'm already hard watching her walk around the room in her sexy silk pajamas. Looks like I wasn't the only one hoping this night might have a happy ending.

"Oh shit." She brings her hand to her forehead, stopping dead center in the middle of the room.

"What's wrong?" I ask, sitting up.

"We don't have any condoms. And I'm not on the pill."

"I have condoms," I say a little too quickly.

"Oh really?" She smirks, cocking her head at me with raised eyebrows. "Well, that was awfully presumptuous of you."

"Always be prepared." I wink, then unzip my backpack. I pull out the condoms and lube, setting them on the nightstand. Even in the candlelight, I can tell Leah is blushing.

"I'm really glad you did Boy Scouts when you were younger. They taught you excellent survival skills," she mocks. I yank her back onto the bed, ensuring she lands on my chest, a leg of hers on each side of me in a straddle position.

"If you're ever in pain or uncomfortable, just say something, okay?"

"Okay, I trust you." Three simple words and the crippling weight on my shoulders evaporates. I am so fucking ready to make her mine. Officially. Physically. All of it. I run my fingers through her thick, soft hair, then pull her face down to mine, my tongue immediately dipping between the seams of her lips. Our tongues meld gently together. Then the calmness is shattered by a starved kiss. Urgent. Exploratory. All-consuming. Once the hunger is satisfied, we start the pattern all over again.

The only way I can describe kissing Leah Stone is to compare it to an ocean wave crashing on the shore. The swell is rough and passionate, moving in quickly. It crashes against the sand ferociously while the shore stands strong in its path, relishing in the collision. Then the tide ebbs and glides unhurried, gently, carefully across the sand before retreating slowly back to sea to begin their love affair all over again. The ocean chooses the pace, retreating but always returning back to the shore, and the shore is always there to catch it. Leah is my ocean. Serene, ethereal, ominous, or turbulent—I will always, always catch her.

My right hand cradles her face while the other caresses her hip. My palm slides slowly under her silky night shirt, memorizing the contours of her back. I graze slowly up her spine, taking the hem of the shirt with me, exposing more delicate skin.

"Do you want me to take it off?" she mumbles into my mouth between kisses. She tastes like peppermint and something else I can't quite decipher. Whatever it is, it's intoxicating as all hell.

"Oh, God, yes," I groan in approval.

If I could live in this moment forever, I would. Leah sits up, and her warm, throbbing center presses flush against my dick. Her mouth curls into a seductive smile as she grinds against me, and I might come right in my pants. She grabs the hem of her silky pink top, inches it up her stomach until her perfect breasts are free, and pulls it over her head, tossing it to the floor. *Holy. Fucking. Shit.* Leah Stone is more stunning than my wildest fantasies. Complete perfection. Her breasts are beautifully formed, full and round, with small, dark pink nipples, begging my mouth to devour them.

Those gorgeous patches of freckles are scattered across her skin like stars in the night sky. In one quick motion, I flip her under me onto her back, a heavy breath escaping her lips from the impact. I lower my mouth to the crook of her neck, sucking gently before I release to return to her lips.

"Oh my god, please keep going," she begs.

If she thinks this is good, wait until I get a little lower.

My wet lips make their way down her neck, and I glide my teeth along her collarbone. My aching dick is pressing against her center, begging for attention.

She arches against me. "Fuck," I rasp, not meaning to say it out loud.

"What?"

"If you keep arching like that, I'm going to come in my fucking pants," I groan, seconds from losing all composure. She giggles and arches into me again, harder.

"Leah, I'm being fucking serious," I growl at her. "Do you really want that to happen?"

"Fine, I'll stop." She pouts at me with a teasing grin but not before one more tiny thrust. Fortunately, I maintain my dignity.

My teeth drag down from her collarbone towards her exposed breasts. Her breath hitches as I pull her nipple gently between my teeth. She doesn't protest, so I suck it harder while giving the other one the attention it deserves with my hand. *Wouldn't want my girls to be uneven.* She trembles beneath me as I glide my mouth between the crevice of her breasts towards the other nipple.

"If you keep doing that, *I'm* going to come in *my* pants," Leah groans breathlessly, throwing her arm over her eyes with a chuckle. I take her nipple in my mouth, giving it one more hard suck before letting it pop free. She releases a sweet little cry, and it's my new favorite sound. I rest my head on her chest, allowing her to catch her breath. Her heart rate steadies, and I know my next plan of action.

"If you think that brought you close to the edge, just wait," I taunt, running my tongue down her stomach towards the hem of her satin shorts, dipping slightly under for a taste.

"Fuck, Jake," she gasps loudly. I'm savoring the empty house we're in, allowing my girl to scream for me as loud as she wants to. I take her shorts between my teeth, tugging them down, but they're stuck on her ass so I'm struggling a bit.

"Just take them off, for fuck's sake," Leah shouts at me breathlessly, sending goosebumps down my spine straight to my dick.

"You're so sexy when you're bossy." I grin.

I scoot back, grabbing both sides of her silk shorts, and yank them off her. She's now lying in bed wearing nothing but a pink lacy thong. If I thought she looked angelic before… Now… in nothing but that? Leah's every man's wet dream.

I hum in approval. "Fucking perfect." I tease her panty line with my pointer finger, then flip her over onto her stomach. My dick pulsates from the sight of her perfectly plump ass and exposed, sun-kissed back. I straddle her legs, lowering my mouth down to kiss her bare shoulder blades. I bite down on the nape of her neck, and she squeals.

"Don't leave a mark," she chastises.

"As you wish." I nibble her neck again before sliding my tongue down her spine to her panty line. I draw the thin thong strap between my teeth and tug it down, my scruffy jaw rubbing against her ass cheek in the process. She lifts her hips off the bed, allowing me to slide the thong down her bare legs and off her feet. I lower down, nipping her ass cheek, and she yelps with a giggle.

I nip the other one too to keep things even. "Do you want me to stop?" I question breathlessly.

"No," she answers firmly.

I kiss the spot my teeth claimed. "Don't worry, no one will see bite marks there."

I flip her onto her back again and for the first time have a complete view of my naked girl.

"Fuck, Leah. You've just been walking around looking like *this* and I had no clue?"

"Guess you shoulda worked your magic a little faster." She smirks, appearing completely carefree and ready for whatever comes next.

"You seem… relaxed." I smile down at her, and my heart swells in my chest.

"Should I not be?" She furrows her brows.

"No, it's good. I'm happy you feel comfortable." I slide my hands simultaneously up each of her thighs, closer to her center.

"Like I said, I trust you." Her eyes go wide for a brief moment when my right hand dips directly between her legs, my other hand holding her hip for stability. I don't take my eyes off her as I begin to swipe her clit with my thumb. I'm wondering if I found the right spot at the same moment her eyes roll to the back of her head.

That's it, baby.

I lower my mouth between her legs and stroke my tongue gently against her inner lips. I then replace my thumb with sucking and nibbling. She grabs on to my hair, tugging left and right until my mouth is in the perfect position on her sensitive flesh. Within seconds, I can feel her body start to tremble.

"Oh my God. If you don't stop, I'm going to come," she whimpers.

I don't stop.

I don't even come up for air.

I couldn't care less if we don't go all the way tonight. I'm going to watch my girl fall apart. Her warm, soaked sweetness convulses against my face, and I push against her ass cheeks to hold her in place.

"Jake!" she screams breathlessly, and the sound is so intoxicating I want to hear it on repeat for the rest of my life. Thunder, lightning, and ocean waves crash in symphony all at once. After one final shudder, she pulls me by my hair up to her face. She's panting and out of breath. So am I.

"Was it good?" I ask confidently between gasps of air as I stare down at her.

"Yes," she pants.

I roll off of her and pull her into my arms.

"So… is that it?" she asks a few minutes later after our breathing finally steadies.

"What do you mean, *is that it?*" I scoff, looking down at her.

"Well, I kind of thought you might want to... go all the way tonight?"

"Oh, I *definitely* want." I hum, pressing my forehead to hers. "I just didn't know if you'd be too worn out from that *mind-blowing orgasm* I just gave you."

She throws her head back, laughing. "That *was* amazing... but I think I can rally."

Before I can reply, she straddles me and yanks off my boxers and sweatpants. My dick stands at attention, and she stares at it with raised brows.

"Wow." Pink tinges her cheeks as she bites her lower lip. "It's bigger than I thought it would be."

"What?" I chuckle.

"I mean, I always figured you were... endowed. I just never would've imagined... Damn." She hums in approval, gliding her wet tongue along her top lip. I definitely don't think I'm above average, but she doesn't have a ton of experience, and I'm not going to correct her.

If she wants to think my dick is God's gift to women, who am I to disagree?

"I'll be careful," I assure her.

"I'm on top. Aren't you worried *I* won't be?"

"That wouldn't worry me in the slightest." I smirk, shaking my head, and her lips curl upwards into the sexiest wicked smile I've ever seen.

Oh, fuck me.

She leans over me, reaching for a condom and lube off the nightstand. Her breasts are dangling in my face, and I'm half a second away from sucking her nipple into my mouth again when she leans away.

Damn it.

Her lips graze my chest, trailing kisses downward until she reaches my hip bones. She sucks on each hip hard enough that she'll definitely give me hickeys, and I have to mentally run through one of the soccer team plays to keep from coming in her face.

"What happened to no marks?" I tease.

"No one should be seeing these," she echoes, giving my right hip bone a kiss before centering her face above my throbbing erection, eyes full of lust. She grasps my shaft firmly, meeting it with her slightly parted lips before encompassing it in her mouth for a hard suck. This time, I force myself to mentally recite all the Marvel movies in chronological order to keep from coming too quickly. She slides her mouth up and down my engorged flesh and just when I think I can't take it anymore, she swipes her tongue around the tip of my dick, plants a soft kiss, and pulls away.

Before I have a chance to be disappointed, she grabs the condom off the bed. Although she seems confident, her trembling hands almost can't get the foil pack open. I don't want to make her more nervous by offering to help, so I just stare and enjoy the show. She finally gets the condom free and rolls it on to my hard dick. She even checks to make sure there isn't any air in the top.

Thanks, tenth grade health class.

I still can't look at a banana the same.

After the condom is securely on, she opens the lube and squeezes a generous amount on the condom, rubbing it up and down my shaft with her hand in a slow, circular motion. She sits up, straddling over me on her knees, and brings her center directly over my dick, brushing it up and down her inner lips before sliding it slowly into her opening. She lowers herself down onto me, allowing me to enter her deeper. A gasp releases from her swollen, wet lips.

"Does it hurt?" I rasp.

"Just stings a little," she pants breathlessly. She grinds against me, and I can't help myself from thrusting deeper inside of her.

"Oww," she yelps, scrunching her face, and my entire body freezes.

"Do you wanna stop?"

"No, I'm okay," she pants, trying to calm her rapid breathing. "It was just a little too deep."

"Sorry." I brush the stray hairs out of her face. "I don't really have much control in this position."

"Well, then let's try a different one." She grins before pulling off me.

I slide off the mattress, walking around to stand at the foot of the bed. I'm thankful for the previous… *research* I've seen, giving me the idea of a position we could try. "Come to the edge of the bed and get on your hands and knees." She happily obliges, and only seconds have passed before I'm sliding slowly into her again as she holds her ass into the air. "How is that?"

"So. Fucking. Good," she moans, grasping the bedspread with both hands.

I pick up the pace, thrusting faster and harder, but making sure I don't press deep enough to hurt her. I reach around her and grab her breast firmly in my hand. A high-pitched whimper escapes her lips, and it's taking all my willpower to hold it in.

"Don't. Stop," she commands with a needy moan.

Thank God.

I can't hold it much longer.

She convulses around me, tugging tightly against my hard, tortured cock. Knowing I'm the reason for the sweet little cry that escapes her pushes me straight over the edge—bursts of pleasure ripple through me.

When both our breaths finally steady, I pull out of her, holding my shaft so the condom doesn't slip off. She flips onto her back, still gasping for air.

"That was the best sex of my life," she says, smiling at the ceiling.

"It was the only sex of your life." I chuckle, grinning ear to ear.

"I'm pretty sure it will still always be the best," she says confidently.

I believe her.

Losing my virginity to Leah. The girl I've loved probably my entire life. I don't know how it could ever get better than that.

I throw the T-shirt from my backpack at her, and it lands on her chest. "I brought that for you."

She examines the shirt and smiles up at me. "Thanks."

Leah gets dressed, and I dispose of the condom in the bathroom, making sure to wrap it in loads of toilet paper so no one finds it in her trash can. When I come back, she's turned the TV on and is sitting on the bed in my T-shirt. Her bare ass is sticking out, and the pink thong is still lying on the floor.

"If you're not going to put any underwear on, this is going to be an exhausting night." I walk over and rub my palm against her soft ass.

"I'm counting on it." She smirks, dragging me down to the bed, and the tide meets the shore all over again.

19
Leah

Light scatters in through the blinds, and I'm trying to recall the events of the night before.

Did Jake really spend the night?

A hot, heavy arm is loosely draped over my hip. *Yep, that happened.*

Did I finally lose my virginity?

The ache between my thighs answers that question. Double confirmed by the two torn-up foil packs crumbled up on the nightstand.

Did Jake really beat the shit out of Cole?

My blood runs hot, recalling the other less pleasant memories of the evening. So yes, that did happen.

Thankfully, Cole hits like a little bitch and only left a small bruise.

I want to relive the positive parts of the night and ignore the worst. Like remembering the refreshing feeling of running into the cool ocean water on a hot summer day. When you think back, you recall how good the water felt on your sun-kissed skin, not the searing temperature of the thick air.

Think of the positives.

Jake protected me and probably (*hopefully?)* broke Cole's nose.

Jake took care of me.

Jake *took care* of me.

I grin at the last thought.

I roll over to face him. As I do, his eyes flutter open. "Good morning, beautiful," he mumbles with a sleepy smile, nuzzling closer to me.

"Good morning," I echo, unable to wipe the giddy grin off my face.

"So it wasn't a dream?"

"Afraid not."

"And we get… how many more days of *this*?" he asks, squeezing me to him.

I tap my fingers against his shoulder, counting to myself.

One.

Two.

Three.

Four.

"Five."

"Not enough." He tugs me closer, lifting his head just enough to glance at the clock on my nightstand. "It's already ten? I have to leave for practice in an hour."

"Ugh…" I groan. "Can't we just stay here all day?"

"I wish." He sighs, tracing my arm with his fingertips. "But I have a really important game this week. A few scouts are coming, so Coach added a Sunday practice."

"Are you nervous?"

"I mean, I'm not really nervous to play. That part I can do in my sleep. But I am kind of freaking out about what it all means. Getting an offer… or not getting one… It's going to determine my entire future."

"I get it," I lie, unable to come up with anything else. I know it's selfish, but I don't want to think about what it all means. For him… for us.

"And it'll affect *us* too, Le," he says, looking at me with gentle eyes, reading my mind.

"I won't be the reason you don't pursue these incredible opportunities. You need to make the best decision for your future. I don't have to prove to you I'm not going anywhere. I'm in this for the long haul."

"You really are the perfect woman." He chuckles, pulling me into a deep kiss.

"Why don't you show me just how perfect you think I am?" I taunt.

"With pleasure," he says, rolling on top of me.

We begrudgingly get dressed after the first and best morning sex I've ever had. I throw on Jake's T-shirt he brought me to sleep in, along with a pair of sleep shorts, and he puts on his sweatpants. We make our way down to the kitchen for a necessary cup of coffee before getting ready for the day. I can't even function until I've had my allotted amount of caffeine. Jake pours us each a bowl of Lucky Charms, my favorite, and we sit down at the kitchen table to eat.

"This is so domesticated. I actually love it," Jake admits between spoonfuls of cereal.

"I know. I could get used to this. You're an *incredible* cook." I dramatize bringing the spoon to my mouth and savoring the sweet flavor on my tongue. "Oh my god, mmm."

"I did attend culinary school in France."

"Jake Cordon Bleu?" I snort. "I'm surprised you could graduate without learning how to cook a proper pancake."

"Hey." He throws a hand over his chest. "You burn a pancake *one time*, and you're the burnt pancake guy."

"Jake, you burn them *every* time." I laugh, shaking my head. "You're a pancake murderer."

"You know what?" He narrows his eyes at me. "That hurts a little bit…" He smirks. "But I appreciate that you still always eat one," he says with a soft smile. I do always eat one, and it's *always* horrible, but Jake tries so hard for their family, I want him to feel appreciated.

Just as I bring the last spoonful of cereal to my lips, there's a knock on the door.

Who the fuck would that be at ten in the morning?

"Want me to check who it is?" Jake offers.

"How would we even explain why you're answering my front door at ten in the morning?"

"I came over for breakfast," he says casually, gesturing towards the empty bowls on the table.

"Half naked?" I smirk with raised brows.

"Fine." He rolls his eyes. "I'll get a shirt, you get the door."

I walk down the hallway, stopping at the alarm keypad to disarm it. Once at the front door, I pause with my hand on the handle and look through the peephole.

Oh, fuck.

I open the door timidly, forcing a smile upon my panicked lips.

"Hey, Chlo," I say.

"Hey." She walks straight into the house towards the kitchen.

"What's up?" I say casually, but hopefully loud enough Jake will hear.

"Nothing… Trey's parents called and said they were coming home earlier than expected, so he brought me home," she replies, looking around.

She glances at the table with our two bowls and pauses, then looks at me with narrowed eyes.

"Well, somebody was hungry this morning." She grins with raised brows.

"Uh, yeah, I—"

"Where is he, Le?" she asks, cutting me off as heat flushes my entire body in panic.

"What?" I say with a shaky voice.

"Where's Jake?" she probes, crossing her arms over her chest.

"Hey, Chlo," Jake says, coming down the stairs fully dressed.

"What are you doing here?" Chloe asks smugly, looking between us and raising an eyebrow as her eyes flick to my shirt.

"Oh, he, uh, he came for breakfast." I gesture to the bowls.

"Then why was he upstairs?" she probes, obviously not buying my shit. "And why are you wearing his shirt?"

"Because I, because he—"

"Because I slept here last night," Jake says, finishing my panicked response.

My eyes go wide, and I inhale sharply.

"And why exactly were you at Leah's house all night?" Chloe pushes, ignoring me and looking directly at Jake.

"What's your fucking problem, Chlo?" Jake snaps.

"What's *my* problem?" she shouts, her jaw ticking. "I want to know how much longer you guys are going to hide the fact that you're *fucking*!"

"What?" My eyes go wide, and I struggle to breathe. "How did you kn—"

"Seriously, Leah?" She laughs. "First of all, we've been best friends for our entire fucking lives, and you didn't think I noticed the second you went from pining after Jake to eye fucking him every time he was in the room? How self-absorbed do you think I am?"

"I just wasn't—"

"Not to mention the fact that Jake couldn't go two fucking minutes without mentioning your name," she says, looking at him with raised brows, and he glares at her. "And third, you idiots were dry humping on top of the fucking Jeep last night. If you didn't want to get caught, you probably should've picked a better hiding spot than in the middle of the damn street." She laughs and rolls her eyes.

"Then why the hell did you try to keep pushing guys in my direction?" I ask, confused.

"I was *hoping* you might eventually grow a pair and say, 'Oh, actually, Chlo, I'm dating your damn brother,' but no luck!" She throws her hands in the air. "Why the fuck didn't you guys just tell me? I've been waiting weeks for you guys to stop hiding this from me, and I'm just fucking over it."

"Not everything's about *you,* Chloe," Jake snaps.

"You're not helping," I spit at Jake. "And I tried to tell you he was my boyfriend last night," I say, returning my gaze to Chloe. "But you were in such a rush to get to *your* boyfriend you didn't bother to let me finish my fucking sentence."

"Oh, he's your boyfriend now?" She scoffs. "Guess I didn't see the status update."

"I'm sorry." I drag both hands down my face. "We just wanted to figure out what it even was before we told you."

"Give me a break," she fumes, with narrowed brows. "You had plenty of chances to tell me."

"I can't believe you're this fucking mad that we're dating," I shout, my voice breaking.

"Are you both seriously that fucking dense?" Chloe shrieks, running her hands through her hair. "I do not give *a singular fuck* that the two of you are dating. In fact, I'm thrilled. What I'm *not* thrilled about is that you guys kept it from me."

"Chlo, we're sorry… seriously," Jake says softly.

"We never wanted to hurt you," I reply.

"I just don't understand why you felt like you needed to hide this from me," Chloe says to me with a pained look in her eyes.

"I mean… you literally forced me to pinky swear I wouldn't date your brother under any circumstances," I say awkwardly. "We're not supposed to break a pinky promise."

"Leah." She laughs, shaking her head. "We were ten."

"I know but—"

"Ten," she repeats, holding up both hands and wiggling her fingers.

"But we're not supposed to break a pinky promise," I say, looking down at the floor, feeling stupid.

"Okay… but you did break it," she says, tipping my chin to look at her.

"I know," I say as my breathing increases.

"And I don't care, okay?" she says, looking at me intently.

"Okay…"

"Seriously, Leah. It's fine." She smiles genuinely. "I'm really happy for you guys."

Relief floods through my anxious veins.

"Good," Jake says with a wide, relaxed grin. "Now that we're done with that. Do you want something to eat?" he asks her, walking to get another bowl.

"Actually, I feel disgusting." She scrunches her face, looking down at yesterday's clothes. "I'm going to take a shower, but how about you come over after Jake goes to practice and we can work in the studio today?"

"I'd love that." I smile softly.

"Okay, see you in a bit, Scaredybug." She winks at me.

"Bye, Lovebug." I breathe a sigh of relief as she turns and walks out of the house.

Jake grabs my wrist loosely and pulls me into his arms the second she's gone. "I told you everything would be fine." He smirks, and I sigh happily against his chest.

He rubs along my back lightly with his strong hands, and I beg the clock in my peripheral to pause so we can stay here the rest of the day. It ignores me, ticking to ten forty-seven instead.

20
Jake

I'm scarfing down a turkey and cheese sandwich, sitting at my usual lunch table with Chloe, Trey, Matt, and some of the other guys from the soccer team. My stomach is twisted in a million knots because Leah and I decided we'd stop hiding our relationship today. With Chloe knowing, there was really no point in us being secretive anymore besides how fucking hot the sneaking around was.

My eyes are flicking uninterrupted between my sandwich and the cafeteria entrance. Leah finally walks through, and I pop up so quickly it startles Matt, who was flanking my side.

"Jesus, dude, what's your deal?" he says, laughing, then follows my gaze, spotting Leah as she walks over to us. "Oh… I see." A shit-eating grin spreads across his face, and I glare at him.

I sit back down, a leg on each side of the bench to make room for Leah, trying to calm my pounding heart. Why the hell am I so nervous about this?

"Hey, guys," Leah says to the table before sitting down next to my open legs. "Hey." She looks at me with a smile.

"Hey." I lean in and kiss her soft lips.

"Finally!" Matt shouts.

"I knew it," Trey says, chuckling.

"It's about damn time," Laura says, smirking at me.

Leah's grinning, and her cheeks are flushed pink. I can't wipe the stupid ass smile off my face as I tug her between my legs, leaving a possessive arm on her lower back as she unpacks her lunch.

I risk a glance at Chloe, who's giggling at the boys' reaction while eating her sandwich. My chest blooms at how supportive she's been. I knew she would be.

"Hey, beautiful," I whisper in Leah's ear, running my fingers into her hair and resting my palm against her cheek.

Finally, I get to show the world she's my girl.

Today is our big rivalry game against Shorewood—aka Cole's school—and I am stressed as hell. I really don't want to see him out of fear I'll lose my cool in front of the scouts.

Leah's been so distracted all week. Chloe is thrilled we're dating, but I could tell she was really hurt that we kept it from her. Knowing that we're keeping an even bigger secret from her is eating at the both of us. I don't know if we'll be able to wait until Christmas to tell the girls about Mom.

"How many scouts are coming today?" Leah asks, her fingers interlocked with mine as I walk her to class.

"I'm not really supposed to know," I say with a grin, taking in a deep breath. "But Coach Hamilton let it slip that three are coming. One from Florida and two from out of state."

"Wow, that's awesome. I'm so proud of you." She beams up at me, squeezing my hand three times, and all my stress is washed away. "Which universities from out of state?"

"The University of North Carolina and UCLA. They have the two best soccer programs in the nation aside from Stanford and Princeton," I say, getting nervous at the prospect.

"That's great," she replies, smiling.

"Yeah..." I stop walking outside the door to her classroom, and she turns to face me.

"Look, Jake, I know you're feeling anxious," she says quietly. "But today is an important day for you. You need to ignore everything that's happening in our lives and focus on the game. Not to add pressure or anything, but your future is riding on this. Just go out there, be you, and kick ass," she says like it's the easiest thing in the world.

God, I am so fucking in love with you.

"You want me to forget *everything* that's happening?" I grin, raising my eyebrows at her.

"Okay, not *everything*." She blushes, biting her bottom lip.

"Are you coming to the game?"

"Of course. I asked Chloe if she wanted to get ready together, but she hasn't answered yet," she says, concerned. "But... either way, I'll be there."

I reach into my backpack and hand her a folded-up jersey of mine. "For tonight."

Leah unfolds the Longwood High Soccer jersey with the number eight prominently on the front and back along with my last name in large block letters.

"This is definitely better than wearing your hoodie." She grins.

"And in case I don't see you before the game, good luck." She gives me a peck before running into class, and my lips tug upwards.

The soft kiss was a searing hot iron against my flesh, and I graze the spot her lips scorched with my fingertips, checking for burn marks.

The guys and I are already getting warmed up when Cole and his team walk onto the field.

My blood boils like lava. It's going to take all of my willpower to remain calm during this game. I've already spotted two of the three scouts sitting in the metal bleachers watching us warm up. I can't let Cole's stupid bullshit fuck with my game. Like Leah said, my future is riding on this. *Our future.*

Between warmups, I spot Leah skipping up the bleachers alone, joining Dad, Sophia, and Sage. Leah's wearing the jersey I gave her earlier, and *damn*, it looks good. Just the brief sight of her steadies my breathing and reduces the temperature of my blood to a normal range. Let's get this fucking shit show started.

We're fifty minutes into the game, and it is hot as hell out here. There's not a single part of my body not dripping in sweat. The score is two to one, with both goals scored by me. Shorewood is putting up a decent fight, but we're definitely the more conditioned and skilled team. I'm ten yards from the goal, waiting for the ball to be kicked to me. Cole is the defender for Shorewood, and he is not letting up. I have to admit, as much as I hate the fucking guy, he's one of their better players.

"You're such a little bitch, Summers. Couldn't stand someone hitting on your new toy?" he hisses, quiet enough no one else can hear.

He's baiting you, Summers. Just ignore him.

"You know she was into it. You should've just let us have our fun," he presses, his sweaty body bumping against mine, the putrid smell of alcohol radiating off of him.

Did he seriously come to this game wasted?

My hands clench into fists at my side. It's taking every single ounce of my willpower not to lay this guy out right now. But with three scouts watching from the best schools in the country, that news would travel, and my hope of a full ride to *anywhere* would be over. There are enough great soccer players out there. No one wants a hothead on their team that can't keep their cool. People talk so much shit during games trying to play the mental game, but my ability to ignore the head fucking is one of my best skills.

"I saw her up there with your jersey on, man. I can't wait to help her take it off later after she realizes what a piece of shit you are."

I'm about to lose the battle to the devil on my shoulder when the ball comes flying towards me. I stop it against my chest, it drops to the grass, and I dribble towards the goal. Cole tries to cut me off, but I spin around him with ease, *accidentally* tripping him in the process.

Oops.

No whistle is blown, and I make my way to the goal, then dodge and weave one other defender before sending the ball sailing directly into the white net. The home team's bleachers erupt in cheers, as do my teammates.

"You should focus more on the game and less on the shit-talking, prick. Then maybe you wouldn't spend the whole game on your ass," I taunt Cole, who's standing a few feet away.

"Maybe you should keep your dick in your pants. I know you're still fucking around behind Leah's back with her friend," Cole snarls.

"What?" I laugh. "You need to lay off the bottle, dude," I spout, turning to walk back to center field.

A firm hand grabs my shoulder, spinning me around, and decks me in the jaw.

I stumble back, rubbing my face.

"*Oww*," I groan.

The entire crowd gasps, an eerie silence filling the air.

A referee blows his whistle and throws up a red card.

"She'll realize you're playing her soon," he taunts so quietly that only I can hear him. "I'll be the first one in line to peel your jersey off her gorgeous body. She'll be begging me for it."

I glance towards the bleachers and spot all three scouts eyeing me intently, arms folded over their chests. I'm sure they're loving every minute of this. Getting to see exactly how I'll handle pressure and altercation. If I didn't know any better, I'd think they fabricated the whole ordeal to test me. Leah is standing with wide eyes and a hand over her mouth like she's about to cry, and I can't blame her. This week's been so mentally exhausting, I feel like I'm close to it myself.

I exhale heavily and continue towards the middle of the field.

The rest of the match goes by textbook. Since Cole got a red card, he was removed, and Shorewood only got to play with ten players, which made our victory laughable. The final score is six to one, with me having scored five goals and assisting for a sixth.

After the game ends, a scout from UCLA, my fucking dream school, walks up and shakes my hand. "I'm Coach Young from UCLA."

Holy shit, the actual coach came to see me play?

"You played a hell of a game, kid. I was pretty impressed how you held your cool out there even after that kid decked you." He smirks.

"Thank you, sir," I say nervously.

"I have to ask… Did you deserve it?" He narrows his eyes at me.

"Partially." I shrug. I mean I did trip him and shit talk back, so I guess it was somewhat deserved.

"Okay... Well, I appreciate your honesty." He smiles ear to ear, and I know I gave the right answer.

"Thank you, sir," I repeat, smiling.

"Listen, I'm gonna cut straight to the chase. You're a great player and one hell of a leader. The way those guys gravitate to you is... well, it's exactly what we're looking for at UCLA. As I'm sure you know, we're one of the best programs in the country, and you'd be lucky to have the opportunity to be a Bruin."

My heart pounds in my chest.

"Yes sir. It's an incredible opportunity," I say, nodding.

"So here's what's going to happen. I'm going to have to make a few calls, but you can expect to hear from us in the next few months."

"Oh wow. Thank you so much. Can you, um, tell me what kind of offer you think I could be receiving?" I probe, unable to help myself.

"The way you played today. How you handled yourself on the field. Keep that up the rest of the season and don't be surprised if your time at UCLA is all expenses paid." He smirks, then reaches up and squeezes my shoulder.

"A full ride?" I ask incredulously, my eyes bugging out of my skull.

This is the best day of my life.

He winks with a grin. "Speak to you soon, kid."

The talks with the next two recruiters are basically the same. UNC hinted that I would get a full ride, as did UM. They're all amazing schools. I'd be lucky to be at any one of them.

Finally, after all the talks with scouts, coaches, and teammates are done, I make my way to Leah, Dad, Sophia, and Sage, who are waiting for me patiently on the sidelines. I was worried when Chloe didn't show up, but Trey said she had some project to work on, which is a little suspicious because she's never missed a game. Especially not for any kind of project.

"You did so good, Jakey!" Sophia squeals, running into my arms.

"Good job, J." Leah grins up at me. I'm aching for her to lean in and plant her lips on mine, but we still haven't informed Dad or Soph on our relationship status update. "No hugs from me. You're a sweaty mess." She scrunches her nose.

"Eww," Sophia says, squirming in my arms. "You are disgusting. Put me down!" she says, making exaggerated gagging noises.

"I'm so proud of you, son." Dad praises, giving me a bear hug, unbothered by my stench. "What did the scouts say?"

"They… they said I should be looking at a full ride," I sputter out as calmly as possible in an attempt to hide the inner freak-out I'm having.

"That's amazing!" They all cheer in unison.

"Which school?" Dad asks.

"Uh, all of them." I shake my head in disbelief and smile from ear to ear.

Holy shit.

This is becoming real.

I'm being prospected by the best soccer programs in the country.

"Well, this calls for a celebration," Dad shouts. "We're going out to dinner. Go get cleaned up, and I'll call your sister to meet us at the restaurant."

Dad pulls out his phone and turns to walk away. I flick my chin at Sophia, gesturing for her to join him so I can have a minute alone with Leah. Sophia narrows her eyes at me, and I raise my brows at her in my brotherly way to say, *I'm serious.* She huffs, then spins around and runs to catch up to him. Leah laughs at Sophia's dramatics, then turns her attention back to me.

"I'm so proud of you," she squeals, jumping into my arms and kissing me firmly against the mouth as I swing her around.

"I can't even believe it." I sigh, shaking my head.

"Believe it, baby." She grins. "You deserve it." She sounds sincere, but I can tell there's also something else on her mind.

"What's wrong?"

"Nothing," she answers with a loose smile that might convince someone who hasn't known her for fifteen years.

"Leah," I warn.

"Do you think Chloe will come to dinner? I can't believe she wasn't at your game. She's not answering any of my calls or texts, and I've sent like a thousand," she says, sighing.

"According to Trey, she had a huge project to work on and that's why she couldn't come to the game," I say in an attempt to reassure her.

"We both know that that's bullshit," Leah says with raised brows.

"You're probably right," I admit. "Maybe we should talk to her after dinner?"

"Yeah… maybe we should," she agrees.

21 Leah

Dinner was nice. Aside from the crippling anxiety burning inside of me every second we were there. Will took us to Seafood Haven, one of our favorite restaurants in the area known for, of course, their delicious, fresh seafood. As good as the food was, it was impossible to relax and enjoy the celebration because as expected, Chloe didn't come.

She gave Will the same bullshit excuse as Trey. That she had a project she just *had* to finish. Seafood Haven is one of her favorite restaurants and although school is really important to her, she has never passed up an opportunity for conch fritters. And I mean *never.*

On top of that, she sent Jake and I a cryptic group text halfway through dinner that just said, *We need to talk*. Then wouldn't reply to either of our hundred texts asking her why.

"Please, please, please can we go get ice cream for dessert?" Sophia begs, jumping up and down while holding Will's arm.

"Sophia, you have to be full from all the food you just ate. There's no way you have more room in that tiny tummy of yours." Will tickles her belly as she giggles wildly.

"There is *always* room for ice cream," Sage says pointedly.

"What do you kids think? Ice cream?" Will asks Jake and me.

"Actually, we have to head home and help Chloe with something for her project," Jake says, the lie floating effortlessly off his tongue. "But you should definitely take the girls. We all know Sophia's going to wear you down anyways."

"Yeah, you're probably right." Will chuckles.

"Yaaaaayyyyyyyy!" Sophia and Sage squeal in victory, sprinting to Will's truck.

By the time we arrive home, it's pouring rain. If I didn't know any better, I'd think we had a tropical storm over us from the heavy wind. I glance up at the Summers' house, and the light is on in Chloe's window. *Thank God.*

"Do you think she knows about Lysa?" I ask nervously before we exit the car.

"I don't know," Jake answers honestly. "If that's not it, we should tell her."

"Are you sure?"

"Yeah. I see how it's eating at you, babe. It's eating at me too. I don't want any more secrets or disconnects between the three of us." He takes my hand in his and kisses the top of it. I buzz with anxious energy. I'm so ready to be done with the secrets.

"Okay, let's get this over with." I sigh, opening the car door and stepping into the rain. By the time we reach the red front door, I'm soaking wet. The blasting AC forces goosebumps to scatter across my skin as we make our way through the freezing house. Chloe is sitting on her bed with her laptop open when we come up the stairs. She catches our gaze, and her face is blotchy like she's been crying.

I walk faster into her room and sit down next to her on the bed.

"What's wrong?" I put my arm around her shoulder, and she leans against me.

"I… I have to tell you guys something," Chloe says nervously.

"What's going on, Chlo?" Jake asks with furrowed brows. The house lights flicker, presumably from the torrential downpour outside. I glance around, but it seems the power has returned to normal.

"You should sit down," she replies to him, gesturing to the foot of her bed. Jake obliges and sits on her white comforter. Chloe pulls her head off me and sits up a little taller. "It's easier if I show you."

She opens a browser on her laptop, and Lysa's mugshot is in full screen.

Fuck.

My eyes connect with Jake's for a brief moment, and neither of us say a word.

"Well?" Chloe says with wide eyes. "Aren't either of you going to say anything?"

Jake sighs loudly. "How did you find this?"

"What?" Chloe asks with furrowed brows. "What do you mean? Arrest records are public." Jake shakes his head, and Chloe's eyes widen. "You already knew," she says quietly.

Jake looks down, ashamed, and her head snaps to me. "Did you know?"

"I, uh…"

"Are you fucking kidding me?" Chloe shouts, jumping off the bed and pacing the room.

"Chloe, calm down," Jake says sternly, and we both stand as well.

"Calm down? She was arrested for drug possession, Jake! How are you not furious about this?" She throws her arms in the air.

"Of course I'm furious! Mom didn't *just* abandon us. Dad caught her popping pills and told her to clean up or get out and, well, you know what she chose. Guess it caught up to her." He rolls his eyes and shakes his head.

"I can't believe this," she says, breathing heavily. "How long have you guys known about this?"

"I don't know. It's been like… a month or so?" Jake says questionably, looking at me.

"Mom's been in jail over a *month*, and no one thought to tell me?" she roars, and Jake flinches, rubbing a hand down his face as his lips twitch into a frown.

"Chlo, don't you remember how fucking gutted you were when Mom left us?" he says sheepishly, stepping towards her. "You barely ate for weeks… You've been so happy lately. I just—I didn't want that ruined. Dad and I thought it would be better to let you and Soph be happy for a little while longer before telling you."

"But you guys thought Leah should be brought in on our trailer park family drama?"

"It wasn't like that," Jake pleads. "I–I had just found out about Mom, and I was going to see her. And Leah found me, and she… and she didn't want me to go alone." He swallows so hard, his Adam's apple bobs.

"Leah went with you to Georgia?" Chloe asks Jake, her face pained.

"Yes."

"To see *Mom*?"

"Yes."

"At the jail?

"Chloe." He cocks a brow.

"I can't even fucking believe this!" she shrieks incredulously, throwing her hands in the air. "Like, are you kidding me? You took Leah and not me? She's *my* mom."

Her reminder twists the knife in my chest.

"That's not fair," Jake says in a sharp tone. "Stop acting like Mom didn't help raise Leah too."

A flicker of regret flashes across Chloe's face but quickly fades.

"God, you guys are infuriating," she yells. "The second I found this I wanted to tell you guys, but I knew how important your game was today, Jake!" she shouts at him. "*That's* why I didn't come. So I didn't fuck up your game. But you guys just fucking kept it from me, and somehow *I* end up being the bad guy for pointing out that her *actual* daughter deserved to be informed before Leah."

"Chloe," Jake snaps, raising his eyebrows.

"You guys have just been walking around for weeks keeping all of this shit from me. I'm supposed to be your best friend, Leah," she barks at me. "We tell each other everything." A single tear drips down her cheek before she pushes past me, hurtling down the stairs towards the kitchen.

"Chloe, wait." I run after her, and Jake is quick on my heels. She pauses when we get to the kitchen and spins around.

"Not one of you thought that I might be interested in joining your little fucking road trip?" Chloe spouts.

"You were with Trey, and Jake was going to go alone, and I just—"

"You what?" she asks, cutting me off. "Thought to yourself, hey, maybe if I go on this road trip with Jake, he'll finally fuck me in the backseat?"

"Chloe," Jake growls.

"What? Oh my God, no," I say in horror.

"You thought I'd get in the way of your one chance for Jake to finally *fucking* notice you," she says, laughing and shaking her head. "Well… I guess it worked. Mission accomplished."

"Chloe, stop being such a fucking bitch," Jake snaps. "I've been in love with Leah since we were kids. Stop talking down to her like she's been pining after someone who didn't give her the time of day."

"Wow, you love her. Well, good for you." She smiles, folding her arms.

"What is your problem?" Jake spouts. "You said you didn't care we were dating."

"Well, I didn't realize your entire relationship was based around keeping shit from me," she shouts.

"The only reason we kept anything from you is because we love you and we just want you to be happy," I shout.

"This is such bullshit," she says before snatching the keys to the Jeep off the counter. I chase after her as she runs out the front door into the pouring rain. She rounds the Jeep and jumps into the driver's seat. I step off the front porch into the downpour. I can feel the water sloshing beneath my bare feet since I didn't have time to put my shoes back on before chasing after Chloe. Jake's footsteps splash behind me.

"Where are you going?" I yell as she slams the driver's side door. I sprint to the passenger side and throw it open before she can lock the doors.

"Where do you think?" she yells. "To see my fucking mom."

"If you're going, so am I." I get into the passenger seat. Jake wedges his body between the door before I can shut it.

"Are you both fucking crazy? It's a hurricane out here. You can't drive in this," Jake commands as the rain blows sideways into the car.

"Luckily, you're not the boss of *me*," Chloe retorts, fire in her eyes. "As for you, Leah, will your new boyfriend *allow* you to go for a ride?" What she really wants to know is if I'll choose to go with her or listen to Jake, who is actually being the reasonable one considering the inclement weather.

"I'm sorry," I sob at Jake with pleading eyes. "I have to go with her."

"Don't waste your time," Jake shouts over me at Chloe. "Mom's a fucking coward who can't even admit she has a problem. She didn't care about us when she left, and she doesn't care about us now."

"Well, I guess that's for me to figure out for myself," Chloe spouts, putting the Jeep in reverse, and Jake jumps out of the door frame to avoid being knocked over. I slam it shut, watching him as we back out of the driveway. He screams something that looks like "fuck" at the sky and kicks the puddled ground, spraying water across the driveway, pulling at his hair as he watches us drive away.

22
Chloe

I'm shivering from the blasting AC on my damp body, but I'm too pissed to reach for the controls.

How could they not tell me Mom was in fucking jail?

I've been worried sick for months, and everyone knew where she was the entire damn time.

I can't fucking believe they've been lying for weeks about my mom.

I was dead on that they were keeping shit from me. I was just wrong about how much shit that was.

My hands shake against the steering wheel, and I'm gripping it so tight my knuckles are ghostly white. The sky is pitch-black, and heavy raindrops lash against the windshield.

Fuck, I can't see at all.

"We should pull over," Leah suggests almost immediately.

Oh, now she wants to tell me what to do?

"You wanted to come," I snap at her. "I'm not pulling over. God, this is such *bullshit*!" I hit the steering wheel, and Leah flinches. The only sound besides the rain thrashing against the windshield is her seatbelt clicking.

I can't believe my mom chose drugs over us. Guess grounding Jake last year for smoking pot was a bit hypocritical now, huh, Mom?

"Chloe, you need to calm down."

She has got to be fucking kidding me.

"Or at least put your seatbelt on," she adds, but the red-hot anger piping through my veins is causing my mind to spin in a hundred different directions, making it impossible to concentrate on a single thought.

"Calm down?" I scoff, tears blurring my already obstructed vision. "My mom is in *fucking* jail, and no one thought I had the right to know. Oh, *and* my two best friends in the world are *fucking* and just kept lying about it. Who do you think you guys are going to choose whenever shit hits the fan like today? Each other, and I'm the one getting left on the outside."

The first thing I did when I saw Mom's mugshot is grab my phone to text Jake. Then I saw my most recent text to him about tonight's game, and I knew there was no fucking way I was ruining that for him. Mom's taken enough from us. Yet their first instinct was to hide it? *Freaking bullshit.*

"That's such bull! I *chose* to get in this car with you, didn't I?" Leah shouts.

"Yeah, whatever. You guys kept this fucking *massive* secret from me. She's *my* Mom!"

"I know that! I really wanted to tell you, I swear. So did Jake. But after we saw Lysa… She acted like it was no big deal. She *lied* to our faces! Will and Jake wanted you and Soph to be happy for a little while longer and not worry about the mess your mom made for herself. And honestly, I don't blame them."

"Well, I'm *real* fucking happy now," I say, flicking my turn signal as I veer onto the dark country road towards the highway.

"Jesus, you're missing the *fucking* point, Chloe," she snaps at me, and my veins bubble with rage.

"No, *you're* missing the *fucking* point. You guys should have *told* me about my mom, Leah."

"I know. We were just trying to protect you," she says quietly. "We were going to tell you after Christmas."

"And I still can't believe you didn't tell me about Jake over an eight year old pinky promise," I say, shaking my head and laughing.

"I know..."

"Do you love him?" I ask timidly.

"Of course I do," she says incredulously. "I always have." Her voice lowers to a whisper. It's been so obvious. I've watched them dance around one another for years. But I sure as hell wasn't going to be the one to encourage my best friend to date my dick brother. *Okay, I adore my dick brother, but still.*

"I meant it when I said I'm fine with it," I say genuinely.

"Really?" she chokes out.

"Of course. You know I am. You're my family. I couldn't ask for anyone better to always have to be around. And if anyone can put up with my brother's shit, it's you." I'm unable to stop my lips from twitching upwards. It's the truth. Jake is a fucking handful, and if anyone can deal with that pain in the ass, it's her. I saw how she leveled him during the whole Cole situation. One look at her, and he snapped right back to reality. The way his hands cradled her shoulders at Trey's house, it was *so* obvious.

Besides, when Jake dated Katelyn, it was complete fucking torture. I'd much rather have to be around Leah all the time. I already love her. *God, I hate fighting.*

"We were just looking out for you, Chloe, I swear," she pleads. "I knew you finding out about your mom would ruin any progress you'd made since she left… You never even mention her."

"I get it." I sigh, aching to be over this stupid fight. "You guys are always protecting me."

"Always," Leah ensures me.

"I'm sorry for what I said earlier… about you only going to Georgia because—well, you know…" I knew saying those things would hurt her the most.

"It's okay, I forgive you," she says.

"I forgive you too." The corners of my lips twitch upwards. *Ugh, I can't ever stay mad at my favorite person.*

"No more secrets?" Leah says, extending her pinky towards me.

"No more secrets," I repeat, releasing my right hand from the steering wheel and hooking my pinky with hers. "I love you, Scaredybug."

"I love you too, Lo—"

23
Jake

I'm pacing the living room like a madman, waiting for the girls to come back, when my phone buzzes in my pocket. I pull it out so fast it almost flies across the room. *Oh, it's just Dad.*

"Hello."

"Jake, it's Dad," he says, his voice trembling.

"I know. I have caller ID, remember?"

"Jake," he repeats. This time there's a break in his voice.

"Dad, what's wrong?"

"You need to get to the hospital."

"Why, what's going on? Are Sophia and Sage okay?"

"Yeah, they're fine. Sage's mom is on the way to pick them up. Just, can you get here? Be careful, okay?"

"Okay… Do I need to call Chloe or did you already call her?"

"I—um," he stutters, his voice cracking again. "I got it. See you soon."

What the fuck?

Sophia's fine... Dad's fine... Mom's in a penitentiary in bum fuck Georgia, and that leaves... *Fuck.* My heart is pounding. All of the oxygen has been sucked out of my lungs.

I can count on two fingers the number of times I thought my life was over. When I broke my leg in the ninth grade and was told I might never play soccer again, and after Mom left. I was so depressed I never thought I'd be happy again. Neither of those things is even comparable to what I'm feeling from getting that call.

I pick up my phone with trembling hands and call Leah—no answer. Chloe—no answer.

I pat my pockets for my keys. I stumble down the stairs three at a time and check in the bowl by the front door—not there. I look in the kitchen...

Not there.

Where the fuck are my keys?

Leah's backpack is sitting on the kitchen island. *Leah...*

Oh, that's right. I don't have any fucking keys because the girls took the damn car.

I snatch Leah's backpack off the counter.

Please, let the keys for her parents' car be in here.

I hear a jingling sound in the front pocket. I unzip it and snatch the keys out. *Thank God.*

I slam the front door and sprint through the torrential downpour to her driveway, sliding into the car sopping wet. I fumble the key into the ignition and turn it. *Click–click–click–click.* The engine sputters. I slam my fist into the steering wheel. "You've got to be fucking kidding me!"

I try one more time, begging any God that will listen. *Click–click–*

click—the engine roars to life.

Thank you, God, Allah, Zeus, Buddha, Jesus, whoever you are.

The entire drive, I'm calling Leah and Chloe's phones with no answer. *Please be a coincidence.* The hospital has bad service. They must already be there waiting. Rain is coming down in sheets, and it's a miracle I make it to the hospital in one piece.

It usually takes fifteen minutes to get to Longwood Hospital. Even in the pouring rain, I made the drive in seven. *What the hell is happening?* It's only been fourteen minutes from the time I got Dad's phone call. Fourteen minutes that felt like centuries. I burst through the emergency room doors, soaking wet, slipping along the linoleum floor, and see Sophia and Sage sitting in the corner clinging to one another.

"I want to see her... *now*!" Dad booms on the other side of the room, arguing with a doctor.

"Dad, what's going on?" I say loudly from across the room as I make my way to him. "Where are the girls?"

"I... I..." Dad stutters as tears prick his cheeks, struggling to catch his breath, then glances at the doctor.

"May I?" the doctor asks Dad with raised eyebrows, and he nods in response. My heart is beating so quickly that I may have a heart attack.

"Hi, I'm Dr. Wilkins," he introduces, outstretching a hand, which I shake by reflex as panicked thoughts swirl in my head. "Leah and Chloe were in a severe car accident this evening."

My stomach drops. "They... they what?"

I fucking knew I shouldn't have let them leave.

This is all my fault.

Why didn't I try harder to stop them?

"Are... are they okay?" He glances back at my dad, who nods

again, apparently unable to speak.

"Would someone just tell me what the *fuck's* going on?" I shout, unable to suppress the emotions bubbling out of me. *The two people I love most in the world are... what? Hurt? Dead?*

"Yes, of course," the doctor continues. "Leah has suffered severe injuries including facial lacerations and a broken femur, and we're also monitoring for internal bleeding. She's shown signs of brain activity; however, we have placed her into a medically induced coma to allow the mild swelling in her brain to reduce, but the prognosis is promising." *Promising? She could not wake up?* Bile is climbing up my esophagus, threatening to burst out at any moment.

"Oh my God," I whisper, covering my mouth, unable to hide the waves of panic over taking me. If I thought oxygen was lacking when I got the phone call, now it's as if someone is pushing my head underwater and I can't even struggle for air, I'm so paralyzed.

I've spent fifteen years being in love with this girl.

Fifteen years.

No one has ever even come remotely close. If Leah and I date, fizzle out, break up, that I can handle. Losing her like this, never knowing what we could have been. I don't think I will ever recover. I *will* never recover. Not to mention it would fucking kill Chloe. *Chloe...*

"And Chloe?" I choke out. The doctor takes a deep breath and cocks his head to the side as his mouth forms a straight line. The face my orthopedic had before he told me I might not ever be able to play soccer again. The face Dad had right before he told us Mom left.

"Chloe's injuries are very severe," Dr. Wilkins says intently.

Dad walks away and rubs his hands over his hair and ears as if he's trying to avoid listening to Chloe's prognosis again.

"What are you saying?" I ask. My hands tremble as I await his reply.

"Chloe wasn't wearing a seatbelt, and because of this, she was ejected from the vehicle. After she was brought in, we discovered internal bleeding and severe swelling of the brain, along with other various fractures throughout her body. Her pupils were unresponsive. We have run an EEG to measure brain activity, which was inconclusive, but we will test again tomorrow to see if there is an improvement."

"And if there's no improvement?" I ask, trying to make it make sense.

"There is a wide array of tests we will be performing to ensure a proper diagnosis… But if Chloe doesn't show signs of brain activity within the next twenty-four hours, this means that the trauma to the head was too severe," the doctor clarifies.

"And then what?" I'm struggling for air.

"Chloe is currently on a ventilator, as she's not able to breathe on her own. Should we certify that she is brain dead, we would come in to discuss with your family the options for Chloe's end of life care."

"End of—" My breathing becomes rapid. I stumble, catching myself on the arm of a chair. "This isn't happening," I say, tears flooding my cheeks. "This is—this can't, no, you're wrong, she's not—there's no way—it can't—I don't—"

"Jake," Dad croaks firmly, pulling me up to look at him. He stares at me intently with his tear-soaked eyes. He opens his arms, and they swallow me whole, like I'm a little boy who's afraid of the dark.

And I am so afraid of the darkness that's coming.

24
Leah

I'm struggling to focus on the blurry shapes around me. The air reeks of ammonia or rubbing alcohol. *Where am I? A doctor's office?* Bright light is slowly infiltrating my vision as my other senses take a list, trying to make sense of it all. My parents' voices are distant, like they're in a different room talking to someone. My left leg hurts like a fucking bitch. I have a splitting headache.

I blink at least a thousand times before my vision comes into focus. *I'm in a hospital bed?* Jake is sitting next to my bedside holding my hand and… praying? That's something I've never heard or seen Jake do. Ever.

"I will do anything," he pleads through quiet sobs while grasping my hand tightly. There's a small object clenched in my palm, but I can't quite tell what it is by the feeling. "Please just bring her back to me."

"Anything?" I croak out weakly and squeeze his hand once.

He jerks his head up to me. "Oh my God. Thank you, God." He sobs loudly into my shoulder as I squeeze his hand a second time. "I love you. I love you." I finally get the third squeeze in. "You have no idea. Oh, thank you, God." I've never seen Jake so emotional, and I don't know what to make of him looking so broken and destroyed. I want to comfort him, but I barely felt strong enough to squeeze his hand.

"I love you too." The words come out quiet and raspy, almost like a rough whisper.

"I know." He smiles and kisses me softly on the cheek, then plucks the object out of my hand, and I notice it's the pearl hair clip I wear whenever I need a bit of good luck. I smile softly at the thoughtful gesture as he places it gently in my hair.

My parents burst into the room, followed by someone in a white coat.

"Oh, sweetheart, I'm so glad you're finally awake. We've been so worried." My mom hugs me tightly as her cool tears soak my hospital gown.

"I love you," Dad croaks out through teary eyes as he kisses me on the forehead. I've never seen my parents so emotional before. I wonder how long I've been out? *What the hell happened?*

"Hi, Leah, I'm Dr. Wilkins," the man says. He pauses for so long I realize that he's waiting for me to speak.

"Hi," I mutter awkwardly.

"Do you know where you are?"

"Uh, a hospital?"

"Very good," he praises like I won a middle school spelling bee. "Do you know why you're here?"

"Uh, no, not really."

"Do you remember anything about the accident?"

What accident? "The accident?"

"Yes." He pauses again, and I look towards the ceiling, trying to sift through the most recent memories in my head.

"Honestly, I don't remember much. I was in the car with Chloe, and it was raining." I frown, hating that I can't remember.

"Is there anything else you remember?"

I close my eyes in an attempt to recall something else, but there's nothing. "I'm sorry, I don't remember anything else," I say weakly.

"That's okay," the doctor assures us all. "It's normal for the brain to suppress traumatic memories after an accident." *Traumatic?*

The doctor continues what I assume is the typical check-up for a person who was unconscious for a few days. Vitals, reflexes, etc.

"Everything looks good so far. I expect the large laceration on your head to heal completely without any need for surgery."

He then speaks directly to my parents as if I'm not even in the room. Normally that would irritate me, but I'm too weak and tired to even care.

"Leah seems to be improving at an expected pace. We will monitor her here for a few more days, and she'll require three to six months of physical therapy." *Months?* "But her condition is promising, and we expect a full recovery." *Well, I guess that's good news.* The doctor walks out of the room, and my parents trail after him. Knowing them, they have a thousand more questions he won't have the patience to answer. *Poor guy.*

"Are you okay?" Jake asks gently as soon as they're gone.

"I guess so… You heard what the doctor said."

"Do you remember anything else, baby?" he asks, brushing a stray lock of hair gently behind my ear.

"I just told you guys," I say, frustrated.

"I know, I just... Was there anything you left out? Did our fight with Chloe cause this?" Jake asks, staring at me intently.

"No," I say firmly. I don't remember much. I know that's true. "The last thing I remember, Chloe was telling me she loves me. And that she would have never been mad at us for being together," I say, smiling weakly. "But I promise I don't remember anything else."

"It's okay, baby." Jake brushes the hair out of my face, and I wince when he lightly grazes a sore spot on my head.

"Where's Chloe? Couldn't they have given us a shared room? We can have our most bizarre sleepover ever." I chuckle. He's quiet and looks like he's about to crumble to the floor at any moment.

"Chloe's..." Jake croaks, unable to continue. He places his face in his hands and then drags them through his tousled hair. Tears are brimming in his eyes, seconds away from bursting out.

"Chloe's what?" My heart constricts in my chest.

"She... Chloe..." He runs his hands over his face, eyes sealed shut.

"Jake," I plead, my voice cracking into a thousand pieces as my body trembles with worry. "Where's Chloe?"

"Her, her injuries, they were much—they were way worse than yours," he sobs. The tears pour from his eyes like a broken dam.

"I don't understand." I shake my head, unable to fight the panic rising in my chest. "What are you saying?"

"She..." He looks like someone is choking him, unable to mutter a word from his tear-soaked lips.

"Where's Chloe?" I shout through blurred vision.

The light fades from his eyes until they're dark and empty.

"She... died."

25

Jake

"Jake, you're up after Matt," Ms. Gibbons, my English teacher, instructs. For Christmas break, she assigned us to write a poem based on someone that's impacted our life. Choosing my inspiration was easy. Getting the words out without a complete breakdown was damn near impossible.

After they declared Chloe brain dead, Dad signed a form at the hospital to donate Chloe's organs, and we got a letter a week later that she'd saved four lives. Four other people got a chance at life because of Chloe. All of their families contacted us in the months following Chloe's death.

Logan Joseph Ends, twelve years old and a lover of building model trains, received Chloe's right kidney. He'd been waiting two years for a match.

Isaac Young, fifteen years old and obsessed with Led Zeppelin and playing guitar, received Chloe's left kidney after waiting six months for a match and undergoing two rounds of chemotherapy.

Sylvie Austin, twenty-two years old and a lover of writing *Harry Potter* fan fiction, received Chloe's lungs after waiting three years for a transplant and enduring four rounds of chemotherapy.

Larissa Mae Underwood, thirty-two years old, a talented painter and a mom of two, received Chloe's heart after being on the transplant list for five years. *Five years.*

Larissa visited us in December to thank us. It felt weird to be thanked for something I had no control over and would have sold my soul to change if given the chance. She allowed us to listen to Chloe's heart beating in her chest. It was one of the strangest things I've ever experienced. Hearing the heartbeat of a stranger, knowing it belonged to someone I loved. Someone who grew together with me in the same womb.

Meeting Larissa helped me feel connected to Chloe, even though she's already been gone for months. When Ms. Gibbons assigned this poem, I knew immediately it had to be about them.

I flip my notebook to the page where I've scribbled it down. My classmates start clapping as Matt finishes his poem and does an exaggerated bow. I wasn't listening, but I'm sure it was cheesy and hilarious.

"Jake, your turn," Ms. Gibbons says. I stand and walk slowly towards the front. I turn to face my classmates, and they're all staring at me intently. "Whenever you're ready."

I take one heavy inhale, then read the one homework assignment I'll never forget.

The Tether Between Us
By Jake Summers

Although it's no longer yours
I have heard your beating heart

It brings me peace to know
That although you had to depart
I can hear you
I can feel you
and pretend we're not apart

For I still sense your tether
Tied to my soul
As strong as a sailor's knot

Knowing your beating heart
Walks the earth alongside me
Even if you can not

My hands are shaking, and I feel a teardrop trickle down my cheek. I take a breath, then glance up at my teacher.

"Jake, that was… Wow," she says, holding a hand over her mouth as tears stream down her face.

I risk a glance at my classmates, who all mirror a similar position. The dam breaks, and tears flood my face.

"Excuse me," I croak out calmly and walk slowly out of the classroom. I lean against the wall and close my eyes, picturing Larissa as a reminder that it was a gift for her to receive Chloe's heart.

When things get dark, I try to think of the positives.

Larissa only had six more months to live without a new heart—now she has decades.

Unfortunately, it's hard to think of the positives when their miracle was our worst fucking nightmare.

"Doesn't it scare you?" I had asked Larissa. "Knowing how much—or little—time you have left?"

She placed her hand on my cheek like a mother would, tipping my face to hers, and said, "A few months ago, I was told I have months, maybe weeks, to live. Now they've given me an extra twenty years. That is a damn miracle. If I can live long enough for my children to grow and become their own people—to buy my daughter a prom dress and watch my son fall in love for the first time—and have thousands of more nights dancing in the kitchen with my husband..." she said with a dreamy look in her eyes while looking towards him. "Then I have lived a full and happy life. It's not about how much time you have on this earth. Time is intangible—it's irrelevant. It's about what you do with the time that you have. Don't waste a second of it."

I wish I had been ready to take her advice. Unfortunately, I was too shattered to comprehend what she *really* meant. I had no idea how it felt to have years of wasted time you'll never get back. All I understood at this point in my life was missed time, the time we never got at all. Those missing years we would never have with her. I was naive to the implications of what it meant to actually have that precious time... and squander it spectacularly.

26
Leah

"Are we almost done?" I groan as every one of my muscles burns like it's on fire. "I don't know how much longer I can do this."

"Just two more minutes," my physical therapist, Dana, assures me while pointing to the countdown on the treadmill that reads two minutes and forty-five seconds. *Liar.*

"Come on, Le. You've got this," Jake encourages from his position in front of the treadmill. Sometimes he dangles a little baggie of Lucky Charms in my face for motivation, like one of those cartoons, and it always improves my mood. "You're almost there, babe."

I glare at him as the stinging ache spreads further throughout my body. It hurts like hell, but it's also a constant reminder that I'm still here. A reminder that the only thing I walked away from the accident with is a six-inch-long scar on my left leg where they had to surgically screw my bones back together so I wouldn't lose the ability to walk.

You are so lucky to be alive.

I've heard it hundreds of times over the past four months. It's hard to feel lucky to be alive when the majority of the time I wish I was the one who was dead.

I fantasize often about how different things would be if it had been me instead of Chloe. Sophia and Jake would still have a sister. Will and Lysa would still have a daughter. Trey would still have an adoring girlfriend. And I wouldn't have this gaping hole where my heart used to be.

I do my best to get through the day without breaking down, even though it's hard, because everything is the same, even though it's not.

I haven't painted since before the accident. I've sat down at the easel in my bedroom, picked up the brush, and just… nothing. I end up walking away an hour later without leaving a single stroke. I tried to go to our art studio in the garage but couldn't even make it to the easel before turning around and running out of the room.

Each day I walk into school, and the same people who used to greet me with a smile stare at me with sympathetic eyes. It drives me fucking mad. Everyone watching me, just waiting for the day I inevitably lose my shit completely. The only person besides Jake who can possibly understand is Trey, and he looks even more broken than we do. *If that's possible…*

Chloe and I were a package deal. I am absolutely *nothing* without her. I'm a shell of a person waiting out my time on Earth until I can finally see her again.

With Jake, it's even worse. We share the grief to such a painstakingly deep degree there's no way for either of us to even support each other. Our grief is out of sync. He's fine, I'm a mess. I'm numb, he's wrecked. We're okay, Sophia is destroyed. It's like we're all drowning, and every time one of us comes up for air, the other drags them right back down with them.

We still see each other frequently, but the tension between us is palpable. We don't talk much, just sit in uncomfortable silence. I just want our relationship to feel normal again. To be around one another without the tension. To be intimately in love like we used to be before.

Jake blames himself for the accident too. He says that he should have stopped us from driving in that horrible weather. I've assured him time and time again it wasn't his fault, but I can tell it does nothing to sway the crippling guilt surrounding him. I felt guilty too for a while, but I realized that whatever the events were leading up to it, they weren't our fault. I have to believe that when the universe decides it's your time, then it's your time.

I wonder when mine will be.

27
Jake

I'm dripping with sweat. My lungs are burning. The heat is beating at my skin.

There are twelve minutes left in the championship game, sealing our perfect record for the year. My entire life is up in flames, but the moment I step on the field, I focus on my breathing, the ball, and the goal.

That's it.

"Summers," Coach yells, then gestures for me to cut across the field.

I sprint as hard as I can until my muscles are screaming at me to stop. Trey passes me the ball, and I stop it effortlessly, then spin towards the goal.

Two defenders are quick on my heels, but my daily half-marathons have improved my endurance, and I'm faster. I dribble effortlessly to the goal, cock my foot back, and send it soaring through the air and into the back of the net, missing the goalkeeper's hands by a mile.

The team and bleachers erupt in cheers, and the guys come barreling towards me.

I plaster a fake smile on my face, but all I feel is numb.

Now that the game has ended, the guilt that resides inside me floats right back to the forefront of my mind.

If we would have just told Chloe about Mom, if we would have brought her with us that first day, she would've never tried to go see her. Leah wouldn't have gotten in the car.

Leah almost died…

Chloe did.

I'm lying on my bed, trying and failing to read *Gone Girl* by Gillian Flynn. Reading was always something that distracted me, but my mind is so foggy I can't even concentrate on the words on the page. Dad and Soph went for dinner, but I wasn't really up for celebrating. The house is uncomfortably quiet, but I don't have the energy to put music on to drown out the deafening silence. My phone buzzes on the nightstand. *Ugh, I don't want to move.*

A few minutes later, it buzzes again. I put the book on the nightstand and pick up my phone.

LEAH

Leah

Hey, can I come over?

Leah

?

I stare at the messages longer than I should. I always want to see Leah, but I don't know what her mood is tonight. I never know when I see her if she'll be that happy, carefree girl I've known since we were in diapers or the depressed, grief-stricken one created from the accident. I love both versions, but it's so hard for me to be there for her when I'm drowning myself. I do my best to shove it down and be there for Leah and Sophia as much as I can. Unsurprisingly, faking it is exhausting. If I'm not grieving Chloe, I'm worried about the girls or Dad. He can't even walk near Chloe's room without breaking down. It's a never-ending cycle.

I glance at the UCLA flag hanging on my wall. I received my official letter of acceptance a few weeks ago. How the hell am I supposed to go three thousand miles away from Leah and Sophia when they could crumble to pieces at any minute? There is no way I can leave them.

After another half hour of staring at the ceiling, I text her back.

Me

Yeah, sure

I send the message, and at the same time, my bedroom door opens.

"Hey," Leah says, walking in with a big smile and closing it behind her.

"Hey," I say, smiling back, trying to match her energy. She pulls the phone out of her back pocket, assumedly having just got my text.

"So I guess your phone *is* working?" She raises her eyebrows.

"Yeah, sorry," I mumble, unable to think of a single excuse.

"That's okay. I know how you can make it up to me." She grins seductively and walks over to the bed, then crawls on top of me.

"Well, hello there," I say with raised eyebrows, holding on to her hips. She's wearing the T-shirt I gave her the first time we slept together and a pair of black leggings. *That shirt sure brings up memories. I'd give anything to go back to that night.*

"I miss you," she pouts, leaning down and kissing me softly against the lips.

"We just saw each other at the game," I tease, narrowing my eyes at her. Something is off. She's acting too happy.

"I know... but I was just watching you from the sidelines," she says, pushing up my shirt and rubbing her warm palms against my stomach, causing my breath to catch in my throat. "But I actually meant, I miss *you*." She scoots down a little and plays with the hem of my sweatpants.

"I miss you too." I sigh, sitting up, and she straddles my lap, throwing her arms around my neck. She presses her lips to mine again, hungrier. Her tongue finds its way into my mouth, and she kisses without coming up for air. She's grinding against my lap and rubbing her hands wildly over every inch of my body. I've never seen her act like this before. She seems panicked, like if she stops touching me, I'll disappear. I'm trying to match her enthusiasm, but my mind is spinning in circles, and my dick refuses to participate. *Something doesn't feel right.* Leah reaches down, grabs the hem of my shirt, and pulls it upwards.

"Leah," I say firmly, stopping her and pulling the shirt back into place. "Slow down."

"I don't want to slow down. I want this. I need this, please," she pants breathlessly into my mouth, leaning in for another kiss. "Don't you want to celebrate your big win?"

I run my palm down her left thigh, and I can feel the raised scar from the accident. She freezes at my touch, her lips mere centimeters from me.

"I don't think we're ready, Le," I say softly.

"God, Jake," she says, her voice cracking as she looks away. *I knew something was off.* "I just want to feel normal for one fucking night! I just want to be a normal girl spending time with my normal boyfriend. Is that too much to fucking ask for?" She shouts the last part as tears stream down her face.

"Please, please, don't cry," I whisper, wiping the tears from her cheeks with my thumbs. "I love you. You know I love you. Please don't cry." I hold her tightly. "I love you."

She pulls away and looks at me. The sound of our breathing is the only noise in the room for what feels like hours. She stares into my eyes like she's searching for the answers to the universe. I can see the moment she cracks in two, just before she falls against my chest, wailing loud sobs.

"I just want a moment of normal." She sniffles and rubs her nose against her sleeve.

"I know, baby," I say, fighting the dam full of tears threatening to pour out of my eyes. *Get it together. You have to be strong for her.* I lay us down on my bed and turn her facing away from me, then pull her flush against my chest. "Someday. Someday, we won't hurt so bad."

Her ribs expand and contract sporadically as she gasps for air between sobs. If I could magically siphon all her pain away and endure it myself, I would.

I would carry every burden if it would just bring a single, genuine smile upon her tear-soaked lips.

Eight Years Later

28
Leah

I wake in a bed I'm unfamiliar with and surroundings I don't recognize for the third time this week. Another night in a random hotel room. My family and friends back home think my life is glamorous. New cities every week, traveling the world "for free," meeting new and interesting people constantly. And I guess they're right. There are a lot of perks to being a flight attendant, but it's also exhausting. Having to pack and repack every other day. New cities, new faces, nothing ever the same. "New" is my ordinary, but I'm actually getting drained by it.

Yeah, sure, when I got to see *The Creation of Adam* by Michelangelo on the ceiling of the Sistine Chapel, I was in absolute awe. The other Italian sights in the shape of tall, dark, and handsome men with seductive accents didn't hurt either—but it's really fucking lonely.

I have a small group of close friends back in Longwood, and I'm starting to hate only being home a few times a month. There's no routine or sense of normalcy.

I never work with the same crew, so I don't really have coworkers in the traditional sense. There is no shortage of staff to be randomly placed on each flight, so every trip has different pilots and flight attendants. Typically, when we have a long-haul flight, like today's from Orlando to Amsterdam, by the time we get off the plane, all the crew is well acquainted. Once we finished our shift, around nine this morning, all undoubtedly exhausted, we made plans to meet up tonight (as flight crews typically do) after a shower and rest. None of us have to fly out until tomorrow afternoon, which means we get to let loose tonight. I'm also looking forward to visiting the Van Gogh Museum tomorrow—it's one of my favorites.

My eyes struggle to adjust to the light in the room coming from the bedside lamp. I was too exhausted to turn it off before my nap.

Ugh, maybe I should just message that I'm not feeling well and stay in.

Then again, the last thing I want to do is lie here and think about my lonely ass life.

I roll out of bed and finish blow drying my hair that was still damp from sleeping on it after my shower earlier and style it into big, loose curls. My hair took longer than anticipated so I dab just a bit of concealer on the excess baggage under my eyes that come from constant international travel, a quick swipe of mascara, and apply my favorite nude lipstick.

The weather will be in the low sixties tonight. I look through my limited wardrobe options in my carry-on and settle on my favorite tight velvet little black dress. It's long-sleeved and dips down like a V shape in the front low enough to show a generous amount of cleavage. The back also dips down towards the middle of my spine, showing off the freckles that I've learned to love so much. I pair the dress with gold jewelry, black, knee-high boots, and a tan, mid-thigh length blazer.

Europeans typically dress chicly with neutral colors, so I try to blend in as much as possible when here. I throw my small clutch over my shoulder, which contains my phone, lipstick, and a condom—always be prepared—and head to meet the others in the lobby of our shared hotel.

"Okay, it looks like everyone's here," Rebecca, one of the other flight attendants, says, clapping her hands together like we're a bunch of kindergartners. "I found this place on my last trip to Amsterdam, and it is *fucking incredible.*"

"How far a walk?" one of the other girls asks, shifting in her stilettos. *Rookie mistake.*

"Only about ten minutes."

The streets of Amsterdam are buzzing with energy. People are going every which way, headed in or headed out.

After a few near-death encounters with bicyclists, Rebecca pauses at a street corner. "It's just around the corner up here."

She leads us down a dimly lit alleyway. The only light is coming from a completely out-of-place, lit-up, cherry-red telephone booth.

"Uh, are you sure this is the right place?" Sam, another female attendant, asks Rebecca.

"Guys, just trust me, okay?" We glance at one another with raised eyebrows and wide eyes.

Just when I think we're about to be mugged, she slides open the door of the telephone booth and steps inside. She pulls the phone off the hanger, bringing it to her ear before typing in a series of numbers. "Hi, it's Becky L. I placed an order today for twelve shots of poison." *What the fuck?* There's a pause. "Okay, great." She beams, shimmying in place, and smiles at the group before hanging up the phone.

There's a clicking noise, and the brick wall next to the telephone booth glides inwards, revealing an entrance to a… I don't exactly know what.

We walk through the door, and there's a small counter with a girl behind it taking people's coats. She gives me a ticket stub, which I store in my small clutch. The room is eerily quiet and completely void of people. There's not even a faint sound of music buzzing. My veins are buzzing with anxious energy.

"Follow me, please." A tiny, cheerful blonde with a thick Dutch accent smiles at us. Her little black dress closely resembles mine. We trail after her down a narrow set of stairs and into a large, empty room with nothing but a large vault door. She spins the safe handle that looks like a wheel, then yanks it open. The second she does, loud music and chattering voices flood my senses, freezing me in my tracks.

Holy. Shit.

We all funnel inside and stare around in awe. The room is massive, with vaulted ceilings, and a wide staircase leads up to a wrap-around balcony on the second floor. The banister is lined with people drinking and dancing.

There are high tops, tables, pine-green velvet chairs, and matching booths along the perimeter of the room. And a large, packed-full dance floor. There's easily a few hundred people here tonight. Even on a Wednesday, this place is packed to the brim.

A long, white marble bar on the left wall extends the length of the room. An abundance of greenery, like succulents and fiddle leaf figs, are scattered around. The walls are painted a soft shade of peach, and a bright neon sign behind the bar says Chloe's, which must be the name of this swanky speakeasy. My lips curl upwards at the name tied to so many memories—full of both happiness and heartache.

I remember the first time I was able to laugh instead of cry when thinking of Chloe.

I was at the park with Sophia, enjoying the spring weather. The sun was kissing my skin as I leaned back against the picnic blanket I brought. I thought to myself, *If I can have more days like this, I'm going to be okay.* We were eating the sandwiches I brought for lunch when we were swarmed by freaking love bugs. Sophia and I jumped up, squealing. I thought she was going to run away just like I was, and then... she didn't. She chased them... just like her sister did when we were kids.

"Leah, come on," Sophia had shouted, waving her hand for me to join her. "Let's dance with Chloe!"

I wanted to cry. I really thought I was going to cry. But a strange noise came bubbling out of me instead. Then it got louder. Then I realized I was howling in laughter and keeled over, holding my stomach because my muscles burned from the foreign feeling.

I ran to Sophia, and we spun around in circles, laughing and dancing with the love bugs. I know that Chloe was right there spinning with us.

It was so freeing to laugh. To think about the person I loved more than anyone in my entire life and remember what it felt like to be loved by her.

"Isn't this place amazing?" Rebecca shouts over the music, ripping me out of my head.

"It really is." I smile.

"Told you guys," Rebecca says, a hint of smugness in her voice. "I reserved a lounge area for us."

The same blonde leads us up the wide staircase to a large sitting area on the second floor with plush couches, a few armchairs, and coffee tables between them. For being in the middle of a crowded club, it's surprisingly cozy and intimate. A few minutes later, a waitress shows up with a few bottles of wine and places them around the table.

All twelve of the flight crew from today's long haul are here tonight, including the pilots who usually keep to themselves. From the outside looking in, we're a group of lifelong friends laughing wildly about our shared years of memories. Having already spent nine hours in a metal tube in the air together, we are thankfully past any awkward "where are you from?" small talk. Everyone is intently chatting, on the dance floor, or getting more drinks from the bar.

Rebecca and Sam are to my right, chatting animatedly about stopping by a "coffee shop" later, and I guess, when in Amsterdam, right?

I jump in place when one of the pilots from today's flight, Joshua, mumbles something in my ear.

"I'm sorry, what did you say?" I ask politely, giving him my full attention.

"Have you been to Amsterdam before?" Joshua repeats, resting his arm on the back of the couch behind me. The sleeve of his soft Armani button-up rubs against the small bit of skin exposed on my back, and the musky smell of his aftershave overwhelms my senses.

"Yeah, and I have three more trips here in the next few weeks," I say, smiling.

"Oh, very nice. I'm mostly between New York City and London. But I'm glad I'm here tonight." He grins, raising his eyebrows, and leans closer to me again. I'm trying to be interested, but there's just nothing there. Is he handsome? Sure. Taller than me, with a muscular frame, brown hair, and the wrong color green eyes, but from the brief interactions we've had, I can tell he is completely pretentious and full of himself. I prefer a man a bit more humble and down to earth. Someone who's not going to scream out their own name during sex.

"Oh wow, is it already eleven thirty?" he states, angling his black-and-gold, diamond-encrusted Hublot watch on his wrist towards my face. I have to clench my jaw to keep from rolling my eyes into the back of my head. "So do you have anyone waiting for you back at home?"

I feel like there's this big misconception that flight attendants just fly all around the world hooking up with random strangers. I guess they're partially right from the body language many of my coworkers are giving off tonight, but I'm trying to reduce the amount I sleep around these days. I visit different cities every week, and I don't want to frequent STD testing centers as often as I do the TSA line.

It never takes me long to realize if I'm attracted to someone or not, and as I said before, Joshua is just *not* it. I have no interest in dragging this out and having to turn this guy down continuously for the next few hours when he knows I'm single… so I lie. A lie I've practiced thoroughly whenever I want to avoid rejecting someone—because the only thing I hate more than small talk is awkward conflict.

"Yes, my fiancé, Jake," I say, toying with the gold ring on my left ring finger. The one thing from Jake I haven't been able to part with. "I actually can't forget to stop by a gift shop tomorrow and pick him up an Amsterdam shot glass. I always bring him one each time I visit a city."

I considered using a different name, but it was the one that rolled off my tongue the first time someone asked if I had a boyfriend, and I just kind of kept it. Having an actual face in mind made it easier to answer people's probing questions.

"Oh." There's an obvious disappointment in his voice, but he recovers quickly. "That's nice. You must have hundreds by now."

"Yeah, we have a whole wall in our house dedicated to them, kind of a 'where I've been' map without the map."

It's only a partial lie. I do have a "where I've been" map made from souvenirs from each new city. But it's not shot glasses, and it's not for my boyfriend.

My first route as a flight attendant was to New York City. On my layover, I went to The Metropolitan Museum of Art and was completely awestruck by the walls and walls of breathtaking art. I bought a postcard of my favorite painting, *Autumn Rhythm (Number 30)* by Jackson Pollock, and stuck it to my wall when I got back home.

I now have 234 postcards tacked to a giant corkboard in my childhood bedroom of my parents' house. Where I still live. It's not worth it for me to have my own place since I'm gone so much.

"Are you guys… *serious*?" Joshua probes.

We were.

"Yes, very. Do you have anyone waiting at home for you?" The tan line on his left hand pretty much answers the question, but I'm curious if he'll be truthful or confirm he's the shady guy I've assumed him to be.

"Nope, it's just me and my ten cats." He chuckles. I pretend to laugh too, because I know it's a lie. He is definitely not the die-alone-with-ten-cats type.

"Oh, okay, interesting, I wouldn't have pegged you as a cat guy."

"Oh really?" He raises his eyebrows. "What did you *peg* me as?"

"Well, considering the still prominent tan line on your left hand, I would have pegged you as married," I say with a cocked brow. He narrows his eyes and grins.

"My wife and I have an open relationship," he says, smirking and scooting closer, trailing his fingertips along the exposed skin of my back. "So I can enjoy you guilt free."

What a fucking tool.

"Sorry, but I'm not comfortable with that," I say, standing abruptly. "I'm going to excuse myself. Enjoy your night, Joshua," I say sweetly with a closed-lip smile. "I'm going to the restroom," I tell Rebecca and Sam. They both give me a tight-lipped smile like they're trying not to laugh, making it obvious they heard my conversation with Joshua.

"Okay," they say in unison and turn back to their conversation. Neither employ the girl code and offer to go with me, which I'm honestly thankful for. I just want to get the fuck away from Joshua, and I actually do need to use the bathroom. I leave the group and make my way through the crowded balcony area.

I spot the women's restroom down on the first floor, or rather, the line to the women's restroom. Shocker, it only wraps around half the room. Do you think clubs will ever realize they need to add larger restrooms? I don't know if I've ever been to one where you didn't have to get in line half an hour before you actually have to pee. You'd think we were waiting in line at Sephora on Black Friday.

I'm a few paces away from the staircase when I slam into a hard, broad-shouldered body directly in my path. "Oh, I'm so sor—" My words evaporate as my gaze connects with a pair of familiar, golden-flecked green eyes.

"Leah." A face I could never forget grins down at me with furrowed brows. Except the face I remember was much younger and still full of boyish charm. I much prefer the grown man version standing in front of me now. "Oh shit, I'm sorry," he says, looking down at my dress now soaked with wine. The cool red liquid glides down my exposed chest, disappearing beneath the fabric.

Fuck, not again.

"Jake?" I gasp, convinced my eyes are playing tricks on me. "Wow, uh, what—what the hell are you doing here?" I stutter out, unable to hide the shock on my face. The scar on my left thigh is pulsating. My dress is six inches shorter than when I put it on earlier. I would blend in with the women in the red light district windows easily. I fumble with the bottom seam, tugging it downwards, but it's no use. His eyes burn into my skin as they linger on the hem of the velvet fabric against my exposed thighs.

"I think the better question is, what are you doing here?" he inquires, narrowing his eyes and raising one eyebrow. I'm too in shock to speak or ask him to clarify when he adds, "I own this place."

I'm sorry, what?

"Oh, wow, I, uh, I didn't know." My heart sinks when I remember the name—*Chloe's*. I glance again at the neon sign in the middle of the bar and notice a small inscription under it: Pick Your Poison.

Of course...

My eyes go wide as I attempt to process the current situation. "I... I, uh... I'm just here with some coworkers," I say lamely, gesturing over my shoulder with my thumb to the rowdy group I just left. Joshua is glaring right at us. His eyes burn into the side of my face. *Jesus, could this get any more awkward?*

Jake's eyes dart between us as an unreadable expression spreads across his face. I assume it's merely curiosity because of our shared past, but I can't help wondering if he's jealous of the man staring at us. Or maybe it's *because* of our shared past that he *is* jealous of the man staring. I don't bother telling him Joshua's definitely not my boyfriend and I'm in fact trying to avoid him. Not only because I'm interested to know if it's jealousy or curiosity, but also in case I need an out to this unexpected conversation. *Okay, I'm lying to myself if I think I'd want an out to a conversation I've been thinking about for eight years.*

The first and only time I tried to contact Jake after the breakup was a few years ago, after Sophia had brought up how much she missed him since he was off playing soccer in Europe.

I haven't been able to stop thinking about Jake since Sophia mentioned him today. I've gone down the rabbit hole of googling him and looked through every website that mentioned his name like a fucking stalker. Most of them were in German, which made it impossible to understand what the hell they were talking about.

So far all I've come up with is that he plays for FC Bayern Munich, which is apparently a big deal, according to my research. All the pictures posted on Jake's Instagram are of him playing soccer, so that was no help. I did go into his tagged photos, and there were hundreds of pictures of him with teammates and various women that look like goddamn supermodels, but I have no clue if they're just fans or he actually knows them. In every photo, he has that signature lazy, come-fuck-me smile on his face, and damn it if it isn't the sexiest thing I've ever seen.

I'm sitting on the bedroom floor with my laptop placed on my thighs. I've been in this position for—I glance at the clock—approximately three hours now.

I've single-handedly destroyed an entire bottle of wine. My heart is pounding out of my chest.

I miss him so badly that my entire body aches.

In a moment of bravery, I snatch my phone off the floor, unlock it, and pull up his contact. My hands shake nervously as my thumb hovers over the call button. My breathing is staggered. After I press this button, I could hear Jake's voice on the other side…

I wonder what he sounds like now. God, I miss his voice.

Fuck it.

I tap the call button as quickly as possible before I can change my mind.

"We're sorry, your call could not be completed as dialed," a robotic voice says on the other end. I gasp and hang up, throwing the phone across the room. It slams against the wall and falls to the ground with a thud. The screen's probably shattered into a million pieces… just like my damn heart.

He fucking ***blocked*** *me.*

After that night, I returned the favor and blocked him

everywhere—Facebook, Instagram, Snapchat, the whole nine yards. I couldn't risk going down the rabbit hole again of cyberstalking him. It hurt too fucking much. Sophia brought him up again a few days later, and I broke down crying like a pathetic loser. Now she rarely brings him up. The only thing she'd mentioned in the last two years was that he had a bar in Europe, but I didn't know what country, and I never imagined it would be something like this.

"You always were a pretty good bartender." I smirk, taking in those beautiful emerald eyes for the first time in almost a decade. "Sophia mentioned you opened a bar. I just thought it would be more of a pub that offered stale pretzels and had huge flat screens around to watch the soccer games. This place is amazing."

"Here it's called *football.* And I have grown a bit more sophisticated over the last eight years." The corners of his mouth crinkle into a teasing smile.

It's so familiar yet completely foreign, reminding me just how long it's been since I've last seen him. Almost an entire decade without hearing his laughter or feeling his gentle lips against my skin. I guess it would take time for the cute, boyish features to turn into the handsome man in front of me. His hair is lighter than I remember and short but tousled in a purposeful way. His jaw is sharper and lined with light stubble.

I wonder how that would feel sliding between my thighs.

He has a tattoo just barely peeking out of the sleeve of his black fitted V-neck shirt.

Oh my god, fuck me sideways.

"So, do you live in Amsterdam?" he asks, snapping me out of my ogling.

"No, I'm a flight attendant, so I'm just here on a layover until tomorrow."

"Oh." His tone is disappointed. "You travel for a living? Sounds fun. Looks like we both got out of Longwood."

Am I really making small talk with a man I've known for over twenty years?

The love of my life.

The muse of my late-night fantasies.

"Yeah, the glamorous life of an international traveler." My lips form into a thin, lined smile.

"You don't seem very excited about it."

"Yeah, well, it just gets a bit *lonely* sometimes. It's hard to form meaningful friendships when you're always in different places with different people." I shrug.

"Yeah, I can definitely understand that." He nods in agreement. This conversation is definitely not over, but I wasn't lying when I told Joshua I needed to go to the restroom.

"Uh, I have a request for the owner."

He chuckles. "Sure, Le. What is it?"

"Can you put a few more restrooms in this place?" I gesture towards the ridiculous line that seems to have barely moved.

He removes the empty wine glass from my hand and sets it on a nearby table, then places his hand in mine.

"Come on," he says, pulling me through the crowd. Memories ricochet through my mind from the contact of his warm hand in mine. One touch, and I'm eighteen again, sitting in the passenger side of Jake's Jeep—windows down, breeze blowing through my hair, George Strait on the radio.

Jake drags me through a hallway and up a narrow staircase. His fingers are still tangled with mine even though we're no longer in a crowded bar and I could easily follow him. It feels natural—*normal*—comfortable. It also feels electric. Heat radiates up my arm from the place we connect. Maybe Jake is as terrified as I am that once he lets go, he'll never get to touch my skin again.

It takes seven years for the body to grow entirely new cells. It dawns on me that this man has never touched me. Not this body. Not this skin. He's never kissed these lips. He's only touched a version of me from a decade ago.

I ache for him to rediscover every new inch of me.

I crave to return the favor.

After four flights of stairs, I open my mouth to jest about the late-night cardio workout when he stops in front of a door and pulls out a key from the front pocket of his jeans. He turns the key in the lock and pushes it open, gesturing for me to walk in first.

"Holy shit," I gasp. The apartment is modern and ridiculously beautiful. The kitchen has a large marble island with a vase of tulips in the middle—interesting—and there's a stainless steel double gas stove and oven, gleaming like they've just been cleaned. The kitchen, living room, and dining room are open concept, with a beautiful, long wooden table and white leather chairs. Out the large window, the lights of Amsterdam are twinkling beautifully on the canal across the way. "It's gorgeous."

"Thanks," he says with a stoic expression, but I can tell by his posture and the slight upcurve of his mouth that he's proud of what he has. "The guest bathroom is down the hall to the left." He gestures towards one of two hallways in the apartment—or penthouse, rather.

"Okay, thanks again."

The guest bath is unsurprisingly as stunning as the rest of the apartment. It has cream-colored walls with golden accented finishings.

I go quickly and wash my hands in the bowl-shaped stone sink sitting atop a wooden vanity cabinet. I spend longer than I should staring at myself in the square mirror, trying to figure out how the fuck I ended up in Jake Summers's bathroom.

The wine has soaked completely through the velvet fabric of my dress and is seeping into my skin. The burgundy color stains the crevices of my exposed chest. As I'm staring in the mirror, I notice a familiar canvas in the reflection. I spin around, my eyes locking on the abstract painting of gold and blue paint splattered across a white canvas.

It's one of mine.

A few years ago, Sophia helped me set up a website to sell my paintings to make an extra income. I earn a decent amount being a flight attendant, but selling my prints allows me to put money to the side so I can eventually have my own place to call home. This was the first painting I ever sold. My website had only been live for two hours, and I couldn't believe I'd sold one so quickly… *Mystery solved.*

My phone vibrates in my purse.

REBECCA

Rebecca

Hey, just making sure you didn't get kidnapped LOL

I'm actually touched that she's checking up on me. Maybe she feels guilty about not offering a safety buddy to go to the bathroom.

Me

Ran into an old friend. I don't think I'll make it back to you guys tonight. 😬Let me know what I owe you for the wine 🍷

Rebecca

Okay, let me know if you change your mind. And don't worry about it, we're going to make Joshua pay 😉

Me

Okay, thanks 😂

The last part makes me giggle. I like this girl. I don't know why I already assume I won't be making it back to the table, but I know I'm not ready for this conversation to be over. This feels like a cosmic opportunity from the universe, and I don't think I could ever forgive myself if I ran out of here like a scared little girl.

29
Jake

I'm pacing the floor of my living room like a psychopath. My stomach is twisted into knots. There's not a single ounce of oxygen left in the entire flat.

Leah fucking Stone is in my bathroom.

My Leah.

The girl I've known since I was three. The love of my life. The one that got away.

She's actually here, in the flesh, and not just a figment of my imagination. It's not just another night of seeing the ghosts of my past. My mind wanders to the last time I saw her "ghost" in Munich. I about lost my damn mind.

I've finally accomplished everything I've been striving for my entire life. I'm playing soccer professionally. I'm living in Germany, playing for

FC Bayern Munich, one of the best teams in the league. I make more money in one game than most people make in six months.

I'm sitting in a crowded bar with a few of my teammates. We won today's home game thanks to the goal I scored.

I should be on cloud fucking nine.

Why do I still feel so damn empty?

The door to the street swings open, letting in a gust of cool air, along with more patrons to fill this already stuffed-to-the-brim bar. There are too many people standing in the walkways to see the faces of the newcomers. A redhead is bobbing through the crowd. Could it be?

My heart races at the possibility. But what in the hell would Leah be doing in Munich?

"I'll be right back," I tell my teammates. They don't even glance my way, entranced in a conversation about what club we're going to later to celebrate.

I push my way through the crowded bar.

"Pass doch auf du Arsch," a broad, angry man says after I've accidentally bumped him out of my way. (Translation: Watch where you're going, ass.)

"Sorry," I mutter without turning around.

The woman vanishes.

I quicken my pace, just a few strides away.

"Leah," I shout breathlessly as I finally reach the spot where she disappeared.

A beautiful woman with the wrong color eyes stares up at me from her seat in a corner booth.

Fuck—my entire body deflates.

It's not her.

Again.

"Sorry," I mumble, before turning to return to my teammates.

I've been seeing Leah for years.

Around every corner.

In every crowded bar.

Every time I close my eyes to sleep.

Chloe may have been the one who died, but it's Leah's ghost that haunts me from the shadows of every room I'm in.

Leah walks into the kitchen, and she's definitely not the paint-speckled eighteen-year-old running around the springs I remember. She's, for lack of a better word, stunning. Her long strawberry hair is curled and still falls to the middle of her back. Her face is the same, but her features have matured. In her boots, she's still several inches shorter than me, but not as much as I remember. The tight black dress she has on shows off her long, tan legs, and the front dips low enough to make any guy in Amsterdam curious as hell. *Except I already know what's underneath.* I grin at the thought.

"Um, Jake. Hey, buddy, my eyes are up here." *Oops.*

I'm usually strategic at checking girls out without them noticing. But there's always been something about Leah that makes me act like a goddamn idiot.

"Uh, yeah, sorry. There's wine on your dress," I say, pointing at her red-stained chest.

"Yeah, that tends to happen when someone barrels into you when you're holding a full glass," she retorts sassily.

"Hey, you ran into me."

That's a bold-faced lie. I watched her from the second she stepped through the vault door. I was walking out of my office on the second story as a copper head bobbed through the crowd. I almost dropped a two-thousand-dollar bottle of whisky when I realized it was actually Leah—in the flesh. I couldn't take my eyes off her the rest of the night. She looked so happy and carefree. I wanted to talk to her desperately, but it was thrilling seeing her interact with her friends, laughing and having the time of her life. Such a different woman than the one I walked away from so many years ago.

"Potato, po-tah-to," she sings songs, and my heart pangs at how much she still reminds me of Chloe. "So what do you do for work these days?" she probes, glancing around the apartment.

"You mean how can I afford this apartment *and* that lame bar downstairs?"

She chuckles. "You caught me. Yeah, I guess that's what I'm asking. I mean, I knew you came to Europe to play soccer. I just never realized it paid so well."

"Well, I am pretty good," I point out, attempting, and failing, not to sound arrogant.

"I know that," she replies softly. "So why the speakeasy?"

"I went to one in Paris right after I moved to Europe. It was one of the most fun nights of my life. The whole experience—and I wanted to create that experience for other people. I knew if I was going to open a bar, it couldn't just be your typical run-of-the-mill sports bar. I wanted it to be classy and fun. Somewhere people can come to have a good time and forget about whatever other shit is going on in their lives. Even if it's just for one night. It also helps me maintain a bit of privacy since I *am* pretty well known around here."

I don't mention that I was nominated for UEFA Men's Player of the Year. According to the press, I'm one of the top *football* players in Europe, and holding that position as an American is really fucking rare. Some of my teammates even thought it funny to nickname me Unicorn, which I despise and they thrive off of.

"And pretty tipsy girls in every corner doesn't hurt, huh?" she teases, and I can't help but notice the bite in her tone.

I laugh. "I have a rule about dating customers."

"Well, it's a good thing I didn't pay for any of my own drinks tonight," she says, smiling, and then her mouth snaps shut. I'm not sure if she was trying to make me jealous, but it worked. I know she's been drinking, so that means someone was buying her drinks. And there's only one reason someone would buy a beautiful woman drinks. It was probably that douchey-looking guy she was sitting with. He looked like he was ready to rip my dick off. *Try me, asshat.*

"Trying to drink and dash now, are we?"

"No, oh my God, no," she stammers out. "I just meant… because you said—"

"Relax, Le. I'm kidding. I saw you talking to that guy before I ran into you."

In fact, I was about thirty seconds away from walking up to the table and snatching her away from that asshole. It doesn't matter if it's been ten years or fifty, I will never be able to watch her talk to another guy without the little green monster waging a war inside my head.

She furrows her brows, and then they shoot to her hairline. "Oh, no." She laughs "I—it's not what you think. I was here with the whole crew I flew with last night, and he was hitting on me… shamelessly. But he's just another douchebag that I have no interest in."

"Oh… Is that because you're already seeing someone?" My heart stops beating in my chest.

She chuckles nervously. "No, definitely not. Single as a pringle."

My heart returns to a normal rhythm.

She's single.

I always worried that whenever I would see her again, we'd be like ships passing in the night. She would have someone, or I would, or we both would. And I am definitely no cheater. Then again, I've never been offered an aged scotch while attending AA, so maybe I'm not as strong as I think—and this woman is a welcome relapse.

"Do you need to get back to your, uh, friends?" *Why do I keep trying to get rid of her?*

"No, I texted and told them that I ran into an old friend and we're catching up."

"Oh... okay." *Old friend, huh?*

"Sorry, was that too presumptuous? I just assumed we'd want to catch up since it's been so long. But I'm sure you're incredibly busy being a professional *football* player and club owner and all that jazz." Her rambling is adorable. She speedwalks to the island, grabbing her small purse she set down when we walked in. I surprise both of us when I chase after her and grasp around her small wrist, spinning her to look at me.

"No," I say firmly, looking down at her as she crashes into my chest. "I'm glad we can catch up. And, Leah, the best part about being the owner is I can come and go whenever I want. I pay people good money to keep things moving no matter where I am." Her wrist is hot coals against my palm. I wonder if she feels the familiar burn like I do. Her cognac eyes look lighter than usual. I can't stop staring at her.

"So do you live here alone?" she asks, gesturing with her free hand at the apartment.

I laugh like an idiot, I'm so surprised at her question.

"Yes, I live here alone. I'm *also* single... as a pringle." I grin.

"Interesting," is all she manages to get out. "I just... the tulips on the island," she says, looking towards them. I furrow my brows, unsure what she means by that.

"They're a bit of a feminine touch," she adds.

"Oh." I chuckle. "My mom used to always do that, and, I don't know, it makes it feel more homey, I guess."

"I like that." She smiles, those adorable dimples making an appearance. I let go of her wrist and instantly regret the loss of contact.

I've fantasized about this moment every day for the last eight years. Every. Damn. Day. But I had given up hope that it would actually happen. Seeing her again, holding her, touching her, feeling her breath against my skin or her smile against my lips. *Her lips.* I can't pull my gaze away from her wet, pink lips. Remembering how soft they felt against mine. How she tasted like peppermint when we made love for the first time. How she branded me with a single kiss. *Fuck, and now I'm hard.*

She brushes a stray hair behind her ear, and a familiar gold ring gleams on her left finger. My heart beats out of my chest. I can't look away even as she drops it back down to her side. "Is that—"

Knock.

Knock.

Knock.

We're both startled by a banging on the front door.

"Jake? Jake, are you in there?" a familiar female voice yells frantically, knocking again.

Fuck.

"I thought you didn't have a girlfriend!" Leah hisses with wide eyes.

"I don't. Stay here."

I stride to the door, readjusting myself on the way, and swing it open. It's one of my managers, Jessica, and I've never been more annoyed by her presence.

"What?" I snap. Jessica winces, and her eyes are wide. I'm a hard ass, but I never get angry with my staff. They're all great. I suppose I'm just feeling especially irritable at this moment.

"Uh, um, sorry, Jake. It's just that uh…" she sputters in her thick British accent.

"Spit it out."

"There's some high shelf drinkers here tonight, and we need a few more bottles of Macallan Double Cask," she replies.

All the top shelf liquors are locked up in my office. I used to let the night managers have keys, but a few months ago, three thousand euros in cognac went missing, and I am in no mood to let that happen again.

It's never bothered me enough to find a different solution—until now. Playing professional soccer keeps me insanely busy and well paid. I could easily make this a hands-off business venture, but being involved in the day-to-day operations allows me some distraction from the parts of my life that are lacking.

"And… one of them asked to speak to you specifically. He said his name is Adrian Schneider?" she adds.

Adrian was an old teammate of mine from FC Bayern Munich. If I don't stop by after he's spent thousands in my place, I'll never hear the end of it.

"Okay, give me five minutes. I'll be right down." I shut the door and walk back to Leah. "I'm sorry, I have to—"

"I know. I heard." She frowns.

Damn it.

This is not how I imagined this night going a few minutes ago.

"I'm really sorry, it won't take too long," I say.

"It's fine, Jake." Her lips curl into a small smile that doesn't reach her eyes.

The hell it is.

There is so much I want to say. So much I don't know if I should.

Leah is staring at me with those same heartbroken eyes she had on prom night. The same ones that cracked my soul in half when they were followed by telling me she needed space to heal. Meaning space apart from me.

I may have been able to keep myself distracted the last eight years, but the second my eyes locked with hers tonight, I was reminded of a truth I'd forgotten—she may not always be mine, but I will always be hers. It's been 2,942 days since we last kissed, and I've belonged to her for all of them.

There is no way I can let her leave like this.

"Stay here," I command, walking towards the door.

"What?"

"Stay here. I'll be back in an hour."

"You'd trust a stranger in your apartment?" she teases.

"It could be a hundred years and you'd never be a stranger to me," I reply firmly. "Make yourself at home."

"Okay." She smirks. "You know I'm going to snoop, right?"

"I'd be worried if you didn't. My bedroom is that way, the last door on the right." I point down the hallway. "You're welcome to use the shower and borrow some clothes if the wine is bothering you."

"Okay." She looks down, giving us both the opportunity to stare at her chest. "Uh, yeah, that would be nice."

I'm already regretting suggesting she change into something less revealing. I forcibly store away the mental image of her undressing in *my* bathroom… without *me*. I walk out and shut the door on the blazing fire that just got reignited in my apartment. I have no idea how I'm going to put it out. I have no idea that I'd even want to.

30
Leah

I'm standing in Jake's massive bathroom, staring at my two options. A glorious gray stone walk-in shower with a golden waterfall shower head or an even more glorious porcelain, freestanding bathtub—both certainly big enough for two. Next to the bathtub is a glass jar filled with salts and a bottle of luxury bubble bath. I ignore that there's usually only one reason a man would have that type of stuff in his apartment and relish in the fact I'm going to be able to finally take a bath for the first time in months.

The hotels they book us in for work, although nice, mostly just have showers or bathtubs that you definitely wouldn't want to sit in. But as Jake said, we're not strangers, and I certainly have no qualms using this *glorious* bathtub.

I fill it with steaming hot water and add a generous amount of the lavender Epsom salts and bubble bath. I slowly undress, my veins buzzing with nervous energy.

I can't believe I'm naked in Jake's apartment.

The door is cracked so I can hear if he comes into the apartment. *Sure, that's why.* Knowing he could walk in at any moment equally excites me and terrifies me. Most people would think you need time to catch up before having these kinds of thoughts, but honestly, there is nothing in this world I want more than to pick up right where we left off. Like a candle left on the shelf—it doesn't matter how long it's been sitting there unused, it'll light right back up with the strike of a match. But Jake isn't just the flicker of a flame, he's the whole goddamn bonfire.

I don't mean where we left off on prom night. I want to go back to the days before the accident. Before our entire lives changed in an irreversible way. I know we can't go back to that time, but after spending years working through my grief, I finally feel like I could be ready to love again. My heart has been dormant for so long, but one look in his emerald eyes was all it took to jump-start it.

I sink down into the tub, with bubbles up to my chin. Even though my mind is flooded with past memories, the warm water melts my muscles like butter, lulling me into a relaxed state. It's almost twelve-thirty in the morning, and I've gotten about five hours of sleep in the last two days. My eyelids are heavy, and I stifle a yawn. I close my eyes to soak in this temporary heaven, trying to suppress the anticipation of seeing Jake again.

The painting I saw in Jake's bathroom comes to mind, and I can't stop myself from wondering what it means—or if it means anything at all. I attempt and fail to ignore the heart-ripping memories popping into my mind of the night we broke up. For most teenagers, prom is the magical grand finale to your high school career. For me, it was the second worst night of my life.

"May I have this dance?" Jake says with a smirk, holding out his hand to me as we stand in front of the headlights at Brahms ranch after deciding to skip prom.

"I would be honored." I curtsy before taking it. One arm is extended like we're waltzing, and his other is placed firmly around my waist. The tighter his grip, the more I feel like my chest is going to crack wide open. My mind wanders to all the things that have happened this past year. To all the things that are going to happen soon and in the future. How as much as I love Jake right now, spending time with him mostly brings up memories and pain I'd rather just forget. It's hard to move forward from the worst parts of your past when you're dating someone who shares them so deeply. I suppose it's good that we understand each other, but we're both in such dark places, and like Martin Luther King Jr. said, "Darkness cannot drive out darkness; only light can do that."

We're both physically incapable of pulling one another out of this darkness. Either one of us has to become the light, or we need to go find the light on our own. Otherwise, we're both going to end up in the darkness forever, and I don't know how much longer I can live like that.

"I got a full ride to UCLA," Jake says timidly, breaking the silence. There's a long pause. I focus on the sound of his heartbeat as my ear rests against his chest.

"I know," is all I'm able to muster up, aware of where this conversation will go. He's talked about UCLA since we were kids.

"I'm not going," he says firmly.

"What?" I jerk my head away to look at him. "But it's your dream school."

"Dreams change, Leah." He sighs, running his fingers through my hair. "Besides, I can't leave you. Not after…" He looks away.

"Jake," I whisper, leaning into his hand. It takes all my strength not to let my voice crack. "We can't stop living. She wouldn't want that. It would

kill her all over again."

"How can I be so far away from you and Soph?" he asks loudly, rubbing a hand over his face, hiding his pained expression.

"Jake. We'll be fine. Besides, you and I barely talk anyways. It shouldn't be that different," I mumble out, regretting the words as soon as they're spoken.

"What's that supposed to mean?" he asks, and his entire body stills as he stares down at me with furrowed brows.

"Nothing." I look away and rest my head back on his chest.

"No, tell me," he commands, nudging me gently away so he can see my face.

"Come on, you can't tell me you haven't noticed how distant we've been," I say, my lip quivering at the honest words. "We're both here… but we're not." I hear actual crickets chirping around us as he tries to come up with a suitable answer.

"It's just so—" His voice cracks.

"Hard… I know, Jake. God, trust me, I know… I love you." I take his face in my hands as tears blur my vision. "If you could only understand how much I love you."

"I love you too, Le. So fucking much." He places a hand over his chest as if for protection.

"I love you so much that the thought of losing you, God, I can't even fucking breathe." I remove my hands from his face and pace in front of the headlights. "But losing Chloe… Sometimes I don't even want to be alive." I exhale heavily, then place my hands on the hood of the car and brace myself so I don't fold over in pain from the memories.

"Don't say that," he croaks, grabbing my elbow and turning me towards him. He cradles my face between his warm palms and angles it up towards his concerned gaze.

"I'm sorry. I–I don't—I didn't mean that," I stutter out. "I used to, but

I don't anymore."

"Good." His green eyes blaze with intensity. Those eyes.

"I just, what I'm trying to say is, I love you, but..." I can see the glitch in his emerald eyes as they switch from concerned to tormented.

"But?" he asks, dropping his hands and stepping away from me.

"When I look at you... When I look into these beautiful gold-flecked green eyes..." I sigh, stepping towards him and brushing my thumbs under his eyes as tears prick my cheeks. "All I see is her." He winces at my honesty. "And maybe someday that'll make me smile, but right now that makes me want to rip my fucking heart out and throw it across this field if only for a millisecond of relief."

"I just, I want to be there for you," he says, reaching out and taking my hand in his. "I already lost my best friend. Am I supposed to lose you too? I know we haven't talked much, but even being around you helps."

"Being around you... it's... It doesn't just hurt me. It's when I'm in the most pain." He winces, and I know the truthful words are a dagger straight to his already bleeding heart. Unfortunately, honesty doesn't always make you feel better. Sometimes it just hurts.

"Jake, please," I beg, my voice still trembling. "You have to go to UCLA. It's been your dream for forever. And I'm not the only one grieving. I know you're grieving too."

"She was my sister," he whispers, his voice cracking.

"I know, baby." I wipe the tears away from his cheeks. "And she'd kick your ass if she knew you were even considering turning down a full ride to your dream school."

"But what about us?" he asks pleadingly, searching my eyes for answers.

"I just, I think I need time. And I think you do too. You can't tell me it's not hard to be around me."

"It's exponentially harder to not be around you... I love you, Leah," he emphasizes, cradling my neck and rubbing his thumbs along my jawline.

"I love you too. God, I love you so much, you have to believe me," I beg. "But I think because of how much we love each other, we need some space to heal..." I can't even believe I just suggested that, but I was telling the truth when I told Jake that right now it hurts me more being around him.

"Unbelievable," he whispers, shaking his head and dropping his arms.

"Jake, please..." I reach for him but he takes a step back.

"No," he snaps. "This is such bullshit. First, I lost Chloe, and now I'm going to lose you too? And why? Because I have her fucking eyes? I can't change my fucking eyes, Leah," he wails, and I've never heard him say my name in that tone. The sound cracks my chest wide open.

"I know that. It's not just your eyes. It's just—it's all too much right now. And you're not losing me, Jake. I'm right here," I sob as I step towards him and reach for his hand. He backs another step away from me, out of reach.

"Yeah, until you're not. Until we're three thousand miles apart and we haven't talked in months because I have soccer and you have sorority parties or whatever bullshit college girls do," he says, shaking his head.

"Jake, I just, I just need a little time. Just for it to hurt a little less." I fold my arms over my chest, hugging myself as tears stream down my face. The salty liquid drips into my mouth, reminding me of our last trip to the beach.

"Time?" he shouts. "How much time? How long does it take to get over the death of your best friend? Do you think I'll ever have a day where I don't think about her? Don't wish I could call her? It's always going to fucking hurt, Leah."

"I know that, I just—"

"Maybe you're right. Maybe we do need some space." He shakes his head again and rolls his eyes. He paces a few strides, steadies his breathing, then walks back to me. He stares at my crumpled, tear-soaked face and reaches up a hand in a failed attempt to wipe them away, then pulls back. "I'll give you the space you're asking for," he says, his tone softening. "I won't call you.

I won't text you. I won't be the one to cause you any more pain, Leah. I love you too much."

"I love you too," I say, reaching for him again, and this time he doesn't back away. He takes me in his arms, wiping the wet hair out of my face so he can look into my eyes.

"You will always be my girl," he says, pulling away and looking down at me again. "Whenever you're ready for me to be in your life again, I'll be here."

We ride home in heartbreaking silence. If I didn't know better, I'd think I held my breath the entire time. He parks the car in my driveway, and we get out. His door slams shut, the loud bang like a gunshot to my chest. He turns and walks toward his house, disappearing into the dark without a single glance back.

Lovers turned strangers, now passing one another like ships in the night.

Except it doesn't hurt to look at a stranger.

"Leah, wake up," a husky voice says as I'm drifting in unconsciousness.

"Leah," the familiar voice says louder, shaking my arm.

My eyes pop open, and I blink them rapidly.

"Oh… hey," I rasp at Jake. I pick up my arms to stretch them. The sound of water jostling in the tub jolts me from serene to high alert. An audible gasp escapes my mouth as I cover my breasts with my arms. I'm still in the bathtub, and Jake is standing right next to me, looking away, trying and failing to stifle a smile.

Please, god, no.

I risk looking down to see that all of the bubbles are also gone, leaving me completely exposed.

Fuck. Fuck. Fuckedy fuck.

"Sorry, I, uh, I tried to wake you up by knocking on the door but I guess you were too deep in sleep. I would've let you rest, but I was kind of afraid you'd drown."

"It's okay. Can I, uh, have a towel?" My cheeks are burning hot.

"I left one on the counter for you. I'll be in my room. You can pick out something to wear from the closet."

I'm equal parts thankful and annoyed by the fact that he isn't even trying to sneak a peek. Either he's over me and not interested or he's being respectful, which I suppose I should appreciate.

I've never wanted someone to disrespect me so badly.

I emerge from the bathroom a few minutes later with the towel wrapped around me. Jake is sprawled out on his bed in sweatpants and a T-shirt, tapping away on his phone. He glances up, only looking into my eyes, and gestures to the closet. "Take your pick."

"Thanks."

I wish I had eyes in the back of my head so I could know if his gaze was following me as I walked away, but apparently, only mothers have that superpower. *Lysa damn sure did.*

My breath hitches as I step into the closet. It's bigger than my bedroom at home, with a small marble island in the middle. There is one section filled with just suits and tuxedos, another with his workout gear, soccer jerseys, cleats displayed, etc., and another section with sweatpants and T-shirts all on hangers.

The rest of the closet is completely bare. *Thank God.* I was half scared I'd walk in here and find a small section of women's clothing from whatever woman he's probably sleeping with right now.

He said he's single.

That doesn't mean he's celibate.

I finger through the T-shirts until I touch one that freezes them still. It's a Longwood High soccer shirt, with the number eight on the back. Summers is blazoned across the top in big block letters. Before I can talk myself out of it, I snatch it off the hanger. I drop the towel and pull it over my head. The comfortable material encases me like my favorite warm blanket.

Shit, I don't have any underwear.

I will never put on the same pair twice. That's where I draw the line.

I guess commando it is…

I browse through his wardrobe, searching for the matching Longwood sweatpants.

He still has those too.

I exit the closet, and Jake's no longer in the room. I walk around, taking in all the touches of him. There's a huge flat screen mounted on the wall above a large wooden dresser, to watch the soccer games, no doubt. On the dresser is the picture of Chloe, Jake, and me in the bubble bath in the Florida Keys. My lips curve upwards at the distant memory.

A floor to ceiling bookshelf takes up the entire wall between the bathroom and bedroom door. I run my fingers over the book spines, taking in the home library that's stuffed to the brim with books from every genre. James Patterson, Stephen King, Harlan Coben… There are a few spicy romances I recognize too. *I'm definitely asking him about those.* There's a brown lounge chair in front of it with a white blanket draped over the back. I smile, imagining Jake sitting there, enthralled in his latest thriller.

Honestly, is there anything sexier than a man who reads?

My eyes snag on a small painting hanging above one of the nightstands. I walk towards it with a hand resting on my pounding chest. It's another of mine. This particular painting is one that I sold a few months ago. It was my most profitable piece to date, and I always wondered who it ended up with. The seller's line just said The Unicorn, and I had no fucking clue what that meant.

"I figured white would be a safer option," Jake says, walking back in the room with two glasses of white wine. I scrunch my nose at him, and when he sees my choice of outfit, his lips curl into a sexy as fuck grin.

"Oh man, that brings back some memories," he rasps out in that sexy, deep voice I'm not yet familiar with. I probably should've chosen literally anything else, but I couldn't help myself.

"Yeah, old habits, I guess," I say, smirking. He never takes his eyes off me as I walk to him and take one of the wine glasses.

"You know," Jake says, grinning, "there's a German tradition that if you don't look in the other person's eyes when you cheers, you'll have seven years of bad sex."

I laugh at his fun fact of the day. "That is *not* an option."

We clink our glasses and both take a sip while maintaining eye contact. I've never been so turned on from drinking a damn glass of wine.

He breaks our trance to walk over to his bed and sets the glass down on the nightstand. He then climbs into it and makes himself comfortable against the pillows. I take that as my invitation to do the same. I walk to the opposite side of the bed and crawl on top of the covers, lying back against the soft pillows to face him.

"So… how did you end up *here*?" I ask before taking a sip of the wine.

"Do you mean in this apartment or in Amsterdam?"

"I guess both?"

"Well, after college, I got scouted by a small team in Germany, where I lived for a couple years. Then I got offered to play for the team here in Amsterdam, and, well, the rest is history, I guess."

"And the apartment?" I ask, taking another sip, then setting my glass down on the nightstand.

"After I started playing here, I quickly became one of the best strikers on our team, so I get paid a pretty good amount of money." He smiles sheepishly. "I was sharing an apartment with a teammate for a while, but he got a girlfriend. And I figured I'll still be in Amsterdam for at least another five years due to my contract, so it made more sense to buy rather than rent." He shrugs. "When I was looking for properties, this building went up for sale and it seemed like a worthwhile business opportunity, so I decided to buy it. There were originally six apartments and a restaurant in this building, but the two bottom floor apartments, just above the club, are too loud at night for anyone to actually sleep." I can't help but feel a sense of pride when he talks about what he's turned this place into. I wish I could've seen it before he bought it. I love watching those HGTV-style makeovers. "So I converted one into an extra office space, and we use the other for storage."

"Wow, that's amazing."

"Thanks." He smiles proudly. "The penthouse is obviously mine." He gestures around. "And I rent out the other three apartments."

"Was it hard to find time to work on starting the club while playing soccer, er, football all the time?"

"Honestly, yeah." He chuckles. "But it was the one thing that brought me joy. I loved figuring out the floor plans and drink menus. It was all creative stuff that kept my mind off... off of all the other stuff going on." There was an obvious pause in his thought, and I can't help but wonder if it has anything to do with me.

"I wish I could've seen this place before you fixed it up."

"Yeah, it was in pretty rough shape. I had a few investors and put every paycheck I made into it for almost two years until it was finally done."

"Well, it definitely paid off."

"Thanks." He smiles.

"Do you like Amsterdam?"

"Yeah, it's nice. Most everyone speaks English, so I get around pretty easily."

"Do you speak any Dutch?"

"I know the important phrases, but not really conversational," he admits. "Do you speak any other languages?"

"I'm learning Italian, but I'm awful at it," I laugh.

"Now *that's* a romance language." He cocks a brow. "Say something."

"What?" I laugh, suddenly feeling shy.

"Come on, practice on me," he begs, fluttering his long eyelashes.

I can think of other things I'd like to practice…

"Fine," I concede. I think for a minute about something I can admit without him understanding. I take a deep breath and pray he doesn't know shit about Italian.

"Ti penso ogni giorno." *I think about you every day.*

I wait to see if there's a flicker of recognition in his eyes. There is none.

"Sei il grande amore della mia vita." *You are the love of my life.*

"I don't know what you said, but it sounds sexy as fuck," he says, laughing and biting his lower lip to stifle a smile. I have to stop myself from crawling on top of him and making up for lost time.

"Have you picked back up the smoking habit being here?" I ask, trying to change the subject.

"Not since Mom grounded me for a month and made me do pee

tests for three." He chuckles. "Thanks for that, by the way."

Chloe and I were the ones who ratted him out to Lysa in the first place. We were such little assholes.

"Oh, come on, I was sixteen." I giggle.

"So was I. And besides, professional athletes definitely aren't allowed to partake in recreational drug use."

"True, true," I say lamely.

"So what about you?" he asks.

"What about me?"

"Why flight attendant? What did you do for college? Sorry… I just feel like we have so much to catch up on. It's been a long eight years."

"Yeah, it has." I sigh, mouth curling downwards. He rolls on his side to face me, mirroring my position. He's so close I could easily reach out and touch his cheek with my hand. "I went to the University of Florida for two years. I was studying business like my parents wanted. But I dropped out. It was just…" I trail off, unable to find the right words.

It's difficult for me to talk about this stuff with Jake. I can't give him the bullshit answer I give everyone else. *Oh, school just wasn't for me. I wanted to travel and experience the world.*

"It was just really hard for me," I continue, fighting back the tears that are already blurring my vision.

Fuck. I haven't cried in years, but I suppose that's because I never really talk about Chloe. Being with Jake, bringing up all these feelings I've pushed down deep over the years, it picks the scab wide open.

He must notice my internal conflict because he reaches out and grabs my hand. An innocent gesture, but I'd be lying if I said it didn't make my entire stomach turn in on itself.

"My entire life I had… I had these two best friends," I whisper with a soft smile, "and I just—a life without you both in it was *awful.* I went to my classes, which I hated. I tried to make Chloe proud, but I couldn't stand being there without her. We were supposed to do it all together... I tried the sorority thing for a semester, but I was too depressed and never went to any events, so they kicked me out. I went to a few parties, but anytime I felt myself smile or have the least bit of fun I just felt..."

"Guilty?" he fills in as if he understands exactly how I felt... and I guess he would. I forgot what it's like talking to someone who understands your grief so well. Who shares it with you instead of simply accepting it as a part of you.

"Yeah, guilty... So I focused on school, which honestly just drained me because I hated what I was studying. For my twentieth birthday, my parents took me on a trip to Greece, and I was so distracted by the traveling that I..." I pause, unsure if I should be completely honest.

"It's okay, keep going." He smiles tenderly and squeezes my hand three times, causing a rush of warmth to spread throughout my body from the familiar gesture.

He remembers that.

He remembers us.

"I honestly didn't even think about you or Chloe for an entire week," I blurt out. "Well, that's a lie. I did think about you both, but it wasn't in a grieving way. It was more like, 'oh, wow, Chloe would've been in awe of this statue' or 'Jake would have devoured this bacon-wrapped chicken souvlaki' and—"

"Damn it, now I'm hungry," he says, chuckling.

I giggle and smile. "I realized that traveling made me feel more alive than I had in years. So as soon as we got back, I dropped out of school and applied to become a flight attendant. I figured it was my best opportunity to see the world and remain in a constant state of distraction."

"What did your parents think about your career change?"

"Honestly?" I smile softly. "They were just happy to see me happy again. It had been so long since I'd genuinely smiled. The day I came home from college was the happiest I'd been in years. It felt like a huge weight had been lifted off my shoulders. I think they could feel it too. Because they never pressured me to go back. They even made sure there was an easel and paint ready in my room when I got home."

I smile at the memory.

"Is that when you started painting again?" he asks with a knowing grin.

"No." I glance at my painting hung on the wall. "After I started flying, I would visit the art museums during my layovers. Going all around the world, seeing all that culture and history, one day I just... picked up the brush and started painting again."

"I'm so happy you got back to that," he says earnestly. "You've always been so talented."

"Is that why you have a Leah Stone original hanging next to your bed?" I ask, unable to contain my curiosity.

"What can I say? I have good taste," he replies, brushing his thumb in circles on the top of my hand. My stomach is doing somersaults. *He must have touched other women like this in the past decade.* The unwelcome thought makes me nauseous.

"Any serious relationships?" I probe as the wine gives me liquid courage. A small smile curves his mouth.

"Just one," he says softly.

My heart drops into my stomach at the thought of him loving someone else.

"Oh... who—"

"In my life," he interrupts.

"Huh?"

"I've had one serious relationship in my life."

Sure, we were serious for teenagers, but we're twenty-six now. Certainly he's had a more significant relationship than ours since high school.

"Who was she?"

"Seriously, Leah?" He narrows his eyes at me. "Come on."

"I want you to say it before I feel like an idiot for thinking it." I bite my lower lip, and his gaze flicks down to it before returning to mine.

"Of course I'm talking about you. Who else?"

"I don't know. We were just kids back then. I figured you'd had girlfriends since then." I shrug.

"Yeah, sure, I've had girlfriends. Hell, one I dated for a year, but it was nothing compared to our relationship. It was light and fun… but that's all it was." I want to be offended that he just inferred our relationship was neither *light* nor *fun*, but sadly, it's the truth. The better part of our relationship was filled with sadness, grief, pain, and darkness. Not a lot of room for fun.

"Why did it end?"

"We dated when I was in Germany, and it wasn't the kind of relationship that would withstand long distance. So we both just agreed to move on." He seems completely unaffected by it, so it must be the truth.

"Oh, okay," I say, attempting to mask my relief.

"What about you?"

I'm embarrassed to even answer him. I've had my fair share of one-night stands. I suppose that's typical for someone who travels like I do, but not one single actual boyfriend. I'm jealous, not really of his ex, but that he had someone he connected with enough to distract him and stick around for a while.

"I, uh, I've dated."

Good. It's not lying but doesn't make me sound like a total loser.

"Anything serious?" *Crap.*

"No, nothing." A wide smile spreads across his face. "What?"

"Sorry. It's just, I was terrified you'd tell me you had this great love and had forgotten all about me." The grin is still plastered across his face.

"Jake. I couldn't forget you even if I tried."

And trust me, I've tried.

31

Jake

"I'm starving," Leah says as soon as we walk into my kitchen to refill our glasses of wine.

"What else is new?" I chuckle.

"Hey!" She giggles and slaps me against the arm. "I didn't eat any dinner tonight."

"Well, I can always eat."

"Do you have anything in this sterile kitchen of yours or is it just for show?"

"I think I can manage to find something."

"If you pull out a jar of pickled herring, I'm going to barf."

"Don't knock it till you try it." *Not that I have.*

"You know what? I'm not hungry anymore." She scrunches her nose up in disgust.

"Le, I'm kidding. I'm not making that." I laugh at her adorable face as I walk to the pantry, grabbing the one thing I know she'll like, then retrieve bowls and spoons from the drawers of the island.

"No way," Leah squeals when she sees the box I've placed on the counter. "I didn't even know they sold that here."

"They sure do." I grin as I pour two large portions of Lucky Charms into the bowls.

"Can I ask you a question?" Leah says timidly as I'm grabbing the milk from the fridge.

"Sure," I reply.

"Why haven't you ever visited home?"

My body stiffens. "How do you know I haven't?"

"Oh, Sophia and I talk… a lot. And although we don't talk about you often, I think she would have mentioned it if you were going to be in town."

"I, uh, I don't know. It's a pretty far trip. And my schedule with soccer keeps me pretty—"

"Eight years, Jake? Come on," she snips, no qualms for calling me out on my bullshit. *That's my girl.* "And when you were at UCLA, it wasn't as far."

"I know… I booked a flight a few times," I admit, sighing. "But I could never get on the plane. Being home, it always reminded me that Chloe was gone. Being in our house without her. I just, I couldn't do it."

I'm doing well. I'm happy… as happy as I can be. I'm terrified of being sucked back down into that black hole.

"They miss you," she whispers as I bring over the bowls to stand by the island with her. Neither of us reaches for them. We just stand there, inches apart, staring at one another.

"I know."

"You can't keep running from this. You have a family that loves you, and they need you. They've spent too much time loving you from afar."

"I'm running?" I scoff. "You're one to judge."

"What's that supposed to mean?" she says, folding her arms over her chest and cocking a hip.

"Oh, come on, Leah. Seriously?"

"Jake."

"You ran from us. It was too painful and real, and it scared you." I shake my head at the memory.

"It's not the same thing," she says quietly.

"How is it not? You said they need me, right? Well, I needed *you*. And you left me. Maybe not geographically, but you still left."

"I just needed time," she whispers, looking down at the floor.

"And has eight years been enough time?" I snap, mirroring her position and folding my arms in front of my chest. Years of suppressed emotions are bubbling straight to the surface.

"Jake..." Tears well in her eyes. *Ugh, fuck.* My stomach drops at the sight.

"You never even called," I point out calmly.

"I never knew what to say." She runs her fingers nervously through her curls.

"Anything would have been better than nothing."

"I tried once," she says so quietly her words are almost lost to the air.

"What?"

"I tried to call you once. A couple of years ago. But—well, the call didn't go through."

"How long ago?"

"I think like two or three years ago."

"I've been in Europe for almost four."

"Okay?"

"I got rid of my number when I moved here."

"Oh," is all she says, but I can see a flash of relief on her face.

"Why didn't you ask Dad or Sophia about it?"

"I don't know. I guess I figured it was a sign that I should just leave you alone. Your soccer career was going so well, and I hoped you were happy, and I was afraid to fuck anything up for you."

"Are you serious, Leah? You're the one thing that would've made everything better." The silence in the air is so thick, I can hear the hum of the refrigerator. "Can I ask *you* something?"

"Yes," she answers timidly.

"Are you happy?"

"I mean, I guess I've found something that resembles happiness. I no longer feel like half a person walking around in a partially empty shell. I've finally figured out who I am on my own. How to make myself feel whole, even if I'm alone. But Jake… I would have been *exponentially* happier with you in my life than I have *ever* been on my own," she says without hesitation, turning her gaze to meet mine.

It feels good to hear those words but also adds fuel to my anger, knowing how different the last eight years could have been had we just fucking talked to one another.

"And you never called either." She's right, I didn't.

"I know." I sigh.

"Why not?"

"Because…" Because I was drowning, and I was a scared little boy afraid that if she rejected me again, it would send me straight down back into depression. I couldn't risk it.

"Because?"

"Because I love you, Le." I sigh, and her pretty lips part open in surprise. "It fucking gutted me that you thought you would be happier without me than with me in your life. I needed you, and you couldn't even look at me. I'm not an idiot. I felt that we were growing more and more distant. What we went through was fucking traumatic. I guess I just hoped that the more time it had been since the accident, that every day apart was a day closer to being together again…"

"Jake," she says quietly, with tears brimming her eyes.

"Do you know how hard it was not to call you? To hear your voice? I spent months, hell, *years*, burning alive from the inside out from the desire to talk to you. But I loved you more than I cared about ridding myself of that pain. You said you wanted space, so I gave it to you. I never wanted to be the person that brought any more pain into your life. All I ever wanted to do was love you."

"I'm so sorry," she says, her voice cracking as tears spill down her cheeks.

"I forgive you," I return, pulling her into my arms, because it's the truth.

She gazes up at me with those fucking beautiful, glossy chestnut-brown eyes. The past eight years of pain and regret vanish in an instant. All that wasted time.

Don't waste a second of it.

The familiar words ring through my head. My eyes drop down to her plump, pink lips as they part slowly. My face draws closer with every breath.

She loved you and left you, the angel on my shoulder warns, begging to protect me.

Don't you remember the last time your lips touched her skin? No? Remind yourself, commands the devil ready to destroy me.

She drags her fingers through my hair, and the devil's already won. I shove the bowls out of the way, then grasp her hips, placing her ass on the edge of the kitchen island. She braces herself on the cool granite, and I wedge myself between her thighs. Our lips are centimeters apart. Her breath is a warm breeze against my skin. She must feel the effect she has on me as I press my stone-hard dick directly against her. My heart is beating so fast I forget basic human reflexes—like breathing. She's panting as I graze my thumb along her bottom lip. A magnet drawing me closer to what I so desperately desire.

Our lips crash together, fusing like hot molten metal. My tongue glides against her lips, begging for entry, and she allows me without hesitation. She wraps her legs around my waist, arching into me. My sweet and gentle exploration of her mouth turns hungry, animalistic, and full of pure lust. I place my palms on her knees, inching them slowly up her thighs towards her center.

I nuzzle her chin to the side with my nose, allowing me better access to the smooth column of her neck. I glide my tongue along her jawline and down to the center of her throat, nibbling gently. My hands are gripping her thighs, and my thumbs are so close I can feel the heat radiating from between her legs.

She places her small hand on mine and lets out a quiet moan. I glance down and see the gold band gleaming on her left ring finger. I pick up her hand and bring it between us, looking down at it, then directly into her eyes.

I knew you still loved me, I say silently while grinning.

Her hand trembles in mine, and I place a gentle kiss on top of the ring, then flip her hand over and kiss her palm, wrist, arm, all the way back to her neck. I slide my hand into her hair and brush her jawline with my thumb.

"Stop," Leah says abruptly.

"What?" I ask, pulling away to look at her.

She nudges me out of the way and hops off the counter.

"I'm sorry. This is all just too much. I can't do this." She turns to walk away, and I grab her wrist, holding her in place.

"Leah, wait," I beg.

"No, it's just all too much," she says, her voice breaking. I see the pain in her eyes, and it cracks me in two. I let go of her hand. She snatches her purse off the counter and runs out of the apartment.

I'm standing there dumbstruck.

I feel like I've been sliced in two.

I can't believe she fucking left me… *again.*

32
Leah

"Hey there, Ladybug," I say to Sophia as she gets into my car. We're going to the mall for the fourth time because she wants to make sure we "blend in with the locals" during our Euro trip in June. We leave the week after her high school graduation—it's a gift I've been excited to give her for years.

"Have you been practicing your Italian?" I ask.

"Buongiorno, vorrei un gelato piccolo, per favore."

"Wow, that sounded perfect. Well, at least we know we'll be able to order gelato, if nothing else," I say, smiling.

"How would you know it sounds right? You don't speak Italian," she teases as her blonde hair falls over her bronzed shoulder.

"Bella, non sottovalutarmi," I respond. *Don't underestimate me, beautiful.*

"Well, I've learned the most important phrases," she huffs.

"Oh yeah, like what?"

"Ciao, un uomo italiano sexy per favore."

I furrow my brows, unsure of the phrase's meaning.

"Hi, one sexy Italian man, please," she clarifies.

I throw my head back, laughing wildly. "I don't think you can just order them at the bar."

"But can't I?" She grins, and we burst into laughter. "How was Amsterdam?" Sophia probes. "Was it cold for late April?"

"It was… a lot," I admit, sighing. "And the weather was okay. A bit cold at night."

"What do you mean it was a lot?"

"Oh, you know, the usual. I'm just exhausted from all the travel…"

"Mm-hmm. There couldn't be any other reason?" she asks suspiciously.

"What would that reason be?" I say, narrowing my eyes at her at a stop light.

Of course Sophia knows Jake lives in Amsterdam. I guess I shouldn't be surprised she never told me after my last Jake-related breakdown.

"I don't know, you tell me," she says, being cagey.

"I saw your brother," I admit.

She gasps. "I knew it!"

"Little Ms. Nancy Drew," I say, chuckling.

"Okay, tell me everything," she instructs.

"There's not much to tell… We talked, he kissed me," I admit, and she gasps. "And then I almost knocked over a soggy bowl of Lucky Charms as I ran out of the apartment like a scared little bitch."

"What?" she asks, laughing. "You wasted a bowl of Lucky Charms? Damn girl, this is why you're the Scaredybug." I narrow my eyes at her. "Why did you run out?"

"I don't know... It was just a lot, I guess. It had been so long since we'd seen one another, and there were just... a lot of emotions under the surface. Like, I'm good, I'm happy, I feel fine overall, but I think seeing Jake brought up a lot of feelings that I'd just completely forgotten I even had."

"Damn..." she says. "So what are you going to do?"

"What do you mean?" I ask incredulously.

"Well, are you going to talk to him again?"

"I wasn't planning on it," I say, trying to convince myself.

"Why not?" she huffs.

"Are you always this nosy?" I narrow my eyes at her.

"Not relevant," she says, waving a hand at me.

"Soph, it was all too much. I started thinking about how I would feel if I ever lost him again, and I just... panicked."

"Well, why don't you guys try to just be friends?" she suggests, as if it's the easiest thing in the world. "I mean, you knew each other your whole lives before you even dated. And you barely even dated for a year."

It's the truth, but it still hurts somehow hearing her point out just how short the romantic part of our relationship actually was. And if Jake and I are friends, *just* friends, I can have him in my life without the risk of the inevitable romantic fallout.

"I'll think about it," I say.

"Pinky promise?" she says sticking out her little pinky to me.

"Pinky promise," I say, hooking my finger with hers.

33
Jake

"Voer het verdomde tempo op!" *Pick up the damn pace.* Coach Roord yells at us from the center of the field as we run laps around it. Our last game of the season in Barcelona is coming up, and our coach wants to make sure we finish on top. I want to win too, but making the entire team run laps until we vomit is overkill. Half the guys have already spent their lunch on the sidelines, and I'm five seconds away from it myself.

I finish the current lap just as Coach blows the whistle. *About fucking time.*

"De training zit erop, tot morgenmiddag. Als ik ook maar één piep hoor dat een van jullie vanavond uitgaat, zit je op de bank, begrepen?" *Practice is over, see you tomorrow afternoon. If I hear a single peep about one of you going out tonight, you'll be benched. Understood?*

"Begrepen meneer." *Understood, sir.* We all chime in unison.

I'm not fluent in Dutch by any means, but I know the standard phrases Coach has said time and time again before every game. Fortunately, most everyone speaks English, but I am on a Dutch team in the Netherlands, after all.

I walk through the front door of my apartment, and every muscle in my body is screaming for relief. My stomach is empty and aching for food. I'm cursing myself for not picking up takeout on the way home. I drop my duffle by the door and go straight to the kitchen to prepare something at least moderately healthy.

It's days like this where I'm sad to walk into an empty house. Not just because I'd love to come home to a freshly cooked meal, because who wouldn't, but because I wish I had someone to share the parts of my day with that no one else cares about or understands. Like how on the way home, I saw a tall blonde laughing with her friend, and she reminded me of Chloe. I have friends here, but not many I can talk to about the real stuff. The things that have happened in my past that still float to the front of my mind from time to time.

Seeing Leah a couple weeks ago gave me hope that I'd finally have someone to talk to again who understood me. And I mean completely understood me. The dark, light, flaws all of it.

But then she ran out before I could blink, and I felt like I'd been sucker punched in the gut.

I guess I could call my therapist if I really wanted to talk about it. I have Coach Young from UCLA to thank for convincing me that I needed to talk to a professional. He was one of the only people at UCLA who knew what had happened back in Longwood. If it wasn't for him, I honestly don't know if I'd still be here.

I can't believe it's been two years since Chloe's been gone. Two years of not hearing her voice or seeing her smile. Some days fly by, and others feel like I'm standing frozen. Going through the motions without even realizing what's going on around me. The one person I want to call to help relieve me of this pain wants nothing to do with me.

The only thing that brings me distraction is soccer. I barely talk to the team outside of practice or games, which didn't make me the first pick for captain like I dreamed, but it does give me plenty of time to practice and hone my skills on my own. If I'm not playing soccer, I'm studying or sleeping.

My coaches think I'm dedicated. They don't realize it's depression.

I haven't told anyone in California my story. Why would anyone care? We all have our own shit.

The rest of the team is already out on the field, and I'm sitting here in the locker room, a blubbering, pathetic mess. Today is one of those rare days when I can't contain my grief. It overwhelms me. It consumes me.

The locker room is eerily quiet aside from my wailing sobs ricocheting off the walls, sending daggers straight through my aching chest.

Pull it together, Summers.

"Fuck!" I scream, dragging a hand over my face, attempting to wipe away the broken dam pouring out of me. I need to get to practice.

"Summers?" a familiar, gruff voice says gently. "You alright, kid?"

I must have taken too long, and Coach Young came to sweep the locker rooms.

Damn it. Pull yourself together.

It's no use. The dam has busted wide open, and nothing is stopping the complete breakdown I'm having in this stinky ass locker room. I'm sure this must be a shock to him. For the last year and a half, I've been as tough as stone. Nothing bothers me. Not coaches yelling at me, not when I got benched for three games because I reinjured my knee—nothing. I've damn sure never cried.

Coach Young comes over and sits down next to me on the wooden bench, placing an arm around my shoulder.

"Tell me about it," he says gently.

I tell him everything. About my sister. The accident. Leah and how we couldn't make it work because it was too fucking painful. All of it. He sits and listens intently as I blurt out the entire depressing saga that is my life. He comforts me and nods at the appropriate times. When I'm done, he pulls me tightly against his side. It's the first time since I've moved to California that I don't feel completely alone.

"Don't ever feel weak for showing your emotions," Coach Young implores. "It's a gift to have loved someone so deeply you ache their loss—whatever the reason. It's okay to allow yourself to feel. It's extremely brave of you to talk about it, and you really need to keep talking to someone about this stuff. I'm going to excuse you from today's practice, but you need to get help, okay? Professional help. I'm going to make an appointment for a campus therapist." I open my mouth to protest, but he cuts me off. "This is non-negotiable."

A fucking therapist? Like I'm crazy or something?

But he's right. I can't go on living like this. I need help. I need someone to talk to who can help me figure out how the fuck to be human again.

I thought going to therapy would mean I was weak, but I learned I was strong for acknowledging all of my trauma and my own personal weaknesses.

Leah ending things destroyed me, but I finally understood. We tried to fill our gaping wounds with each other, but you can't stop a flood by adding more water. We'd never been our own individuals outside of Chloe. She was always Chloe's best friend, her soul sister, and I was Chloe's twin brother. Neither of us had an individual identity outside of the sister between us.

It's almost ten at night, and I'm cleaning my plate from dinner when there's a loud knock on the door.

Who the hell could that possibly be?

It shouldn't be anything urgent from the bar. The day after Leah left, I installed a secure store room for the top shelf liquors with an individual keypad code for every employee and cameras inside.

I sigh, wipe my hands off on a kitchen towel, and toss it on the counter, then stride over to open the door.

"Hi," Leah says, panting, and my heart races at the sight of her.

"Hi," I echo, unable to stop the grin from spreading across my face at her appearance.

She's in her flight attendant uniform and has a small pink carry-on with her.

"Can I come in?" she asks uncomfortably.

"Yes, of course." I open the door wider and gesture for her to come inside.

She walks in and leaves her carry-on by the door, then walks to the kitchen without saying a word.

"Leah, what's going on? What are you doing here?"

"I–It's just that, well, I—" she says, pacing and flustered.

"Leah," I say, grabbing her shoulder and spinning her to face me. "What's going on?"

"I shouldn't have left," she says, looking pleadingly into my eyes.

"You're going to have to be more specific," I reply calmly with my hands still on her shoulders.

"After we saw each other again, and we… well, you know," she says awkwardly.

As if I could ever forget the only woman I've ever loved running out of my apartment after we kissed for the first time in eight years.

"Okay…" I say, unsure where she's going with this. "So you wish you'd stayed?"

"Yes. Just…" She sighs, placing her face in her hands.

"Let's start with why you're in your uniform?" I ask curiously, storing away the sexy image.

"I was supposed to get in earlier today," she says, sighing. "I had a quick layover in Dublin, which turned out to be not so quick. The plane wasn't working and then it was and—"

"Le, relevance," I say, trying to keep her on topic.

"Right, so I didn't get in until an hour ago, and I checked the schedule and saw you're playing a game in Barcelona on Sunday, and I just… I didn't want to waste any time and came here straight from the airport."

"Why?" I ask, rubbing my hands along her arms.

"I wanted to tell you that…" She pauses and sighs. "I don't want to go another decade without having you in my life."

I smile, and it's the most relief I've felt in a long time.

"I'm so happy to hear that," I say, running my fingers through her hair and tilting her face up to mine.

"I think we should be friends," she says, pursing her lips and awaiting my response.

I'm sorry, what?

"Friends?" I say, cocking a brow.

"Yes, *just* friends," she says, unconvinced, with pleading eyes.

"Okay…" I say, trying to mask my confusion and disappointment. "Can I ask why you're friendzoning me?"

"We have a… messy history," she says pointedly as if I'm not already blatantly aware. "And I can't handle losing you again. Especially if we were more… intimate."

Being friends with Leah would be infinitely better than being nothing. I surprise myself by saying, "Okay."

"Oh, thank god!" She smiles widely and throws her arms around me. Her sweet floral smell envelops me, and I realize just how damn hard this "friends" thing is going to be.

34

Leah

Jake and I are sitting in his living room, catching up on the past eight years.

"What's the tattoo on your arm?" I ask, continuing our game of twenty questions. I can see the ink peeking out from his shirt sleeve.

"Do you want to see it?" he asks.

"Absolutely."

He sits up and removes his T-shirt in slow motion—although I'm pretty sure it was just me praying I could slow down time—and throws it on the floor. My mouth goes completely dry.

Being just friends is going to be way harder than when we were in high school with him looking like he walked straight off the set of a fucking GQ shoot.

He sits back down, and I pull my eyes away from his perfect abdomen, sitting up to inspect the tattoo. Permanently etched on to his large bicep is a female angel looking to the side, with her long hair flowing in the wind, sitting on top of a wall that reads "I still sense your tether tied to my soul."

"Jake," I whisper, choking up. I trace my fingers over the black ink and feel closer to her.

I no longer feel debilitating pain from the reminders of Chloe. *At least, not always.* I'm thankful for having loved someone so deeply. Being here with Jake, I feel as if a weight has been lifted that I've been carrying for the last eight years. Or rather, the burden of the weight is being shared, rather than having to bear it alone.

"Do you have any tattoos?" Jake asks, his gaze skimming the length of my body. I've changed into sweats and a hoodie, but even fully dressed, I can feel his eyes burn into my skin.

"I've always wanted to get one, but I don't know. I guess it just never felt like the right time."

"Do you know what you want?"

"Yes," I respond without hesitation.

"Then let's go," he suggests, grinning.

"What?" I balk. "What do you mean, *let's go*? It's the middle of the night."

"Okay, and?"

"And… It's after midnight?"

"I know a guy." He smirks.

"Of course you do." I laugh, unable to help myself. I really do already know what I want, and getting it with Jake beside me couldn't feel more like perfect timing. "Okay, let's do it."

35

Jake

I called my friend, Luuk, to see if he was still at his shop that's only a few streets away from my building. He was, in fact, sleeping in his apartment above it, but he jumped out of bed when I said I'd let him drink free at *Chloe's* for a month. Not to mention he's my closest friend in Amsterdam that isn't on my team or payroll.

We walk into the small tattoo studio, and Luuk is already preparing his work area. Inside, there are two large couches along the windows for people who are waiting and two chairs for artists to work on clients. There's a large wall in the back with an abstract painting that reminds me of the ocean. It's a Leah Stone original.

Have I convinced almost every one of my friends to buy one of her gorgeous paintings to help support her passion? *Of course.*

Do I get a rush from the look Leah just gave me when she noticed it there? *Abso-fucking-lutely.*

My heart swells with pride.

"Hallo, you two," Luuk greets us in his thick Dutch accent.

"Hey, Luuk, thanks for getting us in on such short notice."

"My pleasure. Anything for Amsterdam's star footballer, no?" He winks. I grin and roll my eyes, silently thanking him for talking me up in front of Leah.

"This is my—er, Leah. She'll be the one getting the tattoo."

"Hi, Leah." Luuk smiles. "Jake says you already know what you want?"

"Yes," she says firmly.

"Do you have any pictures?" She pulls out her phone and scrolls through a hundred pictures before pausing and handing her phone to Luuk. "Okay, got it. In the same style?"

"Yes please," she responds.

"How big do you want it? And where?"

"Here," she replies, holding up her hand and gesturing to the length of her pinky finger.

"Oh yes, that will look nice. Let me just make the stencil and then we can get started. You can go ahead and sit over there." He gestures to the empty leather chair by his workstation.

"I can't believe I'm doing this," she says nervously while getting situated against the leather.

"Are you sure you want to? I don't want you to feel like I pressured you into this," I ask, with furrowed brows.

"I'm sure. I *definitely* want… no, *need* this," she says, looking at me assuredly as a soft smile spreads across her face.

"Okay. If you're sure." I smile.

Luuk comes back with the stencil. "Can you rest your arm here?"

She outstretches it on the large, cushioned arm of the chair, and he places the stencil on the inside of her pinky as requested.

"Is this placement fine?" he asks.

She twists her wrist to look at the placement. "Yeah, that looks good," she responds, fidgeting in her seat.

"Okay, let's get started." He rattles around at his workstation, then turns his attention on Leah's hand, ready to begin.

I haven't seen the tattoo she's getting yet, but it must be small if it's on her finger. She winces when the needle first touches her flesh, and I instinctively place a hand on her shoulder. She reaches up with her free hand and interlaces her fingers with mine. *She probably just needs moral support. It doesn't mean anything.* She grips harder as he continues. The muscles in her jaw are tight.

"Are you okay?" I lean down and mumble close to her ear.

"Yeah, it's not that bad, just stings a little," she admits, smiling embarrassedly at Luuk. "I don't know how the hell you sat through yours. It's huge."

"Yeah, me either," I mumble with a small smile. Luuk pauses for a moment and makes eye contact with me. He was the one who did the angel tattoo on my arm last year. He doesn't say anything, thank God, and continues on Leah's tattoo. I don't feel it necessary to tell her it took us three sessions to complete mine. Not because of the physical pain, but because of the meaning behind the tattoo.

Luuk is the only person in Amsterdam who knows about Chloe. At the first session, he was able to do the entire outline of the tattoo before I broke down crying. I tried so hard to fight it, but it was like the needle was poking directly into my soul and extracting all of the grief I had pushed down over the years since Chloe's death. We sat and talked for hours that night, no one else in the shop, and that was the beginning of our friendship. Leah has a visible scar from the accident, and although I wasn't in the car, I lost something that day too. I can't explain why, but I wanted a physical and visual reminder of the pain. A reminder that Chloe will always be a part of me even if she's gone.

I can feel Leah's shoulders rise and fall as her breathing gets more and more unsteady.

"Alright, all done," Luuk says to Leah as he wipes a napkin across her skin. "What do you think?"

She brushes something off her face, then twists her hand to see the tattoo.

"It's perfect," she whispers. Leah turns around, presenting it to me. The word "Lovebug" is etched in script with black ink on the inside of her left pinky. I always thought it was such a silly nickname, but I've never seen any tattoo more perfect.

"What do you think?" she says, smiling as a single tear rolls down her cheek. I brush the tear drop off with my thumb, then take her hand in mine.

"Perfect," I echo, brushing my finger over the word.

The skin is raised from the fresh tattoo, and I close my eyes, reading her flesh like braille. Luuk cleans the tattoo, bandages it, and hands Leah a business card with all the instructions to heal properly.

"Thank you," Leah says to me as soon as we exit Luuk's shop.

"Of course," I reply.

It's now two in the morning, and the city is growing quieter by the minute. It's too early for breakfast and too late to do anything else.

We return to my apartment and decide to watch a movie in the living room. I'm thankful she's not running out the door like last time. Not because I expect something more to happen, but because I'm not ready to say goodbye yet.

I don't think I'll ever be ready to say goodbye again.

"Jake," I hear a sweet voice say, pulling me from a deep sleep.

"Hmm," I hum in response.

"I have to go." She squeezes my shoulder gently. "I have a flight in a few hours, and I have to get to the airport."

I blink my eyes open, and her beautiful face comes into focus.

"Thank you for coming back," I tell her, wanting to say so much more.

"I'm glad we're friends again." She smiles while resting her chin on the edge of the couch, and it's a dagger to my pining heart.

"Yeah." I smile with pursed lips. "Friends."

She stands and I sit up. "Listen… I saw this on your counter." She hands me an envelope, and I glance down at the letter I received from Sophia. With it is a ticket to her graduation in a few weeks. "I really think you should come. It would mean everything to Sophia."

"I don't know if I ca—"

"Just think about it," she says, cutting off my bullshit excuse.

"I'll think about it." I nod my head as my throat drops to my stomach at the thought of returning to Longwood.

I'm a twenty-six-year-old grown-ass man afraid of a dot on a map.

I haven't been able to stop thinking about Sophia's graduation since Leah mentioned it a few days ago. She's right, it would mean the world to Sophia if I showed up. I also selfishly want to see Leah again… even if we're just friends. I spent fifteen years hiding my feelings in the friendzone, and I just agreed to enter it willingly. I'm either a masochist or an idiot.

I pull out my phone to call the only person who could maybe talk some sense into me. The only person who could possibly understand how difficult it would be for me to return to Longwood after all this time.

"Hey, honey," a smooth, feminine voice says on the other end of the line.

"Hey, Mom." I smile as I sit down on my living room couch.

"What's going on?" she asks in an upbeat tone.

"Not much. Just practice… games… the usual," I say, unsure how to approach the subject.

"What's really going on, J?" she asks with her don't-bullshit-me tone, and I exhale loudly as my knee starts bouncing uncontrollably.

"Sophia invited me to her graduation in a few weeks."

"Oh…" She pauses. "That's, uh, that's great, honey."

"I don't know if I'm going to go," I admit, dragging a hand through my hair.

"What?" She scoffs. "Of course you're going to go."

"I just…" I drag a hand down my face. "I don't know if I'm ready to go back there."

"Jacob, you're a grown man. This will be good for you… and it'll mean so much to Sophia," she says, echoing my friend.

"That's what Leah said," I say, chuckling, before I can think better of it.

"*Leah*?" Mom says, and I can hear the shock in her tone.

"Oh, uh, yeah." I bite my lower lip to stifle the smile on my face. Luckily, Mom can't see it. "She visited me this week."

"Oh my goodness, Jacob!" She shouts through the phone so loudly I have to pull it off my ear. "Why didn't you start with that? Oh, honey, I'm so happy you guys are finally reconnecting."

"Yeah…"

"She's always been so sweet on you. I'm so happy you're trying to make things work."

"We're just *friends*," I inform her as my lip upturns in disgust at the word that's going to be the death of me.

"Yeah, yeah." She waves me off. "You two were made for each other. It was honestly such a joy seeing your friendship bloom over the years. When you and Leah came to visit me when I—well, you know… That was such a hard day for both of you. The way you calmed one another… baby, that's special."

"It was high school, Mom." I frown and pick a piece of lint off the couch.

"Jacob, don't even act for a second like you and Leah were nothing more than a high school fling that fizzled out. Life's too short to not take risks on the things that matter."

Life's too short—don't waste a second of it.

"Alright, well, I've gotta go, Mom."

"Okay, love you, baby. Call me anytime."

"You know I will." I smile.

"Bye, baby."

The call ends, and I busy myself by vacuuming the living room and reorganizing the entire kitchen. My housekeeper's going to think I was robbed by Mr. Clean next time she comes.

After I've finally run out of things to move around, I grab my phone off the kitchen counter. My fingers hover over her name, trembling with uncertainty. I look up at the ceiling and curse myself for acting like such a pussy. *Fuck it.*

LEAH

Me

Hey Le, how's the tattoo healing up?

Minutes turn into hours, and she still hasn't responded. I've moved on to reorganizing my bookshelf, and the entire crime section is scattered across my bed when my phone finally bings, interrupting my playlist. I trip over a stack of books like a fucking idiot and snatch it up off the night stand.

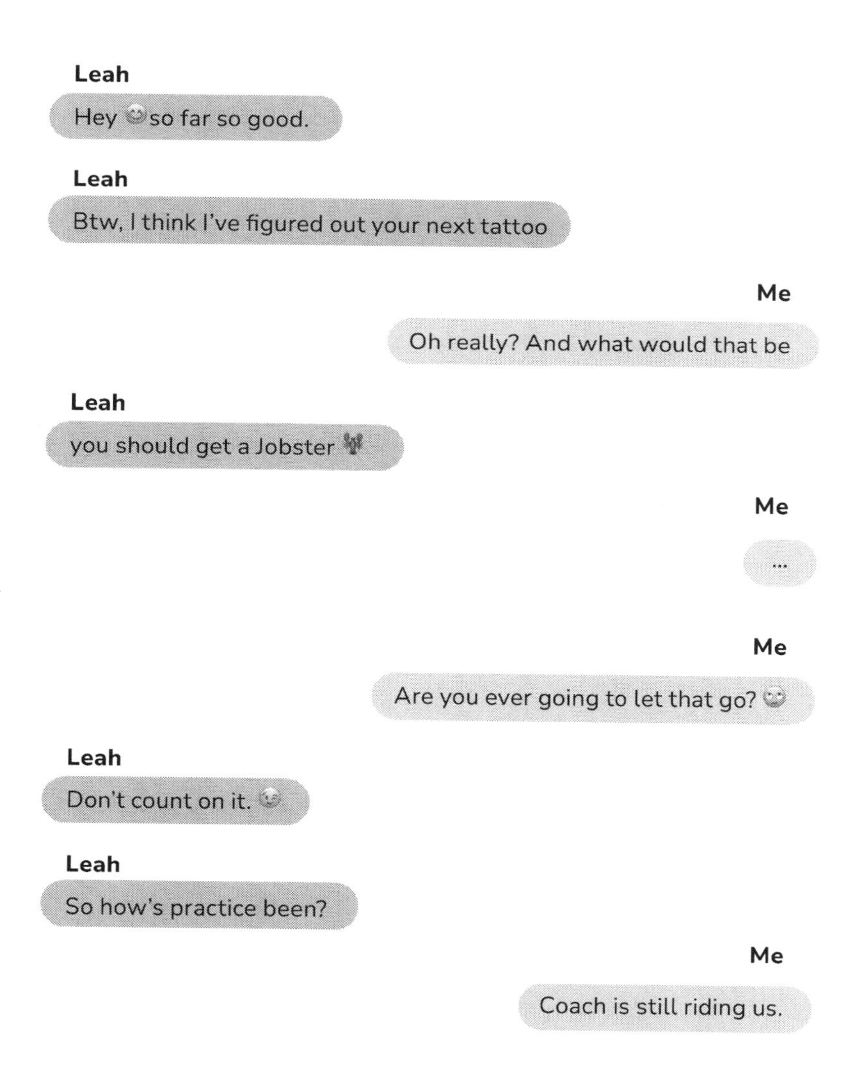

Me

HARD

Me

But it's nothing I can't handle

Leah

I'm sure 😏 Still can't believe you're a pro soccer player

Leah

I mean, don't get me wrong, I believe it. It's just crazy

Me

I know… I get it, trust me. It's my life and I still think it's crazy 😁

Leah

I can actually tell people I knew a pro soccer player. How cool

I knew.

Those two words are a bullet to the chest. I'm sure she's just trying to make conversation, but that sentence doesn't encompass a fraction of what we were to one another. Everything we still are. She should've said, *I can actually tell people a pro soccer player is still in love with me even after all this time*. Now *that's* cool.

Me

Uh oh, is Leah Stone using me for CLOUT? 🤨

Leah

Of course?

Leah

When do you leave for Barcelona?

Me

In two days

Me

Think you can get a layover in Spain for the weekend?

Leah

I wish... I'm taking Sophia to Europe for the summer for her grad trip and I've already got an overload of work trips lined up to make some extra cash 🙁

I want to tell her she can have my credit card and I'll pay for the whole damn trip if she'll just come to Barcelona for my game, but I stop myself. *Just friends, remember?*

Me

Maybe next time

Leah

Yeah

Leah

We'll see each other anyways when you come home for Sophia's graduation

Me

I'm still thinking about it...

Leah

What's the hold up?

Me

Le...

Leah

Jacob...

Me

It's just... a lot being home. You know?

Leah

Not really...

Me

I really don't wanna fight. Can we table this convo for now?

Leah

Sure, I just got home and leave tomorrow for another work trip so I'm gonna get some rest

Me

Okay, sleep tight. I'll call you later this week?

Leah

Sure

Four letters that translate to one word: hope.

36
Leah

I collapse into the bed of my hotel room after a long hot shower. I got into Dublin late this morning and took a tour of the Chester Beatty museum before coming back to the hotel. My eyelids are heavy, and I turn on the TV to Jake's game against Barcelona. Within minutes, Jake scores a goal on live television, and all my earlier exhaustion is replaced by adrenaline. I can't believe I've never watched him play professionally before. He's just as good—okay, better—than I remember.

The game passes quickly and before I know it, the whistle is blown and Amsterdam has beat Barcelona three to zero. I pour a glass of champagne from the minibar to celebrate Jake's win and order room service.

A few hours later, I'm scrolling through the pictures I took in Dublin today when Jake's name flashes across the screen, requesting a

FaceTime call. My heart drops to my stomach as I throw myself out of bed and start pacing the room. I catch a glimpse of myself in the mirror and take in my sloppy appearance. Frizzy hair, no make-up, oversized T-shirt... *Jake's* oversized T-shirt!

I answer the FaceTime call, then throw the phone on the comforter.

"Hey," I say coolly as I rip the T-shirt off over my head and toss it on the floor. I rip my bag apart for a different shirt and only find a tank top. *That'll have to do.*

"Hey... ceiling," Jake says, his tone full of amusement.

"Sorry," I grumble, throwing my hair into a messy bun. "Just give me a second."

He lets out a soft, deep chuckle I can feel in my bones. "Do you always get all pretty before answering FaceTime calls from your *friends*?"

I snatch the phone off the bed. "I am *not* getting all pretty." I narrow my eyes at him. "I needed to put clothes on."

"Then where are they?" He cocks a brow.

I look down and realize the insane amount of cleavage this tank is showing off and angle the camera so he can only see my face. "There. Now it's not a problem."

He rolls his eyes and shakes his head in amusement. "So what did you do today?"

I slide under the covers, pulling them up to my chin. "I'm in Dublin for a layover. I went to the museum here, and then I came back to the hotel room and watched TV."

"Watch anything good?" He smirks.

"Just some guy I used to know kicking ass on the field."

"Ouch." He stabs a fake knife in his chest.

"What?" I giggle with furrowed brows.

"Stop talking about me in the past tense. We're friends again, remember?" My chest aches. I definitely didn't say it that way to hurt him.

"Yeah." I smile with pursed lips. "You're right, sorry."

"So did you enjoy watching the game?" His smile returns.

"Yeah." I laugh, rolling onto my back and holding the phone above my face. "It was actually a lot more exciting than I thought it would be."

"Good." He chuckles.

"Do you ever get freaked out playing in front of so many people?"

"I used to…" He smirks with a shrug. "But eventually, I just got over it. I try to drown out the noise when I'm on the field."

"That's amazing." I laugh. "I can't even drown out my coworkers on the plane when they chew gum."

"You used to scowl at me for eating chips too loud." He smiles and bites his lower lip.

"Yeah." I narrow my eyes. "Because I couldn't hear the movie… Hopefully you've gotten rid of that annoying quirk."

"Guess you'll just have to find out next time we watch a movie." He smirks. "So where to next?"

"I have a flight back to Orlando tomorrow and then leave for Seattle in a few days." I sigh, thinking about how exhausted I am from all the extra shifts.

"Do you always work this much?" His tone is laced with concern.

"No." I smile faintly. "Just trying to make up for the time I'll miss over the summer for Soph's and my vacation."

"Good." He lets out a heavy breath. "It can't be healthy to travel nonstop and never sleep."

"Says the pro-soccer player." I chuckle. "Isn't that in your job description?"

"Yeah." He cocks a brow. "But I get paid enough to lose sleep. Do you?"

"Not really, no." I shake my head and as if on cue, a yawn comes out of my mouth in the least sexy of ways.

"Okay, sleepy girl." Jake laughs. "I think it's time for bed."

"But *Daddyyy*," I whine teasingly. "I don't wanna."

"Sorry, sweetheart," he says, playing along. "It's sleepy time."

I giggle. "Okay, *fine*. If I must."

He pauses and bites his lower lip. I can tell there's something on his mind, so I wait to hang up. "Le?"

I tilt my head to the side. "Yeah?"

"Are friends allowed to tell friends they miss each other?" His voice is low, gravelly, and my god, is it sexy.

My lips curl upward at the corners as I struggle for air. "Yeah… I think that would be okay."

He swallows hard. "I miss you, Le."

I smile softly as my heart pounds wildly in my chest. "I miss you too, Jake."

We hang up the phone and I roll over, staring at the wall until the sun comes up.

What am I doing?

I'm finally back in Longwood after working my ass off the past few weeks, and I'm surprised I don't have to glue my eyelids open to stay awake. Sophia's graduation is tomorrow, and we leave a week later for Europe. I usually hate working so much, but I was thankful for the distraction after seeing Jake in Amsterdam again.

Are friends allowed to tell friends they miss each other?

I'm holding out hope he'll show up for Sophia's graduation, although I know it's unlikely.

Sophia is modeling the fifteenth dress option for graduation, twirling in front of her bedroom mirror.

"Any plans for after graduation?" I ask.

"Just a party at the springs," she says casually, changing back into her pajamas, having still not settled on an outfit.

"Typical." I grin, reminiscing on the olden days.

"Is Will gonna be home for dinner tonight?"

"Nope, he's uh… got a date." She scrunches her nose.

"A *what?*" I squeal.

"A d-a-t-e," she says, literally spelling it out for me.

"Wow." I smile. "Good for him."

"Yeah…" The corner of her mouth curves upward. "But it's still a little weird, you know? He's my dad. And I know he and Mom have been officially divorced for over six years, but I'm used to it being just me and Dad. What if this new lady comes in and changes everything?"

"Just give her a chance. Your dad deserves happiness. We all do," I remind myself.

"Yeah, I guess you're right." She scrunches her face. "He was fighting a smile when he told me about the date."

"Well, how about we have a girl's night tonight to get you ready for graduation? We can order pizza, do our nails, facials, the whole nine yards." I waggle my eyebrows.

"I'd be honored, ma lady." Sophia curtsies, princess style, and I shake my head, laughing.

I love that silly girl.

"Oh my God, what is that?" she squeals, grabbing my hand and prying open my fingers, presumably so she can examine my new tattoo.

"I got it a few weeks ago." I smirk.

"I love it." She smiles softly and grazes a finger over the letters. "It's perfect."

"Me too." I pull her in for a tight hug.

"I can't believe you got it without me though." She puts her hands on her hips and looks at me with raised brows. "I totally would've gotten a matching tattoo." She sticks out her lower lip, pouting.

"We'll find a place on our trip, okay? It'll be our special thing." I wink.

"Pinky promise?" she asks, with raised brows.

"Pinky promise," I reply, hooking my inked finger with hers.

I'm sitting on the couch of Sophia's living room with a slice of pizza hanging out of my mouth when the doorbell rings. "I'll get it," I tell Sophia as I stand up. "I wanted to get another glass of wine anyways."

"Can I have one too?" she asks, and I narrow my eyes at her.

"Fine, one glass. We'll call it research for our trip." I wink.

I walk to the front door and look through the peephole to see Jake standing uncomfortably on the other side with a duffle swung over his shoulder.

Why must he always look so damn sexy?

I take a breath and swing the door open.

"Is *the* Jake Summers knocking on his own front door right now?" I ask, cocking a brow.

He shifts on his feet and shrugs. "I wasn't sure what else to do." He bites his lower lip to stifle a smile, and I open the door wider.

"Well, are you going to come in?"

Sophia rounds the corner as the door clicks behind us. "Who was it?" Her mouth falls open. "Oh my god. Jake!" she screams before running and leaping into his arms. He catches her effortlessly, of course, crushing her in a tight embrace.

"Surprise, Bug." He laughs. "How's our graduate doing?"

"Amazing, now that you're here." She beams up at him.

"So what's with the..." he questions, looking at the two of us and pointing at his face.

"Huh?" I stop at the hallway mirror to see that my face is completely covered in a dark green seaweed mask.

"Shit," I mutter, trying to contain my embarrassment. Although Jake has seen me in much worse shape, this is definitely not how you want your *friend* to see you. Especially not a friend that looks like *that.* I look like Shrek while he's standing there, the embodiment of David Beckham's hotter younger brother.

"We'll be back," Sophia says, laughing and dragging me upstairs so we can wash our masks off in her bathroom.

"Did you know he was coming?" She bursts as soon as we're out of Jake's earshot. My heart is racing. *I can't believe he actually came.*

"No," I say honestly, although it's not the full truth. She narrows her eyes at me.

"When's the last time you saw him?" she probes.

"Soph." I raise my eyebrows.

"Leah."

"Fine, I saw him the last time I was in Amsterdam."

"I knew it!" she shouts.

"Shhhhh!" I chastise.

"Why didn't you tell me you saw him again?" She frowns.

"He mentioned coming home for your graduation, and I was afraid to get your hopes up if he didn't," I lie. I was also afraid to even admit out loud that he was back in my life. I'm not ready to think about what all that could mean.

"Well, he frickin' came!" She beams. "Did he go with you to get the tattoo?"

"Yes." I smile with pursed lips.

"Well, isn't that just the cutest thing since Allie came back for Noah," Sophia squeals.

"Sophia," I snap, unable to keep my lips from curving up slightly. "Don't compare us to a Nicholas Sparks book."

"Sorry," she grumbles, rolling her eyes.

"We're *friends*, just like you suggested," I say pointedly.

"I know. I know." She throws her hands up in defense. "Still cute though," she mumbles under her breath.

We walk into the living room where Jake has already taken over the TV.

"Some things never change," Sophia whispers with a grin. *Isn't that the truth?*

Being around Jake in such a familiar setting is strangely normal. It's like we're in high school again, except Sophia isn't just a little kid anymore and can actually participate in our "grown-up" conversations.

"Think you girls will make it to Amsterdam during your Euro trip?" Jake asks.

"I think we can make that happen," Sophia says, grinning and shooting me a wink. I widen my eyes at her, mentally telling her to *Shut. Up.*

"Oh, that would be awesome. You guys can stay with me." He pauses. "Or there's a really cool hotel my friend owns down the street where—"

"No, we'll definitely stay with you," my wing woman agrees without my input.

"Great." He smiles wide. "And we can run the route by the river you love, Soph."

"Cool beans, I just got new Nikes last week," she says, her face lighting up. Her phone rings on the coffee table. "Oh, it's Sage, I've gotta take this."

She picks up the phone and puts it to her ear. "Hey, I'm just hanging out with Leah… and *my brother*!" She bubbles with excitement. "I know, right?" She glances between Jake and me. "I don't know. I wasn't able to retrieve that bit of… information…" she says, obviously trying to talk in code. "Tonight? Oh, I don't know, I kind of had plans with Leah." She looks at me with a sad smile.

"What does she want, Soph?" I probe.

"She's asking if I want to sleep over tonight before graduation."

"Go," I offer.

"Are you sure?"

"Yeah, of course." I smile softly. "We'll spend plenty of time together this summer. You only have one night before graduation to spend with your best friend."

"Okay." She smiles.

"How about we drive you and maybe Jake and I can go downtown?" I grin at Jake.

"Okay," Sophia says, heading upstairs to pack her stuff.

"What's downtown?"

"Just a local bar, but it's a nice atmosphere. I mean, not as nice as your place, but nice nonetheless."

"Sure. But I need to shower and stuff. I'm covered in airplane germs." He shivers.

"Yeah, I need to get ready too. Obviously," I say, gesturing at my sloppy appearance.

I head over to my house to get ready. My parents are out of town for the next few days, shocker, so I go straight to my room. I'm buzzing with nervous energy at the anticipation of spending a night out with Jake.

Tequila better not make my clothes fall off tonight.

37

Jake

It feels surreal being home for the first time in eight years. I'm exhausted from the long travel day, but Leah's offer was a hell of a lot more enticing than sleep. Since she left, I haven't been able to stop thinking about her. Not that that's entirely different from any other day of my life. There was just new fuel added to my fantasies.

After dropping off Sophia, Leah drags me into the diviest bar in town, Roy's, and it is packed to the brim.

"I can't believe so many people actually *want* to be in a place like this," I grumble in Leah's ear as we make our way towards the bar. It smells like old beer, stale pretzels, and sweat. *Is this the kind of shithole Leah thought I ran? Jesus.*

"Don't be a bar snob." She rolls her eyes, and I grin at her teasing.

We finally make it to the bar, and I capture the attention of the bartender immediately. "Well, if it isn't the heartbreaker of Longwood gracing us mere mortals with his presence." The brunette grins.

"Hey, Laura." Leah smiles at her genuinely. *What the fuck?*

"Long time no see." I smile.

"No kidding. How'd you finally drag this one back to town?" She probes like they're old friends. *Are they?*

"Bribery at its finest," Leah says, briefly flicking her gaze to mine with a sexy as fuck grin.

"What'll it be?" Laura inquires, wiping down the counter in front of us.

"I'll have a scotch on the rocks, and Leah will have whatever the sweetest drink on the menu is."

"Hey." She hits me on the bicep. "My palate has matured since senior year."

"Your usual, Leah?" Laura asks her with a raised brow.

"Yes, please," she replies, then narrows her eyes at me as Laura walks away.

A few minutes later she comes back with our drinks. She places the scotch in front of me and a layered orange-and-red drink in front of Leah, then walks away. I glance at Leah with raised eyebrows, smirking.

"Fine, it hasn't improved that much," she mumbles sheepishly, taking a sip and closing her eyes. The corners of her mouth tug up into a smile as soon as the liquid hits her tongue. "Mmm, so good."

I chuckle at her dramatics as we make our way towards an empty high-top with two chairs on each side. I place the palm of my free hand against the small of her back, guiding her through the crowd, and we sit on the same side of the small table.

"So what *did* you order?" I ask, placing my arm loosely on the back of her chair next to me.

"Tequila sunrise." She smirks.

Tequila makes her clothes fall off. The familiar song plays on a loop in my head.

"You do know what they say about tequila, right?" I ask with a cocked brow.

She smirks at me. "Are you complaining?"

"Not even in the slightest." I grin.

"I'm glad you came," she says, smiling softly.

"Me too," I admit, taking a sip of my bottom shelf scotch. The cheap shit burns all the way down.

"Will's going to freak," she says, shaking her head and laughing.

"I hope so," I say nervously.

"Why shouldn't he? He's your dad."

"I know, he's just been on me about coming home for years. I know he'll give me shit that this is the first time."

"Rightfully deserved shit," she points out in her blunt way that I hate to love so much.

"I guess you're right," I admit.

"What else is new?" she says.

I can't stop myself from reaching up and brushing a hair behind her ear. Her breath hitches at the contact.

"Do you come here often?" I ask, brushing her back with my fingertips. I can feel the goosebumps appear beneath them.

"Is that a pickup line from the heartbreaker of Longwood?" She giggles, covering her heart with her palm.

"Haha. I meant do you frequent this shithole often, or is it just your form of punishment for my decade of absence from our beloved hometown?" I narrow my eyes at her, and she throws her head back, laughing.

"Oh, come on. Trust me, this place grows on you," she says, plucking out a pretzel from the small wooden bowl on the table and popping it in her mouth.

"Is this the kind of place you thought I owned?" I ask, forcibly removing my hand from her burning skin and placing it back on the top of the chair behind her.

Friends, I remind myself. *She just wants to be friends.*

"Maybe." She shrugs.

I scoff. "Were you impressed that it wasn't?"

"Yes, Chloe's is fucking incredible, Jake. I mean, besides your theft problems." She grins, but there's a hint of annoyance in her voice.

"I added a secure storage room so the staff can access the high shelf liquors without me. So that shouldn't be a problem anymore."

"Oh, that's good. No more getting interrupted when you have pretty girls in your apartment," she says, smiling with pursed lips.

"Nope," I say, popping the *p*, enjoying the little green monster dancing in her eyes.

"No *fucking* way," a deep male voice boasts, slapping me on the back. I look up and see a broad-shouldered, blonde-haired, brown-eyed, smirking, lovable idiot that I haven't spoken to in years.

"Matt? Holy shit." I laugh before jumping up to give him a tight hug. When I left for college, Leah and my family weren't the only ones I left behind. Matt tried to stay in contact for a while, but he eventually drifted away too. Although, by his greeting, he doesn't seem to be hanging on to that grudge.

"What the hell are you doing here?" he asks.

"Sophia's high school graduation is tomorrow."

"Ah, okay. Awesome." He turns his attention towards Leah. "And if it isn't the most beautiful girl in every room." He smiles, walking over and pulling her in for a tight hug, then kissing the side of her head. *The fuck?* My blood runs hot, and my hands form into fists at my side.

"Hey, Matty." She beams up at him, starry-eyed. "Where's Jorge?"

"He's on his way."

"Okay, perfect."

"Did you orchestrate this?" I ask her.

"What can I say, I thrive on surprising you."

"Who's Jorge?" I ask Matt.

"Oh, he's my—"

"You'll see." Leah cuts him off with a smile, and Matt winks at her. My shoulders tense.

"So what are you doing for work?" I ask Matt.

"I'm a real estate agent," he replies, smiling.

"That's great, man," I say. It's so weird seeing him after all these years. I feel guilty for letting all that time pass between us when all he ever did was be there for me. "Look, Matt, I don't want to bring down the mood, but I just, I'm sorry I didn't keep in touch."

"It's alright, J. Don't worry about it, okay? Water under the bridge."

He seems like the same old Matt. Light, airy, fun, just way more mature. I can't imagine the man in front of me doing a thirty-second keg stand before streaking into the springs.

"Hey, honey," a tall twenty-something man says, striding up to our table. He has curly brown hair, dark brown eyes, and a coppery skin tone.

"Excuse—" My words escape me as his lips press to Matt's. *What the hell?* My mouth is hanging open, and Leah is giggling into her drink at my reaction.

He rounds the table to Leah and hugs her from the side. "Hey, gorgeous." He kisses her on the side of the head, and she melts into him for a brief moment. *What is going on?*

"Hi, I'm Jorge," the man says, reaching his hand out to me, and I return the gesture.

Leah reaches over and pushes my chin up with her finger. "You're going to catch flies in there if you're not careful," she teases, closing my mouth that was apparently hanging open.

"I'm sorry, I, I just, I guess I missed a lot over the last eight years." I chuckle, shaking my head.

"Well, if you would have ever picked up your damn phone, you would have learned a thing or two," Matt snarks.

Leah smirks and raises her eyebrows while tipping her glass toward Matt. "Yeah, like that Trey's moved to BFE North Carolina after inheriting a hotel from his rich as fuck grandpa."

"Lucky bastard." Matt laughs and clinks her glass.

"Damn. I really have missed a fuck ton, huh?" I smile faintly. "How long have you, er, have you guys—"

"How long have I been dating men?" Matt interjects calmly. An amused smile plays on his lips.

"I guess, yeah," I say sheepishly. "I'm sorry, am I being offensive? I'm totally not judging. I'm just… surprised." *How about completely fucking shocked?*

"Well, you know I've always been a flirt. In college, I got a little more experimental and started hooking up with guys too. Turns out I play for both teams," he says, pretending to throw a football. "I met Jorge a few years ago after I graduated college. Now we live together with our thirty cats." He pauses and looks at Jorge, then chuckles. "Okay that's a lie," he continues. "There's only one, Jose Cuervo, but she definitely eats enough for thirty." They all laugh together, and I feel left out of the inside joke.

"Got any pictures?" I ask the proud cat dad. He shows me his lock screen, and I almost choke on my drink. "Jesus, fuck. That is the ugliest thing I have ever seen." One of those naked hairless cats is lying perched on a bed of fluffy pillows. *Spoiled little shit.*

Jorge gasps, throwing a hand over his chest. "Excuse me?"

"How dare you!" Matt narrows his eyes at me. "She's fucking adorable." He turns the phone back to himself, sticking a pouty lip at it. "Aren't you, girl?" His mouth lowers, kissing the screen like a crazy cat lady. *Bro.*

"But why is she naked?" I ask, trying to understand why anyone would choose to look at something so ugly on a regular basis.

Matt shrugs. "Tequila made her hair fall off."

Leah throws her head back, laughing, and the sweet sound vibrates to my bones.

38
Leah

I walk up to the bar to order another drink and, honestly, have a little girl talk with Laura. I never would have expected she'd become one of my closest friends, but here we are. She's at the other end of the bar with her back to me, talking to a group of customers, so I take a seat on a free stool. She laughs, moving out of the way, and Cole Danvers, surrounded by a few other officers from the Longwood Police Department, sits there sipping on a glass of amber-colored liquid. He's devilishly handsome as always, with a smug smile on his face as he embarrassingly flirts with Laura.

He's at Roy's almost every time I am, but we've gotten used to being around one another over the years. Cole's attractive and really lets it get to his head—he's a hell of a darts partner though. Laura notices me and smiles, holding up a finger.

A few minutes later, she comes over and places a new tequila sunrise in front of me.

"It's from Cole." She points to the other end of the bar. "He said it was his apology for spilling his drink on you last time you were here."

Because apparently having drinks spilled on me is my thing.

"He should be sorry. I smelled like Jack Daniels for two days." I chuckle while picking up the drink and looking over to him. Cole tips his glass in my direction, and I return the gesture of the invisible cheers.

"He does know you're married, right?" I ask her, gesturing slyly at Cole, who's turned his attention back to the only love of his life: alcohol.

"He's harmless." She smirks. "Besides, he was just filling me in on that hit and run case from a few months back."

"Any updates on that?"

She frowns, shaking her head. "No."

"Damn…" I say sadly.

She looks over my shoulder then narrows her eyes at me. "So, how could you not tell me you reconnected with Jake?"

"It's just…" I say, sighing. "It's still all really new."

"Are you guys… dating?" she probes with a wide smile.

"No." I roll my eyes and try not to smile.

"Why the hell not?" she scoffs.

"Laura… you know how hard it was for me to get over Jake. I don't think I can do that twice," I say quietly.

"So you're *just* friends?"

"Yep," I say, popping the *p*.

"And how's that going?" she asks, amused.

"It's harder than I thought it would be," I admit.

"Well, I don't doubt that for a second," she says, laughing. "He's sex on a stick."

"Laura," I squeal, giggling.

"What?" she says, drying a clean glass off and placing it next to the others. "I love James, believe me. But I'm still allowed to admit when a ten out of ten walks into our normally seven—max—bar."

"You're hilarious," I say, shaking my head at her.

"I'm just being honest. You'd be insane to not at least try to make things work with him," she says, shaking her head. "And also, when the hell have you ever dressed like *that*..." She waves a finger up and down at my outfit. "In here."

"Just cause we're friends doesn't mean I can't look nice," I say pointedly.

"Girl, you look *hot*. And not an innocent oh-you-look-amazing-nice-outfit kind of hot," she says, bobbing her head sassily. "You look fuck-me-in-the-bathroom-right-now hot."

"Laura," I giggle. "You're too much."

"I'm just saying. Friends? With him?" She shakes her head. "Such a waste."

"Why are you shitting on this friend thing so hard?" I ask her with furrowed brows.

"Leah," she says, taking my hand and looking at me intently. "I just don't want you to waste time pushing away the beautiful inevitable." She pauses and takes a deep breath. "You guys were friends for years before you took the next step. And I know that everything with Chloe hurt like hell... but y'all are so much further down the road now. Give the poor guy another chance."

I squeeze her hand. "I just... What if it doesn't work out?"

"Babe," she says. "You cannot play the what-if game here. You can't avoid this because you're afraid. Think about how you'd feel if Jake called you up one day and invited you to *his* wedding... with another woman." Bile rises in my throat at the mere thought, and my face twists into a look of disgust. Laura bursts out laughing at my reaction.

I scrunch my face at her with narrowed eyes. "He probably doesn't even feel that way about me anymore," I say quietly.

I know we kissed, but maybe it was more of a caught-up-in-the-moment kind of thing. And that was before I friendzoned him.

"I need you to be cool when I tell you this, okay?" she says, giving me a pointed look.

"Okay…" I say hesitantly.

"It's so indisputably obvious Jake is still into you." She flicks her gaze behind my shoulder, then back to me. "He hasn't taken his eyes off you since the moment you walked over here."

My head snaps in his direction.

"Way to play it cool." She laughs.

Laura's right. Jake's eyes are glued on me. Heat flushes throughout my body from the intensity of his stare. He cocks his brow, and his mouth turns up into the sexiest damn smile I've ever seen.

"Girl," Laura says, chuckling. "If you think that man isn't still in love with you, you're an idiot. And if you think you're never going to want more than friendship with him, then you're just straight crazy."

"I am so fucked," I say, unable to pull my eyes away from Jake.

"You are so fucked," she agrees, laughing.

39
Jake

"Here you go." Laura places four tequila shots on the table.

We each take one and lift it in the air. "Here's to those who wish us well, all the rest can go to hell," Matt says, winking at me. We clink glasses, and Leah downs hers without even a flinch.

Fuck, why was that so sexy?

The conversation is so easy, it feels like we're back in high school again. Except the topics of conversation would bore the shit out of a teenager.

Do you own a house?

Have you been investing in crypto?

Did you see who's running for president again next year?

Yes. Yes. And unfortunately, yes.

Leah is sitting across from me, listening intently to Matt drone on about his latest house up for sale. I can't stop staring, memorizing the features of that pretty face. It's like I'm rewiring my brain to stop thinking about the eighteen-year-old girl I lost years ago and start picturing the bombshell sitting in front of me.

"So what's with you two?" Jorge inquires, gesturing between Leah and me.

"What do you mean?" I ask.

"Like, are you guys a thing, or…?"

"Jorge," Matt chastises.

"What? I'm curious. You're, well… delicious looking," he says, eyeing me up and down. I fold into myself at the compliment, my cheeks flushing with heat.

"Hey," Matt chastises again.

"Oh, calm down, honey, you know I only have eyes for you. Also, my gaydar is sadly unmoving on this one." He pouts.

"You guys are hilarious." I chuckle, and Leah is giggling wildly. She's drunk, and her giddiness is contagious. I've smiled so much tonight my face hurts. Leah shrugs off the jean jacket she had on, and it looks like the tequila is doing its job. I smirk to myself, and she narrows her eyes at me before taking another sip of her drink.

"So as I was saying before I was so *rudely* interrupted," Jorge continues, shooting Matt heart-filled dagger eyes. "*You're* delicious looking, and Leah is, well, Leah." He gestures up and down at her. I certainly don't need him to point out how stunning she is. "You'd be an idiot not to snatch her up."

"Jorge," Leah snips with wide eyes. "Leave the poor man alone."

"Hey, I'm just talking facts. There's nothing I love more than two pretty people being together." Jorge grins, looking at Matt, and then plants a soft kiss on his lips.

"We're just *friends*," I say, smirking in an attempt to mask my disappointment. "Should there be a status update, I promise you'll be my first call."

"That's all I ask." He winks, tipping the edge of his glass towards me.

I can't wipe the stupid grin off my face as my gaze returns to Leah. She's staring at me with those come-fuck-me eyes while biting her lip, and *fuckkkk meee.* My erection strains painfully against the fabric of my tight blue jeans. She places her hand on my knee and squeezes it three times.

If this is how she acts with her friends, I'm going to lose my fucking mind.

"I have to go to the bathroom," Leah tells us, hopping off her stool. "I'll be right back."

"Okay," I say, apparently being the only one who was paying attention to her. She grins at me, then saunters away.

"Okay, spill," Matt says, leveling the second Leah's out of earshot.

"Spill what?" I ask with a cocked brow.

"You show up all these years later with that woman, her looking at you like that. Come on, spill."

"We're just friends," I repeat, sighing.

Matt and Jorge look at one another with wide smiles.

"Jake, I know how crazy you were about her. Don't fuck this up again," Matt says, scolding me like a school child.

"Wow, no foreplay with small talk, huh? Straight to the deep shit." I chuckle.

"Hey, what can I say? I'm dating a man who has a lot of opinions that he is overly vocal about." Matt laughs. "I guess it's rubbed off."

"You know what? I have to go to the bathroom too," I say as I hop off the bar stool. "I'll be right back."

"Mm-hmm… Have fun in there."

"Oh, shut up, Matty." I laugh.

I walk into the hallway just as Leah exits the bathroom.

"Hey," she says, stopping in the door frame when she spots me. She bites her lower lip to stifle a smile.

"Hey," I say with a crooked grin, narrowing my eyes at her.

"This is the ladies room, you know?" she teases, grinning

seductively. I take a step toward her, and she steps back into the bathroom. It's a single stall bathroom with a lock. *Thank God.* I twist it before turning around to gaze at her gorgeous freckled face.

"Can I help you with something?" she says, unable to stifle the playful smile upon her pink lips.

"You can't look at me with those come-fuck-me eyes in the middle of a crowded bar, slide your hand up my leg, then run off and not expect me to find you the second you're alone."

Her lips curve into a wide smile, those gorgeous dimples on full display.

"I don't know what you're talking about," she says, placing her arms around my neck.

"Uh-huh. Sure." I lift her by the hips and unintentionally slam her back against the wall, encouraging her to wrap her legs around my waist. It knocks a breath out of her, but she doesn't seem to mind. The heels of her boots dig into my ass, and my dick twitches at the sensation. "You're telling me you *weren't* hoping I was going to follow you in here?"

"Didn't even cross my mind," she says, shaking her head unconvincingly.

"You weren't hoping I'd slide my hands inside your little silk dress." I graze a warm hand up her thigh, under her dress, and rest it on top of the thin string on her hip. She squirms beneath me as I angle my hard dick against her warm center.

"Lucky coincidence," she says, her breath hitching as a provocative smile gives me encouragement to continue her torment.

"I'm sure you weren't fantasizing I'd do this." I angle my mouth down to the valley of her neck, flicking it lightly with my tongue. I trace the notches of her throat down to the center of her chest, between her breasts, tugging down the material of her dress with my chin. I use my thumb to rub on top of the silk fabric over her hardened nipples, and she arches into me in response. I hold her against me by her ass cheeks, her dress sliding up to her stomach, then carry her over to the countertop and set her down on the edge.

"I'm sure you haven't been fantasizing for weeks about continuing what we started in my kitchen." She's wearing a black lace thong, and I can see through the sheer material. "You certainly didn't put *these* on just for me." I rub my thumb over the thin lace above her most sensitive spot. She's already soaking through the fabric and squirms under my touch. "You're dripping wet, baby," I mumble into her mouth. "Are you still sure you didn't want me to follow you in here?"

"Like I said, it was a happy accident," she pants.

"Admit you'll never be satisfied with us *just* being friends."

"We can be friends with benefits." She grins.

The fuck we can.

I lower my face down directly in front of her center, inhaling deeply through my nose. I tease the edge of her thong with my fingertips before pulling it to the side, exposing her swollen wet lips. "Mmmm," I hum in approval. I explore with my tongue, memorizing her new taste as the sweetness coats my lips.

"Oh my God," she whimpers. I flick my tongue against her swollen bud, and she thrashes against me. I pull my mouth away abruptly, and she stares down at me in shock.

"What are we?" I stare up at her with my mouth just inches from her sensitive skin. I breathe out a warm breath, and she squirms impatiently.

"We're friends." She smirks, knowing exactly how much she's driving me crazy.

"Do all your friends know how sweet your pussy tastes?" I ask, narrowing my eyes and licking the taste of her on my lips.

She bites her lip and throws her head back in frustration. "Jake, please." She arches her back, then angles her glistening lips toward my face in invitation.

"Admit you still want this. Admit you still want me as more than a fucking friend, and *maybe* I'll keep going." I breathe a hot breath against her while squeezing her soft thighs.

The war is waging behind her smoldering eyes. Love versus lust. She knows once those words escape her pretty little lips, there's no going back. But I know Leah, and I know for us love and lust go hand in hand.

I slide up her body and grab her left hand, bringing it between us.

"Why have you never taken this off?" I ask, grazing my finger against the gold band I gave her for her eighteenth birthday.

"Jake," she says, her breathing heavy.

"You say you want to be friends. Why have you never taken this off? Why do you keep it on your wedding finger, showing the entire damn world you're already claimed?"

She glances down at her finger, then back to me. She bites her lower lip, then releases it slowly.

"Because I am," she admits. "Because I always have been."

"Tell me what you want me to do to you." She squirms in search of my thumb as I glide it along her wet entrance.

"I want you to claim me again," she whimpers, gasping for air.

"Baby, I already own you."

I grab her chin in my hand and pull her lips to mine, kissing her deeply as my thumb runs along her clit towards her dripping wet entrance. I slide back down her body and kiss the insides of her thighs, taking my time towards her perfect pink pussy.

"I'm soaked for you," she rasps. "Show me how much you missed me, Jacob."

"That's my dirty girl." I grin, sliding two fingers into her opening, and she gasps. I stroke against her inside walls and bring my hungry mouth back to taste her.

"Oh *fuck*," she moans loudly. I cover her mouth with my palm, stifling her whimpers.

"Quiet, baby. I'm the only one allowed to hear you fall apart."

I increase my pace inside of her as she clutches around my aching fingers. I remove my palm from her mouth and glide it down her chest, taking her breast in my hand, then pinch her nipple, and she lets out a quiet squeal.

"I'm coming," she pants.

She convulses around my fingers. I slide my hand to her back, holding her against my face so I don't lose the spot that's carrying her to heaven, allowing her to ride out the euphoric wave. When her breath steadies, I remove my fingers and bring them to my mouth, sucking her sweet juices off of them as she watches while breathing heavily. I plant a kiss on her throbbing flesh, then place her thong back in place before standing up to her eye level.

"Wow," she says, still breathless. I kiss her softly on the lips, allowing her to taste herself, my dick twitching in my jeans.

"Don't ever lie to me again." I raise an eyebrow with a smirk.

"Why not? Are you going to punish me again?"

"I just might," I say with a smirk.

"Do you have a condom with you?" She rubs her hand along the front pocket of my jeans.

"Why?" I ask, pretending to be surprised.

"I just thought you might wanna…" She waggles her eyebrows at me, and her adorable antics *almost* have me break my pretend-to-be-serious facade. "You know."

"Leah." I run my hands through her hair and angle her face so I'm looking directly into her lust-filled eyes. "When I fuck you again for the first time, it's not going to be on the floor of this shitty bar bathroom."

Her eyes widen as she drags her lower lip between her teeth, and I may in fact be fucking Leah on this floor in approximately thirty seconds.

"I can take care of you in other ways." She smirks, placing her hand against my dick that's straining against my jeans.

Pull yourself together, Summers.

As much as I want to give in, I already can't believe no one has banged on the door since we've been in here. I don't want to get interrupted mid blowjob.

"How about I pay the tab and we get out of here?" I offer, cupping her face in my hands.

"Deal." She grins, kissing me on the lips.

After I readjust myself, we walk out of the bathroom to a surprisingly empty hallway. I glance at the bathroom door and see a handwritten Out of Order sign taped to it. It looks like it was written by a five year old. I chuckle quietly and shake my head.

"We're going to get the bill and head out," Leah says to Matt and Jorge when we get to the table.

"Mm-hmm, okay," they say, smirking at us.

"Here, go pay the tab. I'll be right there," I tell Leah, handing her my credit card.

"Sir, yes, sir." She grins, disappearing towards the bar.

"Did you tape a sign on the women's bathroom?" I accuse Matt, unable to wipe the grin off my face.

"No," he says with a straight face. "But Jorge might have noticed that the bathroom was undergoing a little… maintenance work."

"I thought it would be more effective than a sock on the door." Jorge tips his glass to me with a cocked brow.

"Touché." I chuckle and shake my head. "You guys are… thank you."

"We might be close with Leah now, but I'll always be your wingman, J," Matt says, pulling me in for a hug.

"Love you, you idiot."

"Love you too, asshole."

"Awww, I love both of you," Jorge says, pulling us both in for a hug and rubbing his palm along my back muscles.

"Okay." I spring away, "Let's catch up again before I leave, yeah?"

"Hell yeah," Matt says.

"Nice to meet you, handsome," Jorge says, smirking at me as I stumble away to meet Leah.

We finally pull into the driveway half an hour later. The headlights hit the front porch. *What the fuck?* There's a man and woman sucking face under the porch light. They break away abruptly, staring towards the car.

"Uh-oh." Leah laughs. "Caught in the act."

"Shut up, smartass." I chuckle as we get out of the car.

"Jake?" Dad shouts, looking at us, squinting as we stride towards the front porch. "What are you doing here?" he hoots, yanking me in for a tight hug.

"I came for Sophia's graduation."

"That's great, Jake," he replies, holding my face in his hands.

The woman is standing next to him, waiting patiently with a smile.

"Oh," Dad exclaims. "This is Diane."

"Hi, Diane," I say, reaching out my hand and shaking hers gently.

"Hi, Jake," she says in a familiar way like she knows me.

"Well, I, uh, we were just—" I stutter.

"Have a nice night, Diane. See you tomorrow. I'm going to go catch up with my boy," he says with a huge smile while swinging an arm over my shoulders tightly. "See you tomorrow, Leah." Dad waves at her.

"See you in the morning, Le," I say, then mouth the word *sorry* at her. Her laughter echoes in the air as Dad drags me into the house.

After an hour of catching up with him, I finally walk into my room. The jet lag combined with two scotches and a shot of tequila has the bed calling my name.

Before giving in, I go to my window, looking across the way into Leah's room. The curtains are open, and her bedside lamp is on, emitting a yellow glow in the room. I don't see her, but there is a light coming from the bathroom. I need to get some sleep, but I can't seem to pull my eyes away.

A few minutes later, the bathroom door opens, and Leah walks out with wet hair and a towel wrapped around her.

Fuck.

It's the second time in a month I've seen her this way, and it still affects me like we're eighteen. Except we're not eighteen, and after getting a taste of her fully matured body at the bar, I'm dying for her to drop that damn towel.

She picks something up off the bed and turns around, facing away from me before dropping the towel.

Double fuck.

I should walk away, but I can't pull my greedy eyes off of her.

She swings her wet hair over her shoulder towards her chest, allowing me an unrestricted view of her bare back. My eyes wander hungrily from the base of her neck downwards, memorizing her gorgeous curves.

She bends down slowly and pulls on a thong, situating the string directly between her cheeks. I feel like she's putting on a seductive dance just for me.

Leah grabs something else off the bed and pulls it over her head. The tight fabric of the lace dress fits her curves perfectly. She turns around slowly, making direct eye contact, and her lips curve into a seductive smile.

She's trying to kill me.

Leah takes slow, deliberate steps towards the window until she's standing directly in front of it. Her fingers play with the bottom hem of her lace dress, dragging it up against her thigh, revealing more golden skin. She stretches her arms out and… *What the fuck.* The curtains to her bedroom close in a blink, ending my… *What's the opposite of a strip tease?*

I pull out my phone and search for her contact.

LEAH

Me

What the fuck was that?

Leah

I don't know what you're referring to

Me

Mhm, sure. Giving the neighbors a show?

Leah

Just one 😏

Me

You better be careful or I'm going to spiderman my way up the wall and through your window

Leah

We're adults

Leah

I think you can at least get a ladder from the garage

Me

Ha ha, very funny

Leah

See you in the morning. 😇😘

Me

You're cruel...

Me

Goodnight, Babe. 💕

Eight years and that woman still knows how to drive me fucking crazy.

40
Leah

"It doesn't freaking fit," Sophia says, throwing her head back with a groan. It's the morning of her graduation, and she's five seconds away from a meltdown because none of her outfits are perfect enough. She was supposed to get ready with Sage but begged me to pick her up after swearing up and down that her dress didn't fit.

"You bought two new dresses last weekend alone. *None* of them work?" I ask.

"No," she says dramatically.

"I think I have an idea," I say, leaving her room as she picks up dress number six.

I walk into Chloe's room, and it looks exactly the same as it did in high school, except our bathtub photo on her pottery shelf is missing. *I now know it's because Jake took it.* And there aren't clothes scattered in every corner of the room. It's actually organized and clean, which feels unnatural, but I've gotten used to it. Sophia and I have tried to go through Chloe's things with Will, but he's never been ready to really get rid of her stuff, so Sophia and I come in here to feel closer to her.

It's been over eight years since she died, and every time I come into her room, I miss her. Not the eighteen-year-old girl from the pictures on the walls, but the versions of her that I'll never get the opportunity to meet.

Chloe—my college roommate who drags me to tacky bars, with our fake IDs, to fend off dumb drunk guys.

Chloe—the award-winning sculptor with pieces in the Met, the Louvre, and other world-renowned art museums.

Chloe—the beautiful bride marrying the love of her life in the fitted A-line dress that she picked out when we were fourteen.

Chloe—the mom of twins who loves her life and sends me updates every time her kids poop, laugh, or cry.

I'll never meet any of those versions of Chloe, or the versions of myself I could have been before a wrecking ball came in and destroyed everything. Sometimes the thought of all of the things we'll never do or have together hurts worse than the shared memories from our past. But then I remind myself how thankful I am to have known her, because half a life with her was exponentially better than having never known her at all.

The pink, upholstered armchair in the corner has Chloe's favorite plush pink-and-white striped blanket thrown haphazardly across it, telling me Sophia's been in here since the last time I was home.

I go to the closet and finger through the hangers until I find what I came in here for. I turn to walk out and pause at the chair before leaving. I set down the dress and fold the blanket, setting it back neatly on the chair. Sophia might not realize I even do it, but I like being able to tell when she's spent time here too.

I walk back to Sophia's room and hand her the dress. She looks at it with furrowed brows.

"Just try it on," I say, smiling softly.

Sophia shimmies into the fitted, satin, spaghetti-strap, forest-green dress that brings back a flood of memories. She looks in the mirror, turning to the side and scrunching her nose.

"That's the one, Soph." I walk over, place my hands on her shoulders, and find her gaze in our reflection. "This was Chloe's dress for homecoming senior year," I tell her, brushing hair off her shoulders. I don't need to clarify that Chloe never got to wear it. We're both well aware of that fact.

Sophia studies her reflection, rubbing the fabric gently between her fingers, and then her lips curve into a soft smile. "It's perfect," she whispers.

"Yeah, it is."

Chloe's death was tough on Sophia. She's spent a lot of time in therapy. Hell, we both have. I've tried to be there for her as much as possible even though I'm gone a lot. I can tell it helps her to have a sister figure around. I would never try to replace Chloe, but I know she would want someone to be there for Sophia like I've been.

"I've gotta head next door and grab my purse. Will you be ready to leave in twenty?" I ask.

"Yeah, I'll be ready," she says quietly, still staring at herself in the mirror with a faint smile. I walk out and close the door behind me, making my way towards Jake's room. His door is slightly ajar, and I nudge it open to find him clad in black dress pants and… that's it. My mouth goes dry at the sight of him, and I'm thankful we called off our friendship pact yesterday.

"Hey, beautiful." Jake grins. "Are you just going to stand there eye fucking me or are you going to come give me a kiss?"

I can't stop the full-toothed grin from forming upon my aching lips. I walk closer, and he slides his fingers into my hair and pulls me in for a deep, soft kiss.

"What was that for?" I ask, nuzzling his nose as he brushes my cheeks with his thumbs.

"It's been eight years since I've been able to kiss you whenever I want to," he points out. "I'm just catching up."

"Kissing isn't the only thing we have to catch up on." I grin as the heat pools between my thighs.

"Trust me," he rasps out with a seductive smile. "I am *genuinely* looking forward to the makeup sex." I burst out laughing, and he hugs me tightly, joining in. "You can laugh all you want, babe. But you won't think it's so funny later when you're screaming my name."

I bite my lip and nuzzle my beet-red face into his chest. I glance towards the open door, then stand on my tiptoes and whisper in his ear, "If you don't stop talking like that, we're going to end up fucking under the bleachers at Sophia's graduation."

He stares down at me with lust-filled eyes while biting his lower lip. "Now that's a fantasy I wouldn't mind fulfilling." I'm fighting every urge to push him on the bed as my hands explore his muscular abs.

Fuck me…

Please.

"Are you guys almost done in there or should I start preparing the nursery?" Sophia shouts from down the hall.

"Oh my god." I laugh, nuzzling my embarrassed face into Jake's chest.

"We'll be right there," Jake calls out, chuckling, then kisses me on top of my head.

I could get used to this.

41

Jake

Sophia's graduation was excruciatingly long and hot as hell. Florida in June is like willingly diving headfirst into the devil's asshole. I could tell how excited Sophia was that I made it for her special day. Looking back, graduating high school doesn't seem like anything important from my life, but at eighteen it's the *only* important thing. The whole day was a bit of déjà vu, except there was, thankfully, no memorial tribute to an incredible girl who died too young. It's especially trippy as Leah and I drive Sophia to the springs for her graduation party where we've spent so much time.

Sophia, Leah, Dad, and I all had lunch after graduation at Seafood Haven. Then Dad went to meet Diane for a late afternoon coffee date. Dad admitted that they've been dating for a few months now. She's a teacher at the local elementary school, which is why she was so familiar with me. She was my first grade teacher. Dad seems to really like her, and I'm just grateful he's found someone to bring joy into his life again.

"Do you have a ride home?" Leah asks Sophia as we get to the parking lot filled with giddy teenagers.

"I'm sleeping at Sage's house again tonight. Her mom is getting us."

"Okay, be careful but have fun. And don't do anything I wouldn't do," she says as Sophia jumps out of the car. I adore how protective she is of Sophia. It's exactly how Chloe would have treated her.

"Okay, *Mom*. Then that leaves me *plenty* of *Le*-way. Bye guys." She waves and winks at Leah before slamming the door and running away to catch up with a group of girls walking towards the springs.

"What?" Leah probes, eying me curiously.

"Huh?"

"You're smiling," she points out.

"Oh yeah." A full-toothed smile is plastered across my face. "I guess I am."

"Why?" She smiles, cocking a brow.

"This place just brings up a lot of memories," I admit, grinning.

"No kidding." She laughs, shaking her head.

"Do you ever come here?"

"Sometimes, if I want to think."

I consider suggesting to Leah that we go for a walk to the rock where we had our first kiss.

"Fuck yeah!" an acne-faced teenager yells, running past the car without his shirt on. "We graduated, *bitchessss*!"

Yeah, no, fuck that.

After a quick stop by BCD, we finally pull into my driveway. Leah said she was feeling inspired, and I wasn't about to deny her need for fresh paints.

The sun has long set, and both of our houses are pitch-black.

"Nobody's home," she points out.

"Looks that way," I say, shooting her a smirk.

We get out of the car, and just as I'm about to ask her if she wants to come inside, the front porch light flips on. *Fuck, Dad again?*

"I'll, uh, see you tomorrow?" she says with a sigh.

"Yeah." I frown.

She turns to walk away, but I grab her wrist gently, tugging her to me. She gazes up at me, smirking with narrowed eyes.

I cup her face in my hands and kiss her gently. When our lips separate, she smiles up at me, those dimples on full display, and all the breath is sucked out of my lungs. I brush my thumb against her lower lip and she nibbles my finger gently, then sucks it into her mouth, hard.

Jesus Christ.

"You're trying to kill me, woman." I chuckle as all the blood in my body rushes south.

"I don't know what you're talking about." She smiles coyly.

I spin her around, press her torso against the hood of the car, then lean down to her ear and whisper, "If my dad wasn't waiting inside for me, I'd be taking you right in the goddamn driveway."

Leah giggles underneath me, and I spank her ass, then pull her back up and spin her to face me. She puts her arms around my neck and pulls me in for another deep kiss.

"Bye, Jacob." She smirks before pulling away and disappearing into the darkness towards her house. I wait until I know she's inside, then go into mine.

Dad's waiting for me in the kitchen when I come inside. "So how's it feel to be home, son?"

"Weird," I reply, unable to find any better word to describe exactly how I'm feeling.

"I'm sure. Eight years is a long time."

"Dad…" I sigh.

"Hey." He puts his hands up in defense. "I'm not trying to start a fight, Jake. Just making a statement. We miss you."

"I know. I miss you guys too." I look at him with a half smile.

"I know you're busy during the season, but it would be really nice if you could visit more on your off time."

"I'll do my best, I promise."

"That's all I ask." Dad beams, throwing an arm around my shoulders and kissing me on the forehead.

"Diane seems nice." I cock a brow.

"Yeah," he says with a wispy look in his eyes, sporting a dreamy smile. "She's pretty great."

"You heard from Mom lately?" I ask, and his smile flips immediately to a deep frown.

"We don't have anything to talk about," he says sadly.

"Yeah, I guess not."

Mom's been sober since the day she went to Athens County Jail, but she never stepped foot in Longwood again. I think she was too embarrassed. Up until Chloe's funeral, it was barely noticeable that Mom was gone. But how could someone not show up at their own child's funeral? After that, her criminal record spread like wildfire.

"You?" he asks.

"We actually talk a lot," I admit with a tight-lipped smile.

"Oh, good. I'm glad she is staying in touch with you." His response seems genuine. Then again, Dad did always only want what's best for us.

"Is she there for Sophia?" I probe.

"As much as Sophia lets her."

"I'm surprised she didn't come for her graduation."

"Sophia didn't invite her," Dad says, with a frown.

"Why not?" I ask incredulously. *I can't believe Mom didn't mention that to me when I called.*

"She said that Lysa didn't deserve to celebrate the big stuff if she couldn't bother to be there for the small stuff."

"I guess I get that."

Even though I've forgiven Mom and we're forming our own relationship again, I can completely understand how it feels for Sophia. Mom never came back to Longwood. She never came back for *her*.

"Alright, I'm gonna hit the hay," Dad says after another hour of catching up in the kitchen.

"See you in the morning."

"I have the early shift, so I'll be gone before you wake up. But we can grab lunch?" he asks hopefully.

"Yeah, I'd like that." I smile.

I go to my room and switch out of the button-up and slacks I wore for Sophia's graduation into something more comfortable and walk to my window. Leah is lying on her bed, sketching in a notebook, wearing a tight white tank top and gray sweatpants, looking like a goddamn angel. I've waited years to be in the same zip code as this woman again. I'm not wasting time watching through the window like a Peeping Tom.

LEAH

Me

Is your house alarm on yet?

Leah

No, why?

She eyes her phone curiously, lips in a half smile, then glances my way. Before her gaze can meet mine, I'm gone, taking the stairs three at a time. I'm out the front door and across the lawn in seconds, searching through the potted plant out front for the key. *Fuck yes. Still there.*

I slip quietly inside her front door, locking it behind me. I can hear music playing as I make my way quietly up the stairs towards Leah's bedroom. When I finally get to her door, she's lying across her bed like a Victoria's Secret model—only with a lot more clothes on.

"Hi," is the only thing I'm able to muster out through my panting, shit-eating grin. I may be a professional athlete, but the speed plus the adrenaline running here was next level.

"Hi?" She raises an eyebrow, unmoving from her position. "What are you doi—"

"Don't ask me that."

"Okay…" Her gaze drifts away from my eyes, moving further down my body. "How can I help you?" she asks my abdomen with a mischievous smile.

"I could think of a few things."

"Oh really. Like what?" There's a fire scorching in my gut. My heart works double time as my mind considers the possibilities.

"We could watch a movie," I suggest innocently, raising my eyebrows, sprawling across the end of her bed, facing her. I move her legs so her feet are pressing against my chest.

"A movie, huh?" She pokes me with her big toe.

"Yeah." I smile innocently. "A movie."

"What did you have in mind?" *Fuck, I didn't think this far ahead.*

"Your choice." I rub my thumb in circles on her foot, and she presses it deeper against my chest. Her gaze scans from my toes, pausing for a moment at the straining erection in my sweatpants, then wanders back to my eyes. She makes no movement towards the remote sitting visibly on her nightstand.

"It's been a long day." She sighs, then bites her lower lip.

"Do you want me to leave?" I taunt, gliding a hand up her calf.

"No," she answers without hesitation. A wicked smile forms against her lips as she wiggles her foot in my hand—the same way she did when we were teenagers. "But a foot massage would be nice."

42

Leah

Jake sits up at the end of my bed and crosses his legs. He picks up my right foot and kisses each of my toes before placing it in his lap, massaging gently with both hands. Sure, the massage feels nice, but all I can think about is how good his hands would feel rubbing along other, more sensitive parts of my body. I can't deny that may have been part of the reason I suggested this in the first place. When we got home, I took a shower and shaved *everywhere.* I'm talking hairless as a dolphin. I left my curtain open, hoping he would see me on my bed and make another move. *Step one, success.*

I was the one who suggested we take a break all those years ago. Never did I think it would have lasted eight years, but we can't change the past, and here we are. It's strange how surprisingly normal this all feels. Jake here again, in my room, taking care of me like nothing has changed. So far, our time together has been exhilarating. But this feels much more… intimate.

"Do you have any lotion?" Jake asks.

"Um, yeah, here." I reach into my nightstand drawer and pull out a small bottle. He squirts some of the white cream in his hands and starts massaging my ankle and calf, nudging my sweatpants up a little at a time.

"That's not my foot," I say teasingly when he's fully moved on to my lower leg.

"Are you complaining?" He cocks an eyebrow.

"Not at all. Just observing."

"Mm-hmm. Although… it is a bit difficult to massage your legs with these sweatpants on."

"Oh, is that so?" I smile with pursed lips.

"Yes, that *is* so." He bites his lower lip as his gaze scans the length of my body.

"What do you suppose we do about that?"

"Well, I am a problem solver," Jake says, cocking a brow, and my heart accelerates at the insinuation.

"Then please, do share your solution." I smile.

"I can show you better than I can tell you." He crawls up the bed and on top of me until his face is directly over my center. It throbs at last night's memory of his mouth on me. He maintains eye contact while breathing me in deeply. His shoulders are tense. His green eyes smolder like a forest fire.

Jake sits up on his heels, straddling me, and his eyes drift from my face towards my partially exposed breasts, down to the hem of my sweatpants. Rough hands push the hem of my tank top up a few inches, exposing my stomach. A finger drags between the hem of my sweatpants and skin, leaving a trail of goosebumps in its path.

He lowers himself back down, lips mere inches away. His mouth trails the line of goosebumps with light kisses, causing them to multiply like a tsunami from my neck to my toes. Even my nipples are puckering through the thin fabric of my tank top. He uses his teeth to grab the hem of my sweatpants, tugging them slightly downward.

I lift my ass off the bed, enabling him to drag my pants lower as he uses one hand for assistance. Once they're to my knees, he runs both hands down my calves, pushing the pants all the way off and throwing them in a heap on the bedroom floor.

Thank God I went for another black lacy thong instead of my usual comfortable granny panties tonight.

"Fuck," he rasps to himself as he scoots off and stands at the foot of the bed. "You still look so fucking perfect."

"Are you so surprised?" I tease. Although perfect is never a word I would use to describe myself. Jake always makes me feel like a hard ten—even when I'm dressed like a two.

Especially when I'm not dressed at all.

"Not even in the slightest." He exhales heavily, pulling his hair with his hands, not breaking his gaze. "You're a goddamn masterpiece, baby."

"What about my foot massage?" I mock pout.

I can think of much better ways to occupy your hands.

His mouth twists into a seductive, crooked grin as he cocks a brow before grabbing both my ankles and pulling my ass to the edge of the bed. He steps between my legs and even with the few layers of clothing between us, I can feel his rock-hard dick pressing against me.

"How flexible are you?" He bites his lip, staring down at me.

"Excuse me?"

"You heard me."

"I don't know?" I chuckle. "Like a normal person."

Both of my legs are lifted up to the middle of his chest. He takes my right foot in his hands and begins massaging again, resting the free leg against his shoulder. His hard dick is pressing directly against my ass.

This is absolute torture.

He's massaging the entire length of my bare leg, dragging his calloused hands up and down the top and inside. He trails his hand slowly up my left leg and when his warm palm glides over my outer thigh, his entire body stills, eyes flicking to mine. His fingertips explore my damaged skin, memorizing every inch of it.

I've never experienced this level of intimacy. Sure, I've had sex in the last eight years, and they've touched my scar, but none of them knew where it came from. None of them understood my scar goes much deeper than the surface. Jake does. He saw it during doctors' appointments, but we broke up before it had completely healed. He's never felt it so tenderly, so thoroughly, not like this.

Jake drops my legs onto the bed and lowers his head towards my center. He plants a kiss on the inside of my left thigh, then trails outward, placing kisses over and around my entire scar. Taking his time. Other guys I've been with avoided it. Rushed past it. Made me feel like it was a flaw, a disfiguration, something to be ashamed of. Jake's tenderness and attention to a spot that's caused more pain than I've felt in my entire life combined has tidal waves of love and healing pounding into me with every touch of his lips to my damaged flesh. I fight back tears begging to escape my eyes.

He grazes his wet mouth along my stomach, and I ache for it to brush against my lips as lightly. We've kissed only a handful of times in the last eight years, and my body is begging to make up for lost time. I'm an addict on the verge of total relapse, and I have no intention of being sober ever again.

"So fucking beautiful," he murmurs against my skin, continuing the trail of kisses towards my breasts while fighting against my tank top. He places his warm palms flush against my stomach, pushing the fabric up and over my breasts. My breath hitches at the exact moment his eyes flicker from gentle and carefree to smoldering and hungry.

"*Fuck*," he gasps, biting his lower lip as his thumbs trail my ribs, lightly grazing the underside of my aching breasts. I must look like a goddamn idiot. Unable to speak. Unable to move. Unable to do anything but eagerly stare at the hungriest man I've ever seen in my entire life. Jake is starved, and I'm his all-you-can-eat buffet.

I lift my hands to his waist, playing with the hem of his T-shirt.

"I think it's a little unfair." I pout, and he pauses his exploration. "I'm wearing a lot less clothing than you are."

"Well, I suppose that can be easily rectified." He grins, tugs the hem from my fingers, rips it over his head, and throws it to the floor. My mouth goes dry instantly. I tried to avoid looking in Amsterdam, but I'm not going to miss this opportunity to ogle.

Wow.

My eyes are glued to his perfectly toned abs. He was in good shape when we were younger but… *Damn. That's a man's body.*

"Damn." I smirk. "I don't even want to know how much you have to work out to keep these."

He grins with pride, flexing as I brush my fingers along the ridges of his abdomen, counting.

One.

Two.

Three.

Four.

Five.

Six.

Seven.

Eight.

Damn.

I memorize the feeling in case it's the first and last time I get to live the porno that's played out in my head on repeat over the last eight years whenever I need a release. I shed my tank top and scoot backward, lying against the pillows. Jake stands up and drops his sweatpants, revealing the tight black Calvin Klein boxers he's wearing underneath.

Fuck's sake.

If my mouth was dry before, it's the fucking Sahara now. He crawls up the bed after me until a leg of his is on each side, straddling me. His hard cock brushes against my pulsing center, only two thin scraps of fabric separating us. It'll be a miracle if I can refrain from seeing stars before he's even kissed me. He leans forward, *finally*, towards my desperate mouth, veering off to nibble at my neck. *Are you fucking kidding me?*

"Are you avoiding my lips?" I blurt.

"Which ones?" Jake counters with a wicked grin. "Are you talking about..."

He slides down my body, his stubbled chin scratching against my skin.

"These?" he finishes, just before dipping downwards and letting out a warm breath against my lower lips. He plants soft kisses against the fabric of my thong. "I can promise I'm not avoiding them." He grazes his pointer finger against the fabric before pulling it to the side. His lips devour my sensitive flesh as he tongues my opening. Every touch shoots shocks of electricity throughout my body. "Mmmm." He returns the fabric into place, crawling back up my body until we're nose to nose.

"I'm not avoiding," he declares, our lips brushing with each word. "But teasing you. That's my favorite fucking past time. I'm making sure I still know exactly what makes my woman squirm."

His woman.

My heart works double time to make up for the knots twisting endlessly in my stomach. He grins wickedly, and the sight causes all the blood in my body to rush south to his latest conquest. He rubs his lips against mine lightly, careful not to pucker them. I don't understand how he can maintain so much composure when I'm about to fucking explode. He tastes along my lower lip, sucking it between his teeth. My tongue escapes, entangling with his, and our lips *finally* connect. For mere seconds, it's gentle and soft, in rhythm with our panted breathing. Then, as always, it turns hungry. Animalistic. Apparently, I'm not the only one making up for a decade of irrecoverable kisses.

He rubs his hard length against me, and I mentally recount all of the flights I've taken in the last month to maintain my composure.

Amsterdam.

London.

Amsterdam.

Dublin.

London.

San Francisco.

A little trick Jake taught me back in high school.

Jake must be getting impatient too because the next thing I know, he's moving his mouth down my neck, along my stomach, and settling just over my throbbing center. He grabs the side string of my thong between his teeth, tugging at it. He releases his bite, and it snaps against my skin.

"Oww!" I yelp with a giggle.

He chuckles against my hip, sucking the strap back between his teeth. Like before, I lift my ass off the bed so he can strip me bare, but he uses his large palm to push me back onto the bed.

"Uh-uh," he hums, leaning down and taking the side of my thong between his teeth. His stubble scratches my skin as he tugs it down and off.

Fuck, that's sexy.

He climbs off the bed, shedding his final piece of clothing. My heart stops beating in my chest at the sight of Jake as a grown, well-endowed man. *Damn.* His thick, swollen masterpiece is completely exposed.

"See, we're even." He smirks. "I'm naked. You're naked. Everyone's happy."

"I can't believe we're doing this," I blurt, unable to stop the words from escaping my mouth. He bends down and pulls a foil pack out of his sweatpants, eye fucking me with a crooked grin. Showing the condom between his two fingers as his only response.

"That was a bit presumptuous." I bite my lower lip to stifle a smile, almost drawing blood.

"Always be prepared." The words echo with my memories.

He rips open the foil packet, removes the condom, pinches the top, and rolls it over his hard cock. He grips the bottom of his shaft, rotating his hand up and down the engorged erection. I'm trembling with anticipation.

I spread my legs wide, inviting him in. A devilish smile forms upon his lips before he reaches for my right leg.

"Jake," I yelp with a giggle as he drags me all the way to the edge of the bed like our earlier massage. He bends down to my mouth, slipping his tongue between my aching lips while rubbing his flexed abs against my sex.

"Tell me how badly you want me inside of you," he groans into my mouth.

"How about I show you?" I flip onto my stomach and raise up on all fours. My naked backside is on full display. I glance over my shoulder, and I can tell by the look in his eyes that he's about to show me exactly what I've missed out on these last eight years.

He takes both of my ass cheeks in his hands, squeezing them firmly, and I moan in pleasure at the pain. He grabs my hips, pulling me flush against his front, then swipes between me, guiding his hard length towards my opening.

"You're so fucking wet," he rasps.

"All for you, baby."

"Once we do this, you're mine. Only mine. Forever. There's no going back. No running." The possessiveness in his voice shoots goosebumps down my spine as his tip presses directly against me. "You're *mine*."

I lean back, forcing him inside. My mind is so consumed with lust and love it's the best reply I could give. Once he's filled me completely, he wraps my hair around his hand and tugs as he thrusts deeply, stretching me open. I'm already panting when he slips back out, and I whimper at the loss.

"Tell me you're mine." The tip of his hard cock taunts my opening as my inner walls pulsate with desire.

"I'm yours." The words aren't even off my tongue as he thrusts back inside of me, hitting my deepest point.

He rotates his hips in gentle rhythm, like the flow of small ocean waves against the shore. So peaceful you almost lose yourself in the calmness. Soft kisses along my neck and back, sweet wandering hands—steady and slow.

Jake yanks my hair at the same moment he thrusts in deeper, and I let out a moaning cry.

In.

Out.

In.

Out.

He quickens his pace, finding the perfect rough tempo, and the gentle waves now roar and crash violently against the sand.

"Play with yourself," he rasps.

"What?" I ask breathlessly.

"Use your hand and play with your clit," he commands through heavy breaths.

I fucking love when he's bossy.

I do as I'm told, finding a rhythm that syncs with his as our bodies clap together with each thrust. My arm is getting tired, but I'm so close to nirvana I'll deal with the aftereffect later.

"*This* is mine." Jake delivers a stinging slap against my ass cheek with his open palm. The delicious pain sends me gloriously over the edge. My breath is ragged, legs shaking, body convulsing as I pulsate around his hard, throbbing cock. He finds his release shortly after me as I milk him empty from the inside.

Jake holds me to him by my stomach as our breathing steadies, then slips out, and I collapse to the bed. He walks to the bathroom to discard the condom. It's déjà vu from our first time. Except this was *way* fucking better.

I ignore the nagging feeling in my gut, making me question just *how* he got so good at it. He returns to the bed, pulling my arm and leg over his still naked body, then tugs the covers over us.

"That was…"

"Incredible," I pant. He chuckles, planting a wet kiss on my forehead.

"Best sex you've ever had?" He grins.

"It's in the top ten," I tease, and his muscles tense beneath me. "Kidding." I kiss his exposed chest, and he relaxes immediately, then tucks his left arm behind his head. I spy another tattoo on his inner bicep and sit up to get a better look. I run my fingers over three tulips drawn in a fine black line on his skin. "I didn't notice this before."

"You usually get pretty distracted when I take my shirt off." He smirks, and I scrunch my nose at him.

"Three tulips," I say out loud as if he doesn't know what's permanently tattooed on to his skin.

"Mm-hmm," he hums.

"For Lysa?" I ask, smiling softly.

"Well, I chose tulips because they're her favorites, yeah... but that's not why I got it." He closes his eyes, enjoying my gentle exploration of his skin.

"So why?" I probe, and his eyes flick back open.

"*Three* tulips, Le," he emphasizes as if the number should mean something specific to me.

"I can count." I smirk down at him.

"For the *three* people I've loved most in my life," he continues with a pointed expression.

"Chloe, Sophia, and your dad?" I smile. "That's sweet."

He pushes a stray hair behind my ear and shakes his head with a chuckle. "For the three *girls* I've loved most in my life."

"You said it wasn't for your mom?" I say with furrowed brows.

He chuckles and shakes his head again. "Chloe, Sophia, and *you*." He picks up my hand and places three soft kisses on my wrist. "You're the third tulip, Le." My lips part at his admission as he flips our position and smirks down at me. "*My* three girls." He drags his mouth along my neck, leaving goosebumps in its wake. "I got it the day I opened Chloe's... I needed my good luck charms. All three of them." He doesn't give me a chance to respond before leaning down to kiss the shock right out of me.

43
Jake

I'm awoken by an irritating incessant buzzing. I crack my eyes open, and my phone is lighting up on the nightstand. I grab it before it wakes up Leah.

SOPHIA

Sophia

Can you pick me up from Sage's house this morning? 🙏

Me

What time?

Sophia

10:30?

Me

See you then 👍

It's only nine right now. There's still plenty of time to enjoy another round with Leah before we have to leave. She rolls over, her naked body wrapped up in the sheets, and blinks at me with sleepy eyes.

"So I didn't dream it?" She grins up at me, her voice still gruff from sleeping.

"Nope." I drag my fingers from her neck and along her exposed shoulders, connecting her beautiful patches of freckles like constellations in the night sky. I brush some stray hairs out of her eyes, tucking them behind her ear. "Sophia asked me to pick her up from Sage's house at ten thirty. Wanna come with me?"

"Throw in a stop at The Brew House and you have yourself a deal. I need an iced coffee, and I need a big one." The Brew House is a local coffee shop we used to frequent when we were younger. They have good coffee and even better pastries.

"Deal," I say easily, pulling her closer to me and kissing her gently on the mouth. "You know, we do have a little time before we have to leave. Do you want to take a shower?"

"I would *love that*," she mumbles into my chest.

"Man, that place has not changed a single bit," I tell Leah after we pull out of the parking lot from picking up our breakfast at The Brew House.

"Yeah, it's one of its best qualities," Leah responds, taking a long sip of her massive iced coffee.

I make a sharp turn onto the country road towards Sage's house, and my phone flies off the center console and under my feet.

"Damn it." I reach down, grabbing it off the floorboard. The car veers just barely over the center line, and I jerk it back into the center of our lane.

"Jesus," Leah says, holding on to the handle and breathing heavily.

"Shit," I say, looking over at her terrified expression. "I'm sorry, Le." I place my phone back on the center console, then place my palm on her knee. She interlaces her fingers in mine and squeezes them tightly.

"It's okay," she replies after catching her breath and relaxing. "I still get freaked out sometimes, I guess."

A few minutes later, I notice a police car is following us. "For fuck's sake," I mumble.

"What's wrong?" Leah asks.

"There's a cop behind us."

"Were you speeding?"

I glance down to check the speedometer, which reads five under the limit. "No."

"Then I'm sure it's fine."

"You're right." I squeeze her hand. "Probably just a natural human response."

I glance again in the rearview, and flashing red and blue lights are now blinding my eyes.

"Fuck," I groan, pulling off to the shoulder.

"It'll be fine," she assures me, placing her hand on my thigh. "You weren't doing anything wrong. Probably just a routine stop."

The officer strolls up to the car and before he can look inside, I see the name tag: Danvers.

You have got to be fucking kidding me.

He bends down to the window, and his mouth curves upwards.

"Well, well, well. The great Jacob Summers."

"Cole," I quip.

He eyes me up and down and raises an eyebrow. He glances to the passenger seat and smiles widely at Leah, giving her the once-over.

"Hi, beautiful." He smirks at her. "Did you enjoy the drink I bought you at the bar the other night?"

The what now? I snap my head to Leah, who rolls her eyes, then mumbles something under her breath.

"Do you know why I pulled you over?" he asks smugly.

"Because you're a cop with a superiority complex?" I don't know why those words come out of my mouth, but I blame it on the jealousy flowing through my veins from his comment to Leah.

What does he mean he bought her a drink?

"Have you been drinking today?" Cole asks.

"Excuse me?" I balk.

"Have you been drinking?" he repeats.

"No, it's ten in the morning. All I've had to drink is this black as dirt coffee," I snap, holding up the to-go cup.

"Mm-hmm... Well, you were swerving back there. That's why I pulled you over," he says, pointing his thumb towards the road we just came down.

"My phone fell, and I didn't want it to slide under the brake." I shake my head and exhale loudly. "Next time I'll be sure to make a complete stop even though there wasn't a single other car on the road."

Cole breathes in, then exhales heavily. "You are aware that texting and driving is illegal in the state of Florida," he says pointedly.

"Seriously?" I raise my brows at him, unamused.

"I'm going to have to ask you to step out of the car," he says calmly.

"Under what grounds?" I scoff.

"You can't be serious?" Leah asks from the passenger seat.

"Sorry, but this is a serious offense." He raises his eyebrows. "You should be more aware than anyone how dangerous reckless driving can be." My blood boils with rage.

How dare he.

"Cole," Leah snaps at him.

"Please step out of the car," he repeats, the corner of his mouth twitching as he rolls his eyes in annoyance.

This is un-fucking-believable.

I unbuckle my seatbelt. Before I can exit the car, Leah grabs my arm. "Just stay calm," she says with raised brows, looking at me pointedly.

"It'll be okay." I lean in and kiss her on the cheek as Cole says something into his walkie-talkie in the background.

"Please place your hands on the front of the vehicle," Cole instructs robotically, attention solely focused on me. He pats me down looking for, well, I don't even know what he's looking for, honestly.

"Why are you doing this?"

"I'm just doing my job." He sighs.

"You are so full of shit, man." The anger is bubbling out of me, and I can't contain it. "It's been eight fucking years. Aren't we past this?"

"Past what?" Cole asks, continuing his pat down. "If you're talking about the shit in high school, that's ancient history now... *man*."

"Well, I'm sure you're still a piece of shit who doesn't respect other people's relationships," I scoff at him, unable to bite my tongue.

"Relationship?" He laughs in my face, and his breath smells like a goddamn whiskey distillery. "I was doing that poor girl a favor by trying to get her away from you."

"Me?" I laugh. "I'm a pro soccer player, and you're a washed-up, small town cop who apparently can't get through the day without hitting the bottle."

His jaw clenches, and he rubs his hand against the sidepiece on his hip. I'm not sure if it's a habit or he's actually considering using it. He grabs the handcuffs off his belt, then yanks my arms together and slams my face against the metal hood. "I'm going to have to cuff you while we finish our questioning."

"What the fuck?" I yell, squirming against him. *I do not trust this dick.*

"I guess Leah's not as smart as I gave her credit for. I thought she was long over you," he says into my ear as the potent whiskey smell floods my nostrils. "Are you still fucking her friends behind her back?" He whispers and then laughs.

He fucking laughs.

"What the hell are you talking about? You have seriously got to lay off the whiskey. It's making you fucking delusional." I spin around with one handcuff swinging from my wrist as an elbow accidentally slams into his ribs. *Fuck.* "Oh shit, I'm so—"

He presses my shoulders back down against the hood and flips me over, locking the other handcuff in place.

No. No. No.

"Will you just fucking stop, Cole," Leah shrieks, jumping out of the car.

"I'm going to need you to stay where you are unless you'd like me to cuff you too," Cole says sternly. Leah puts her hands on her hips as my veins ignite with jealous rage, burning me from the inside out.

"Seriously?" she says, unamused. "You're going to handcuff me?"

"Like you haven't thought about it before." He chuckles.

"Only in your fucking dreams," she spits out.

"Only every night of my life," he says seductively, yanking me to a standing position.

Am I fucking hallucinating this right now?

"Jacob Summers, you are under arrest for assaulting a police officer and resisting arrest," he spits, tugging me towards his cruiser.

Fuck.

I don't even put up a fight. I'm not ending today with a bullet in my back. The only thing more dangerous than someone with a gun is someone drunk with a gun.

"You have the right to remain silent. Anything you say can and will be used against you in a court of law. You have the right to an attorney. If you cannot afford an attorney, one will be provided for you."

"You're such a fucking prick," I mumble as he drags me over to his car, making sure to put as much strain on my shoulders as possible, and throws me into the back seat.

"Just for the record," he says, looking down at me with murderous blue eyes. "The only reason I even came on to Leah like that at that party was because your ex-girlfriend, Katelyn, told me that Leah was waiting for me in the bathroom. Oh, and that the two of you were still fucking behind her back. Leah was pretty shocked when I told her that bit of information a few years ago." I'm stunned silent, unable to produce a response as he slams the door in my face.

How the hell is my ex-girlfriend from ten years ago still fucking up my life?

44
Leah

"This is ridiculous," I snap at Cole.

"Leah," he says, exhaling heavily. "I'm just doing my job."

"Bullshit. I saw that smirk you had the entire time you were dragging Jake to the car," I spout with narrowed eyes. My heart is pounding so hard my eyes hurt.

"What can I say? Ensuring people abide by the law makes me happy." He grins devilishly.

"You're such an ass sometimes," I say, pointing my finger at him.

He grabs my finger and stares down at me with a lazy grin. "You know, you're pretty cute when you're mad."

I yank my finger away. "Cole." I exhale loudly, shaking my head.

"I'm an honest man." He shrugs.

"Am I free to go?" I ask, exasperated.

"Yes." He sighs. "Drive carefully, okay?" he says with furrowed brows as his arctic-blue eyes bore into mine.

"Sure," I grumble, rolling my eyes as he walks away. I get in the car and glance at the clock. It's now quarter to eleven. *Shit. Sophia.* I pull out my phone and dial her number.

"Hey, Soph, sorry we're late. There's been, uh, an issue. Is there any way you can stay at Sage's till tonight?"

"What's going on?"

"Nothing for you to worry about."

"Leah, please. I'm not a little kid anymore. Can you just tell me what's going on?"

After everything with Lysa and what happened to Chloe, Sophia always wants to be in the loop. She was angry that she didn't get to say her goodbyes to Chloe in the hospital, only finding out afterward what really happened. But I understand why they did it. Jake described the situation to me, and it sounded horrible. Chloe's body was completely torn up. Bandages all around her head. A tube down her throat and other wires sticking out of her. Definitely nothing a nine-year-old needs embedded into the brain. Hell, I had nightmares myself just from the description.

"Jake was arrested," I say with a sigh, choosing honesty.

"What?" she shrieks into the phone. "For what?"

"It's a long story."

"Great. You can tell me when you come pick me up. Now."

"Alright, fine. I'll be there in fifteen minutes. Be ready."

As soon as we hang up, I scroll through my contacts again, my finger landing on Will Summers before I put the car in gear towards Sage's house.

"Hey, Leah," he answers in a cheery voice.

Man, I hate being the one to fuck up people's day.

"Uh. Hey, Will."

"What's wrong?" he asks immediately. It's crazy how that paternal instinct extends to more than just your blood children.

"Uh, Jake was arrested."

"Jake… what?" he shouts, in the same shocked fashion as Sophia.

"By Cole Danvers."

"That fucking prick."

"Will…" I giggle, unable to hold it in at his out-of-character use of profanity.

"Sorry. But he is."

After Trey's party, it was impossible for Jake to hide the large black-and-blue bruise on his face. I tried with makeup, but Will noticed the swelling immediately. We told him about the fight, and he said he wasn't surprised considering who Cole is related to. Whatever that means. I may have forgiven Cole, but Will certainly hasn't moved on.

"Yeah… he can be," I agree. "He accused Jake of reckless driving, which I guess he did a little bit. But only on accident," I add quickly. "Then he kept provoking him, and Jake accidentally elbowed him, and then he arrested Jake for assaulting a police officer and resisting arrest."

"Good Lord," Will scoffs. "Don't worry. We'll get him out. Where are you right now?"

"I'm on the way to get Sophia. Jake and I were on our way to pick her up when we got pulled over. Should we meet at your house?"

"Let's meet at the police station. I have a few choice words to share with the chief," Will says sarcastically.

"Do you think it'll help?" I ask.

"Well, the chief is his dad, so I'm hoping so." Will sighs.

"Cole's dad is the *police chief*?" I balk incredulously.

"Yep. I've known him since high school. He's a real selfish son of a bitch. Nepotism at its finest."

"Are you sure that's the best idea? Don't you think he'll just take Cole's side?"

"I just want to have a little friendly chat. Father to father," Will says, seething.

"Okay, meet you there," I say, a sinking feeling in my stomach.

My phone buzzes in the cup holder.

Sophia

How much longer??

45

Jake

I don't know how long I've been sitting in this cell, but it feels like days. I can't fucking believe I'm in here. I'm supposed to be back in Amsterdam for summer training at the end of the week. *How could I explain this?* It's such bullshit.

There are three other men locked in with me. They all reek of piss and vomit. I almost threw up four times so far. *I counted.* I've asked for my one phone call five times, and every time I've gotten "in a bit."

There's nothing in this tiny ten-by-ten cell to distract me from mentally replaying the whole ordeal over and over again. Getting pulled over. Cole forcing me out of the car. Him and Leah chatting like they're… what? Friends? And the bomb about Katelyn… What the fuck was that?

God, I hope Leah doesn't actually believe that shit. I'm not sure how I know that Cole is telling the truth about that, but it seems too specific to make up. Especially all these years later, why lie?

Is that why Leah never called? Because she thought I'd cheated on her?

"Summers," a guard shouts, pulling me from my self-inflicted rage spiral.

I walk to the gate. The guard unlocks it and lets me out before relocking it.

"Follow me please," he says gruffly. I trail after him as we walk down a poorly lit hallway that looks like it would be on an episode of *Stranger Things*. We finally stop at an old phone, and he gestures with his hands that I can use it. I type in the one phone number I have memorized and record my name to be played when they decide whether or not to accept the call.

"Jake?" Dad exclaims.

"Hey, Dad," I reply, sighing.

"I'm on my way to the station. It took a little longer since I had to bring the rig back to the hospital," he says.

"Leah called you?" I say, not the least bit surprised.

"Of course. What happened?"

"He just..." I exhale heavily. "He just made me so mad. He said some stupid stuff, and I just—"

"It's okay. I'll be there in half an hour," he says, cutting me off.

"Okay, but Dad, there's one more thing," I say quickly, hoping he's still on the other end of the line.

"What?"

"Cole's breath reeked," I say quietly, unsure if the guard watching me would relay the information I'm sharing. "Like, I'm telling you, he had an Irish coffee for breakfast."

"Okay, thanks for letting me know," he says, sounding somewhat relieved. "I'll see what I can do."

"Well, if that isn't the biggest load of bull dookie I've ever heard," Sophia exclaims after I've filled her in on the eventful morning. "What do you think Dad's going to say to the chief?"

"I have no clue, but I hope he doesn't make it worse. I don't think the chief would take too well to his son being accused of anything."

We're waiting in the parking lot of the police station for Will to arrive. I gnaw on my fingernails like I haven't eaten in weeks. A nervous habit I quit years ago, but it seems to have returned in an instant due to the overwhelming stress. I pull my hair up into a ponytail. Let it back down. Pull it up into a sloppy bun. Let it back down. Put it in a braid. Let it back out. *Where the fuck is Will?*

"You seem anxious," she points out.

"Wow, what a keen observation," I say, scrunching my face at her.

"You're worried about him," she says calmly.

"Of course I am. Aren't you?" I ask incredulously.

"I mean, I don't like that he's sitting in jail. But obviously, if he really only elbowed him like you said, I don't think they can consider that aggravated assault," she says, nonchalantly playing with the ends of her golden hair. "He could maybe even claim it was self-defense, that he felt threatened."

"What? How do you even know that?" I laugh.

"Google… duh," she says, angling her phone towards me as if I'm an idiot.

"Okay, yeah. Good. I guess that's true." My nerves calm by half a percent.

"What's going on between you two anyways?" she probes as her green eyes bore into mine.

"Honestly? I don't even know." I sigh.

"I mean, I don't need the dirty details… but I know something is going on. I see the way he looks at you. The way you look at each other. Act around each other. Deny it all you want, but you totes still have serious feelings for each other."

It's obvious after what we shared last night that we mean something to each other. What that is exactly? I have no clue.

"He lives in Amsterdam, and I live here. It would never work." I shake my head and toy with the gold ring on my finger.

How could it work?

"Oh, bullshit," she says, unimpressed.

"Excuse me?" I scoff.

"You *barely* live here. You're always jet-setting all over the world. There's no reason you couldn't be a flight attendant from Amsterdam,

Munich, or wherever he plays. Besides, in case you didn't realize it, Jake is hella loaded. Like, you could be his trophy wife and never have to lift a finger for the rest of your life kind of loaded." Her arms are folded over her chest, and she's staring at me like I'm crazy.

"I don't care about his money," I say genuinely.

"I know that. That's not what I'm saying." She relaxes her arms and picks her fingernails in her lap. "I'm saying is work a factor or a cop-out? Because if you guys *really* wanted to be together, you could be. Or if you're so dead set on being a working woman, I'm sure you could bartend at Chloe's." She smirks.

It feels weird hearing her say that name, knowing she's referring to the club.

"And you've sold tons of paintings on your website. You can totally make a living with your art," she says enthusiastically, opening her arms wide as if to say *duh.*

I've sold tons, thanks to Jake. I noticed them all over his apartment and even at the tattoo shop, and I'm sure my art display in Amsterdam doesn't stop there if I know my man.

My man.

"You've really thought this all through, haven't you?" She shrugs. "When did you get so grown up?" I reach over to ruffle her hair, and she dodges away.

"What can I say? I love a good rom-com, and this just seems like the time where the guy is supposed to get the girl." She looks at me pointedly with raised brows.

"I suppose so," I say, the corners of my lips curling into a soft smile. "How was the party last night?"

"It was good," she says, blushing sheepishly.

"Oh my god," I squeal. "Who is he? Or she… no judgment."

"I don't really know."

"What do you mean?"

"I mean, I didn't even get his name. We talked for an hour, and somehow I didn't even get his fucking name," she says, groaning and hitting her head against the headrest.

"Aww, well, if he's from around here, you're bound to cross paths again. Trust me, it's a small town."

"He's not really from around here. But he does have family in town, so I guess he could visit again. But we'll be gone for over a month this summer, and then in August I'm going off to school."

"Don't worry, those things have a way of working themselves out. And besides, if you started dating someone before our trip, you wouldn't be able to order un uomo italiano sexy, per favore."

"True." She chuckles while picking at the corners of the sketchbook she carries everywhere. "But I don't even know if I want to see him again. You know how I feel about relationships."

"Don't be a hypocrite. It's okay for you to get a happily ever after too, you know? Not all guys are like Liam," I say pointedly. "And not everyone leaves." I reach over and squeeze her hand.

Will's truck pulls up next to us, ending our heart-to-heart, and Sophia and I both open our doors to exit the car.

"Stay here," Will commands, freezing us in place. Will is laidback to a fault. He never commands or yells.

"Are you sure you don't—"

"No," Will cuts me off. "Stay here. Like I said, I want to talk to him father to father. I'll come get you girls when I'm done."

We slump back into the car, waiting anxiously for their conversation to be over.

47
Jake

"Fuck off," an inmate who I've learned is named Jim says to another before spitting on their shoes.

"You really wanna do this?" a tall, burly guy says, standing up and towering over Jim, whose arms are so skinny it looks like he hasn't eaten in weeks.

Somebody get me the fuck out of this boxing ring.

"Summers," a guard bellows, cocking his head for me to come to the gate. He unlocks it and lets me out before locking the door behind me.

"Where are you taking me?"

"Your charges have been dropped," he says, unamused. A rush of relief floods through me, and I feel like I can breathe for the first time in hours. He leads me through the hallway, and I collect my belongings that were taken during booking.

The guard unlocks a large metal door and allows me to exit the holding area. I walk unescorted through the precinct towards the front doors. A few officers are glancing in my direction as I pass. Cole is sitting at a desk with his back to me on the other side of the room. He doesn't even have the fucking gall to look at me as I walk out.

Fucking pussy.

Just as I think macho bravado will get the better of me, I spot Dad sitting in a waiting area by the exit. I've never been so happy to see him. It feels like being picked up from preschool by your favorite person. Pure happiness and relief. He jumps to his feet when he spots me. Once I reach him, he grabs me by the shoulders, pulling me into a tight hug. I want to feel embarrassed. Eyes around the precinct are burning holes in my back. But the comfort it brings me is too good to ignore.

"Told you I'd take care of it," Dad whispers into my ear, then kisses me on the side of the head.

"Thanks, Dad."

We break the hug and make our way to the front doors, exiting the building. Outside in the fresh air, the sunshine on my face, it's like recharging a battery—and I only spent a few hours in that place.

I descend the concrete stairs to the parking lot, looking around for Leah and Sophia. I know they must be here. I spot them talking animatedly in the car. As stressed as I am from the day's ordeal, I can't ignore the swelling in my chest from how well they get along. I never knew how close Leah and Sophia were. Sophia never mentions her. I guess my family was walking on eggshells around me more than I realized.

Leah turns her head towards the precinct and notices Dad and me walking towards the parking lot. In unison, they hop out of the car, barreling toward me. I open my arms, welcoming Sophia and Leah under them, pulling them close to me.

"Oh my God. We were so worried, Jake," Sophia exclaims while crushing my ribs.

I look down at Leah, who is nuzzled into my right side. Our eyes meet and lips connect too by reflex. It's short and sweet but just enough to say *I missed you.*

When we break the kiss, Dad and Sophia are grinning at one another. No doubt they'll have loads of questions later.

"So how much was my bail?" I ask Dad. "I'll pay you back."

"You'll do no such thing," Dad retorts.

"Dad, seriously, I can afford it."

"Well, considering I got the chief to drop the charges, you don't owe much of anything. But if you really want to pay up for my excellent services of persuasion, you can fill your debt by coming home for Christmas this year."

"Deal," I respond easily. There's really no reason I haven't made it home for holidays in the past decade. I just always found excuses. Winter practices. Required press meetings. Whatever it took to stay out of Longwood. Sophia and Leah both grin and high-five one another. If I didn't know better, I'd think this was all a ruse to force me home more often. "And wait, how did you get the charges dropped completely?"

"I've known Chief Danvers since high school," Dad replies. "Let's just say we came to an understanding about protecting our children."

"Okay..." I say curiously. "Works for me."

"You're probably starving," Dad adds. "Why don't we head home and order some pizza?"

"I'll ride with Dad. Give you two love birds some alone time," Sophia teases with a wide-toothed smile. Leah shifts uncomfortably on her heels and gives me a weak smile before throwing me the keys and getting in the passenger side.

"Are you okay?" Leah asks as soon as we're seated and buckled in the car.

"Yeah, I'm fine." I smile at her weakly. I pull out of the parking space and onto the main road towards home. I keep both hands on the steering wheel, trying to calm my nerves. I have so many questions for Leah, but I don't even know where to start.

"Jake," Leah says softly, placing her hand on my thigh. "Talk to me."

I sigh heavily. "What the fuck was that with Cole today?"

"You're going to have to be a bit more specific."

"I mean with him acting like he knows you and saying he bought you a drink the other night? Is it true?" I ask as I white-knuckle the steering wheel, attempting to maintain my composure.

"I mean, technically, yes…" she says, shifting uncomfortably in her seat.

"What the fuck does that mean? Have you *slept* with him?" My veins are boiling, and I hold my breath, awaiting her response.

"No, of course not," she assures me. "Last month when I went to Roy's, Cole accidentally spilled his whiskey all over me."

"What?" I glance at her with a furrowed brow.

"He bought me a drink as an *apology* for spilling the drink on me last time."

"I'm the only one allowed to spill drinks on you," I say firmly, and she giggles. "This is *not* funny."

"Actually." She laughs harder. "It is… and I hate to break it to you, but it happens *a lot*." I scowl at her and attempt to stop my lips from curling up into a smile, but it's no use. Her laugh is infectious. "Your possessiveness over having drinks spilled on me is humorous."

I bite my lip to stifle a smile. "Fine. Other guys can spill drinks on you since you're clumsy and it's bound to happen again."

"Hey!" She places her hand over her chest.

"But I'll be the only one buying them, okay?"

"You got it, dude." She shoots finger guns at me, and I chuckle at how much the gesture reminds me of Sophia.

"There is one other thing though," I say as my heart pounds hard against my chest. "Cole mentioned something kinda… weird before he put me in the back of the cruiser."

"What do you mean?"

"He said…" I shake my head at how ridiculous it is to even be discussing this after all this time. "He said that the only reason he came on to you at that party is because of Katelyn."

"Oh, trust me, I know." She laughs. "Your bitchy ex really fucked us hard on that one, huh?"

"You knew?" I ask incredulously.

"Yeah?" she says as if it's obvious. "It's a small town. Eventually Cole and I compared notes and figured out what didn't add up."

I drag my fingers through my hair and let out a loud exhale. "God, I feel like such a prick… I beat Cole's ass over a stupid miscommunication."

"Aww, a real-life miscommunication trope." Leah giggles. "How cute."

I chuckle at her. "You read too much."

"Never." She scrunches her nose at me. "And besides, I saw you have some smutty smut on your bookshelves too, mister."

I narrow my eyes at her. "Well… you did always talk highly of the paper porn."

She rolls her eyes and bites her lower lip.

"There's one more thing…" I say, needing to clear up the last bit of the bomb that Cole dropped. "Katelyn told Cole that she and I were fucking behind your back… But Leah, you have to know I never—"

"Jake," she says as I pull into the driveway and park the car. I turn to face her, and she's smiling at me. "Of course I didn't believe that for even one second. Katelyn was toxic and manipulative and willing to say anything to fuck up other people's happiness… Also, it was pretty clear you were a virgin our first time." She smirks.

"Excuse me?" I scoff. "You said, and I quote 'that was the best sex of my life.'"

"What did I know? That was the *only* sex of my life." I glare at her, and she reaches over and touches my arm. "Jake, I'm kidding, obviously. I *promise* you're the best I've *ever* had."

I narrow my eyes at her. "You better not just be stroking my ego."

"I wouldn't dare." She smirks devilishly. "But I'd be more than happy to stroke something else."

I throw my head back, groaning. "You're trying to kill me, woman. If you keep saying things like that, we'll never make it inside."

She giggles and reaches out, placing her hand gently on the side of my cheek. "I was so worried about you today," she says softly. I place my hand over hers, then bring it towards my mouth, planting soft kisses on her palm and the inside of her wrist.

"I can handle myself," I reply between kisses.

"I know." She sighs. "But still, I was worried. It was all so chaotic and crazy and… I don't know."

"Hey…" I grab her chin and pull her in for a soft kiss, then pull away and analyze every inch of her beautiful face. "I'm right here, okay? Everything is fine."

"Okay," she says, looking away.

"Le," I rasp, trying to get her attention. "Stop looking away. You don't need to hide from me."

"I know." She smiles softly, returning her gaze to mine.

“You can’t push me away again if things get hard.”

“That’s not fair.” She sighs, tapping her forehead to mine without breaking eye contact.

“No matter what happens in our lives, grieving or not, I can’t let you go again. Do you understand me? I let you have your space before, but I won’t repeat that. I need to know you’re not going anywhere. No matter what life throws our way.” I look at her intently, holding my breath for her response.

“Of course I’m not going anywhere. It’s you.” She smiles softly. “It’s us. It always has been.”

I lean in and brush another soft kiss against her mouth. “I love you,” I mumble against her lips before pulling away.

Her beautiful doe eyes stare deep into mine. “I love you too, Jake. Forever and for always.”

“I could stare into your beautiful emerald eyes for hours,” Leah whispers as we’re lying intertwined in her bed, with nothing but a sheet covering our exposed skin. I rub my thumb along her jawline. “They’re just so… beautiful.” She smiles, and I laugh. My heart swells knowing that she no longer feels pain from the one feature that I shared with Chloe. I guess we’ve both done our fair share of healing over the past eight years.

“Well, you can stare into them all night if you want.” I open my eyes wide at her to give her a better look, and she bursts out laughing.

“Stop,” she says between fits of giggles. “You look insane.”

I relax my face muscles and kiss her nose softly. “I just love hearing you laugh, that’s all.”

"There's only one problem though." She frowns. "You're leaving in a few days."

"I know." I exhale heavily, and my heart breaks wide open at the reminder. I've been thinking of every possible way I could extend my trip, but I'm expected for summer training next week, and it's just not possible.

"What's going to happen when you go back to Amsterdam?" she asks softly.

"I don't know..." I say honestly. "What do you want to happen?"

"I don't know either... But I know what I *don't* want to happen," she says as her head rests against my chest.

"What's that?" I ask, trailing my fingertips along the freckles on her shoulder.

"I don't want to go another decade spending every day wondering where you are and who you're with and what your lips taste like. It was only a few hours today when I couldn't get a hold of you, not knowing what was happening, and I was going insane. I can't live like that." She nuzzles her face into my side.

"I know, me either."

"But I also don't know if I could manage being long distance. Having you but not having you? Always wondering if some fangirl or drunk girl from the bar is going to find her way into your bed... Oh my god, I sound like a crazy jealous girlfriend," she groans, throwing an arm over her face to shield her eyes.

"No, you don't," I assure her, removing her arm from her beautiful face. "Leah, when I think about another man having his hands on you, it puts me into a full-on rage. You know what I did while I was sitting in that cell today?" She looks up at me with those gorgeous chestnut eyes. "I spent the entire time talking myself out of wringing Cole's neck with my bare hands."

"I mean, he did arrest you."

"No, that's not why I wanted to do it. It's because he... he kept undressing you with his eyes, and it drove me fucking mad. I'm the only one allowed to eye fuck you like that." I grin, knowing I sound like a possessive asshole, but I don't care.

She laughs as her body melts deeper into mine at the confession.

"We still haven't decided anything..." Leah pushes.

"Well... I could sell the business and move home. My contract with the team is for three more years, but I can see what—"

"Are you insane?" she interrupts.

"What?"

"I'm not letting you give up your dreams, Jake."

"Dreams change, Le. I'm living the dream I had ten years ago. Now? My only dream is you. Falling asleep next to you every night. Having our annoying ass little kids waking us up at the crack of dawn by jumping on our heads in our perfectly nice, normal house."

"Jake," she croaks, tears brimming her eyes.

"Could you change your main airport to Amsterdam for now?"

"You want me to move to Amsterdam?"

"I want you to move in with me."

"How would that even work? Don't I need a visa or something?"

"Marriage visas are pretty easy to get," I say, unable to hold in a grin.

"Oh, be real." She rolls her eyes.

"I *am* serious," I say, gazing into her chestnut eyes.

"What?" she scoffs.

"Marry me." I smile.

Her mouth hangs open. "You're crazy."

"No, I'm serious."

"We've only been back together—er, doing whatever this is again for like a week now?" she says incredulously.

"So?" I shrug casually.

"So aren't you scared it's not going to work out?" she asks in a high-pitched voice.

"No."

"How can you be so confident? We barely know each other anymore," she says quietly.

"I know everything I need to know." I pretend to be thinking hard, tapping my finger to my mouth. "I know that you prefer purple Skittles over the other colors even though they basically all taste the same."

"They do not!" She giggles and nudges me with her shoulder.

"I know that you like to dance in the rain because it makes you feel like you're the main character in a sappy rom-com. You hate scary movies, but you love to read thrillers. You spent three months in the fourth grade trying to learn how to do a rainbow kick to impress me."

"How would you even know that?"

"I have my ways," I say, booping her on the nose. "When we were twelve, you found that injured bird in the woods with Chloe and brought it home. You stayed up all night feeding it with a syringe and nursing it back to health. I know that you are confident and independent but always make time to care about the people you love. I know that you are the first and only girl I have ever loved. That the last eight years of my life were by far the hardest I've ever gone through, and they would have been exponentially better with you by my side. I know that I can't fucking stand the thought of any other man ever laying a finger on you. I know that I need you in my life more than I need water or food or oxygen. God, I know I sound like a sappy fuck, Leah, but for fuck's sake, you are the love of my entire damn life. I don't even remember a time before you, and I don't want there to be an after you. I just want you. All of you. Forever."

"Jake." She rolls on top of me to stare directly into my eyes. "I love you too. With every single fiber of my being. And please, please, don't take this the wrong way, but… no."

"No?" I ask incredulously, my heart dropping to my stomach.

"No, I won't marry you." *Fuck.* "Not right now at least."

"Okay?" My brows furrow in confusion.

"Jake, we've missed out on so much over the last eight years. And—"

"But I—"

"Let me finish." She tilts her head, holding a finger to my lips. "We missed out on so much the last eight years. The majority of our relationship, I was learning how to walk again, and we were depressed and grieving. I don't want to get married right now, but I do want to date you." She places her warm hand on my cheek. "I want to take our time to get to know each other again. And when you *do* propose to me and we *do* get married in the future, I want it to be because we're ready. Not just because we want to do it for some visa."

I shake my head. "I don't want to marry you just because of a stupid visa."

"I know that, but it's a factor." She smiles with pursed lips. "And like I said, I don't want to rush this. I want to savor it. Savor you. Have our first date. Meet your friends. Learn your new annoying little habits, like whether you're a leave-the-toothpaste-cap-on or off kind of guy." She grins, and I chuckle. "Go on adventures. Take over your place, drawer by drawer. And when we do get married, I want to be able to say my vows to the Jake who is my very best friend. The man I know *everything* about. Not the one I'm just getting to know again. I want it to mean something to say, 'I'm *your* wife. I'm *your* person.'"

I rub my hands up along her shoulders and down her arms. "So what do you want to do then?"

"I *will* move in with you. If I need a visa, I'm sure I can get one through my job. Or maybe a student visa. We'll figure it out. In case you forgot, I fly for free. So I'll come to see you as much as I can, and you'll see me and your family here in the off-season. Trust me… I can't wait for that gorgeous stone bathtub to be mine." She throws her head back, humming in pleasure.

I take her hand in mine and toy with the gold band still on her ring finger. "I promise you, in the near future, there'll be a wedding ring on this finger. One that tells the whole fucking world you're mine. Forever."

"Forever and for always." She smiles softly. I pull her flush against my naked body, and the tide meets the shore all over again.

48

Leah

"Hey, babe," Jake says as he walks through our apartment door with a bouquet of fresh tulips in one hand—our Tuesday tradition. He's smiling like he just won the lottery.

"Hey?" I look at him with a wide smile and narrowed eyes. "What has you in such a good mood?"

"Practice went well, and I just had a great day, that's all. Happy to be back home with my girl." He walks over to my position at the stove and pulls me in for a long, gentle kiss, then hands me the bouquet. "I'm going to shower, be out in a few." He gives me one more quick peck.

"Alright, dinner's almost ready… I made your favorite." I smile, picking up the tulips and taking in this week's color—pink.

"Oh, trust me babe, I could smell the bacon as I walked up the stairs."

I grab the vase I'd already prepared earlier with fresh water and place the tulips in it. "So *that's* why you were all smiley when you walked in?" I cock a brow as I set them in the center of our kitchen island.

"Maybe." He shrugs, then disappears down the hallway to our room. It still feels crazy to say that…

Our room.

The last five months have been a blur. We spent the rest of Jake's time back home catching up and making love in just about every random private spot we could find.

The stargazing field at Brahms Ranch.

The big rock by the springs where we first kissed in high school.

The dressing room in Target.

Hey, no judging.

After that, I flew to Amsterdam as often as my schedule allowed, and Jake came home twice between training camps. Sophia and I also stayed with Jake for a few days during our Euro trip. We brought her to Luuk and got her the Lovebug tattoo to match mine.

I moved in two months ago after my visa was *finally* approved, and it's been heaven ever since. Waking up to Jake every morning is the highlight of my day. We wake up, cuddle, have sex, eat breakfast, and go off for the day. Him to the stadium and me to the University of Amsterdam for my classes. Instead of getting a work visa, I opted for a student visa so I could go back to school and finish my degree. It's a great school and one of the few in our area that offer a bachelor's degree in Art History taught in English.

It feels incredible to be learning about the things I love instead of a getting a degree I was forced into.

Today, it's been exactly five months since we got back together, and it might be stupid, but we never celebrated any of the small stuff when we were younger. Actually, six out of the seven months of our relationship was spent helping each other work through our crippling grief. I want to revel in this part of our relationship—savor these moments of bliss.

I flip the bacon in the pan, then place it on a paper towel. It's not as good as the maple bacon from back in the states, but I've been able to find something pretty damn close. Sometimes I even add a little maple syrup, and Jake swears it's even better than the real stuff.

I think he's just trying to appease me. I'm not the best cook, which is why I'm thankful Jake's all-time favorite meal is breakfast for dinner. Eggs, bacon, fruit, pancakes that *aren't* burnt, toast -- the works. Just like we used to have every Sunday at the Summers house.

I know it reminds him of home.

I set the dining table, which is starting to feel way too big for just the two of us in this huge apartment.

Maybe I'll suggest to Jake we exchange it for a smaller one.

I know I don't actually need to ask. The day I moved in, Jake said, "This place is ours. Change anything you want. I want you to feel at home." But honestly? I love this place. His style, or his interior designers' style, I should say, is impeccable. I'm speechless every morning when I wake up here and make myself a coffee in the early Amsterdam morning light. The only thing we've really changed to the apartment is a guest room. The day I moved in, Jake surprised me with an art studio, complete with blank canvases and a ceiling to floor shelf filled with every color of paint I could ever need. He poured me a glass of wine, told me to paint what sets my soul on fire, then shut the door.

That canvas hangs on the wall next to our dining table. It's an abstract painting that has a baby pink background and three large golden circles, tethered together by a knot.

My phone rings on the kitchen island. I wipe my hands on a towel and pick it up, accepting the call.

"Hey, Mom," I say, holding the phone between my shoulder and my ear as I scramble eggs in a frying pan.

"Hey, baby girl," she says, her tone excited. "How are you both? We miss you."

"I miss you guys too," I reply honestly. It's still taking some getting used to this being my home now. "And we're good, how are you guys?"

"Also good… So I was calling because one of the girls from my book club has been begging me to ask, can she buy a painting? She adores the one in our downstairs hallway and was hoping you could make a similar one with pinkish hues. I told her your work doesn't come cheap, and she said she doesn't mind."

"Mom," I say, laughing. "You act like I'm Picasso."

"You're our little Picasso, baby, and you should be compensated as such. We're so proud of you."

"Thanks, Mom," I say, blushing. "Yeah, I can paint one and bring it when we come for Thanksgiving next week."

"Oh, Leah, your dad and I are so excited to see you both. Do you need a ride from the airport?"

"Actually, we'll just rent a car so we have something to drive while we're home."

"Okay, See you next week. Love you."

"Love you too, Mom," I say before ending the call and placing my phone back on the counter.

"I'm starving," Jake says, appearing from the hallway clad in gray sweatpants and nothing else.

Damn, do we love a man in gray sweatpants.

"Jake, are you trying to seduce me?" I cock a brow.

"What?" he asks, chuckling.

"You know gray sweatpants are the equivalent of lingerie on women, right?"

He grins and walks over to me just as I've set the last of our food out on the table.

"I guess I'm going to have to order a pair for every day of the week," he says, pulling me in for another long kiss. He's so affectionate tonight, and I'm definitely not complaining.

"That was incredible," Jake says, wiping his mouth with a napkin, then throwing it on his practically licked-clean plate.

"My specialty," I say, tipping my mimosa towards him.

"I'll clean up. How about you go take a bath?" Jake suggests.

"That's fine, I'll help. I know you had a long day," I reply as we both stand to clear the table. We walk to the kitchen and deposit our plates in the sink.

"I don't mind, Le. You're really going to tell me you're not tired after working at the bar last night?" he asks, leaning against the counter and facing me.

"No, actually, it was a lot of fun," I say honestly. "And it's not like I'm working late. I clocked out by eleven since you're a baby and can't sleep alone anymore," I tease, nuzzling his nose.

He narrows his eyes at me. "Hey, I spent enough nights sleeping alone. And what can I say? I'm a cuddler."

I kiss him softly on the lips, then pull away, looking up at him. He pulls me close to him, lifts me by my hips, sets me on the counter, and settles between my legs.

"But you know… I feel like a schmuck," he says.

"What?" I laugh. "A schmuck? Really? Who even says that?"

"Yeah, I mean… You know I make more than enough to support us and our eleven kids," he says, pointedly gliding his palms along my thighs.

"Eleven?" I scoff in shock. "Jake, you do realize the more children we have, the less time I'll have for you. And I am *not* having that many little ones naturally."

"We just need enough to get a team together. Besides, we can adopt some," he says casually, waving me off. "And I guess that's true… I need mommy time too." He puts his hand on my belly, rubbing small circles, and I swat him away.

"Oh my God!" I squeal. "You did not just say that. Mommy time?"

"Yes, Mommy," he says, chuckling with a wink. "Anyways… I feel like a schmuck because I make more than enough money to support us and our hypothetical family, and my girl is in school full time while also maintaining a job. Why are you doing that?"

"You're so busy in season, J. It gives me something to do." I sigh. "And I love being back in school."

"I'm not suggesting you drop out of school, Le, but you don't have to work at Chloe's."

"I know… but I really like the girls there. Jessica is hilarious, and she doesn't mind that I give her endless shit for cockblocking us."

"Okay, but—"

"Jake," I say, sighing. "I like feeling like I'm earning my way, okay? It's still taking some getting used to this whole… lifestyle of yours," I say, looking around at our gorgeous apartment.

"Fine," he says, conceding. "But the second you start to get overwhelmed, you're becoming my trophy wife, and I don't want to hear a single protest." He smirks, holding up his pointer finger. "Alright, so it's settled, my hardworking woman is going to take a bath in the only thing she loves more in this house than me." He cocks a brow and I shrug, not arguing. What can I say? I do love that damn thing. "And I'll come join her when I'm done."

"*Ooooh*, I'll be waiting," I say seductively, with a grin.

He pulls me in for a hug and squeezes my ass cheeks firmly.

"Oww," I yelp with a laugh. It's a little tradition he started a few months ago that's somehow stuck. Whenever one of us leaves a room, he hugs me and squeezes my ass three times. Like a reminder that I'm his.

"Love you," he says as I look up at him.

"Love you too… Jacob," I say, smiling sweetly.

He narrows his eyes at me, and I turn towards our room, laughing the whole way down the hallway.

I lie in the bath, the warm water enveloping me like a cozy blanket as I lean against Jake's muscular front. Our legs are tangled in front of us, and my head is resting on his chest as he plays with my hair.

If this isn't heaven, I don't know what is.

"I think I could stay here forever," I say as Jake glides his fingertips along my neck, sending goosebumps across my entire body.

"Your wish is my command," he says, and I feel him smile against the top of my head as he plants a soft kiss.

"Do you think you'll want to stay in Amsterdam forever?" I ask.

"Honestly, Le, wherever you are is where I want to be," he says, tilting my chin up towards him, and I angle myself to give him a long kiss. He glides his tongue into my mouth, entangling it with mine, and my breath hitches like it's the first time. We've known one another for over twenty years, and he still turns my insides to pudding.

"Am I your best friend?" Jake asks while playing with my hair.

"What? Of course you are," I respond incredulously, entangling his fingers with mine.

"Do you feel like you know everything you need to know about me?"

"I mean, I'd always like to learn more, but the important stuff… sure?"

"Okay, great." Jake removes one of his hands and grabs something from next to the bathtub. He slides the object into my hair, and I lift my fingers to examine it. My fingers trace the familiar texture of my grandma's pearl clip—my lucky charm. "I love you, Le." He kisses my hair, and I melt into him.

"I love you too."

He pushes me off him and rotates my body so I'm lying flush on top of him in the tub. The position is a bit awkward, so I straddle him instead. He pushes a stray lock of hair behind my ear and cups my face with one hand while holding my waist with the other. "I've known you were the one for me since we were stupid kids chasing each other around the playground," Jake says.

He smiles, and I peck his grinning lips.

"I know you said you wanted to wait until you knew more about me again," he continues. "But I know *everything* I need to know, Le. I don't want anyone else. I want you by my side forever, through everything. It's always been you. It will always be you. And there is no chance in hell I'm going to fuck this up and let some other idiot steal your beautiful ass away from me."

He stares up at me with those intoxicating emerald eyes. "Leah, you're my best friend, my favorite person, my whole fucking world. I can*not* imagine my life, let alone a single day, without you. I want to wake up with your auburn hair spread across the pillowcase. I want you to teach our kids how to paint while I burn the pancakes for our weekend breakfast buffet. I'll count every new freckle on your perfect body and keep counting every damn day until we die. I'll be your person. The only one in the world who knows you completely. Every thought, every laugh, and every beautiful mark on your skin. Please, will you *finally* put me out of my misery and marry me already?"

How did I not realize this is where he was going with this?

Tears slide down my cheeks, blurring my vision so much that I *almost* can't see as he reaches on the stool next to the bathtub and produces a tiny white box with gold sides. He pops the box open, revealing a large, singular emerald-cut diamond on a gold band, actual emeralds flanking each side. The exact color that reminds me of the people I love more than anything.

I gasp.

It's gorgeous.

"Leah?" Jake questions, with pleading eyes, and I realize I've been stunned silent.

"Oh my god, yes, of course. Of course I'll marry you." I nod my head as tears stream down my face.

He plucks the ring out of the box and slides it onto my finger above the small band that I've carried with me for the last nine years. The unfamiliar weight is a welcome change. He throws the box on the floor, then sits up and cups my face in his hands.

"Finally," he says, staring down at me.

"Finally," I repeat, kissing him for the first time as his fiancé.

EPILOGUE

Jake

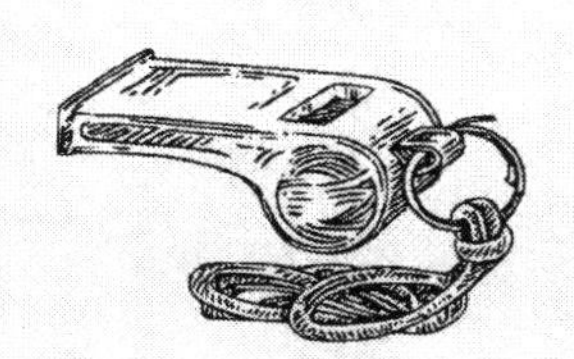

TEN YEARS LATER

"Jackson's open!" I yell as loud as my tired lungs will allow. It's been eighty-eight straight minutes of action aside from the short break between halves, and I haven't stopped screaming for a single second of it. The guys are kicking the soccer ball around the field like a bunch of drunk toddlers.

"Nathan! Get back to center field!" I scream at my midfielder, who's running like he has bricks strapped to his feet. They all look completely exhausted, which is causing them to be sloppy. I'll definitely be adding some endurance drills for our next practice. This team will be playoff ready by the end of the year. I'll make sure of it.

Three long blows signal the end of the game, and the team comes barreling over to me a sweaty, exhausted mess. They won the game two to one, but they almost let it slip away from lack of stamina. "Alright, boys," I bellow as they surround me. "You played a good game, but there's a lot to improve on. We'll discuss it at practice tomorrow."

"Stallions on three," my team's captain, Elliot, yells, commanding the attention of the team. "One, two, stallions!" the boys all yell, then break for their weekly treat.

"Good job today, *Coach*," my beautiful wife says, saddling up next to me after setting down a tray of cupcakes for the boys, who descend on it like vultures. She's brought them every week since I became head coach for the Longwood High Soccer team, and it still brings a smile to my face.

A soccer mom that bakes cupcakes? I've hit the damn jackpot.

"It's been three years, and I'm still not used to that." I smile, placing a soft kiss upon her lips.

When we moved back to Longwood, I didn't need a job considering the money I made playing in Amsterdam was enough to retire on even at thirty-three years old. But I'm way too high energy to sit around all day, and I was driving Leah crazy with my hovering. I also needed a connection to soccer somehow, even if it was coaching hormonal, back-talking teenagers.

"Daddy! Daddy!" says a precious little four-year-old, holding on to my leg like her little life depends on it.

I reach down and scoop her into my arms. "Hey there, princess, how's my favorite cheerleader?"

She throws her arms around my neck and hugs me tightly. "I'm good. Mommy said I can have ice cream for dinner tonight." I pull her away just enough to look into her face.

"Amelia Chloe Summers," I say sternly with raised eyebrows. "What did we tell you about lying?"

"Okay, okay, sorry, Daddy." She bats her long eyelashes at me. "But she did say I could have it for dessert." Her lips curve into a devilish smile.

"Fine, for dessert," I say, looking into her sparkling green eyes. I can never say no to her when she looks at me with those big, beautiful eyes that match her aunt Chloe's so perfectly.

"Dad! Look!" Thomas shouts at me from the field, where he's practicing with one of my players, Lawrence. He dribbles the ball between his feet, running towards Lawrence, then spins around him effortlessly, even though he's only seven years old and half his size. He cocks his foot back and sends the ball soaring through the air into the net. *My mini-me.*

"Good job, buddy!" I yell back, smiling. He loves coming to help out with games and practice, and the boys adore him. They're always letting him join in and helping him improve his shot. I hope he has a passion for soccer like I do because he's going to be one hell of a player someday.

"Come on, Thomas," Leah calls to him. "We have to get to Aunt Sophia's for dinner."

"Coming, Mom!" He waves to Lawrence before running back over to us.

"Hi, Mrs. Summers," says a young girl around Thomas's age, running up to Leah and hugging her side.

"Hi, Jasmine," Leah replies. "See you Monday."

"See you Monday," she says, smiling before skipping off.

Turns out I wasn't the only one going stir crazy at home. As soon as Amelia started preschool, Leah began working as an art teacher at the local elementary school. She still sells her own paintings too but feels teaching art to a new generation gives her purpose. She comes home every day with new little paintings from her students, taping them up in her art studio. The paintings are awful, but it lights Leah up, and happy wife, happy life.

"Mama, can we go swimming later at Aunt Sophia's?" Thomas

asks the second we're in the car.

"Did you bring their suits?" I ask Leah, who's sitting relaxed in the passenger seat.

"Yes," she replies to me. "And yes, you guys can go swimming tonight," Leah says to Thomas, who wiggles with excitement.

"Yay, swimming!" Amelia cheers.

"Did you bring our suits too?" I ask Leah. "I could use a dip myself."

"Of course I did. You know, you're welcome to pack the bag yourself next time, Jacob, if you want to be sure," she says, teasing me.

"If you want to make sure we have absolutely nothing we need when we get where we're going, I'd be happy to," I reply, smiling and placing my hand on her thigh.

"What would you do without me?" she asks, looking over at me with a wide grin on her face.

"Honestly, I have no idea." I squeeze her leg—one, two, three—and she places her hand on mine. I flip it upwards, and our fingers entangle together.

"Are you looking forward to seeing everyone tonight?"

"Definitely. I hate that we rarely get to see them during the season," I say.

"Yeah, I love when they're back home. So do the kids," Leah says, looking back at Thomas and Amelia, who are fighting over who gets to draw in the coloring book.

"Why don't one of you rip a page out and you can color on that?" Leah suggests to the kids.

"Yeah," Thomas grumbles, crossing his little arms. "That could work."

Sometimes the best part about being a parent is solving their simple little problems and feeling like a genius.

"Well, if it isn't my favorite brother." Sophia grins when we walk into her backyard.

"Nice try. I'm your only brother." I laugh.

"And you'll always be my favorite." She stands on her tiptoes and plants a kiss on my cheek. "Dad and Diane should be here soon."

"Okay, great."

"Hey, Jake," Sophia's husband says from across the yard, smiling as he flips chicken breasts on the grill. "I heard the boys kicked ass tonight. Good job, Coach." *I really want to hate that dickhead, but he makes it impossible not to love him.*

"Grandpa! Grandma!" Thomas screams, running up to Dad and Diane as they walk into the backyard. Dad scoops him up and gives him a big bear hug as the three of them laugh wildly.

Leah hands me a beer with the top removed. "Thanks, beautiful," I say, putting my arm around her and placing a kiss on her head. Amelia runs up to Leah and grabs her hand, tugging at it. Leah smiles back at me, then lets Amelia drag her away willingly.

I never thought that I could love Leah more than the day we said "I do." Then I saw her become a mom. It was like I'd been living life in black and white, and the color flipped on. I'm excited to wake up every day and be with my family. Even the boring shit like going to the grocery store or taking the kids to school, I fucking love it.

Thomas was born after Leah graduated from art school, which was a few years after she moved to Amsterdam. We traveled all over, showing him the beauty of Europe. He might not remember it, but we do. Once Leah got pregnant with Amelia, I knew we needed to be closer to our families. I wanted our children to grow up surrounded by the people who love them, just like we did.

Leah talked often about how she missed Sophia and our parents, how she wished she could visit Chloe's grave, but she was just being open about how she was feeling. That was something we both learned in therapy, to communicate openly even if it may be difficult for others to hear. She never once made me feel guilty for living out my dreams. We visited Longwood when we could and brought our family to Amsterdam to see us.

A few years ago, my dad sent me a listing for the house down the street from him that was up for sale. "In case you need a vacation house," he said, but I knew his real motives. He'd been casually suggesting for years that we spend more time at home so he could see his grandkids. He also expects us to have ten more, but I think we'll have to negotiate on that one. I called up the realtor and put in an offer that night.

"You bought this for us?" Leah says as tears stream down her face. A set of keys are clenched in her trembling palm attached to a keychain that says The Summers House - Longwood, FL.

"I didn't want to make it official without talking to you first. But the paperwork is all drawn up. It just needs your signature. I thought it was finally time we had a real home. One with a backyard for Thomas to play in. Where I can teach him and our new little one soccer someday." I smile and place my hand on her round stomach. "Our parents would be right down the road, so they could see the kids anytime."

"But what about your contract?"

"It's only for the rest of this season, and then I'm done. I've already informed my coach I'm not renewing," I say without a single ounce of regret. "After Amelia is born and you're healed enough, we can move."

"Are you sure you want to move back to Longwood?" she asks, staring up at me with furrowed brows. That's my girl—always worrying about everyone else above herself.

I cup her face in my hands. "I've never been so sure of anything in my life."

It turns out everything I never wanted when I was eighteen is all that matters to me now. To be surrounded by the ones I love and care about. And being back in Longwood makes me feel closer to Chloe than I have in a long time.

There are people in life who are imprinted on your soul. Into the fiber of your DNA. Chloe will always be one for me. It doesn't matter if it's been twenty years or a hundred since she's been gone, she will always have a tether tied to my soul. After Leah ran into me in Amsterdam, I knew that she and I were tethered just the same.

When we were younger, I had this idiotic notion that Chloe was what kept Leah and I apart. She was my twin sister and Leah's soul sister. Our grief over losing Chloe separated us more than ever. Sure, it wasn't Chloe's *fault*, but it still always felt like it was about *her* all the same.

When she died, it broke me.

It broke *us*.

But our tether was never broken.

After twenty years of healing and learning to love ourselves again, I finally feel that the love we share for Chloe strengthens the love we have for one another instead of tearing us apart. Healing doesn't mean that the grief is gone. It just means it no longer controls our lives.

It's because of the sister between us that we have a love so strong.

We are the ocean, and Longwood is our shore.

After all these years, we've found our way back to where the sea kisses the sand.

We're finally home.

Also by Hailey Dickert

Return Policy

Sophia Summers is all grown up and has her own story to tell. *Return Policy* will be the first installment at Crystal Bay University—a football romance series full of funny banter, angst, friendship, and open-door spice.

Releasing June 23, 2023!

Scan the Link to Pre-Order on Amazon

Acknowledgements

There's a whole lot of people to thank for the creation of my debut novel, both in giving feedback and simply supporting me behind the scenes, so stand by.

First, I'd like to thank my husband for supporting me endlessly throughout this entire process. Many long nights and weekends were spent laboring over this novel, and your support allowed me to fulfill a lifelong dream of being a published author by creating a story I'm proud enough to share with the world.

Thank you to my parents, Monique and Scott Bruhn, for teaching me that I can be anything and do anything I put my mind to. Without these instilled beliefs, I may have never had the courage to start writing this in the first place.

Thank you to Alli Morgan, who not only put up with late-night chats and daily check-ins, reading updated chapters, and everything in between, but welcomed it with open arms. Your lifelong friendship and support on this journey are unmatched. I'm blessed to have you and your creative mind in my life.

Thank you to my dear fellow author friend Sarah E. Green for your guidance in this process and your instrumental suggestions. Your book, *Breakline,* was the first I picked up last year after a long reading drought and after that, I was hooked.

I want to thank a few authors for writing stories so beautiful that I was inspired to write a love story of my own to share with the world. You each ignited that creative fire in my soul, and I'm thankful for having found your work, which led to my new incredible career: TL Swan, C.W. Farnsworth, and Monica Murphy. After finding and bingeing a majority of your work, I decided to take the leap and give writing a try myself.

Thank you to my beta readers, who have assisted in improving this novel to the very version you have in your hands today. Without you, this book simply would not be the same. Thank you Liz R., Anna K., Katie C., Carolyn H., Stevie H., Diane G., Heather H., Tia M., Josie J., Sarah W., Tara B., Megan L., and Jane G. I would especially like to thank Sandra G. Your feedback was the absolute hardest to hear, but it was the most instrumental in improving my story. Sometimes the most painful advice is the most needed, so I'm thankful for your honesty and assistance.

Thank you to my final betas and bookish friends. Because of you all, I have the motivation to keep going every day: Chiara, Maeve, Mel, Kas, Lexie, Rhianne, Katie, Anna, Mikaela and Gracie. I'm so grateful for our friendships.

Thank you to my incredible editor.

Lastly, I would like to thank you, the reader, for taking a chance on a new indie author and reading Jake and Leah's story. I hope you enjoyed it because this will be the first of many to come.

About the Author

Hailey (Bruhn) Dickert is a contemporary romance author born in a small coastal Florida town who grew up writing songs in her bedroom. She previously maintained a personal blog documenting her journey of moving abroad to her adopted hometown in Germany.

The Sister Between Us is Dickert's debut novel, and her second book will be released June 2023.

When she's not writing at her kitchen table or in her favorite local brewery, Sailfish Brewing Company, Dickert spends most of her time reading, making memories with her husband and young son, and traveling. An admitted sports fanatic, she feeds her addiction to football by watching the Miami Dolphins and Minnesota Vikings games on Sunday afternoons.

Keep in touch with Hailey Dickert via the web

Website: www.haileydickert.com

Facebook: https://www.facebook.com/haileydickert/

Instagram: @haileydickertauthor/

TikTok: @haileydickertauthor/

Made in the USA
Columbia, SC
28 March 2023